She Belongs
to Me

Other Titles by Debby Topliff

And the Word Became Color
Painting Revelation DVD
Trespassing
Squirrel Tales
Hiding

She Belongs to Me

a novel

Debby Topliff

Published by Firefly Life
730 North Maple Street
Saugatuck, Michigan 49453

ISBN: 978-0-9975889-2-7 (softcover)
ISBN: 978-0-9975889–3-4 (ebook)

Cover art and design: Todd T. Norman
Interior design: Beth Shagene

Printed in the United States of America
2017 — First edition

For John,
the one with whom I belong

Prologue

IN 1955 WHEN ALICE WAS SIX her parents built a modern house in the muddy outskirts of Ann Arbor where streets had no sidewalks and dead-ended in the woods. The house perched on a hill making a stylish statement, a glass cage with giant windows that turned into mirrors when the sun went down. The wooden siding was tree-trunk green and the front door was red, like a kiss.

Alice was happy when she was the only one home. She turned on her father's hi-fi and danced from room to room, catching her blurred image in the blackened windows, practicing pirouettes, pretending she was beautiful. She sang along with strangers' voices and swayed to the mournful longing of "Blue Moon." She closed her eyes for "Kisses Sweeter than Wine" as Burl Ives became the Everly Brothers who turned into the Kingston Trio. By the time Joan Baez sang "Sad-eyed Lady of the Low Lands," Alice's breasts were beginning to bud.

Her real home was outdoors where she waded through tall weeds and crouched behind the thick row of arborvitae lining the drive. She rested in the crook of an apple tree at the abandoned orchard down the street and forged trails through sumac woods, braving thorns to pick black raspberries and crushing them on her tongue while they were still warm. She would go anywhere to escape the probing daytime eyes of the house. In winter she ice skated on a flooded, low-lying plot of land across the street, grabbing maple saplings with mittened hands, making mock turns and twirls. In spring she put on rubber boots and headed across mucky fields of quicksand to explore the new subdivision popping up a few blocks away.

In the middle of the woods behind her house, up on a little rise, grew an enormous copper beech. Its lower branches swept almost to the ground and she could nestle underneath, leaning against its odd trunk that was in some places smooth, some places wrinkled, like an elephant's knee. She called it her fairy tree because even on dark, cloudy days, its silver bark glowed like moonbeams. The leaves, too, were magical, flickering from bronze to purple as they caught the wind. It was a European copper beech; no one knew how it got to Michigan. Sometimes she wished she could live under that tree and fall asleep and wake up in a land of fairies where she would be a princess and ride on the back of a flying squirrel and never have to go back to the glass cage again. But the dinner bell always clanged its angry notes, calling her back *right now*. She would scramble to brush moss and pine needles from her lap and run through the woods, around the side of the house, and in through the big red door.

* * *

"Up here. Right now," her mother's voice spat as Alice stepped inside. Her mother was upstairs, getting ready to go out. Her parents' room was on the third level of the house. Their bathroom had a glass ceiling—a sky light, her mother called it—and that's where Alice found her, leaning over the vanity to apply her lipstick.

"But what about airplanes?" Alice said. "Or helicopters? They could look out their windows and see you getting undressed." Or sitting on the toilet, she wanted to add, but that was an activity they didn't discuss.

"Impossible," her mother said as she finished off her Old Fashioned and set the heavy glass next to her sink. "They fly much too high." She swept past Alice and into the dressing room. "Here, help me with this hook." At six Alice was already tall and leggy. "Bean pole" her first grade friends called her. Her mother, on the other hand, was pretty and petite, with bone china skin and a halo of shiny black hair. Alice was covered with reddish-brown freckles and her hair, the same coppery color, grew needle straight and needle thin. Pale pink ears poked out from the sides of her head like twin thumbs. "Can't you pin those ugly things down?" she had heard her father ask her mother one night when she was crouched outside their bedroom door. Sometimes when she walked by his chair he grabbed her ears and said, "Let's take these off and put them in a drawer."

She reached up and closed the top of the zipper on her mother's black velvet dress. "But what if they fly low? What if one pilot looks in and then tells his friends..."

"Don't be ridiculous. You should be using your own bathroom anyway—or the one downstairs."

She hated the downstairs bathroom, the powder room. It was in the center of the house and had no windows, so she couldn't avoid turning on the light with its automatic fan and she couldn't keep from seeing the French can-can girls wallpapered on all four walls. They wore ruffled dresses and kicked their feet high above their heads while the fan taunted her in a sing-songy voice: *There's a place in France where the ladies wear no pants.* She tried not to look at the ladies or listen to the song, but something sinister lived inside the powder room that she couldn't escape.

Her mother dabbed Shalimar on her wrists and behind her ears. "Only a drop," she winked at Alice with one of her green eyes. That was what she and her mother had in common, emerald eyes. "Too much perfume and you're advertiseing. A man likes to feel special. Make him think he's the only one who knows your secret."

Alice shrugged. What secret? She followed her mother downstairs. "When will you be home? Will you be here before I go to bed?"

Her father was already dressed and in the front hall, holding a dark mink jacket open for his wife. She slid her slim arms through the quilted satin straps. "Stop whining, Alice. Mrs. Monsler will be here soon. We won't be late." She smiled over her shoulder at her husband and walked toward the door, her high heels clicking on the brick entryway.

"Mrs. Monsler? No! Please, not her. She hates me."

"Don't be silly," her father said and opened the door to the garage. "She's just a little gruff; German's are like that."

"But she told me I'm going to go to hell."

"Nonsense," he said as he ushered his wife through to

the garage and pushed the button to raise the big door. "No one believes in hell anymore."

"But what time will you be back?" Alice begged. "Tell me. Please!"

"By eleven for sure," her mother said as she slid into her seat. "Twelve at the latest," said her father over the snug chunk of his air-tight door. The Ferrari growled and then purred as it crawled down the drive.

Mrs. Monsler was working her way through a large bag of saltwater taffy—"Not for young girls; they ruin your teeth"—while watching an episode of *Alfred Hitchcock Presents* on their black and white tv. Alice was happy to get ready for bed by herself. Mrs. Monsler was not one for reading bedtime stories and Alice preferred to say her prayers alone. The television was in the make-shift family room on the lower-level of the house, underneath Alice's bedroom. She could hear the eerie music coming up through the floor as she finished brushing her teeth in her bathroom and then jumped from the hall carpet to the center of one hooked rug, and then the next, until she was close enough to lunge on top of her four-poster bed. There she was safe from the alligator who might be hiding behind the eyelet skirts. As long as she kept her toes on the rugs she was safe from its jaws and teeth. She was glad her room was at the back of the house where the windows were smaller and where a robber might forget to look for survivors after he stole Great-grandmother's silver from the bow front chest and Mother's strands of pearls.

She shimmied under her sheets, careful not to untuck them from the sides of the mattress. Then, before she switched off her light, she adjusted her life-size Raggedy Ann. The doll was nearly as big as she was, with elastic under its feet so they could dance together. Alice always slept with Raggedy Ann beside her, on the outside, closest to the door. When the robber came and lifted his blade, he would stop and wonder, which one is the little girl? With any luck, he would plunge the knife into Raggedy Ann and Alice would be saved.

She curled her legs and rolled onto her side, slipping her thumb into her mouth and sliding her other hand over her friend. In the dark she straightened the apron and fingered the long striped legs above the pantaloons with their elastic waistband. Under the dress Alice found the rough little heart that said, "I love you."

Alice woke with a start and lay perfectly still. No, not the garage door. She reached for her bedside clock. One-thirty. They were already home. She slid from her bed and ran from her room, down the hall, and up the short set of stairs to her parents' level. Please, she prayed under her breath. Some nights the door was locked from the inside and she would have to bang and call and even cry to get one of them to let her in. On those nights they let her sleep on the love seat under the window in their room. It was cold and too short and her toes poked out of the afghan, but at least she was near them.

Tonight the door handle turned easily in her fingers and she crept past the dressing room, hoping to crawl into the vacant space between the pushed together twin beds. She didn't mind the crack or the stiff edges of the mattresses and didn't care there was no pillow for her. But as her eyes adjusted to the darkness, she saw that the beds were empty.

She ran out of the room and onto the landing. Her night-gowned reflection in the tall front window laughed at her like a ghost. She grabbed hold of the wrought iron railing and looked down to the first floor. There, below her in the brick entryway, filling the entire space, crouched a gigantic green dragon. The hideous monster curled its spiked tail over its back and flexed its yellow claws. A fiery tongue darted out between its teeth. It looked straight at Alice and growled.

She shrieked and flew back to her room, climbed on her bed and jumped up and down, screaming. There was no one to save her. Then a weary and disheveled Mrs. Monsler appeared at the door and turned on the light. "Hush!" she commanded. "Stop that ruckus this instant." Alice obeyed and climbed under her sheets, clutching Raggedy Ann and sucking her thumb.

.

Chapter 1

ALICE BLANKWELL SAT CROSS-LEGGED on her bed in the cinder block dorm room in Ann Arbor. Her long coppery hair, the color of winter oak leaves, hung like a veil around her freckled face. The contents of a bag of M&Ms lay on the bedspread in front of her, sorted into piles by color. "I eat the green ones first. They're Eskimos," she said to her roommate and tossed the entire green population into her mouth.

"Eskimos?" Yvonne Irving said without looking up. She was perched on the desk, next to the stereo with her feet on her American flag bedspread, stringing glass beads onto a thin strip of rawhide. A poster of Jimi Hendrix loomed like a dark halo behind her blonde curly hair while Judy Collins sang about clouds. A blend of over-ripened pears and decaying apples from trees on the edge of town wafted through their open window on the warm October air. Outside chlorophyll was draining from the trees, leaving them quivering and naked in their true colors.

It was 1968. Alice had survived four years at an all-girls

boarding school in Massachusetts, and even though the University of Michigan lacked the luster of Ivy League, Alice thought she was in heaven. She had spent the past few weeks darting around campus on her bicycle, pollinating boys like a bee in a field of clover. She found them in calculus and physics, under the Engineering arch, at the corner newsstand, in the dusty stacks of the graduate library. Boys were accessible day and night. They littered the campus like wrapped candies tossed from a Homecoming float. In lecture halls the back of their heads and the jut of their shoulders drew her away from academics like magnets. Their laughter added flavor to cafeteria food. Best of all they draped their limbs on the Naugahyde sofas in the common rooms of her dorm and watched her as she passed by.

"Green's the only cool color in the bag, and who could be cooler than an Eskimo?"

"*Hmmm,*" Yvonne purred while she carefully slid a peace symbol into the center of her beads. "And the other colors?"

"Then brown, yellow, orange, and finally red. The red ones are Communists."

"Something you learned out East, I suppose, along with your steel-shank shoes and your homemade blue-jean skirt. Not to mention your proclivity for marijuana." Yvonne tied a knot in the rawhide with her teeth and looked up. "But what about those?"

A pile of six or seven light brown M&Ms were all that was left on the bed. Alice cupped them in her hand like jewels.

"Aren't they beautiful?" she said. "I call them Chigaroes.

Chinese Negroes. And I don't eat them. At least not now. I save them in this special box." She reached down to the crate next to her bed and picked up a tin Band-Aid box covered with wrapping paper. "Then when I need a little magic, I eat just one. Or maybe two." She was contemplating popping one into her mouth when the phone rang. Alice scooped the phone off the wall by the door where it hung. "Sure, she's here," she said with a quizzical look. "Male," she whispered handing the phone to Yvonne whose face spread into one of her Cheshire cat smiles.

"Oh, Bruce." The smile faded. "Unhuh...unhuh... unhuh." Yvonne was one of those good-listener types who took forever to answer.

"Unhuh...unhuh...."

Alice was thinking her calculus homework would be fascinating compared to Yvonne's conversation until she heard her name.

"Friday?....Yup....I'll tell her." She hung up the phone.

"So? So? Who's Bruce? What was that all about? Why did you mention me?" Alice perched on the edge of her bed.

Yvonne held up her palm

"If I tell you, will you do me a tiny favor?"

"Who is he?"

"Just a tiny favor."

"Okay."

"It was my cousin Bruce. He's a junior. He needs a date."

"You never mentioned a cousin."

"We're not close. He's from Grand Rapids and we hardly see him. My mom detests her sister-in-law."

"So what makes you think I'd like her son?"

"You probably won't. But he's kind of cute. And it's just one night. I guess he wants someone new to take to a fraternity gig this Friday."

"Fraternity?" Alice shook her head. "You're crazy. I'm not the Greek type."

"You don't have to marry him, Alice. He just wants a date. And you promised."

Alice rolled her eyes but smiled to herself. She loved a challenge.

Chapter 2

WHEN THE PHONE RANG the following Friday night at eight o'clock Alice was ready.

"You answer it," she told Yvonne.

"No. I'm sure it's Bruce, down in the lobby." The phone rang again.

"Exactly. You keep him busy while I check him out." She grabbed her straw bag and darted under the phone cord, and ran out into the hall.

"You're nuts," Yvonne shouted.

Alice smiled and opened the door to the stairwell. It didn't take her long to get down the six flights of stairs; she'd had four years of practice at boarding school. She stretched her long body, slid her hands nearly halfway down the banister, and spun herself onto the next landing. At boarding school they had only had twenty-five minutes at night, after study hall and before lights out, to use the showers in the basement. There were four showers for a hundred girls, and she lived on the fourth floor. So she'd perch at the top of the stairs waiting for the bell, then fly down and reserve a stall for herself and her friends. No room for modesty if you wanted clean hair.

Tonight she was wearing her favorite Indian cotton dress, deep lilac with turquoise embroidery. Its pleated front turned her into a parachute as she glided through the stuffy air of the stairwell. On her finger was the scarab ring her Nana had given her, and each wrist bore a turquoise bracelet. Her new party shoes from Boston, with a half dozen buckled straps across the top, made a slapping sound each time she landed on the stairs.

Once on the main floor she gathered her hair in a knot and held it away from her sweaty neck as she peeked around the wall of the commons room to the phone booth. She knew him at once. He leaned on an elbow, head cocked to the side, one saddle-shoed foot crossed in front of the other, propped on its toe. His khakis had cuffs, and a golden glint from his wrist told her his shirt did too. He turned slightly in her direction. A blue and yellow striped tie blinked Morse code across his blue blazer. What was she thinking? He was dressed just like her father.

Now was her chance to disappear. This guy wasn't going to like her anyway. Why should she add to his unhappiness? She started to turn when he spun on his heel and looked directly at her with a wide grin and eyes that sparkled the color of bittersweet chocolate. Did he know it was her?

He said something into the phone, then rested the receiver against his lapel. "Do you need to use this? I should be off in a minute. I'm calling to see if my date is ready."

Considerate. A gentleman. She was the one caught off guard.

"Oh...no...thank you." Her words stumbled out. What should she do? "Maybe she's down here already. What's her name?" No, that's a stupid thing to say. He spoke into the receiver, then looked at her again. She took a step toward him. She could smell his aftershave, Bay Rum. His fingers had clean nails with pale moons rising from their cuticles.

"Maybe I'm your date," she whispered just loud enough for him to hear.

"Alice?" In an instant she saw his face change: from recognition to embarrassment to a flash of anger. Color rose out of his collar and into his ears. He looked like a little boy. His eyes narrowed and grew dark; they took her in. She could feel him inspecting her odd dress and shoes, the feather earrings jutting out from her crazy red hair. She thought she saw a glint of disappointment. She heard him exhale and take in another breath, a slow, deliberate one. And then he extended his hand and smiled with his eyes. "Happy to meet you, Alice."

His skin was warm and moist, like hers. He was just a little taller than her but his frame was bigger, and his fingers encircling hers felt safe and strong.

He drove her over to his fraternity house in one of "the brother's" cars. It was one of the older houses on Hill street that she had walked past on her way home from school during her elementary days. She'd never actually been inside a fraternity, or sorority for that matter. She'd given up Shetland sweaters and her string of pearls when she left boarding school, just like she'd given up beer for marijuana and thrown out curlers and make-up for the natural look.

As they pulled up out front of the house she heard

drums and guitars beating through the night air. Every window glowed; the house looked like it was alive. As she fumbled with the door handle, Bruce came around to her side of the car and opened the door. "Here, let me help."

"I'm not crippled," she said, but secretly she admired his manners. He took her arm and led her up the narrow brick walk. She could tell this had once been a lovely old mansion, but now the grass was worn thin and beer bottles stuck out from under the scraggly shrubbery that skirted the house.

"Hope you like to dance because we've got a great band tonight. They play the latest hits." The front door swung open and a couple lurched out, hands groping each other. Bruce coughed.

"Dance? Sorry. Unless you count the cha-cha and box step I learned in seventh grade at the Women's City Club. All white gloves and short boys."

They stepped into the dimly lit foyer. The smell of beer rose like sewer gas.

"Yuck. My shoes are sticking to the floor," she said scrunching her nose.

"I'm afraid it only gets worse as the night goes on. The Monday clean up crew has to swab the whole place down with bleach. Lucky these are stone floors. Let's go see the band."

She followed him down the hall and around a corner into what must have been the dining room. Red and blue lights hung from the ceiling and blended with the rising streams of cigarette smoke, creating an eerie glow. The band in the front bay window was nearly blocked from view by clusters of pulsating bodies. The boys had on sport coats; the girls wore above-the-knee straight skirts with sweater sets and Capezios. She felt like a clod. The band sang, *"I see a red dress and I want to paint it black."*

"How appropriate," she said to Bruce.

"What? I can't hear you."

She leaned closer. "The song. *Paint It Black.* Every color looks black in here." His short hair brushed against her as he ducked to avoid a flailing arm. It felt prickly against her skin.

"Sorry Brucey Baby," purred the fluffy coed belonging to the arm. "Save me a dance?" She looked over her shoulder at Alice, eyeing her outfit. "So what house are you from?"

"Sigma Epsilon Chi," Alice said. It was a joke from boarding school. SEX. But the girl didn't get.

"Ignore her." Bruce grabbed Alice's hand and pulled her toward an open spot on the dance floor. She leaned back, trying to dig in her heels like a stubborn schnauzer, but her leather soles slid. "Whoa!" She said as she started to lose her balance. But Bruce turned and caught her other arm just before she fell. He pulled her up and held her for a moment against his chest.

"You okay?"

"Can we get some fresh air instead?"

"Sure." He started to pick up a couple beers from the bar but she shook her head no. He led her to the back terrace where the music wasn't so loud.

"Hey look." He pointed westward between the triangle tops of two evergreens. "There's even a star out here."

She moved closer to him to warm herself in the chilling air. "That's not a star; it's Venus." She pointed to other dots of visible light overhead. "Stars flicker; planets glow. And their colors are different: Jupiter and Saturn are yellow; Mars is definitely red. And Venus—the one you found over there—is pure white."

"So you like astronomy." It didn't sound like a question to Alice, more like a mental note: dresses weird, can't dance, trips over own feet, refuses beer, science nerd. Night over.

"That's right, I love science—and nature and puzzles and math. Want to know my SAT scores too?" She reached for his cup and took a swallow of the bitter beer.

"Did you see the harvest moon a few weeks ago?" he said. "I was back home in Grand Rapids, at a football game, and this huge orange ball lunged over the field just as the sun was going down. It was out of sight."

She was embarrassed to admit she'd missed it so she gestured to the west. "Look over there at that crescent moon. It's just filling up. See how it curves to the south to hold the light? When the moon is full it rises at the same time the sun sets, but when it's thin like tonight and waxing, it rises early. When it's on its wane it rises late." She sighed. "I love the sky."

He rubbed her arm gently. "Hey, you're cold. Let's go inside. It's my turn to teach you something—the boogaloo!"

"No thanks. I don't fit here."

"When you're with me, you fit. Just give it a try. I promise you'll like it."

Chapter 3

ALICE CLOSED THE DOOR to her room carefully so as not to wake Yvonne. She could hear her slow breathing and the funny raspy noise that turned into Chinese torture in the middle of the night. She felt her way over to the closet, kicking off her shoes and sliding out of her dress. She found her nightie on its hook inside the door and slipped it over her head.

Why does the heart beat so loudly in the dark? she wondered. Turn out the lights and breath takes on a life of its own. Like outside just a few minutes ago when Bruce Bradford had leaned toward her in the shadow of the entryway, his arms braced against the brick wall of her dorm. He hadn't tried to kiss her, though she would have welcomed it. And what did he mean when he said, "I see you"? At first she thought he had said, "I'll see you." But no, he said, "I see you." What did he think he saw?

She tiptoed in the direction of her bed, arms extended, anticipating the desk, her bedside crate, Yvonne's discarded clothes always clumped on the floor. She edged toward her pillow and lowered herself down, sliding under the sheet. Then she reached for Raggedy Ann. Alice felt heavy and warm all over, like the hood of a car that had just made a long journey, her emotions clicking and quivering inside like an engine trying to cool down. She lay back and lifted her hair off her shoulders, spreading it behind her on the pillow.

Bruce likes my hair, she smiled to herself. He kept wrapping it around his fingers, even rubbed the tips under his nose and over his lips as if he was smelling her. She reached back and found a tail of hair and brought it to her own lips. He sees me. But did she see him? Did she want to?

Chapter 4

As DAYS PROGRESSED from Saturday to Sunday to Monday with no phone call from Bruce, Alice had to admit she did want to see him again. The fourth day of silence felt like a week and the fifth a month. Her ego clung to the precipice of her pride while she nonchalantly explained to Yvonne he was not her type. Beyond the obvious—his fraternity allegiance and Republican clothes—he'd never smoked a joint and was slower than a snail about sex. He even confessed he was flunking Spanish, the world's easiest language, while Alice belonged to the honor's college. But when the phone rang Wednesday night and Yvonne handed it over with a smirk, Alice let pretense slip away and said hello with a smile.

He invited her to the Grad Library to study. They met on the Diag in front of the building and he led her upstairs and showed her a trio of desks tucked in an out of the way corner. He sat behind her while she faced a glass case housing a fire extinguisher. She worked on her physics while he was supposed to be doing accounting. His mother had dictated his major: pre-law. Every time Alice looked up from her work she caught his reflection in the fire-extinguisher cabinet across the aisle. He wasn't studying; he was staring at the back of her head.

Finally she closed her book and twisted around. "What is it?"

"Huh?" His face had a dull, faraway look, so different from the confidence he'd worn at the dance.

"What's wrong?"

"Nothing." His voice came out flat and small. She knew he was lying.

"You aren't studying."

"It's not your problem."

"You can tell me."

"No." This time he sounded angry.

"Is it accounting? Maybe I can help."

"You think you know everything."

The aggression in his voice surprised her. "You don't have to be mean."

"Sorry," he back pedaled. "But just leave me alone. It's not your problem." He got up from his chair and disappeared into the stacks. The competitor in her rose like a shadow in bright light. He couldn't brush her off so easily. She got up and went to find him. It wasn't hard. He was sitting on a desk in an empty carrel, away from any other students. She stood in front of him.

"I know we just met. I know we're really different. But Friday night you said you knew me. Now it's only fair you give me a chance to know you." She was surprised she sounded so caring.

"Don't get involved. You won't want to know me."

"Yes I do. Every person has something special about them, even fraternity boys." He didn't laugh.

"Not me."

"Yes you do. You have to."

"What makes you so sure?"

"Something I read when I was a kid. It said, 'How can we say we love God, when we've never seen him, if we don't love people, who we do see?' That's my mission: trying to see God in people." She'd never said this out loud before. Why was she telling him? When she looked up he was crying.

"What?" she asked again. This time she really wanted to know.

He turned his head away but she took his face in her hands and kissed him. Just a soft kiss on the lips with a tiny taste of salt. A taste of the ocean within his body.

"See." She let go and smiled. "I already am involved, so please tell me what's making you so sad."

Then he poured out his fears. His dad had left them, his parents were getting divorced, he had no money, his mother demanded everything from him, and he was going to be kicked out of school if he flunked Spanish one more time.

She felt the weight of his worry press against her like a child's hand imprinted in clay. He had opened the door to his pain and she walked in. Now they were friends, mismatched yet yoked together by his dark tears and her tiny faith.

Chapter 5

As THE DAYS OF FALL SHORTENED into winter and then began lengthening again, Alice spent time with Bruce, waiting for something to happen, for passion—or just plain old chemistry—to take their relationship to the next level. He wasn't cold exactly, but timid, and she was getting antsy.

"Phone's for you," Yvonne said coming into the bathroom where Alice was just stepping out of the shower. Yvonne stood in front of the mirror fussing with her hair, pulling out clumps of ringlets and mashing in the sides. "Got to run. Don't forget the SDS candlelight vigil on the Diag . Maybe you can drag Brucey boy along to continue his higher education." Yvonne held her thumb and forefinger up to her mouth, pretending to smoke a joint.

Alice frowned as she wrapped a towel around her wet hair and put on her terry robe. Was Yvonne right? If she was responsible for Bruce's reformation, she was failing. He wouldn't even try marijuana, much less sex.

She went into their room and picked up the phone. "Bruce?"

"Almost ready?" he said. "I'm downstairs waiting."

"I just got out of the shower. Why don't you come up?" She untwisted the towel and began rubbing her hair. "I'm all clean and Yvonne just left."

"No, I'll wait down here in the lobby. And you might want to wear your boots. It's starting to snow."

"Bruce!" She put an angry spin on the syllable. "If you ever came up here you'd know I actually have windows in my room. I can see the snow." His thoughtfulness was becoming irritating. So nice, so polite, so kind. So boring. He opened every door for her. He walked on the outside. He held her elbow when they crossed the street. He was always on time. And—the deadly clincher—he avoided sex. Once she'd asked him outright if he was a virgin. He'd scoffed and said no, but she knew he was lying. He wouldn't tell her when and with whom. He was hiding the truth and she was sick of it.

"You don't really like me, do you?" she said into the phone.

"Of course I do. But aren't we supposed to be at your parents' by six? I don't want to be late and give them the wrong impression."

"Of course you don't." She left her meaning ambiguous. "But you'll just have to wait." She hung up the phone and went back into the bathroom. She draped her wet towel over the shower bar and let her robe drop at her feet while she combed the snarls out of her wet hair. At least she could be naked here.

As she went into the bedroom and opened her closet and wondered what was wrong with Bruce? She knew he felt passion for her; no one could kiss they way he did without it. But he was different from all her other boy-friends who were eager to go as far as she'd let them. He was making her mad.

She dressed quickly pulling on a turtleneck and cor-duroy skirt, topped with her fringed-leather vest so her mother couldn't tell she wasn't wearing a bra. You'll have droopy breasts when you get old, her mother said. Like a curse. So I should wear a French push-up bra like you? she wanted to say, but she had learned at an early age to keep her mouth shut. Tonight mother would be thrilled to meet a shorthaired, well-mannered boy. She checked the mirror again, fluffing the sides of her hair the best she could to cover her ears, then snatched her winter jacket and went to meet Bruce.

"You smell good," Bruce said as he opened the passenger door. Another "brother" had lent him his rusty Ford for the evening. "Watch out for your fingers. I've got to slam the door hard to make it stay shut." She slid over to the middle of the bench seat and waited while he brushed fall-ing flakes from the windshield. He tapped the snow off the brush and stashed it in back. "Well, hi," he said climbing in next to her.

Without speaking she reached up, cupped her hand around his neck, and pulled him over for a kiss. "Just checking," she said when they parted.

"Checking?" he asked.

"Yeah, to see if you still want to know my secret."

He took hold of her shoulders and kissed her again.

"Oh," she said.

He started up the car and pulled away from the curb. "Locust, right?"

She nodded. "Number 12. Just past Chestnut." He stopped at an intersection. "Bruce," she began. "How come you never want to…you know." There was a long pause. He didn't answer. The light turned green and he gunned the engine. "Why wouldn't you come up to my room?" His jaw looked hard and sharp under the passing streetlights. "What's the matter anyway? You've never had sex, have you?" He slammed on the brakes. The car skidded on the slick pavement and bumped against the curb.

"I guess not," she said.

"It was a squirrel," he said, his voice rising. "You wouldn't want me to run it over, would you?"

"Of course not," she said.

Chapter 6

HUNDREDS OF TINY WHITE CHRISTMAS LIGHTS draped the shrubs and evergreens lining the Blankwell' driveway even though it was nearly mid March.

"You're getting the royal treatment, Bruce," she said with a smirk. "They don't plug the lights in for just anyone. Not for me, that's for sure. But now that I'm finally letting them meet you, they want you to know what an honor it is. Not to mention the way the lights accentuate the length of the driveway."

"Do you have to be so caustic?"

"Just pent up frustration, I guess." They had had fights before, but now the stakes felt higher. This wasn't a misunderstanding; it was a battle. And she wasn't used to losing.

He ignored her comment. "Do I really have to call them Simone and Lincoln? That sounds so weird."

"Right-o. But Mother feels old when people call her Mrs. Blankwell. And everybody calls Dad Linc."

Bruce pulled the car into the turnaround area as she instructed. Alice jumped out of the passenger side before he'd put on the emergency brake and he had to hurry to catch up with her. He grabbed her hand. "I do really like you, Alice," he said. She gave him a saucy smile and pushed the doorbell. A moment later her mother opened the door. Simone Blankwell looked the same as always. She sported the same smooth pageboy captured in her high school yearbook. Except lately Alice, who was nearly six inches taller than her mother, could sometimes see grey roots peeking out of the inky black hair at the part. Simone was wearing her signature Peter Pan collar with a silver brooch right at her throat. A youthful kilt blushed the top of her knees. People were always surprised at how small her mother was, as if Alice was a misplaced giant, like the European copper beech in the woods behind their house.

"Heavens, Alice," Mrs. Blankwell said, raising perfectly plucked eyebrows over emerald-green eyes, the same color as her daughter's. "You don't need to ring the bell; you live here."

"Sure, Mother. There'll always be room for me in your house, if not in your heart."

Her mother ignored the comment. Instead she beamed as she held out her diamond-ladened hand to their guest. "Don't be rude, Alice. Introduce me," she said while squeezing Bruce's hand and tugging him into the foyer.

"Mother, I'd like you to meet Bruce Bradford. Bruce, this is my mother, Mrs. Blankwell." Alice stepped past them and draped her coat over a Hitchcock chair in the entryway.

"Enchanté Bruce. Alice said I'd like you, and I already do."

"Thank you Mrs. Blankwell."

"Simone. I insist. Now tell me. Bradford. Grand Rapids.

Is that the furniture family? Or maybe…wasn't there a congressman?"

"Well, Ma'am…"

"Simone."

"Yes, Simone. Bradford's a common name. I'm afraid those famous Bradfords are from a different limb of the tree."

"Oh." She made a quick swallowing sound. "Well I, if anyone, know what it's like to have a difficult name. My maiden name was Pratt. Everyone asked about Charles— you know, of Standard Oil and the Pratt Institute in New York?" She had slid around to the back of Bruce and was helping him off with his coat. "Can you imagine combining a refined Christian name like Simone with something so coarse-sounding as Pratt? I'm sure I was the result of a Mediterranean cruise. Oh, but you don't want to hear about me. I want to hear about you." She steered Bruce toward the living room and into one of the overstuffed chairs flanking the fireplace. "Alice, go get Bruce a drink and see what your father is up to. We two are going to get acquainted." Simone sat on a footstool in front of Bruce's chair, within reach of her martini, and patted his knee.

Alice passed through the dining room where the table was covered with linen and set with the special Pratt sterling and the twin candelabras. The mint julep cups were fogged with condensing ice water. The silver butter plates with two pats each and the silver salad plates with avocado and grapefruit sections were graciously approaching room temperature. She didn't need to see the fresh horseradish to know they were having roast beef; she had smelled it the moment she walked in the door. Besides, Yorkshire pudding was one of her mother's specialties. She'd bet ten dollars there'd be peppermint ice cream and chocolate sauce for dessert.

She pushed open the swinging door to the kitchen and found her father just where she thought he'd be, hiding in the breakfast nook with a gin and tonic, a bowl of peanuts, and *The Ann Arbor News*. He liked to be near the garage, close to his precious Ferrari. The kitchen radio was tuned to the local jazz station. When guests were important, he'd be the one out in the living room and Simone would be in the kitchen. Her parents were good at switching roles, pinch hitting, scratching each other's back. She didn't know how to parse their relationship, but it didn't look like fun.

"Alice! I didn't hear you come in." He started to scoot out of his chair.

"Hey, Dad, don't get up." She went over and gave him a hug. He'd just turned fifty and the peanuts were beginning to show. His sandy hair was diminishing from front to back, but he still had his dark bushy eyebrows that made his aura teeter between ferocious and comical.

"How's my little girl?" He folded the paper and stood to hug her. It was always a joke, his "little" girl. By the time she turned fourteen she was five ten and taller than him. "So we're finally getting to meet your boyfriend, huh? Bet Simone's got him corralled by the fire. She's been cooking and setting the table for two weeks."

"Oh, Dad, you exaggerate." Though she knew he wasn't far off the mark. For her mother, the appearance of competency came with a high price.

"How's school? All A's?"

"Latin's tough. I'm getting a B+."

"Who cares? As long as you pull A's in math and science you'll be set."

"But I'm not so sure I want to be a research scientist. So much of the University's work is geared to the war. Napalm and...."

"Alice." He cut her off. "Tell me this guy you brought home isn't some pinkie commie."

"No, Dad. He's a dark brown Democrat."

Her father's eyebrows rose.

"Just kidding. Come out and meet him," so we can get this whole evening over with, she thought. She grabbed two Cokes from the refrigerator and headed back to rescue Bruce.

Chapter 7

WHEN ALICE AND BRUCE finally broke away from dinner at her parents it was nearly ten o'clock and the snow flurries had changed to big, heavy flakes. Alice clung to Bruce's arm on the sidewalk to keep from sliding. In defiance to his advice, she hadn't worn boots. "I'm exhausted," she said. "Anything over an hour with those two is too much for me. But you, you fit right in. Passed the table manners test with all A's. I didn't know your dad was in the Air Force. They loved that. And you actually canvassed for Goldwater in '64? I thought you were conservative. I'm surprised you didn't go all out and volunteer to say grace."

"Your mother said the same one mine does."

"Short and sweet so the dinner won't get cold?" she said. "When I was young my parents dropped me off at Sunday School every week, but they never stayed for church. '*Do as I say, not as I do*,'" she chanted in a sing-songy voice.

He put his gloved hand over her mouth. "Slow down, you sound like your mother."

She feigned a knife stab to the chest.

"I don't mean you're really like her, you're just too revved up. Maybe it's contagious. I think you should be glad they sent you to prep school. Except for the cooking. That was a great meal."

"Yeah, but only once in a blue moon. Mom's just earned herself a two-week vacation from the kitchen and a fresh pitcher of martinis. Then it'll be another fancy spread to impress someone else. Feast or famine." She climbed into the car while Bruce coaxed the wipers to clear off the snow.

"Your dad doesn't look like he's starving." Bruce pumped the gas pedal and ground the ignition.

"I'm sure he's got other sources to satisfy his appetite." Bruce's face fell flat and his jaw tightened. Immediately she regretted what she said. Just a few days before he'd found out his dad was living with a thirty-year-old waitress up in Muskegon.

"Since you're so tired, I'll drop you off. I've got to return the car anyway."

"Fine." She wanted to be alone anyway. She needed to think. While Bruce had been playing gentleman and help-ing her mother with the dishes, she secretly asked her dad if she could go to England next fall to study for a year. And amazingly he'd said yes. It had been almost too easy. She knew he was anxious to get her away from what he called the campus rabble-rousers. He'd been appalled by the Chicago Democratic Convention. And the Detroit race riots had practically been in their own backyard. The war was getting too close to home. But her desire had nothing to do with racial tension or politics. She just wanted to get away. She thought that maybe if she went to another coun-try she'd be able to look back and see her life more clearly.

She was confused about school and what she wanted to do with her life. The University had nabbed her into their fast track math and science program, but she was tired of spending afternoons in the lab while everyone else was having fun. There was a lot more to do in college than study. She wanted out. Tonight at dinner, watching Bruce and her parents talk, she knew she had to get away from all three of them. Their little world of conventionalities was holding her back from becoming her true self.

"So I'll see you," Bruce said as they pulled up to the curb in front of her dorm. He leaned toward her for a kiss but she backed away when she smelled her mother's perfume on his sweater. She hopped out of the car and gave the door a big slam, just like he'd said it needed.

Chapter 8

THE FOLLOWING TUESDAY MORNING in Philosophy class, while Dr. Rosenberg sawed on about the Socratic method, Alice let her mind wander to Will Fowler. He'd intrigued her since the beginning of school. She'd seen him around in the honors lectures first semester and noticed him in the special room reserved for them at the library. He had a different sort of look about him, aloof and mysterious. She liked the way he slouched in back rows, propping his chin on a hand or combing his fingers through his long, unruly hair. She liked the rumpled tweed jacket he wore every day over wrinkled button-down shirts. She liked the way his grey, restless eyes were magnified behind his wire-rimmed glasses. He was always alone.

Second semester she had moved him to the top of her "find-out-about" list when he turned up in her philosophy seminar. He couldn't hide in the back since the dozen or so chairs were arranged in a semi-circle. But he usually sat with his head pitched between the tent of his forearms. Every once in a while he'd look up at the professor and utter some comment about the futility of reason. His insolence drew her like the edge of a cliff.

When the bell rang she slipped her notebook into her backpack and rushed to the door. "Don't forget," Dr. Rosenberg's voice rose above the bell. "Next week we enter the cave with Plato." Will was already gone. She squeezed past some students arguing about the existence of God and caught sight of him down the hallway, just turning toward the stairs. She hurried, but kept a safe distance behind, not that it mattered. He didn't know she existed.

He was easy to track. She'd done it before. Even one time when Bruce was with her she'd maneuvered him to follow Will on his route. She knew that when he left the LS&A building he went directly to a drug store on the corner of campus, emerging with a cup of coffee and a newspaper tucked under his arm. Then he headed straight down the street to one of the freshmen men's dorms and disappeared inside.

This Tuesday morning Bruce was doing his work-study job at the law library. The late snow from the weekend had melted and early bulbs were poking out of the lawns. She was free. So when Will turned and went into the drug store, she followed. She stood in line a couple of people behind him to buy a roll of wintergreen Lifesavers. She imagined showing Will how they sparkled when you crunched them between your teeth in the dark, that is if she ever got a chance to talk to him. She watched as he ordered black coffee and *The New York Times*. Impressive. Not like Bruce who read James Bond and drank beer out of cans. Will was intelligent and sophisticated. Worldly. The only time she looked at that paper was to count the number of "Ninas" in the Hirchfield caricatures.

A girl in line ahead of her was taking forever so Alice waved her Lifesavers in front of the cashier and left her nickel on the counter. Will was halfway out the door but he stopped and held it open for her. Then he looked her in the eyes and nodded in recognition as he pursed his lips and blew across the top of his paper cup. She breathed in the earthy scent of coffee as the woolly fabric on his elbow brushed against her wrist like a kiss. Then he was gone. She grinned. This was a tricky assignment, but she was determined to get an A.

The following Thursday was the first day of spring. In philosophy seminar Dr. Rosenberg handed out a surprise quiz. Will happened to be sitting next to her in the small circle of desks and when the professor left the room Will turned to her and said, "You're Alice Blankwell, right?" Her heart thumped.

He knew her name!

"I didn't do the reading. Can I copy your paper?" Her face went slack and her heart sank. Did he just say he wanted to cheat? He wanted *her* to cheat? This was the first time he took any notice of her and he wanted her to cheat with him? Cheating was one of the few rules she held sacred. Cheating, lying, stealing—those were things she wouldn't do. She had thought she was hunting him and now he was baiting her!

She felt him studying her face. It's just a quiz, she told herself. Not like a final exam. She checked to make sure no one was watching, then silently turned her paper toward him. He gave her a wink and a bright, toothy grin.

She dropped her quiz paper on the teacher's desk and hurried out of class. Her heart was beating fast, maybe irregular. Could she have an arrhythmia? From the corner of her eye she saw that this time Will was following her.

He touched her shoulder. "Can I repay you with a cup of coffee?" Feelings of conquest and disappointment fought within her as she allowed him to steer her along his regular route. Did she want to go with this boy? Where would it lead?

But all of a sudden they stepped out of the LS&A building and into a perfect, cloudless blue morning. The warm southerly wind promised seventy degrees by afternoon. She shrugged her dilemma aside like a winter coat. This was the first day of spring after all. She took a deep breath of brand new air. She felt like a horse released from a long winter in the stable with no fences in sight. She could run headlong in any direction and the warm currents would lift her like Pegasus into flight. She deserved an escapade. "Sure," she said. "As long as I can have cocoa instead."

They wound their way through the center of campus that was quickly filling up with students and Frisbees and dogs. It was only eleven o'clock on Thursday but the weekend had begun. She jumped on a stone bench and twirled around, head tilted back, palms lifted to the morning sun. Will reached out as she hopped down. They stood for a moment, hand in hand, eye to eye. They were almost a circle. Then he started talking.

"I'm from Manhattan." Of course. "I live with my mother on the Upper West Side. My dad's a number one jerk, a rich attorney in Westchester with a duplicate family.

But at least he pays for my education. What I really love is guitar, blues guitar." He faked a little riff on his notebook.

"I play," Alice said, "but only folk. I'd love to learn some blues. Do you play slide guitar?"

"Do I! Want to go to my room? I'll show you. I just live over there in East Quad." He pointed down the street.

She uttered a fake "Oh" as if she didn't know exactly where he lived. He headed toward the familiar route but she stopped abruptly and looked at the sky.

"Will," she tried out his name, "it's too nice to go inside. Let's just walk around." Since she had grown up in Ann Arbor she knew all its ins and outs. They wandered through the campus and into the overlapping business district. Will talked on and on about New York and museums and concerts in Central Park. He liked sushi and Thai food. She had never tried either. He had gone to a private school in the city where he wore a blazer and tie every day and rode the bus. He oozed sophistication.

She decided to take a risk. "I've got a joint in my bag. Want to share it?"

"Are you kidding?" He pulled a lighter out of his pocket. It gleamed silver in the sun.

She led him down the street and behind the Natural History Museum, back to a deserted corner where there had once been a tiny zoo—a circular cement building that housed wild animals native to Michigan. It had been one of her favorite spots to visit when she was young, to see the badger and bobcat, the porcupine and raccoon. And the pair of black bears, Maize and Blue. It was perfect except for the rank smell of dirty fur and scat and animal fear.

They lit up and smoked quickly without talking in case

someone happened to walk by. When the joint was burned to its end, Will snuffed it out with his fingers and popped it in his mouth. "A New York tradition," he said.

Soon the marijuana worked its magic and she began to feel giddy. "It's spring!" she shouted. "I wonder if they've got daffodils at the dime store. Come on." She took his hand and they ran back to the shopping area. Will bought her a bunch of daffodils and stuck one in his lapel. They crossed the street and wandered into the old Nichol's Arcade lined with some of Ann Arbor's most esoteric shops. They stopped in front of a travel agent's window and stared at a poster of the Picasso dog sculpture in Chicago.

"I've always wanted to see that," she said, "but I've never been to Chicago."

"We'll have to go sometime," Will said.

"Let's go now. Today. I can skip the rest of my classes. We can fly this afternoon with a student ticket and take the train back tomorrow night." Her spring fever was rising.

"Today? Where would we stay?"

She thought fast. "You know Michael from Honors English? His sister goes to the University of Chicago. I'm sure we could stay in her dorm. I saw him on the Diag when we walked by. Let's go ask." This was just what she needed. She barely noticed the part of her brain scanning the campus, on the lookout for boring Bruce.

It wasn't hard to find Michael sitting with his golden retriever in his usual spot in front of the Grad Library. "That's cool," he said when she told him her plan. "I'm sure you can crash at my sister's place." He wrote her name and address on a slip of paper and they hurried back to the travel agent to make arrangements to leave later that day.

She dashed to her dorm room, slipped a few things into her backpack, and jotted a note for Yvonne. *Gone to Chicago for an overnight—with someone new! (Don't tell Bruce.) Happy Spring!* Then she went to meet Will at the shuttle bus stop outside the Student Union.

Chapter 9

BY THE TIME THE AIRPORT BUS deposited Alice and Will in Hyde Park the flirtations of spring had withdrawn completely behind the cold, rainy cloak of winter. The buzz of marijuana had worn off and left an unhappy blend of weariness and depression. The campus was deserted and after wandering for a few blocks they found Michael's sister's dorm. Locked.

"What's that sign say?" she asked, pulling her light jacket over her head to keep the rain off.

"Closed until April 2nd," Will read. "They're on spring break." He looked at her with hooded eyes. "Now what?" His voice was gruff, even angry. "This was your idea, you know."

"Don't worry, I'll think of something." Her mind raced. "I've been in spots like this before. Missed trains and airplanes...."

"Why didn't you tell me I was in such good hands. It's nearly ten o'clock and we don't have enough money left for a hotel."

"No, not a hotel," she agreed. Not with someone she

just met today. Not with a stranger in a strange city. She needed a safe solution. "I've got it. My friend Julia from boarding school is from Hyde Park. Her father teaches ethics at the Divinity School. They took me out to dinner once senior year. I could call him." Did she have the nerve? She had no choice.

They found a pay phone and a phonebook and she took a dime out of her coin purse. "Dr. Lewis?" Thank God they were home. She explained her predicament, careful to leave out a few details. He gave her directions to the apartment and told her to come right over. She almost hugged Will. "We've been saved—by a theologian!"

Dr. Lewis met them at the door, pipe in hand. "Always happy to be of assistance," he said sticking the pipe back in his mouth and showing them in. "Too bad Julia's not here. Off to Germany this semester. And all four of her sisters are married. Ah, here's Grace." He motioned to a tall, attractive woman in a lilac-colored kimono approaching from the back of the apartment. Her silver hair was swept up in an elegant French twist and a pair of reading glasses hung from a chain around her neck. "She'll show you around. Please excuse me," he grinned, bowing slightly, revealing a small tonsure on the top of his salt and pepper head. "I'm in the middle of a chapter. Propitiation."

Alice looked down the hall that ran along one side of the spacious apartment. It connected their living room with the kitchen way at the other end. "Alice!" Mrs. Lewis exclaimed, smooth as silk, as if this unexpected late night meeting was afternoon tea. "How lovely to see you again. And how nice to meet your friend."

Mrs. Lewis showed them each to one of the vacant

bedrooms that branched off the hallway. She brought two sets of clean towels and pointed them to different bathrooms. Will disappeared. Mrs. Lewis gave Alice a key to the apartment and showed her where to find cereal and eggs for breakfast. She and her husband had to leave early in the morning.

"Your friend seems very nice," she said. "Have you been together long?" How did mothers know everything?

"We've had philosophy together all semester," she answered, hoping this passed for the truth.

"Well, you can stay with us as long as you need to. Good night, dear."

Alice closed the door to her room and set down her backpack. She looked around. A row of cheerleading ribbons and trophies on a shelf above the desk assured her this was not Julia's room. A collection of pristine Madame Alexander dolls sat in a glass-doored case next to the bed. She looked over the titles on the bookcase that served as a bedside table. The complete works of Virginia Woolfe, a dog-eared e.e. cummings, and Sylvia Plath's *The Bell Jar* proclaimed the cheerleading phase was over.

She slipped out of her sweater and corduroys, promising herself she'd brush her teeth in the morning, and crawled under the rosebud sheets, too tired to read. She puffed up the feather pillow and curled on her side.

She watched as the crack of light under the door disappeared. She heard a toilet flush and a door snap shut. From a distance she caught the faint stirrings of a symphony. It reminded her of the bitter-sweet songs her mother played on the piano late at night when Alice was young. A clock ticked somewhere down the hall. Feeling a little too warm, she stuck an arm on top of the sheet and turned over to face the wall. I'm so lucky, she thought. Lucky to have a safe place to sleep. Lucky to have old friends. Lucky to.... Her quasi-prayer was interrupted by a soft scratchy sound at her door. She lifted her head. Did the Lewis' have a cat? A dog? Then she heard the door handle turn slowly, almost imperceptibly. She held her breath and lay perfectly still. Someone entered the room. She pretended to be asleep.

"Alice?" A low whisper brushed her ear. "Alice?"

She tried to keep her breathing slow and shallow. What was he thinking, risking getting caught in her friend's parents' house?

"Alice." Now the word was no longer a question but a statement. Suddenly she felt warm fingers against her shoulder. Warm, but not soothing. She tried not to move. She felt his weight sink down on the mattress behind her. His body leaned toward hers. Her heart began to race. What had she gotten herself into?

She faked a sleepy sound, then scrunched her shoulders and turned away from him. She pulled her arms tight beneath her and lay rigid on her stomach.

"Alice?" His voice was not so near; he must have sat up. She waited.

"Alice?" She felt the bed move. Now he was standing.

She yawned and lifted her head and looked in his direction. "Will?" she said, "Is that you? Is something wrong?"

"I just wanted to say good night."

"Good night," she said. "See you in the morning." She heard him turn and leave the room as quietly as he had come in. She waited for the soft thud of his door, then crept out of bed and twisted the lock above the door handle. He could be dangerous, she thought, and sunk under the covers into a fretful sleep.

The Lewis' apartment was silent when she woke the next morning. Pale daylight cut through the blinds in her room. She pulled clean clothes out of her pack and got dressed. Then she tiptoed down the hall to the kitchen where she found a note on the counter: We drove to Madison for the day. Make yourselves at home. Home? She shivered. She wasn't ready to play house with this boy she barely knew, this midnight intruder. Just then she heard water noises in the bathroom and quickly wadded up the note and tossed it into the wastebasket under the sink.

Will yawned as he shuffled into the kitchen, scratching his armpits Cro-Magnon style. It looked as if he had slept in the clothes he had worn the day before. He scanned the room with his eyes, then raised his eyebrows in a question.

"Gone," she said, "they went out for a while." That could be the truth, couldn't it?

He took a step toward her.

She turned and leaned over the sink, looking out the window. "It's crummy outside again. I guess spring was a premature fluke."

"*Ver equinus interruptus*. Never mind. We can make our own sunshine." He rested his hand on the back of her neck. She flinched away.

"How about something to eat?" she said changing the subject. "Or coffee?"

"Food? No." Will said. "Coffee, yes. This man needs coffee." He stretched his arms above his head and yawned.

"Good idea," she said. "Let's go find a coffee shop. There must be some cool places in Hyde Park." They grabbed their jackets and the house key and scuttled down three flights of stairs to the first floor.

A cold, wet wind hit their faces as they pushed open the lobby door. "So this is the Windy City!" Will said, holding his jacket close at the neck with one hand and pulling her to his hip with the other. She spun out and away from his grip, like an awkward figure skater doing a turn. She tried to give him a leave-me-alone look, but the wind made a bronze mask of her long hair.

"Here's a drug store with a counter. Want to go in?" she said, knowing this was just his thing.

"Great," he said. "I can get a paper, too. I always like to check the home teams."

"Home teams?"

"You know, the Dodgers, the Mets, the Knicks—what the heck—even the Jets. We're into basketball now, and spring training." He searched eagerly for *The New York Times*.

"Oh. Sports." She deflated like a balloon from last week's birthday party.

After breakfast they took the El up to the Loop, rattling past prison-like housing projects and rundown frame houses until they got to the downtown.

"Want to go to the Aquarium?" she said. "I hear it's really nice." She loved fish and seals and dolphins, all kinds of animals.

"Nah, I've seen aquariums," he mumbled, still busy with his fancy paper.

"The zoo's too far away." She was looking at the map she had picked up at the travel agent's. "What about the Planetarium? Do you like the stars?"

"Always gives me a crick in the neck."

"The Art Institute?" she asked sheepishly. He stared at her and she folded up the map.

"Look." He turned toward her. "We came here because you wanted to see the Picasso, right?" He put an arm around her shoulder and gave her a brotherly hug. "And then I thought we could walk over to Soldier Field. You know, home of the Bears."

The Bears. The Chicago Bears, of course. She pushed away from him and curled up her fingers like claws. "Grrrrr," she snarled, feeling gruff and growly herself, as if she'd been tricked into leaving hibernation too soon.

Before they got off the train at the Civic Center and dove into the wind, she put her hair in two ponytails, one above each ear. Will laughed when they came around the corner and saw the Picasso. "You look just like the red dog," he said. "Go stand by it; I'll take your picture."

"I don't think so. It's miserable out here."

"Come on, be a sport."

She walked up to the giant piece of metal and put her hand on its cold surface. "You know some people say it's a woman, not a dog."

"That's even better," Will said clicking the shutter on his camera. "I like dogs, but I love women." He didn't seem daunted by the weather or her refusals. He must be used to big city inconveniences and big city girls.

"I'm too cold to go to the staduim," she said. "We'd better pick up our stuff at the apartment and find a train back to Ann Arbor." She was surprised when he agreed.

On the way back to Hyde Park Alice stopped in front of a florist's window. "Oh look, aren't those tulips beautiful?

Let's get some for the Lewis'. That deep pink would look great in their kitchen."

"Eight dollars a bunch?" Will read. "What a rip off."

"Not really. They had to be forced."

"Forced?"

"You know," she explained, "someone had to plan ahead, keep the bulbs in a cool dark place, make them think winter was over ahead of time. I've got five dollars left. Do you have three?"

"Just barely," he grumbled.

"Well, they did let us spend the night in their home— uninvited. I think we should thank them somehow."

"Yeah. Whatever." He handed over the bills.

She arranged the flowers in a glass milk bottle she found on the drain board and set them on the table on top of a note of thanks.

They collected their backpacks, left the key on the hall table by the door, and went out again into the wind. They walked a block and turned the corner. "Hey," Will said, stopping in front of a phone booth. "We forgot to call about the train schedule. Do you have any change?"

"Eight pennies and our train tickets." She was surprised how fast her money had disappeared.

"No sweat," Will grinned. "I know a trick." He tore a thin strip of paper off the edge of the phone book hanging under the phone by a metal cord. Then he jammed it into the quarter coin slot and dropped in a penny and called for the train schedule. "Anybody else you want to call?" he said after he hung up. "We've got seven cents left."

Suddenly Bruce flashed into her mind. Had he tried to find her? He would be worried. She wished she could let him know she was all right, but she didn't dare call.

Chapter 10

THE TRAIN FROM CHICAGO TO ANN ARBOR was warm and cozy. There were a couple of families scattered across the aisle of the passenger car, their children bouncing up and down on the upholstered seats. A single man was busy with the Tribune. The conductor walked toward them punching tickets. They found an empty set of four seats at the front end of the car, away from the other passengers, where they could sit facing each other. She slipped off her shoes and stretched her legs on the empty seat next to Will. She got out her copy of their textbook on Plato and her notes and the study questions that Dr. Rosenberg had assigned. "Do you think he's right," she asked Will after she'd read for awhile. "Do you think that happiness is the natural consequence of a healthy soul?"

"Who said that? Rosenberg?"

"No. Plato. Haven't you read this?"

"How quickly you forget. Remember yesterday and the quiz? I didn't spend last night in bed catching up either."

The quiz was yesterday? It seemed weeks ago. But last night…she just wanted to forget.

"But I think happiness has more to do with the body than the soul," he said. "Who knows what a soul is, anyway."

"Plato says moral virtue makes a healthy soul."

"That's a laugh," Will snorted.

She shook her head and looked back at the book. "He says the only reason people aren't virtuous is they don't realize it would make them happy. It's all a question of knowledge."

"I thought you told me you wanted to learn the blues." Will smiled. "Maybe this is the sole that matters." He reached out and grabbed one of her stockinged feet and began to massage it. She pulled away and folded her legs under her.

By the time they crossed the Indiana border the sun was going down. A porter came through the car with a tray of sandwiches suspended from a strap around his neck. "Tuna, egg salad, ham and cheese," he sang out. "Last call for the dining car."

"I wish we had some money left." Will crossed his arms and looked disgruntled. "I'm starved."

"I've got an apple in my pack. Would you like that?"

"If that's all you've got." She fumbled around in her bag and handed it to him. Without even shining it up he took a big bite. "Ach," he said shaking his head. "How long have you had this in there? It's bruised and mealy." He dropped it into a waste can built into the side of the train. "Thanks anyway, but I'll just get some shut eye." He leaned his head against the darkening window and closed his eyes.

The rhythmic sound and sway of the train helped

her relax. The trip was almost over. She closed her eyes and remembered her first year at boarding school when she met Julia on the overnight train from Chicago and Detroit to New Haven. They each had their own sleeping compartments in the Pullman car with fold-down beds and fold-down sinks. It had been glorious, to lie in bed with the lights out and the shade up, watching towns and crossroads fly by in the moonlight. The train had been full of prep school boys with Madras jackets and summer tans, and a few were friends of Julia from Chicago. They squeezed into one guy's room, supposedly the heir to Droste Cocoa, with some other boys and listened while he played Bob Dylan songs on his guitar. His voice was beautiful, smooth like melted chocolate. After a couple bottles of beer Julia blurted out that her mother, with five daughters, was sick of estrogen and that's why she'd been sent away. It had made Alice wonder about the true reason her parents insisted on sending her to boarding school. If they really believed Ann Arbor High was too big, how did sending her 1,000 miles away solve that problem?

Alice felt the train slowing down and heard the high-pitched screech of the wheels against the track. "Kalamazoo. Kalamazoo. All out for Kalamazoo." Will stirred in his seat but stayed asleep.

She needed fresh air, so she slipped from her seat and headed for the open door. Clouds of oily exhaust hung around the train as she stepped down the metal stairs to the platform. She stretched her arms behind her head and yawned. This trip was taking an eternity. She wandered into the station. It was dirty and dimly lit, with a not-so-faint smell of urine. Kalamazoo? She might as well be in

Timbuktu. What had she been thinking, going off with some guy because he read *The New York Times*?

The station was nearly deserted. She checked out the magazine stand. *Time, Vogue*, and a whole section of dirty magazines. She turned away and went looking for the ladies' room.

She heard the Chicago-Ann Arbor train whistle its five-minute warning and was bending over the sink washing her hands when the door pushed open. She glanced up, expecting the usual train station patron, but saw a greasy man with stringy hair and a broken front tooth staring at her through the mirror. The left half of his mouth moved up in a crooked smile. She held her breath and saw her own eyes go wide. What was a man doing in the ladies' room? Before she could turn around, he grabbed her from behind, trapping her arms against his body. Fear shot up her spine and down to her fingers and toes. She was paralyzed.

She opened her mouth to scream but could only make a garbled squeak.

"Shut up!!" he commanded. "Shut up and do what I say." He smelled like whiskey, whiskey and something worse, some horrible body smell that made her want to gag. O God, she prayed silently. O God, help me! "Git in that stall," he ordered and pushed her toward the toilet. She took a step backward, and as he let go of her she grabbed the stall door from the top. Before he could follow her inside, she slammed it shut on his fingers and slid the lock.

"You Bitch!" he yelled and kicked his foot against the door.

Please God, make the lock hold, she prayed as she

climbed on top of the seat. She took a deep breath and was able to yell. "Help!" she called at the top of her lungs. "Somebody help me!"

She could see the man in his skimpy jacket over the top of the stall. He looked at her with his horrid face. "Bitch!" he spit, then lunged onto his hands and knees to crawl under the door.

"Help!" she screamed again, watching in terror as his head and then his shoulders wriggled into the stall like the Beast from the Book of Revelation oozing up from the abyss.

Just then the bathroom door swung open and in came Will. He acted instinctively. He grabbed the man by his ankles and pulled him back into the room. Then he flipped him over onto his back and gave him a solid punch in the jaw. The man let out a groan and kicked at Will's knees. Will staggered and fell against the sink. The man was on his feet, his fist cocked.

"Watch out!" she yelled.

Just as the man swung his fist, Will grabbed hold of his wrist with both hands and propelled him, face first into the edge of the tiled wall. With a horrible thunk the man was knocked unconscious and slid onto the floor.

"Will!" She was overcome with relief and amazement.

"The benefits of Karate," he said. "Go get somebody in charge. I'll keep this slime bag immobile."

The engineer delayed the train long enough so she could tell her story to the officials and Will could get his hand bandaged up. Once back on the train the porter brought them sandwiches and coffee, on the house. She leaned, exhausted, against Will's shoulder. He patted her arm.

"I woke up and you were gone. Don't you know train stations are notoriously dangerous—even in the Midwest?" He planted a platonic kiss on her cheek.

"I don't know what I would have done if you hadn't showed up." She began to cry.

"You would've kicked him right where it counts," he grinned and pushed the rest of a tuna fish sandwich into his mouth.

"I don't know. I hope so." She blew her nose into a napkin and wiped her eyes. The train gave a whistle and pulled away from the station. The lights of the car were switched off as they headed east into the night. The families at the other end of the car were quiet. Just one passenger, a dozen rows behind them, was reading with his small overhead light. It was as if they were alone.

"Why don't you get some rest?" Will said. "I'll keep my arm right here around you." He crumpled his empty coffee cup and tossed it on the seat facing them.

Exhaustion swept over her. She had to put her head down. She curled her legs under her and slid down so she was resting in Will's lap.

"That's good," he said, running his hand lightly over her arm. "Here." He covered her with his jacket. "You go to sleep."

She snuggled under the rough wool and closed her eyes while their small, dimly lit cave tunneled into the night.

She felt safe now. Safe and warm. The train wheels clattered underneath her like the chatter of cocktail guests at one of her parents' parties. Sometimes when she was little she would sit at the top of the stairs at home, hugging her nightgown around her knees, and watch the strange ritual of her parents' friends. Grownups dressed in ties and high heels, ice cubes clanking in amber-filled glasses, mothers with red lips, fathers without their five o'clock shadows. Lighters flared, heads bent close, smoke streamed from nostrils or puckered lips. Jazz on her father's hi-fi. Smiles and winks and finger tip kisses. Someone crying quietly in the front hall.

Sometimes she snuck downstairs into the guest room where furs and topcoats lay like tired cats on the four-poster bed. She buried herself in their arms and breathed in the heady, mingled scents of Shalimar and Channel No. 5. This is love, she thought as she stretched a bare foot inside a mink wrap and stroked its satiny coolness with her toes.

She felt the rise and fall of Will's breathing against the back of her head. She switched her hands from between her legs to under her cheek. Then his hand moved from where it had been resting on her shoulder to the hollow of her waist. It felt good to be close. She was in good hands.

The train rocked gently in rhythmic motion between the parallel rails. Will's hand was heavy on her. She felt a slight pressure as his fingers drummed to the beat of the train. Did he say her name? She craned her neck to look at his face, but his head was back against the seat, his eyes shut. She settled again under the warmth of his jacket.

She remembered one time when she hid in the guest room during a holiday party. Her mother's best friend came into the room and Alice was about to say hello when someone else came in and closed the door. She couldn't see who it was and neither person was talking. She sensed a strange current flowing through the candle-lit darkness, then heard odd noises. She didn't dare look; she didn't want to see. She knew it was something bad, something bad and wonderfully exciting. One of the grownups bumped against a lamp in the corner. "Damn," said a man's voice. "Don't," said a woman's. Then all of a sudden the door opened and he was gone. Her mother's friend lit a cigarette and went back to the party.

Will's hand was on her hip. Was that the hand with the bruised knuckles? He had been so brave. He'd rescued her, protected her. Maybe she'd judged him too harshly. Maybe he wasn't so bad after all.

"Next stop Ann Arbor," a voice called over the loud-speaker and the overhead lights flickered on. She sprang from Will's lap. What was she doing? She bent down to find her shoes under the seat, hiding her face. Will stood and gathered his backpack from the overhead rack. Without a word he headed toward the exit. The train blew its whistle again and as it slowed to enter the station she saw her own reflection, ghost-like, in the window.

Chapter 11

IT WAS ALMOST MIDNIGHT when Alice got back to her dorm room. She was so tired she barely acknowledged Yvonne who was sitting on her bed writing. She just dropped her backpack on the floor, slipped off her shoes, and plopped onto the bed.

"Boy have I been through a disaster," Alice said. "First I meet this guy I think is so cool, then we go on this crazy trip, we get stuck in the city, I call Julia's parents, he tries to seduce me while I'm sleeping…"

"Stop!" Yvonne yelled.

"…then I almost got raped in the Kalamazoo train station…"

"Alice," Yvonne said in a commanding tone, "Look." She pointed around the room.

Alice looked up. "Where's your stuff? Your posters? Your bedspread? My stereo? Did we get robbed?"

"That would have been better," Yvonne said.

"And why are you home studying on Friday night?"

"I'm not studying; I'm writing a letter. To the Dean."

"Why?"

"Because of you. You and your impulsiveness. You started this big snowball of disaster rolling and now I'm crashing along with you."

"Me? Come on, Yvonne, what happened?" She had never seen Yvonne so mad.

"First, you go off leaving me some cryptic note. But did I find it? No. Bruce did."

"He came up here?"

"Looking for you. And not only him, but your mother happened to choose yesterday, the first day of spring, to drop by with a bundle of daffodils as a six-months-late dorm warming gift. She didn't find you or me but she found Bruce—"good god, a boy"—in our room, and a worried one at that. By the time I got here, not only was the RA in the room, but also the dorm director. I'm sure your mother would have called in the Chancellor if she could have."

Alice started to laugh, not because it was funny, but because it was so, so awful. "And our stuff?"

"Well, the dorm director seemed to think using the Stars and Stripes as bedding was a capital offense. Your mom thought Jimi Hendrix' leather pants were too tight. And she confiscated your stereo just to be mean."

"And what about Bruce?"

"You'll have to figure that out for yourself."

"Oh, Yvonne. I'm sorry." She sunk next to her on the bed and gave her a hug. "What are we going to do?"

"What are you going to do is more like it. I'm writing a nice little apology to the Dean for misusing the flag in hopes he won't cancel my scholarship. Then I'm applying for co-op housing as soon as the semester ends. We're no longer welcome in the dorm."

"You're not going to leave without me, are you?" A lump rose in her throat.

"Don't cry. I assume you'll come with me. And don't worry about Bruce. He's as devoted to you as your shadow. I'm sure you can get him to forgive you—if you still want him."

Alice tried to sleep but one bad memory piled on top of another until she felt trapped behind the brick wall of her mistakes. She had to see Bruce and try to explain. Quietly she pulled on some clean jeans and a sweatshirt and slipped out the door. She hurried through the dark campus, not afraid of the empty streets, but of what Bruce would say, what he would do. She'd been bad to him. That was the truth. She was bad.

Only a couple of lights were on in the fraternity house. Bruce's window was black. She let herself in the big oak door, wrinkling her nose at the Friday night stench, and tiptoed up the main staircase. His room was on the second floor. She tapped the door lightly. No sound. She turned the handle and went in. As her eyes adjusted to the darkness she could see that the top bunk was empty, but Bruce was asleep on his stomach on the bed below. Without thinking she kicked off her sneakers and slid under the sheets. Her hand found his tee shirt and the small of his back. She didn't mean to, but she started to cry. "I'm sorry," she whispered into his warm neck.

Bruce made a rumbling sound and rolled over. "Huh?" he said, lifting his head a bit. "Alice?" At least he didn't push her off the bed in disgust.

"Bruce, please forgive me. I'm so sorry. I made a bad mistake. I'm bad, bad, bad." She was crying hard now.

He pulled her against his chest. "You're not bad, you're just...impulsive. You don't think about the consequences of your actions."

"I'm sorry. I know I hurt you. I wanted to call. I missed you...."

He rolled over on top of her and put his mouth over hers, runny nose and all. Oh no. His hands slid under her sweatshirt. She couldn't do this, not now. "You think I don't want you?" he said with an intensity she'd never heard before. He kissed her instead of letting her answer. She pushed him away. "Wait," she said. "We have to talk."

"Talk?" said Bruce. "Isn't this what you've been talking about? Isn't this what you've wanted? For me to prove to you that I'm a man, a man in love with you?"

She rolled away from him and sat up. Tears spilled down her cheeks.

"What's wrong?" he said. "What did I do?"

She shook her head. The words were too hard to say.

He wiped her tears with his thumb. "It's all right; I understand. It's really love you want, not sex."

With that she broke down sobbing. He held her gently until her pain ebbed. He pulled off his shirt and gave it to her so she could wipe her eyes and blow her nose. Always a gentleman. He sat holding her hand until she calmed down and was able to talk. She told him what she had done—most of what she had done—and how wrong and foolish she had been. They talked about the fiasco with her mother at the dorm. Then Bruce told her about his dad's unfaithfulness and why he didn't want to have sex before marriage. When they were all talked out and the birds were beginning to sing, he told her she might as well spend the night. They lay down and he curved his body around hers like a wing.

Things went fairly well the next day when Alice met with her parents, though they didn't talk about love like Bruce had, just their disappointment with her inexcusable, irresponsible behavior. Her father gave a speech about the absolute value of reputation. Her mother sobbed on and on about what good girls did and didn't do. She sat as still and quiet as she could, apologizing at appropriate moments. Then they meted out her punishment: they were sending her to Outward Bound for a month beginning in mid June. Her father had read somewhere, probably *The Wall Street Journal*, that the Outward Bound Survival Course was the modern cure for delinquency. It was even being used in place of reform school with excellent results. It sounded like a blast to her.

"Oh, but I was planning to...." she started to say, feigning resistance. Her parents wouldn't feel justified if she seemed eager to go.

"No, Alice," her father said. "This is a unilateral decision. You are going. The check is in the mail."

"Okay, Dad. If you think that's best. But what about May and the first part of June?" she asked. "Maybe I should go to summer school, keep myself busy." She knew they'd fall for that. Sometimes she surprised herself with how fast her mind worked.

"Right," said her dad. "Busy. Study. But where will you

live? Not in some co-ed dorm, that's for sure. And you know your mother and I will be in Italy for three weeks."

"I could probably find some all-girl housing. I'll look into it," she said, keeping a straight, penitent face. In her mind she was shouting hallelujah.

Chapter 12

IT DIDN'T TAKE LONG for the campus to empty when second semester ended in May. One day the streets of Ann Arbor were double-parked with station wagons, the next day the locals had their parking spaces back until fall. Bruce helped Alice and Yvonne move into their co-op before he left for his summer job in Grand Rapids. The co-op was near his fraternity house, just up the corner from the Blue Front where her dad bought his Formula One race car magazines.

"So will I get to see you?" Bruce asked, resting on a box of books he'd just carried to their third floor room. He had to spend the summer doing shift work in a furniture factory in Grand Rapids to pay for college. "Or are you planning to disappear on another sudden trip, like maybe New York this time?"

"You know that's all over," she said. He had forgiven her for the trip to Chicago, but she still felt uneasy. Would he ever really trust her? Should he? She went to the small dormer window and shoved it open as far as it would go. "Hey look, I can see the roof of your fraternity house."

He got up and stood behind her, resting his chin on her shoulder. "I wish I was still living there." He slipped his arms around her. "I don't want to be jealous, but you're crazy sometimes. I never know what you're going to do next."

She turned in the circle of his arms and laughed. "Neither do I." She lifted her chin to kiss him, but they heard voices in the hall and he pulled away.

"I'd better go. I start the graveyard shift tonight. I'll let you know when I get a day off." He squeezed her hand and turned quickly to leave.

She watched out the window until Bruce emerged from the front porch and headed toward the bus stop at the Student Union. He was wearing her favorite shirt of his, a red Izod with a tiny alligator on the chest. "So long. Farewell," she called but he didn't hear her. She unwrapped the purple scarf holding her ponytail and waved it after him. She did like him; he was so sweet. But one thing she knew for certain, she would never marry him. All he had was a good heart.

She was about to duck back inside the room when a voice called from somewhere nearby, "Rapuntzel, Rapuntzel, let down your hair." She looked around and there, out of the first story window of the house next door, was a woman looking up at her.

"Hi," Alice said. The woman, probably twenty-five or older, had an enormous mane of thick blonde hair with bangs cut straight across her wide brow. Sections of her hair were braided with pieces of ribbon. Her eyes were lidded with heavy turquoise shadows and her mouth was painted siren red.

"Welcome, neighbor," said the woman. "Your guy just leaving? Bet you want some company. Come on over and set a spell."

"Really?"

"Yes really. I'm Zelda deWitt. My old man's out on a job. I'll fix you a cup of my homegrown tea."

"Thanks."

She hadn't noticed it before, maybe because the co-op itself was bright purple, but Zelda's house looked like a rainbow. All the gingerbread around the big front porch was painted in bright candy colors. Zelda stood with the screen door open as Alice walked up the steps.

"Hey there, partner," said Zelda, taking Alice's hand before she had a chance to offer it. "Oh yes," she muttered, drawing her inside, still holding her hand. "I feel good vibrations, yes I do. Knew it when I saw you, when I saw that violet scarf. This is a woman of the seventh dimension, I told myself."

"What...?"

"Now just wait," Zelda ordered. "Don't spoil it. Don't tell me your name. Let's see what I can find out from the spirits."

She directed Alice to a chair in the living room while she sat down, Indian style, on a shawl-strewn sofa. There was a large, low table in the middle of the room, carved to look like a mushroom with a flat top. Strange cards with figures of people on them were lined up on the table, along with candles, an incense burner, dirty ashtrays, a bowl of smooth stones, and a vase of dried flowers. The walls were covered floor to ceiling with psychedelic posters. A huge piece of gauzy material hung from the upper four corners of the room.

"Is that a..."

"Parachute? Right. You can ask questions later. I just love this get-to-know-you part." She gathered up the cards and began to shuffle.

Alice felt weird and a little frightened, as if she'd entered a time warp but didn't know if she'd gone forward or backward.

"All right," Zelda said. "I do this my own way. I like to mix and match when it comes to magic, don't you? Don't answer that," she said quickly. "I want to sense your essence without the confusion of words."

Alice sat still. What danger could there be? She was next door to her own house. And it did smell good in there, vanilla and rose petals and a strong undercurrent of clove.

Zelda laid out the cards, nodded, then went to the pile of stones. She tossed four or five of them in her palm, like a gambler shaking dice, then held them still and examined them. She broke three sprigs off the dried flowers and put them in Alice's hand. "Crush this lavender gently, then hold out your palm." She did as she was asked and Zelda studied the bits of leaf and stem. "Now, just one more thing. Don't be afraid, I won't hurt you." She got up and walked behind her and put her hands lightly on her forehead, keeping them there for a minute or two. She made a low humming sound when she was done and sat back down at her place on the sofa.

"Okay," she said. "The gods have spoken. You are a

Gemini. You were supposed to be a twin." That was her zodiac sign, but she didn't know anything about another baby. "Just wait, you can say whatever you want when I'm done. I see you under a big purple tree. You are hidden and happy. There are wolves in the hills and snakes in the grass, but you will be safe as long as you stay with the tree. All that glitters is not gold. I know your name begins with an A. I'd like to say Angelina, but that's not right. Maybe that's what you should have been named. You used to draw straight lines in black and white, but now you're into color.

"How am I doing?" Zelda asked. "No, don't tell me. There's one more thing, and this is from the spirits, because I know you just moved in next door. But soon you are going on a long journey, up and down and up and down. Beware of the cracks. That's all I can say. Beware of the cracks." She clapped her hands twice and took a deep breath.

Alice was stunned. "Should I talk now?"

"Yup. Go right ahead and then I'll make us some tea."

"My name is Alice and I am a Gemini. My birthday's in May. I used to have a fort under a copper beech and its leaves were sort of purple. But I don't know about wolves and snakes."

"Just wait, you might not recognize them right away," Zelda said.

"I am going on a trip, to Colorado and then to England, but I don't get the black and white drawing stuff."

"You will, you will. You're a smart girl. Right?"

"I guess so. But what about you, what do you do?"

"Oh, this and that. Jerry, that's my old man, he's a roofer, a good one at that. He pays the bills, I provide the thrills."

Zelda was a funny woman. It was hard to tell how big she was under her flowing robe. Her fingers were covered with rings, silver and gold and all sorts of colored stones. She had high cheekbones and large, blue-green eyes, like her make-up.

"How did you know all that about me?"

"It's in the cards, girl. It's in the stars. It's everywhere if you know how to look."

They drank herbal tea and talked about the teach-ins on campus. Zelda told her the war in Vietnam came from the position of the planets.

"How about a smoke offering to placate the gods?" she asked lifting the top off a wooden box on the table and taking out a pre-rolled joint. Alice never turned down marijuana. As the drug encircled them with a veneer of mystery, Zelda told her about astral projection and other psychic things she was experimenting with. Alice wanted to listen but her mind was on overload. Her eyes settled on a thin slice of the western sky glowing through the window. It changed from blue to purple to deep red to orange, just as Zelda's stories grew more strange and intriguing. Then, in a blink, the sky lost its color. She realized with a start: it was night. Yvonne would be wondering where she was.

"I'm sorry but I really must go." She stood up quickly and nearly blacked out. Her long legs had been folded under her and her heart didn't have time to pump blood all the way to her head.

"Whoa, take it easy," Zelda said as Alice caught her head in her hands and wavered over the chair.

"I'm okay," she said. "This happens all the time." But

this time it felt different, as if her head and her heart were not quite connected.

"Wait, I've got something for you." Zelda went to a bookcase over against the wall. "This is an extra copy. It's been waiting for you." She handed a thick, stubby book to Alice, soft-covered but with flaps like a hardback. The title said *I Ching*.

"For me?"

"It's an ancient book of Chinese wisdom. You throw three coins six times and get a hexagram, then you look up your fortune. You can do it yourself."

"A hexagram, like the song from *Big Pink*?

"Bingo," Zelda said.

"Can I pay you for this?" The *I Ching* felt sleek yet heavy in her hand.

"Just do me a favor when you get to the UK. Send me a copy of *The White Goddess* by Robert Graves. It's only published in England."

Alice promised she would, though England seemed eons away.

"Now you come back anytime, sweetie. My door is always open and my cupboard is always full."

Chapter 13

IN EARLY JUNE Alice borrowed her mother's car and went to visit Bruce to say goodbye before she left for Outward Bound. She hadn't known Grand Rapids was so big. She'd never been west of Lansing and didn't have a clue about the other half of the state. She saw some nice houses, but the farther she went, the smaller they got. Small and boring. Not like Ann Arbor where individuality was the religion.

She slowed down at a stoplight. There it was, Bruce's mother's apartment complex. Nondescript brown brick. The only plus, he had promised her, was the tiny swimming pool. That's where she'd find him. Since he worked all night he slept by the pool in the day. He said the sun helped him relax.

She pulled the car into a parking space labeled 14B. His instructions had been very precise. She left her bag locked in the trunk and walked toward the sound of splashing children over beyond the chain-link fence.

Would his mother like her? She looked down at her pink polka-dot dress and turquoise sandals. Maybe she should have toned herself down. She entered through the gate and saw Bruce lying on his stomach on a flattened-out chaise lounge. His face was turned in her direction, but his eyes were hidden behind sunglasses. She lifted a hand and waved. He must be asleep. Then, just as she came within two feet of him, he sprang up, grabbed her around the thighs, tipped her over his shoulder, and spun her around.

"Bruce! Let me down!" She eyed his dark tan and strong arms.

"You're not the only one with surprises!" he said setting her back on her feet. "I'm a factory man." He flexed his arm. "Gives me money and muscles." He took off his sunglasses and she saw the familiar gleam in his eye. "Let's go back to the apartment. I need to shower before my mom gets home from work." He grabbed his towel and her hand and headed through the parking lot.

"I missed you," she said getting her keys out of her bag. "I never thought you'd work twelve days straight,"

"I take all the overtime they'll give me. Did you park in 14B?"

"Is it really that big a deal?"

"To my mom everything's a big deal. Dinner's at six, exactly. You have to dry the sink with a towel after you wash your hands, sponge down the shower...."

"What?"

He went on, seeming not to hear her. "No shoes in the living room. She doesn't even like me to go into the living room. No food outside the kitchen. Don't leave anything on the counter. Let's see, what else...?"

"Did your mom freak out after your dad left or something?"

"She's always been like that. A neatnik, she calls herself. But don't worry, I'll watch out for you."

They entered through a side door into the single-stall garage. A rake and a snow shovel hung from peg board on the wall. A garden hose was curled neatly in the corner. The one, small shelf held an ice scraper, a watering can, and a pair of canvas gloves. The floor was spotless except for a drip pan sitting squarely in its center.

"Wipe your feet on the mat," he said unlocking the door to the house.

"You don't have to tell me; I get the picture." But she didn't. Even with everything he had told her, she was unprepared for the feeling inside the apartment. It was dead. Before she could stop herself she blurted out, "Did someone die? It's like a mausoleum in here!"

"You're right," he said with a deep sadness in his voice she'd never heard before.

"I'm sorry. I shouldn't have said that. Did your mom just move in?"

"Are you kidding? My parents moved here four years ago, when I was a senior in high school after my dad admitted he was having financial problems." Bruce was an only child too. Maybe that was part of what held them together: they both needed a family.

"Four years?" Another stupid comment slipped from her lips. It was just that she'd never been in a place quite like this. She'd seen messy and dirty, and fancy and clean—and the crazy emotional whirlwind of her own parents' house, but she'd never been in a home that felt like a vacuum.

They passed through the kitchen. Like Bruce had said, nothing on the counter. No cute canisters or souvenir napkin holder, no toaster or salt and pepper shakers, not even a sugar bowl. "Where's your room?" she asked, almost afraid she'd find more of the same.

"Down here, past the morgue." He pointed into the living room. She punched him on the arm. "Hey," he said and spun toward her. She grabbed him round the neck and hooked her foot in front of his ankle, tripping him. They fell together onto the white carpet in the restricted area. She scrambled on top of him and he reached for a kiss. They rolled, out into the middle of the room, and then again, over next to the piano. Bruce ended up on top. "You're a naughty girl, Alice Blankwell."

"Isn't that what you like about me?" she asked and squirmed from his hold. "You'd better get dressed. I'll put on my white gloves and inspect your room while you wash up. And don't forget to tuck in the shower curtain!"

His room was brown and small. Most of the space was taken up by a low-hung bunk bed, the kind with not enough room to sit underneath, and a matching Leave-it-to-Beaver-vintage desk. There were two pictures on the wall, twin Cocker Spaniels, one with a blue background, one red. She didn't have to ask who had picked those out. All his clothes were neatly hung in his closet, shoes on a wire rack on the floor. But next to his bed was a tiny bookcase that made her smile. His favorite butterflies were mounted and framed under glass. A velvet lined box held his Petoskey stones. He had a collection of miniature art books, Klee and Miro, Kandinsky and Chagall, stacked next to Ezra Pound and Robert Frost. And there was a picture of her, perched on the landing in his fraternity house, posing in her floppy-brimmed red hat. At least there's a heart beating somewhere in this apartment, she thought.

A clank and a rumble interrupted her thoughts: the garage door was going up. Bruce was still in the shower. What should she do? Her own parents forbid boys in the bedroom. She knew the living room was off limits. God forbid she dent a pillow or leave tracks on the carpet. She ran to the bathroom door and opened it a crack. "She's here!" she half whispered, half shouted over the pelting water. Then she ran into the kitchen and slipped into a chair just as the door from the garage was opening.

Mrs. Bradford's face was obscured by the two bags of groceries she was carrying, but Alice could see she was short and solid, dressed in no-nonsense shoes and a navy blue suit, probably J.C. Penney's, with car keys gripped in her fingers and a sturdy straw purse hanging from her wrist. She let out a "humph" and pushed the door shut with her rump.

"Here, let me help you," Alice said and jumped up from the table.

Mrs. Bradford made a little barking sound as she set the heavy bags on the counter next to the sink. Then she turned and looked Alice full in the face. His mother wore no expression. She kept her lips in a straight line and stared right into her soul. Alice felt creepy, almost paralyzed. She didn't know what to say. Mrs. Bradford was a pit bull and Alice was an Irish setter who had trespassed on her property. There was no question as to who was in charge.

Finally Mrs. Bradford broke the silence. "That won't be necessary, dear. I've got everything under control." Her voice was surprisingly melodic, in a Lawrence Welk-ish sort of way. It sounded acquired, unlike Bruce's voice, which she realized just then was one of the things she loved about him. His was deep and a tiny bit raspy and completely real. She imagined it resonating through his lungs and past his heart on its way out to her. So this was his mother?

"Hello, Mrs. Bradford, I'm Alice Blankwell, Bruce's friend from University." She offered her hand.

Mrs. Bradford ignored Alice's hand and reached behind her to pull a carton of cigarettes out of one of the grocery bags. "Of course I know that." Her voice turned hard and flat. "I saw the Oldsmobile in the parking space. Let's get one thing straight. I depend on Bruce. He's my only child and unlike some people," she paused and unwrapped the cellophane from the top of the Pall Malls, "I have to work for a living. " Her eyes flicked down the hall. The shower had been turned off.

"Hi Mom," Bruce called. His wet head was sticking out of the door. "Oh good, you met Alice. I'll be right out to start the grill." He shut the door.

"So," Mrs. Bradford lit a cigarette and switched to her sugar voice. "I hope you and I will be very good friends."

Alice was speechless. Her breath seemed constricted as if something heavy was sitting on her chest. She began to cough.

"Oh," said Mrs. Bradford. "Does cigarette smoke bother you?" She blew a stream of grey smoke straight at her.

"No, I'm used to that. My mother smokes too."

"But as I understand it—you know, Bruce tells me everything—you haven't been living at home, not for a long time."

"Well, I guess that's kind of true," she said.

"Kind of true? Like a little white lie?" Mrs. Bradford had placed all the groceries on the counter and was putting them away. Alice gaped at the inside of the cupboards. She'd never seen such tidiness, if tidy was the right word. Tightiness seemed better. And the refrigerator looked like every inch of shelf space had been mapped out. She hoped there was a guide somewhere so she didn't put the Miracle Whip back where the pickles belonged.

"Are you sure there isn't something I could do to help? Set the table?" She floundered around for a snatch at normalcy. It was hard to believe this woman was related to Yvonne's mother, even by marriage. She wished Bruce would hurry up.

"How kind," Mrs. Bradford said in her company voice again. "That would be nice." She showed her where to find the place mats and utensils. Alice gave a silent prayer of thanks to her parents for their insistence on proper table manners. At least she would pass that part of this domestic exam.

Finally Bruce emerged, his skin glowed beneath his yellow shirt. He gave his mother a kiss on the cheek while he winked at her. She took a deep breath. He would protect her.

"Alice and I have been getting to know each other, haven't we dear?" Mrs. Bradford smiled at her, if you could call lifting the corners of her mouth a smile.

"Right," she said. "Can I help you with the grill?" Get me out of this kitchen, she begged silently.

"You two young people go right on ahead. The Jell-O

salad is in the refrigerator. I'm just going to heat up some beans and make the hamburger patties."

Since their apartment was at ground level, they had a tiny patio and a little patch of grass surrounded by a white picket fence, the kind that came in a roll at the hardware store. A three-inch border of marigolds lined the inside of their yard. She smelled their caustic scent as she stepped out through the sliding glass door. "Did you know marigolds are a natural insect repellent? If you plant them in a vegetable garden, you don't need to use sprays."

"We have a natural repellent inside the house too," he said with a grin. "How did it go with my mother? She prefers me to date girls she picks out, daughters of her friends—or people she wants to be her friends."

"You didn't tell me you were given birth by a Nazi."

"Shhhh. She has CIA-enhanced hearing."

"Maybe I should drive back tonight." She was dreading the thought of a whole night in that house. "Where will I sleep, anyway?"

"On the couch, in a sleeping bag. I hope that's okay."

"How about the garage? I could hang myself from the peg board. Then I wouldn't crease the pillows."

"Don't worry. She won't stab you in the night. After dinner we'll go to a movie, or at least I'll tell her that. We won't come home until she's snug under the sheets with Johnny Carson."

They did go to a movie, *Blow Up* with Vanessa Redgrave. It was shocking to see she didn't wear a bra. Bruce wanted to kiss, but Alice was too mesmerized with the story. When they got back to the apartment a blue glow showed under his mother's door just as he'd said. "She doesn't like to be disturbed after eleven," he whispered. A sleeping bag and pillow were set out on the sofa along with a note: "The maroon monogrammed towels in the bathroom are for Alice. Breakfast at seven."

Alice fell asleep quickly despite the clock on the fake marble mantle that ticked away the minutes with annoying regularity and chimed every half-hour. But when the clock struck four she awoke, panicked, unable to breathe. She was wheezing, struggling for breath. Her lungs felt heavy with fluid and she coughed up wads of phlegm. This had never happened before and she didn't know what to do. The more she coughed, the more scared she got and the shorter her breath became. She felt like she was drowning.

She crawled out of the sleeping bag and made her way to Bruce's door. Just as she reached to turn the handle, the door opened from within. He had sensed her need. He led her back to the living room and turned on a small lamp in the far corner of the room, away from the hallway.

"You're wheezing, aren't you?" He put his hand lightly on her chest.

She nodded. She couldn't speak.

"Do you have asthma?"

She shook her head.

"Well I do. I'll go get my inhaler. You just sit here and try to relax."

He was back in an instant and showed her how to use the medicine. Then he sat on the floor in front of her and held her hand. "Don't try to talk; that only makes it worse. I've had this since I was five, when my grandmother died. It's no fun, but you'll be better soon. I bet that sleeping

bag is full of mold. It was my dad's from the Air Force."
He talked to her then, told her about his grandmother,
her tiny farm by the river, her ducks and geese. The clock
marked off half-hour after half-hour, until the sky outside
lightened to grey, then mauve, then pink. Her breathing
grew still and she told him she thought she could sleep. He
covered her with a blanket from his own room and kissed
her forehead.

Mrs. Bradford had left for work the next morning
before Alice awoke. Slothful girl, she could imagine his
mother saying as she passed her sleeping on the couch.
Bruce fixed her breakfast and they took a swim in the
apartment pool before he left for work. Muddled feelings
tugged on her all the way back to Ann Arbor: Bruce was
a kind caretaker, but his Nazi mother—what did that say
about him? He was stuck all summer in a factory job while
she was flying off to the Colorado wilderness. How much
did they have in common?

As soon as she drove into Ann Arbor, her confusion
lifted. For the next twelve months at least, she had a bright
future ahead of her. She returned the car to her parents'
house and road her bike into town for an appointment
with Dr Winston, her religion professor. She hoped to talk
him into letting her change her major. The religion department had the fewest number of required courses, and she
wanted to say goodbye to endless afternoons in science
labs. Plus she wouldn't have to worry about getting behind
in credits while she studied in England.

Chapter 14

DR. WINSTON'S DEPARTMENT of Religious Studies office was slightly off campus in the shopping district that thrived on the overflow of student money. She locked her bicycle to a lamp post and walked until she found his number painted on a narrow door between a used bookstore and a dentist's office. She had passed there a thousand times, on the way to ballet lessons when she was little, on junior high trips with friends to the listening booths at Liberty Music across the street, and recently on her visits to the newly sprung-up head shop where she bought cigarette papers and tie-dyed clothing.

She pushed open the door and climbed the steep stairs to the second floor. "Samuel R. Winston, Ph.D., D.D. " was painted in gold letters on the door to her left. Doctor of Divinity?

She knocked on the cloudy glass door.

"Enter," a high-pitched, British-sounding voice said. She was sure Dr. Winston was American, but he clipped his words and held up his chin in a distinctly Anglican manner while peering through wire-rimmed spectacles perched on the end of his long nose. Dr. Winston was a tall thin man in his late forties with a cap of tight greying curls. "Just one moment," he said, not looking up from his book-bound desk. Alice glanced around the dark room. The window was shuttered and no daylight could penetrate. Bookcases stood from floor to ceiling and the upright books had others lying across their tops. Thick, important-looking magazines were stacked on the floor. Against one wall, below a print of "The Garden of Earthly Delights" by Hieronymus Bosch, was a day bed covered with an Oriental rug and edged with a dozen exotic pillows. The whole room gave off a near-Eastern aroma, camel dust and pomegranates mixed with body odor and dried figs. In fact Dr. Winston looked like a camel, a dromedary, the kind with one hump.

"Ah, Miss Blankwell. Do sit down." Dr. Winston raised his bony elbows and arched his back like a crane getting ready to fly. But his hands, drooping from his wrists, looked like spiders about to drop silk.

She sat on the edge of the day bed. It sunk beneath her weight. She wished she hadn't worn her short shorts for this meeting; she looked all legs.

"Ah hem." Dr. Winston cleared his throat. "So this meeting is concerning...?" He waited for her to fill in the blanks.

Suddenly she was drowsy. It was so stuffy and strange in there.

"Ummm," she tried to recover. "About my major. I've been thinking of changing from Unified Science to Religion." Now Dr. Winston had his two clawed hands perched on the sides of his head like reverse antlers. Did camels have horns? Did spiders live on birds? Her mind kept wandering.

"That's a considerable leap of faith," he said and chuckled. "What motivates you?"

She knew better than to tell him it was hedonism and sloth. "I want to understand the meaning of life. The ontological meaning. Where it all started. Who started it. Science looks at what we can see and measure. I want to explore the unseen." She was amazed she could say all that, since she didn't know what she was talking about. She sounded like Zelda.

"Ah ha, young lady," he smiled his strange toothy grin. She had seen it in class yet it still amazed her that all his teeth were the same small size. Didn't camels have big teeth? "The angst of your age. I comprehend completely. But why religion? You've ruled out science. But what about the pleasures of the flesh? You look like one acquainted with the *Zeitgeist*." She scrunched her face and he translated, "The spirit of the age."

She crossed her legs and covered her thighs with her hands. "The spirit of the age?" she asked. "You mean the chaos of our time. War, genocide, riots, rebellion, student demonstrations…." Now she was echoing Yvonne.

"Mini-skirts, birth control, marijuana, rock and roll." He finished off her litany. "So you think there might be answers in two or three thousand-year-old religions?"

"They're still thriving today, aren't they?" she said feeling defensive. She fumbled with her scarab ring. Why was he making this so hard?

"True, true. Soup kitchens and redaction criticism.

You've got a point. And my department is the smallest one at the University. An intimate group. Did you know that?"

"No."

"That's why we have so few required courses. You did know that." It wasn't a question. She would have blushed but she was already so hot her face was red. "I'll be happy to send a letter to your advisor. Fill out this form and bring it with you to our next class."

She stood and took the piece of paper he held across his desk. "Thank you, Dr. Winston." She went to the door.

"And next time, Miss Blankwell," he said as she was stepping into the hall. "Consider the appropriateness of your dress. If it's on display, it's usually for sale."

Chapter 15

SHE SHUT THE DOOR to Dr Winston's office and closed her eyes. She leaned against the hallway wall, trying to gain composure. She was confused by her ambivalent feelings: repulsion and attraction at the same time. She was intrigued by religion, but somehow Dr. Winston didn't fit her idea of a holy man, a Doctor of Divinity. More like a doctor-er. Maybe Zelda was right, maybe there were snakes in the grass.

As she turned to go down the stairs she noticed another room, one she hadn't seen before, further down the hall. The door was open and sounds of soothing music seeped from inside. She walked over and peeked in. "Hello?" she called out but no one answered. The room was the same size as Dr. Winston's, but that was all they had in common. This room was bright with lemon yellow walls. It even smelled like lemons, real lemons and oranges, not a fake dish detergent smell. Bookcases lined the bottom half of the room, but above them were wonderful posters: a lion curled up with a lamb, a shepherd looking for his sheep.

She recognized a print of Rembrandt's "Return of the Prodigal Son." Its deep colors reached out into the room. But what drew her most was a large panoramic poster of a mountain scene with several chalets perched on a steep hillside. Must be the Alps. Someone had attached a piece of paper to the bottom of the picture: "He who dwells in the shelter of the Most High will rest in the shadow of the Almighty. Psalm 91"

"L'Abri," said a voice behind her.

She jumped. "Oh, I'm sorry. The door was open and I heard music..."

"That's fine, child." A tiny black woman who hardly reached to her shoulder stood in the doorway. "I left the door open for you." A broad, quiet smile spread across her wrinkled face, more wrinkles than Alice had ever seen before. Her eyes were like the flame of a candle, flickering golden. A bright amethyst sparkled around her neck. Her voice was soft and liquid, like the music that came from the stereo in the corner. Alice felt like she had slipped into a calm, clear lake on a hot afternoon. The peace in the room buoyed her up like water.

"For me?"

"Yes," the woman said. "Do you like that picture?"

"It's wonderful. It looks so pure and clean."

"Ahh, child, it is. It's L'Abri."

There was that word again. "Doesn't that mean shelter in French?"

"Yes. A shelter for every nation, tribe, tongue, and people." They stood in silence for a moment. The music hung at a crescendo of high violin and slow, deep cello.

"Have you been there?" Alice asked, turning from the

poster to the where she thought the woman was standing behind her. But no one was there. She went out into the hall. It was empty. No sound came from the stairs either. That was odd. Wasn't this the woman's office? She looked on the front of the door for a name. It was blank. A strange feeling came over her, like a rogue puff of warm air in the middle of winter. She went back into the room and over to the neatly ordered desk. A Bible lay open to Psalm 91. "He will save you from the fowler's snare...He will cover you with his feathers...He will command his angels concerning you to guard you in all your ways."

She couldn't find any signs of identification, but she had trespassed enough already. She took a little notebook out of her bag and jotted down a note. "To the woman with the amethyst necklace: I would like to learn more." She wrote her name and home address and left it on top of the Bible. Then she scuttled down the stairs, unlocked her bike, and rode as fast as she could all the way back to the coop.

Chapter 16

By 10 am on the second Sunday in June the sun had marshaled its forces for a blistering day in Utah when Harold Reed, a college friend of her dad's, dropped Alice off in a vacant parking lot behind the Salt Lake City Montgomery Wards. About fifty girls stood scattered around the back of the building, each with a lumpy duffel bag, each wearing an Outward Bound tee shirt and Vibram-sole hiking boots.

An exotic girl with caramel skin and a Mia Farrow pixie haircut walked up to Alice. "Is this the bus for Outward Bound?"

"Apparently," Alice said. "But who's in charge?"

"Must be part of the mystique." The girl smiled through almond, almost Asian, eyes. "I'm Audrey from Annapolis."

"I'm Alice from Ann Arbor. Double *a* and triple *a*. We should get to sit at the front of the bus."

"But my last name's Xiang, with an *x*. It means Peace."

"Chinese?"

"My dad was. My mom's Black. I guess you could say I'm a freak."

"No way," Alice said. "That's cool. Very cool." Wow. A real Chigaro? She thought they were something she'd made up with her M&Ms but now here was one standing in front of her.

"Maybe we can curl up in the back," Audrey said. "I'm dead tired. Zonked by the zone." She crossed her elegant black eyes and Alice knew they would be friends.

"I'm not just tired; I ache all over. My father's college roommate took me skiing yesterday."

"Skiing in June?" Audrey pulled her tee shirt away from her rib cage. "It must be ninety degrees on this asphalt."

"Skiing was weird, but good old Harold thought he'd acclimate me to the altitude. We hiked up the trail with twenty pounds of gear, then skied down the patches of snow still left in the hollows."

"Aren't you lucky," Audrey said with a roll of her eyes.

"No really, I think I am lucky. When I flew into Salt Lake City Friday I saw a double rainbow out the airplane window. And then yesterday on the mountain I found a pile of coins and a folded up twenty dollar bill."

"The pot of gold."

"I feel as if something good's about to happen." Just then an unmarked bus drove into the lot. Audrey pointed and laughed.

"Not that," Alice said. "Something really good, something mystical."

"*Da dum,*" Audrey sang, "the Magical Mystery Tour is waiting to take you away!" They hoisted their bags and ran toward the bus to claim the wide back seat.

The five-hour bus ride went quickly as Alice and Audrey learned about each other. They both had known how to work the high school system but didn't care about grades anymore. George Harrison was their favorite Beatle, cheeseburgers were their favorite food, they thought Simon and Garfunkel were emotionally manipulative and Bob Dylan was the ultimate. When the bus finally stopped, it opened its doors at a barren stretch of desert. No buildings. No shelter. Only some weather-worn people in faded Outward Bound tee shirts standing behind piles of gear.

"This is it?" Alice mumbled to Audrey as they got into line with the other girls to receive their supplies.

"Pretend you're Neil Armstrong waiting for the lunar landing," Audrey said.

A burly woman in dark green hiking shorts and hairy legs barked out their names, dividing them into four patrols of twelve each. "Get into groups of three and put up your tents. Then come meet your leader and get some grub at the campfire down in the gully. Better get a move on," she added, "looks like rain."

Alice eyed Audrey and they nodded. Then she saw a square, heavy-set girl with thick glasses standing alone. "Want to be our third?" she asked. "I'm Alice; this is Audrey."

"Okay," she said. "I'm Peter."

"Peter?" Alice looked again. She was a girl.

"That's right. Peter. You have a problem with that?" She drew her eyebrows together in a hard, straight line.

"Not if you don't," Alice shrugged. "Let's get going on our tent. I'm starved."

"What tent?" Peter said. "They didn't give us a tent."

"No one got one. But look over there." Alice pointed to some girls who were fashioning a shelter out of the large square of plastic they'd each been given. "I guess we have to make our own. You go gather some long sticks," she told Peter. "Audrey, you pick up some little stones and a rock to use as a hammer. I'll clear a flat area where we can sleep."

"Hurry," Audrey said. "It's starting to rain." Big drops of water splattered the ground. Peter ran down into a gully while Alice and Audrey lumped their backpacks and supplies under the thick piece of plastic that was their only protection. As Audrey rummaged around in her pack for her rain parka, two small vials of brownish-leaves fell out.

"Is that what I think it is?" Alice said. Her eyes lit up.

"Not unless you had oregano and basil in mind."

"Bummer!"

"I could do with some relaxation right now too," Audrey said. "Enough of this natural high. Where's the Holiday Inn?" The rain was pelting down harder now.

"Think there's any chance peyote grows this far north?"

"I doubt it," Audrey said. "Here comes Peter."

"Just my luck," Peter said, rain running down the front of her glasses and dropping off her puggish nose. "There's not a tree in sight. All the long sticks were taken." She dropped six scraggly pieces of wood at their feet.

"Those aren't even two feet long. What are we going to do with them?"

"Improvise," Audrey said.

They dug holes in the rocky ground with their pocket-knives to anchor the flimsy sticks. Then they tied little bundles of stones in the corners of the plastic and balanced the sheet on the tops of the sticks. They made the two middle posts a couple inches higher than the end ones so the water that was quickly collecting on their so-called roof would drain off. Their sorry-looking shelter was only fifteen inches off the ground.

"As long as the wind doesn't blow it away," Audrey said.

"As long as we sleep flat on our backs," Alice said.

"As long as the glory covers the tabernacle," Peter said.

"What?" Alice said as the three of them hurried down to the campfire.

"Tabernacle. Tent. Same thing," Peter said.

"I thought tabernacle had something to do with the Holy of Holies—like in the Old Testament," Alice said. She'd learned that at boarding school. They were the last ones in line for damp hot dogs and cold beans.

"It does." Peter said. "The word became flesh and tabernacled among us."

You sound like a Sunday school crossword puzzle, Alice wanted to tell her, but just then a small woman approached.

"You must be my stragglers," she said bouncing on the balls of her feet as if her legs were coils of steel. "Welcome aboard, girls. I'm Leigh, your patrol leader." She shook their hands with a rock climber's grip and they knew they were in for a real trip. She'd been an Outward Bound instructor for seven years. Her sun-streaked hair hung in one long braid down her back and her skin was the color of clay, with friendly squint lines at the corners of her eyes and mouth. "We'll get acquainted along the trail," she said. "Better gobble down that grub and hit the hay. Dawn strikes quicker than a rattlesnake."

By the time they found their tent again it was dark. The rain had let up a bit, but the ground was gritty and there were puddles suspended from the ceiling of their make-shift home. They had to shimmy into their mummy bags and lie perfectly flat so the water couldn't wick through the plastic and soak their sleeping bags.

While it was still pitch black a sharp whistle trilled above their heads. "Get up, ladies. Boots on," sang out Leigh like a cattle driver. "Mile run before sun up." The hard floor of the high desert came alive with groans. "No run, no food. If you're not back in twenty minutes we douse the fire and you wait for lunch."

"What is this, boot camp?" Alice said looking at her watch. "It's half past four. I need to sleep."

"But you need to eat too," Audrey said. "Let's get this over with." Alice found her heavy boots where she'd tucked them under her backpack and wiggled them on her feet. Audrey was already up and stretching her hamstrings, but Peter had rolled on her side and pulled her sleeping bag over her head. "Hey Peter," Alice poked her shoulder. "Aren't you coming?"

"No." A voice gruffed from inside the bag.

"Didn't you hear Leigh? No breakfast if you don't run."

Peter raised up on an elbow and poked her head out. "Yes, I heard. But for your information, and I'm only going to say this once, I fast on Mondays. Besides, I need to have devotions." She rolled back into her cocoon.

Alice stifled a snort. Fasting? Devotions? Did people really do that sort of thing? Maybe Peter had a secret stash of manna from heaven.

They spent the first few days getting used to their forty-pound packs as they hiked up steep trails and broke in their boots. One good thing about having so few possessions was it was easy to keep track of them: One pair of jeans, one pair of shorts, two pairs of underpants, two tee shirts, a sweatshirt, a wool shirt, and long underwear. A rain parka, sun hat, bandana, and four pairs of heavy wool socks. Canteen, mess kit, pocketknife, journal, pencil, pen, and a bar of soap. Most precious of all, Leigh assured them, was the compass and the small waterproof case that held a handful of matches. The dehydrated food, the number-ten-can cooking pots, the first aid kit, ropes and pylons and other special things they needed were divvied up between the patrol.

Leigh kept them going at a snappy pace. Alice loved the feel of using her muscles, of swinging her heavy-booted feet one after the other up the rocky grade. She felt tall and strong. One hundred percent alive. As the days progressed her stamina increased and the pure mountain air cleared her head. There was so much to see and feel around her she didn't really miss getting stoned—or boys. The higher they climbed the better she felt. They crossed wide tracts of big boulders and she lobbed her body from one rock to the next. No matter where she started out in line, with her long legs and wide stride, she always ended up at the front of the group. The girls called her Pioneer.

She loved the days they got to go rappelling. She'd be the first one to stand on the edge of the cliff with only sky visible below her. Then she would jump into space, bouncing her feet off the rock face like a spider building a web. She loved the darkness that fell at night. They were so high up on the mountain, so far into the range, that they couldn't see one single human light, just stars and moon. Her eyes grew more and more used to the dark. She moved about, cat-like, almost by intuition.

Even the food took on wonderful flavors and textures. The trail biscuits she had complained about in the beginning became rich and satisfying the farther they walked. She savored each bite. Their nightly stew, made with mashed potato-mix and various dehydrated meats and vegetables was heavenly, especially with Audrey's spices.

Her body began to change. Muscles thickened and her skin grew taut as the layer of fat thinned beneath it. She got used to being dirty all the time, just washing her hands with sand from the riverbed. She kept her thickening hair pulled back in a pony tail. Audrey said that with her sunglasses Alice could model for *Vogue*. At the end of the day when she crawled into her mummy bag it felt like a feather bed. She was where she belonged. She could do anything.

One afternoon their patrol came to a deep gorge with a stream running through it. The only way over was to walk across a fallen tree trunk, ten feet above the water. Some of the girls crawled on hands and knees clinging to the trunk, but Alice strode across without fear. Then, when everyone was on the other side she went back across again, just to show off. "Simple," she called from the other side.

"Okay, hot shot," Audrey said. "Let's see you do it again."

Alice stepped onto the log, arms outstretched like a tightrope walker. She looked straight ahead with a confident smirk on her face. But when she was halfway across she lost her balance and began falling to one side. She broke into a run and managed to land parallel to the stream, flat on her side, in a thick carpet of moss growing on the opposite bank. She stood up and bowed to a spattering of applause.

"Pride cometh before a fall," she heard Peter say under her breath.

There was plenty of time for the girls to talk while they hiked or had meals or before they fell asleep at night. They took turns telling their stories, why they'd come to Outward Bound, where they'd come from. There were two foul-mouthed sixteen-year-olds from Boston who had opted for Outward Bound to avoid reform school. Alice knew her dad would be impressed: *The Wall Street Journal* had been right. Outward Bound cured a hundred ills. A couple of chubby girls were hoping to lose weight and one skinny girl wanted to gain it. One girl was an outdoor education major getting three hours of college credit. Someone else was being kept away from her boyfriend. Audrey had chosen Outward Bound; she wanted to explore the mountains and strengthen herself physically and spiritually. Alice told them the story of her trip to Chicago with Will on the first day of spring and how her parents were using Outward Bound as punishment.

Then it was Peter's turn. But she wouldn't get personal. "For the moment all discipline is painful rather than pleasant," she said. "But later it yields the peaceful fruit of righteousness to those who are trained by it."

"*Tu penses que Pierre est folle?*" Alice whispered to Audrey.

"Do I think Peter's crazy? No, but it's like she's from some other century. Evolution skipped right over her."

"I'm sure she's never been stoned."

"Never been kissed."

"Exactly," Audrey said. "What we need are a few guys around here."

"A whole patrol rappelling down a cliff."

"Or dropping in parachutes from a low-flying plane."

"Let's ask Peter to put that on her prayer list."

Chapter 17

FOR THE SECOND LEG of their wilderness trip Alice's Outward Bound patrol went rafting down the Green River, which eventually joined the Colorado River and formed the Grand Canyon. The girls loaded their gear in the center of six-man army surplus rafts, just glorified inner tubes, and straddled the sides, armored with life jackets and armed with paddles. The current, when it cut deep and narrow, ran twenty-two miles an hour. They took turns being captain and calling out directions so all six girls would paddle in sync, moving faster than the current so they could control their position.

The river was fierce. It hooked and jagged. There were waterfalls and rapids, and sometimes the current ran straight to the edge of a sheer face of rock with only a foot of clearance between an over-hanging canyon wall and the water. If they got sucked into the current, someone could get badly hurt or worse. Every so often the river widened into a quiet stretch where they could let down their guard while the raft gently floated along. But gradually they'd notice a rumbling sound in the distance that quickly grew to a roar. Leigh warned them to tie their rafts on the river's edge and walk along the bank to see what was ahead. They'd find that huge boulders jutted out from the river's belly or lurked just below the surface of the channel. The water bounded up over the boulders, then dropped into a deep hole on the other side. If a raft got caught in a hole, it would buckle in half, closing up like a giant clam, then spring back open with enough force to throw riders and gear into the froth. When that happened they would be swept down the rapids, tennis-shoed feet in front of them, dodging the rocks until they could climb back in the raft. Alice loved it. It was the most dangerous and exhilarating thing she had ever done. Her arms grew strong from paddling. She felt like she was reaching her body's potential. She was becoming one with nature.

Late one afternoon when they had quit for the day and were setting up camp, a lone kayaker sped by on the river. "What's that guy doing?" Alice said, "I thought we were alone out here in the wilderness."

"Listen," someone said. The girls stood still and heard a whirring sound in the distance. They stopped what they were doing and looked at the sky. A helicopter was approaching from upstream, tracing the path of the river. The wind from its blades sucked at the tops of the trees.

"We're being invaded!"

"Maybe they're bringing some real food," Audrey said.

"Fresh peaches and gallons of ice cream."

Peter spoke up; "Maybe it's the army of locusts and the tribulation has begun."

While the girls went on with their speculation, more familiar sounds started coming from up river: laughter and loud voices and music from a radio. They hurried to the edge of the water. A huge raft, at least ten times the size of their tiny Army surplus ones, bumped its way around the bend maneuvered by a man with a long pole who stood on a platform in the middle of the raft. Around him lolled a dozen or so men and boys, all holding cans of various beverages and bags of chips like they were having a picnic. They spotted the girls and whooped and waved wildly.

"Girls!" squeaked an adolescent voice.

"A dozen Barbarellas," another said.

"Pull over here," one of them yelled to their guide.

"What's going on?" Alice said.

"Oh no," Audrey said. "Isn't that Teddy Kennedy?"

It was Senator Kennedy and his nephew, Bobby junior, and a slew of other cousins and friends with their famous mop tops and square chins. They looked like a floating party barge, not a serious voyage of survival. "Might as well set up camp here," they heard someone say as the big raft drifted around the next bend and out of sight.

"I can't believe it." Alice threw a rock in the river. "This is our territory. Who let them down the river?"

"You're just pissed it isn't a raft full of guys our age," Audrey said, "holding reefers instead of beer."

"That's not it." She stamped her foot. "That's not it at all. I'm insulted. We've been paddling hard, even risking our lives, and they float by on some big marshmallow of a raft eating and drinking. It's disgusting."

"But Alice," Audrey said, "It's only been a year since their father's assassination. Can you imagine?"

The two young juvie girls from Massachusetts ran up, out of breath. "They're setting up camp," said one. "They've got cases of Oreos and huge bags of chips and everything you can think of to drink."

"And this really cute guy jumped on shore and said we should come back after dark to roast hot dogs," her friend said. "Can you believe it? Hot dogs with the Kennedys? Real food. Real guys. It's a dream come true!"

"Hush," Alice said, lacing her boots. "Or it'll turn into a nightmare. If Peter hears you she'll consider it her moral duty to report you to Leigh."

"Where are you going?" Audrey asked as Alice started walking toward the woods. "You want to spy on them too?"

"No way," she said. "I need to be alone."

Alice headed upstream, away from the intruders. She climbed over big red boulders that edged out from the river, pieces of canyon wall that had broken off and tumbled down thousands of years before. She was glad to leave the silliness behind. What was this hard knot of feeling inside her that made her want to run and hide? Why had the sight of those boys on the raft, passing by them like some television cartoon, made her so mad? Was this all just a game? A set-up? Was any of it real?

Keeping her eyes on the ground, she placed her feet carefully, shifting her weight from one uneven surface to the next. Lichen and moss clung to the rocks. White primrose and tiny blue-eyed flowers reached up from the sandy soil. She was heading west, into the sun. She could feel its late afternoon heat hitting the top of her bowed head. She lifted her face. Pink and blue streaks smeared the horizon ahead of her. She wanted to keep walking, to reach the source of light before it disappeared. She came to a giant boulder at least ten feet high, with a flat top facing south. She climbed up and lay down on her back, craning her neck to keep watching the western sky.

After a few minutes her neck started to cramp. Why did she always value what was bright and beautiful? What about the plain grey sky above her? She looked straight up and saw the faint crescent of a waxing moon. It has no light of its own, she thought. Just what it reflects from the sun. Or steals from the earth in its new moon phase. Then it becomes invisible, almost as if it's dead. Buried. In just a couple weeks astronauts were going to land on that moon, walk on it for the very first time. She felt so small, lying on that huge rock in a deep canyon. Above her another rock orbited, one without life, without air or wind or water. One that hid its dark side, only showing the earth its ever changing face.

A chill brushed over her. Dusk was falling. Her back was cold against the sandstone. She sat up and looked around. Grotesque shapes of charred trees surrounded her, mocked her. Somehow without realizing it she had walked into the middle of a burned-out forest. With mutilated trunks and branches contorted into swirls of black velvet and deadly white. Hiroshima and Nagasaki. Sodom and Gomorrah. She slid off the boulder with a shudder, as if she'd been lying on some sort of altar, a sacrificial slab. As she landed on the ground she heard a rustle at her feet. A long black snake slid away in the grass.

The Kennedy clan continued to dog them down the river, but it wasn't as bad as Alice had imagined. The floating fraternity partied at night and slept late into the mornings so the girls always had a head start of an hour or two. Their patrol would be leaving their lunch site just as the others arrived. At night the Kennedys wouldn't catch up to them until they had finished dinner. The girls who did sneak over to rendezvous got their reward of stomachaches and diarrhea from all the junky food. Alice did her best to ignore the intrusion. They were just the Democratic version of her parents and their friends.

Besides, the river had mellowed out again. After running treacherous rapids for four days—places with names like Disaster Falls, Desolation Canyon, and Hell's Half Mile—the water cut a wide path through the mountains. The girls stowed their paddles and laid back sunning themselves, letting the current drift them past walls of vermilion and ochre sandstone fifteen hundred feet high. The surfaces shifted in and away from them as the river gently spun their rafts around. Nature's own psychedelic trip.

Chapter 18

FOR THE THIRD PORTION of Outward Bound the girls were paired off and assigned to small sailboats and told, without any instruction, to sail through Flaming Gorge Reservoir. Alice got stuck with Peter, but decided to set herself a challenge. After all, she'd told Bruce every person had part of God in them, so she was going to try to crack open Peter and find her secrets.

"What's the name of your college?" Alice asked on the last afternoon as they dawdled through the cutbacks in the narrow canyon, falling behind the rest of the sunfish. It was sunny and calm as it had been their whole voyage. Peter's aloofness and Alice's boredom combined into a comfortable lethargy. Let the others pass us, Alice thought. We'll get to the end eventually.

"Wheaton," Peter said. "Some people call it the Harvard of Evangelicalism."

"Well, I've never heard of either," Alice said. "Wheaton or evangelicals. Have you even been to Harvard?" Peter's silence was a no. "I snuck into a men's dorm once," Alice said, "with my boyfriend from boarding school and spent the night. There were three bedrooms and a huge living room with paneled walls and a fireplace. And a butler who served tea and toast for breakfast."

"A butler?"

"No, I made that up. But the rest is true." Alice trailed her fingers in the water as she pushed the rudder hard to the left to come about.

"I never know if I can trust you," Peter said.

"And I never know if you're actually talking or just channeling some Bible verse. Do you believe all that?"

Peter didn't answer. Another no? Alice wondered. "So what's it like at your Harvard? Do you have any fun?" A bank of clouds had moved overhead and the breeze picked up. Alice pulled her sweatshirt out of her backpack and put it on.

Peter turned from the bow and looked Alice in the face. "Actually not much. No drinking, no smoking, no dancing, and no playing cards."

"Are you kidding? Sounds like a penitentiary."

"Did I mention no movies either?"

Suddenly a stiff gust of wind took hold of their sail and drove their small boat toward the canyon wall. "Let out the line," Alice yelled, "or we'll keel over." Sailing in the canyon with a strong wind was a hundred times trickier than sailing in a lake. The straight, high walls amplified the conditions and the current played havoc with the rudder. All at once thunder cracked and the sky poured rain. Alice couldn't control the boat and they were driven sideways against the canyon, their sail plastered against the wall.

"I don't see any of the other boats up ahead," Peter said,

calling through the wind. "We're stranded here. What are we going to do?"

"Sit low in the boat," Alice said. "Try to keep balanced." She braced with her hands to keep the boat from being dashed against the rocks.

Just then Leigh and another patrol leader appeared upriver, around the bend, in a small outboard.

"We're saved!" Peter said and waved her arms at Leigh. But Leigh's eyes were focused forward and the boat hurried past them as if they weren't even there. "Hey!" Peter yelled. "Come back!" The wind blew stronger and stronger and waves broke over the gunnels. "We're going to drown!"

A vision of Jesus walking on the water flashed through Alice's mind, but she was too scared to taunt Peter. Then as suddenly as the squall started, it abated. The rain stopped, the clouds moved away, the wind calmed, and the waves settled to a manageable chop. The sun even came out and began warming their drenched clothing.

Alice and Peter looked at each other and shook their heads. "What was that?" Alice said

"Wow," Peter said. "We are saved."

Together they pulled the lines and steered the sunfish into the middle of the river. When they gathered enough speed, Alice showed Peter how to open the valve in the bottom of the hull to drain the water they'd taken on. No other boats were in sight, but not far ahead was another sharp bend in the river.

"Boy do we have a story to tell," Peter said. "Leigh's going to hear from me, ditching us like that in our distress." As they maneuvered around the bend, the walls of the canyon dropped sharply and they found themselves sailing into what looked like a small lake with a dock and some low buildings at the end.

"Where is everybody?" Alice said. "There should be twenty-three boats ahead of us, all four patrols."

"Look." Peter pointed in the water to their starboard. "That looks like a backpack."

"Yikes!" Alice said. "There's another one. And over there, that looks like a upturned hull." As they sailed through the lake and got closer to the dock they saw all twenty-three boats capsized in the water. They passed floating daggerboards and rudders, more backpacks, and even a couple of broken masts still attached to their sails. Leigh's outboard was tied at the dock and a gaggle of soggy girls clustered around the buildings.

"You're right," Alice said to Peter. "The two of us were saved. By the rock."

Chapter 19

THE FINAL OUTWARD BOUND EVENT was a three-day solo. All they were allowed to take with them was their ground cloth, knife, journal, nine matches, and a jug of water. They wore a whistle around their necks in case of an emergency. Leigh deposited each girl in a secluded spot.

"What about our sleeping bags?" Peter asked. "Won't we freeze?"

"That's up to you," Leigh said and hustled them off, away from the canyon edge, and out into the sagebrush desert of southwestern Wyoming.

Alice was the last of the twelve to be dropped off. "See that tree on the side of the ridge?" Leigh pointed a few hundred yards away. "That beauty is a lodgepole pine. They thrive in this sandy soil and only release their seeds in a wildfire. That's your spot, Alice. Stay there until I come back in three days. And don't go walking around; you could sprain an ankle." Before Alice could protest Leigh was gone.

She hiked over to the tree and set down her jug of

water. She pulled off her jeans and sweatshirt; the July sun was rising overhead and soon it would be blistering. She looked around her. Hard, rocky sand, some wisps of grass, tumble weed, sagebrush. She could probably find a small cactus or two if she got desperate. Leigh had shown them how to burn off the prickers and eat the wet green flesh. The lodgepole pine was the only tree in sight, her only shelter.

She reached out and broke off a branch. If I strip these dead lower branches, she thought, then I'll be able to sit with my back against the trunk and stay in the shade all afternoon. She began to clean up the tree, piling the dead wood over by a flat rock so she could use it for firewood.

All of a sudden a shadow crossed her face and she heard the caw of a raven. She looked up. The bird was a speck in the distance, but the top of the pine was still quivering from where it departed. She took a step away from the tree with a sense of dread and stood motionless. At once she felt small and alien in this deserted place, this land where dinosaurs lay buried under eons of rock and dirt. Who was she to denude this tree, this lodgepole pine? She looked again up into its branches. It stood at least ten times her height.

If it wanted, she thought animistically, this tree could fall right on me. It could drop a branch or shake loose its roots or crack right in half and snuff me out. She shivered despite the heat. She was all alone. Or was she? She looked at the tree and began to reason: if I only remove dead branches, that won't hurt the tree. And if I use the branches for my fire and burn some pinecones, then I'll be helping the tree reproduce. A peace settled on her as she started to carefully clear away a temporary home for herself under the great pine.

The first day of her solo went by slowly. She smoothed a level area under the tree for a bed and padded it with tall grass from the hillside. She moved a flat stone and placed it at an angle to another one so that the heat of her night fire would be reflected back at her. But that was all she wanted to change. She was a visitor, not the owner.

She spent time writing in her journal, resting in the shade. She watched a green and black insect crawl up her leg. A wave of emotion overcame her and she cried, stroking her forehead with her own hand to comfort herself. She recited the Lord's Prayer. She listened to the buzz of black flies as they circled her body and landed in her sweat. She was lonely. She cried again. She walked partly up to the ridge and found a smooth white stone to give Bruce when she got home.

When the sun began to set the temperature dropped. She put on all her clothes and boots and built a fire with the branches she had taken from the tree. She lit a fire with one match and marveled at how each piece of wood had its own unique sound as it burned: hissing, spitting, crackling, but mostly deep low rumbling, tiny wind storms and light shows, each a universe all its own. She tossed in some pinecones and watched as the fire spread from petal to petal, and then, when it was through burning, the whole cone glowed in tricolor beauty. She followed the shadow of the fire, a dancing ghost on the ground. She went to sleep under the tree, her boots on her feet and her face on the dried grass.

The next afternoon she climbed to the top of the ridge where she could see a bit of the river and then the mountains beyond the gorge. She thought about the other girls under their trees and didn't feel so lonely. She lay back on the grass, watching the clouds slowly disappear and then reappear, tiny wisps of water vapor reinventing themselves. As she lay there for awhile, weak from not eating, she felt herself sink into the side of the hill. A rhythmic cycle began to circle through her torso and limbs. She became heavy, immobile, as if she was becoming part of the ancient ground. She felt herself drawn into a trance. Then, from nowhere, a voice spoke:

Do you want to leave your body?

Who had spoken?

The voice came again: Do you want to leave your body?

The heaviness she was feeling began to lift, to lift her up, up on a cushion of warm, thick air. Leave my body? She hesitated only a moment. Why not? Why not let go, why not sail on in this dreamy state of suspension. Why not rise into another dimension? I am part of this mountain, part of this world. She rose higher and higher into a relaxed, weightless state. Her body began to rock. A current of energy buzzed through every muscle, every nerve. She felt herself float up off the ground. Like the game they played at slumber parties in grade school. "Light as a feather, stiff as a board" they had chanted, lifting with fingertips the girl who lay within the magic circle. Or the Ouija board, its pointer gliding their hands to spell out answers to their prayers.

Prayers?

All at once something passed between her and the sun. A cloud, a shadow, a giant wing. She became conscious of her own concentration. She dropped back into her body. The ground felt hard and real beneath her. She was back in space and time. As she sat up two white feathers floated into her lap. She had not been alone.

That night as she lay under the tree, she remembered a German prayer her grandmother had taught her when she was four. Nana would bend over her bed, the loose folds of her papery skin hanging like a Chinese lantern from the frame of her face, and whisper strange guttural sounds, making Alice repeat them until she knew the prayer by heart: *Ich bin klein, mein Herz ist rein, soll niemand d'rin wohnen als Jesu allein.* "I am a little child, my heart is good. No one shall live there but Jesus alone." Now she was confused. Who had spoken to her on the hillside? Who wanted her to leave her body? And the feathers, did angels really have wings?

Wind rustled through the branches above her. She felt more than heard the swift black swoop of a bat. She tucked her hands into her armpits and nestled into the dry grass under her head.

Before dawn the next morning, while it was still dark, she awoke to thunder. But the sound wasn't coming from the sky, but from the ground. It rose through her body. A roar, a drumming, a rumble of feet. She lifted her head just in time to see three deer, white tails flagging, running up and away from her, their path no more than six feet from the tree. A visitation, she thought. Wild-hoofed angels. In an instant they were gone.

Chapter 20

WHEN ALICE GOT BACK TO ANN ARBOR after Outward Bound she kept busy getting ready for her year in England. Bruce was preoccupied with classes and a night job and she was just as happy to keep her distance. He was way too tame, too ordinary, too sweet. But one September afternoon, not long before she was to leave, she waited for him outside his Economics class. He seemed happy to see her so she took his arm and led him over to a grassy area beside Martha Cook, one of the old women's dorms.

"How many days in a month are chocolate days?" she said sitting down, legs Indian-style, leaning her head against the brick wall.

"Chocolate days?" He rolled over from his back and looked into her face. He was fingering the smooth stone she had brought back for him from the desert. He carried it in his pocket with his change.

"I was just wondering, you know, about vanilla and chocolate. Black and white. Dark heavy feelings or those sort of light days when you just seem to float by on air, hardly needing any flavor, or any food for that matter."

"What are you talking about? Are you hungry already? You want to go get a cheeseburger?"

She inhaled deeply, stretched her body up, and twisted yoga-style toward the wall. She twined her fingers in the thick leaves of the ivy covering the bricks, adding to the campus' pseudo Ivy League air.

"Okay Bruce, do this: lie down and look at the sky." She reached out and pushed him toward the grass. "See, straight above you, that clear blueness and those wispy clouds that just hang there, happy and content? They don't cast any shadows. They don't threaten rain. They're just light and free flowing. They're vanilla. But then look over that way, past Angell Hall." She unwound her legs and pointed a wool-socked toe over Bruce's head in the direction of the English building. He raised up on his elbows and peered toward the horizon where the sun was sinking into the end of the day.

"See those big dark clouds? They're piling up like some kind of army, ready to march in here and wreck our afternoon. Those are chocolate clouds. Bitter chocolate. They could have lightning and thunder inside, rain and hail, even an avalanche of snow ready to drop down on us and change everything."

"Snow in September?" he said. "Alice, you always exaggerate. Besides chocolate's your favorite flavor. The darker the better you always tell me."

"True." Her hair brushed across his cheek as she peered into his face. "Like your eyes. But I'm wondering how many days in our lives are chocolate and how many are vanilla."

He took hold of her blue-jeaned leg and pulled her over next to him.

"You're crazy, girl," he whispered and stuck his nose behind her ear and encircled her waist with his leg. "And I'm crazy about you."

A calm settled over the two of them as they lay still on the leaf-speckled lawn. "Look at that squirrel," he said, "winding head-first down the trunk of that maple. The tree looks as if it's holding out a palette of leaves, as if it were getting ready to paint the sunset."

She hugged him tighter. He was a gentle boy. He treated her as if she were special. Carried her books, gave her the last bite of his ice cream sundae. Just ordinary things, nothing exotic. But they told her he was paying attention; he cared. Do my parents have this? she wondered. This wonderful feeling of someone pressed close to your side? The safety of being wrapped in a blanket of arms and legs?

He poked his nose through her hair. "I smell the earth getting ready for winter," he said.

She started to tremble. Her belly shook.

"What's wrong?" He pushed away from her and tried to read the expression on her face. "Are you laughing or crying? Is this a vanilla day or are you starting to rain?"

"I don't know," she said sitting up. "I think maybe this is a whole new flavor altogether. Something more complex, more natural. Maybe strawberry. Or raspberry. Yes, raspberry. With tiny seeds in sweet soft juice. Raspberry. I think that's the flavor of love."

And all of a sudden she began to sob. He put his hand on her shoulder and waited.

"Bruce?" She wiped the tears off her cheeks with her sleeve. "I can't believe I'm leaving for England in less than a week." She took both his hands in hers and looked at him with sad eyes. "I'm going to miss you."

He turned his face away from her gaze. She saw his jaw shift as he clenched his teeth. "Now look at that squirrel," he said. "He's digging a hole and burying something at the foot of the maple."

"Will you write me?" she asked, not sure why he was avoiding her. "You will have graduated by the time I get back."

"Of course I'll write." He drew her close and pressed something hard into her hand.

"What's this?" She held up a small oval stone cracked through the middle.

"A fossil," he said. "See the fern? It's 300 million years old. You keep one half; I'll keep the other."

"So you think we'll see each other again?" She held back her tears.

"Alice, we can't see the future." Just then clouds in the distance rumbled a warning. Heavy drops of rain began to fall. They grabbed their jackets and ran for cover, hoping not to get drenched.

Chapter 21

HEATHROW AIRPORT bustled with travelers and British customs agents as Alice emerged from her plane. She was exhausted from the overnight flight and felt totally foreign, not because she was an American, but because of the hideous wool suit her mother insisted she wear on her trip across the Atlantic. And a detestable fake silk blouse. Alice moaned at the ugly chartreuse bow knotted in the middle of her chest. *I look like a frumpy secretary.* She dropped her bags on the concourse floor and turned to face what she thought was west. *No more!* she silently mouthed across the ocean. *I'm free of you now.*

She passed through customs and exchanged her dollars for pounds, then stood outside the airport and hailed a taxi, just like she'd seen in the movies. Two blank days lay in front of her like a brand new notebook. She didn't need to be at the University in Exeter until Wednesday. She would buy new clothes, go to the zoo, and look up the places Audrey had told her about. She would throw off the old and put on the new. It was the middle of the night back in the States, but here it was a bright, warm October morning.

She crawled into the backseat of the London cab that stopped to pick her up and checked out what she could see of the driver. Didn't that cloth wrapped around his hair mean he was religious? Maybe he would help her. Maybe she could trust him.

"Excuse me," she began. "Do you know of an inexpensive hotel where I might get a room?"

He eyed her through the rearview mirror. "You want something cheap?" His voice was surprisingly high-pitched. He sounded like a baby chick saying cheep, cheep, cheep.

"Something not so expensive. But safe."

He turned in his seat and gave her a scrutinizing look. "I know a place." Twenty minutes later he dropped her off in Earl's Court at a hole-in-the-wall where the bathroom was down the hall and there was only enough space on the side of the bed to walk into her room. Oh well, it was somewhere to sleep and she was tired. She lugged her suitcases into the corner, then stripped off her suit jacket and skirt and the horrid blouse and stuffed them under the bed, a present for the next guest. She crawled between the rough sheets and fell asleep.

It was almost dark when she woke at 3:30. I guess I was tired, she said to the dingy window that looked out over the street. But the shops were still open so she pulled on Levis and a sweater and her Nana's boxy car coat from the 40s and went out to concoct a new identity.

She found a boutique on King's Road with the latest fashions. The skirts were even shorter than at home. She picked out a knit lilac suit with a long buttoned jacket and tiny skirt. She found a slinky maroon dress with a wide zipper down the front, and two pairs of velveteen overalls, one bright pink and the other turquoise, and some white lace body suits to wear underneath. To top it off, she bought a long lavender coat, stretchy and tight fitting, with cutaway tails like a man's morning suit.

Now, she told her reflection in the shop's mirror, no one will know I'm not British.

When her shopping was done she discovered she'd wandered far from her hotel. Her feet were sore so she decided to take the tube back to Earl's Court. When she emerged from the Underground station the city had grown dark. Miniature-sized cars and giant double-decker buses, headlights beaming, came at her from the wrong direction. She walked by a cafeteria where they sold pre-wrapped sandwiches in glass-doored compartments and realized she was famished. She got in line and asked some boys standing in front of her for help. They turned out to be Americans, incognito, just like her. They had been studying English literature at a London University all summer and knew their way around the city.

"Hello," one boy said in a gentlemanly fashion and offered her his hand. "I'm Luke, Luke Kinsman. Come sit with us." He was a safe-looking boy; he reminded her of Bruce. "We'll get you pointed in the right direction."

"Oh yeah, Luke," his friend said, "Up, up, and away!"

"Better than being 'hurled headlong flaming from the Eternal Sky!'" another boy said. "'With hideous ruin and combustion down to bottomless perdition.'"

"Yikes," Alice said.

"We've just come from our lecture on *Paradise Lost*," Luke told her.

They crowded around a small wooden table and she watched the four of them as they teased one another, spouting off more Milton.

"Hey, she's staying at the King's Acre!" an open-faced boy reported to the others. "One of those Pakistani cab drivers took her there." They all laughed.

"You know why it's called the 'Acre'?" asked another boy as he smoothed his long blond hair away from his eyes.

"Well, it can't be the size of the rooms," she said.

"You've got that right," he agreed. "Wait'll you wake up tomorrow morning. Then you'll find the acher! And when you pay the bill, you'll wish you were the king!" They all laughed again. She knew they were making fun of the hotel, not her. These were nice boys.

After the meal they invited her back to their flat on Cheney Walk. "The very same street where the Rolling Stones used to live," they boasted as they walked down the cobbled sidewalk where street lamps were half-hidden behind wide branching trees.

"Of course, we don't know which flat was theirs. Not our dump, to be sure. Except the smell is right!" They laughed again, but she didn't get the joke.

Once inside they piled their jackets on the only chair at the cluttered kitchen table and settled down on low sofas around a square coffee table. It was littered with stubby candles and dirty ashtrays, packets of cigarette papers and a big brass hookah. A fat tabby cat slept under the table.

"Care for a smoke?" Luke asked. She kept noticing him, the quiet one with solemn eyes. He seemed to be searching her face for some answer, like a man at the shoreline waiting for a ship to appear. His words were deliberate, his movements steady and solid as he cut off a chunk of hashish and fit it into the bowl of the pipe.

She was happy to accept their offering as it made its way around the circle, the smoke enclosing them in its sharp aroma. "I wondered how I'd find the freaks here in the UK," she said and then filled her lungs with smoke. Soon a dreamy cloud descended on the room. The only sound was a rhythmic purring coming from under the table.

She spoke into the silence and began telling them stories of Outward Bound, the Rockies and the rapids, the charred forest and the bull snake.

"Tell us more about the snake," one of them said.

She shuddered as she pictured it in her mind. "It was a six-foot long bull snake. Harmless. We found it near our camp one morning and carried it with us for several days, taking turns letting it hang from our arms and around our necks. Then Leigh, our patrol leader, said we had to kill it and eat it."

"Gross!" groaned one of the boys.

"No kidding," she said. "It was weird. One girl held the snake against a log while someone else used the hatchet. One decapitating chop and 'Agh, agh, agh.'" She imitated the snake's mouth. "The head was only attached to two inches of neck, but it snapped its jaws and scooted along the ground."

"Like a chicken with its head cut off?"

"Yes, but this was just a head biting at the air. The body

was something else again. After we skinned it and gutted it, it kept curling and tightening around our arms."

"Yikes," the boys said.

"It was eerie," she said. "That headless, heartless creature was more frightening dead than it had been alive."

The room grew still. One of the candlewicks sizzled.

"I must be boring you," she said. She always worried that she talked too much. Her parents were never interested in her stories. "Do you want me to stop?"

"Oh no!" the four chimed together as if a grandfather clock struck the hour. "Tell us more."

So she described rafting down Hell's Half Mile, how she had thought she was going to be crushed under the canyon walls. And the slow lazy days when they floated on their backs and felt stoned just from watching the reds and oranges of the Flaming Gorge spreading up a thousand feet above them.

She looked around in the candlelight; they all had their eyes closed. "Now I've put you to sleep."

"No, we're in the canyon with you."

"Shall I stoke up another round?" one of them said. "I bet Alice could talk all night."

"Thanks, but I'd better get back to my room. I'm really tired." She straightened her legs and stood up. "Thank you all for being so welcoming."

"I'll walk you home." Luke was by her side. Thoughtful, like Bruce.

The night air was cool and clear as they wandered down the empty streets.

After a couple of blocks of walking in silence, he stopped and turned to look her in the face. "There's one thing about you that doesn't make sense," he said in a gentle tone. She could tell he had something serious to say but he didn't want to hurt her feelings. He put his hands on her shoulders. He smelled of acorns and broken twigs. She heard him take a deep breath. "You're such a purist," he said. "So natural, so free. And yet..." he hesitated.

She backed away. More criticism. "And yet what?"

He addressed her straight in the eyes. "I'm surprised you smoke dope. That you need a drug to get high. That's all."

"You smoke dope!" she blurted. "You're the one who offered it to me."

"I know," he said. "And I like it." He reached out and took her hand. "And I like you too. It's just that you're so, I don't know, different. You're courageous—all that stuff at Outward Bound, then coming to England by yourself. It seems like you could be happy without drugs." His words sunk to the back of her mind. When they reached the King's Acre she invited him in.

Chapter 22

THE TRAIN TRACKS seemed to converge, getting closer and closer together while the train became smaller and smaller. Alice felt as if she were going back in time, leaving the sixties, the fifties, a skipping stone across the blank surface of the decades until she reached Devonshire with its sheep strewn hillsides, narrow cobbled streets, lanes barely wide enough for one car to brush through thickets and brambles. Great high hedges blocked her view. All was windy, hilly. Clouds cantered overhead then reared, dropping their heavy, wet burden. Racing off they left a trail of rainbows in their wake. It must be the ocean so near, she thought, and the moor, like a giant airfield where weather from the south and west took off and landed without warning any hour of the day.

As the Exeter taxi wound its way up Crescent Drive and down Sargent's Lane students began to appear, popping out of holes in shrubbery, stepping from brightly colored doors. "Here we are, Miss," the driver said as he pulled to the side of the road next to a towering bank of rhododendron.

"I don't see a dormitory. Are you sure this is the right place?"

"If I'm not mistaken, Miss, it's that house over there." He pointed beyond the wall of flowering bushes. "I'll ask that bloke with the pink scarf. What's the name again?"

She fumbled in her bag for the slip of paper where she'd written the address. "Grove Hall, Willoughby Annex, 24 Chilbury Court," she read.

A thin, elfish boy with decidedly pointed ears assured them they had found Willoughby. Alice could hardly believe it. She was in a dream. She passed under the tall bowering trees and made her way up to the front door of the grey stone mansion. Everything was so old, so pretty, so much more lush and romantic than she'd ever imagined. She found her name along with "Rowena Bickle" posted on the door of a room on the first floor. The driver set her bags down inside the room. "May it be all that you desire, Miss," he said with a nod of his head, "and more." When he'd left she stood still, simmering with excitement. Then she ran to the French doors at the far end of the room. She turned the brass handles and burst into a walled garden. Two rows of pear trees marched down its middle, their fruit-laden branches intertwined in an arbor above. The smell of ripening fruit buzzed in her head like the swarms of bees dancing through the branches. There were roses in bloom and tall hollyhocks along the wall. A fountain in the shape of a swan stood off to one corner, encircled by low stone benches. Thick spongy grass blanketed the ground. She turned and looked back to the house. Above and to one side of her room was a balcony; on either side of her doors were espaliered trees. She could live here forever. Reluctantly she went back inside to unpack.

There were two beds, two dressers, two desks. Rowena had already arrived: one bed was covered with a plain wool blanket, one desk held a stack of neatly lined up notebooks and a coffee mug full of pens. Two pairs of clunky-heeled shoes stood at attention under the bed. Dullsville. But she shouldn't judge by appearances. This was a whole different culture. She could get along with anyone. She'd had all kinds of roommates from six summers of camp, four years of boarding school, and then college. But there did seem to be a peculiar odor coming from the other girl's side of the closet. And everything hanging there was dark and drab.

She was relieved to see her big black steamer trunk that she'd shipped weeks ago had arrived safely. She couldn't believe how much stuff she'd brought. At least she was prepared. She found the key to her trunk in her coin purse, but when she went to unlock it, it was already open. She undid the clasps, lifted the lid, and drew back with revulsion. Something horrible was right on top of all her clothes: a filthy, holey pair of tennis shoes. Where did those come from? She picked them up by their grimy laces and flung them at the door.

Gingerly she searched the trunk to see if there was anything else foreign, but the rest of the things were just as she had packed them, only now they had a sinister tinge. Then she remembered—her new pair of deerskin moccasins—they were missing. She'd had them made for her by a Ojibwa man in downtown Ann Arbor. Someone stole her moccasins before she even got a chance to wear them.

She laughed as the irony hit her. The thief took hers and left his. But she had plenty of other shoes. She could buy more. That person obviously needed new shoes. She tried to be reasonable. But she couldn't shake the feeling deep inside that she had been violated, her privacy broken into, her treasure taken. And in its place was something old and dirty and used.

Chapter 23

ALICE'S PARENTS told her she could buy a bicycle in Exeter to get around campus. But they hadn't known the University sat on top of a steep hill. Bicycling was out of the question. So when she saw a movie poster for *A Girl on a Motorcycle*, starring Marianne Faithfull, Mick Jagger's girlfriend, she took it as a sign. She didn't care that the movie showing conflicted with the Christian Students' Service and Fellowship Newcomer's Tea. Veronica, the dowdy girl who had hand-delivered the formal invitation didn't look like someone who would be her friend anyway. So instead meeting a roomful of social outcasts, she sat alone in the small auditorium off the side of the Student Union and watched as Marianne slipped into a one-piece leather suit and sped off on a motorcycle to meet her lover. The next day Alice took a bus to a used motorcycle shop on High Street where the mechanic showed her a glittering red BSA 175.

"It's a 'Bantam,'" he said with a twinkle. "Light weight, like a bird, but flies like the wind."

"I'll take it," she said, stroking the smooth rounded surface of its heart-shaped body. She wasn't sure how many pounds equaled how many dollars, but it seemed cheap enough to her. She wrote him a cheque from her new back account.

"Ta," he said. "We'll deliver it this afternoon. You be sure to get a helmet. And a leather jacket. That's an order."

"Thanks." At least he hadn't suggested a leather body suit.

Later that day she approached a boy who lived in one of the annexes at Grove Hall. She'd seen him riding a motorcycle and asked if he'd teach her how to handle her bike. He was shy, but kind, and a string of boys came out to watch as she practiced kick-starting, changing gears, and rocking the bike off and then back onto its stand.

"The guy said this is lightweight!" she said struggling.

"You'll get used to it," the boy said with a grin. "You'll be soaring down the lanes and off to the moors like a seagull, you will." And she did. Her bike became her best friend, its low hum a mother's heart beat. She hugged it with her legs, coaxed the throttle with her hand. It took her away from the strangeness of people, carried her out under the open sky, introduced her to the same stars that just a few hours later would look down upon her own home back in the States.

Chapter 24

AT GROVE HALL all the students from the five annexes ate together in a main dining room. At one end of the room was a raised platform where the faculty sat in chairs around the long head table. Students squeezed together on benches at tables down on the floor. Thursday night was High Tea. That meant everyone had to wear academic gowns to dinner and suffer through a disgusting-looking molded paté with whole boiled eggs, pimento olives, and sweet pickles appearing randomly when the loaf was sliced. Alice always went to meals alone. Rowena, her roommate, made it clear she wasn't keen on sitting with her in the dining hall or walking with her to class. She would offer only the slightest help as to British customs and colloquialisms. What were the gods doing when they paired us together? Alice wondered. Rowena was a gruff, mannish girl from one of those northern cities covered with soot. Her chin stuck out like a lump of coal and the sounds that came from her mouth all rhymed with arrhh and grawwhh. She had her own group of friends from home who zipped their lips and nodded at each other knowingly whenever Alice walked in the room. She and Rowena were only together when asleep. That was all right with Alice. She was more interested in meeting boys anyway.

Not long after she arrived she spotted an interesting prospect: a boy with wavy shoulder length hair that floated like a halo around his dark-eyed face. He had the loveliest mouth, deep red like a Christmas bow. Alice thought he looked like an angel, or at least the angel in Antonioni's, *The Gospel According to St. Matthew*. She and Bruce had seen the movie together just before she left home. Bruce, she thought wistfully, was so far away. And she was all alone.

It only took her a few days to maneuver a place at the table where the angel boy sat with a group of his friends. She listened to their conversation for awhile, then took the plunge and spoke to the boy sitting next to the one she fancied. "What do you call this green fruit?" She pointed to the bowl in front of her.

"Gooseberries." He gave her a curious, what's-wrong-with-you look.

"And you pour this white sauce over them?"

"I always do." By now the whole table of boys were looking at her. She knew her accent would draw them if nothing else did.

"Are they sweet?"

"The sauce is sweet, but the berries are rather tart, wouldn't you say so Graham?" He looked over at the angel boy. So his name was Graham.

"My advice," Graham said with a sardonic tone, "is to

taste them." He looked her in the eye as if he could see right into her mind. A chill went down her neck.

"So where are you from?" a curly-headed fellow to her right chirped out. "The U.S. of A.?"

"Um hum," she nodded, her mouth full of gooseberry.

"My aunt lives in New Jersey."

"I'm from Michigan." She glanced at her audience.

"Mitch-i-gan," Graham said. "The Great Lakes State. Erie, Huron, Mitch-i-gan, Ontario, Superior."

"Impressive," she said. "How do you know all that?"

"Geography," he clipped.

"Oh." He didn't waste words. She looked at him in his academic robe with his choir boy hair touching his shoulders and a sprinkle of freckles on his cheeks. His dark eyes drew her like a well. She glanced from his face down to his hands and caught her breath: he had the longest fingernails she had ever seen. They extended half an inch past his fingertips. Suddenly she felt dizzy.

"What course are you reading?" someone was asking her.

"Reading?" she mumbled distractedly. Graham was pushing away from the table.

"You Yanks call it studying."

For the moment Graham was all she was studying.

Chapter 25

ALICE STOOD IN LINE at the Student Union with her package of chocolate-covered biscuits and ordered a cup of tea. She was anxious to read the new European edition of *Time* magazine. So many things were happening on the campuses back home. Sit-ins and teach-ins. The My Lai massacre. A national Moratorium Day. She wondered if Yvonne was still involved with SDS. Hundreds of thousands of people were planning to march on Washington D.C. and at Golden Gate Park. She was missing so much. The students at home were a unified voice demanding the end to the Viet Nam War. And what was she doing? Life was going on without her. Everything was evolving so fast back home and here she was alone and unconnected. She didn't have one friend.

She settled down in an empty spot on one of the semi-circular benches near the windows and unwrapped the biscuits. Whenever she was on campus to study or attend a lecture, she tried a different snack, hunting for something to satisfy her craving for comfort and familiarity. British biscuits were really cookies. Some were sweet and soft, others hard and full of fiber, like bad graham crackers back home. Graham. He didn't seem like he would be very sweet. But would she ever get a chance to find out? She balanced the magazine on her crossed knee and dipped her newest experiment into her tea.

"So how's Estelle?" The young man sitting next to her lowered his newspaper and spoke, seemingly, into the empty space in front of him.

"She's getting on," said a plump girl with kinky hair sitting three seats over on her left.

Then another voice spoke up from across the circle of seats. "I went to see her yesterday. She looked bloody awful." Alice noticed this third voice came from a thin bloke with pointy ears. A pink mohair scarf was draped around his neck. He was the one who'd given her directions the day she arrived on campus. It was dawning on her that most of the students only wore one or two outfits: the boy in the striped sailor pants, the girl with the corduroy vest, the teacher with the olive green jacket. The boy with the pink mohair scarf had it wrapped around his left hand. But as he said "bloody awful", he flung his hands forward and she saw with alarm what the scarf had been hiding: a withered hand.

"Well how would you look, Seth, if you'd fallen under a bus?" Yet another student joined the conversation.

That's mean, she thought. What if this Seth guy had fallen under a bus. Or his mother. Maybe that's why his hand was deformed. And then she realized: she was sitting in the middle of a group of friends who all knew each other. And they all knew she was a stranger. Why didn't they say hello or introduce themselves? She wished she could shrink to the size of a mouse and crawl away under her seat.

Even though she was having trouble making friends, it didn't take her long to find a source for buying drugs. There was a guy in the annex next to hers who wore tie-dyed shirts and a dopey grin on his face. He was short and spidery and seemed to have more than two arms and legs. He jittered when he walked and jittered when he talked. She spotted him alone after dinner one night and decided to introduce herself. "Hello," she said. "I'm new here."

"Yeah, well I'm new here myself. Why else would anyone live on campus?"

"You've got a point," she said. "But I thought you looked like someone who might know where it's at."

"You're that American girl I've heard about."

"Right. Alice."

"Cool. Wonderland and all that. They call me the Joker." He stuck out his hand. It was small like hers. She could see tell-tale yellow smoke stains between his fingers. "So," he said, "are you hip? I mean being from the big country and all that. This is the backwoods here. Not like London where I'm from."

"Oh, London." She thought of Luke and the night they'd spent together. He would have been her friend. "Mind if I sit?" She hoisted herself up on the garden wall. Joker pulled out a funny cardboard box that British cigarettes came in and offered her one as was the custom. She shook her head.

"Yeah. London's totally other. Totally cool. This place

is nearly dead. More like not yet born." He chuckled at his own joke. The Joker.

"So what do people do for recreation around here?" she said. "I noticed there's an official tiddly winks club. They even have officers."

"That's a laugh."

"No, it's true. I read it in that little handbook they gave us."

"Well, here's the scoop. Most of these sods go down to the pub on weekends and fill up on Scrumpy. Had any yet? It's the West Country specialty. Extra hard cider. Still has the worms in it," he chortled. "But me and my mates, we prefer to breathe our fun, if you get my drift."

"I do," she said. "That's what I'm looking for."

"Come by sometime. My room's at Bentley." He sounded like he meant it. "In fact, come by Friday before the evening meal. I'm expecting a delivery. Plenty of free samples."

"Thanks, ta, I'll see you then." She skipped back to her room. Things were looking up.

Chapter 26

ALICE PARKED HER MOTORCYCLE on the cobblestones
of the Cathedral Close and checked the sundial mounted
above the tiny 13th century door. Quarter after two, late
again. She took off her helmet, shook out her hair, unzipped
her leather jacket, and pulled her academic gown over her
turquoise overalls. Theology was the only department that
still insisted on gowns for lectures. But this was hardly a
lecture, just she and Veronica Primly from the Newcomer's
Tea sitting in Canon Shawcross's study talking about the
Person and Work of Christ. She turned the little crank next
to the door and waited for the Canon's housekeeper to let
her in. All her other classes were in the "red brick" English
department. This one theology class was the highlight of
her week. She didn't understand much of theology, but she
appreciated the atmosphere.

"Ah, Alice." The Canon always had a sparkle in his eye.
He was white-haired and round-headed. At least eighty.
She didn't even know what an Anglican Canon was. Of
course Veronica was already there, sitting neatly in her

beige houndstooth skirt that hung well below the hem of her gown.

"Hello Alice," she said talking through her nose.

"Hello Canon, Veronica." She gave a little bow and made her way to the empty chair in front of the leaded window. "I'm sorry I'm late."

"Only fourteen minutes," Veronica said.

"Don't worry, child," the Canon said. "We were just discussing the Atonement."

She settled into the worn chintz. Soon her black gown absorbed the afternoon sun streaming through the window and her eyelids grew heavy. She focused on the books lining the shelves and scanned their titles to keep awake. *The Historicity of Christ, A Harmony of the Gospels, Melchizedekian Archetypes.* Many of the titles were in Latin or Greek.

"What do you think, Alice?" Canon Shawcross was speaking to her.

"Excuse me?"

"Veronica was saying that Jesus performed miracles through his divinity. What do you think?"

She twisted a strand of hair between her fingers and stalled for time. "Of course he was divine, but he was human too."

"Yes."

"Could his humanness also have something to do with the miracles?" She scanned through the Apostles' Creed in her head. Conceived by the Holy Ghost, born of the Virgin Mary. "Didn't his power come from the Holy Spirit? Maybe it was the Spirit in the man that made the miracles possible."

"Yes." The Canon nodded, always so affirming. "Very good."

"So, do we," she stumbled with her words, "do we have the Spirit in us too?"

"If we confess with our lips and believe in our hearts." The Canon smiled.

"Then can we do miracles?"

"Ah, Alice. That's a good question. Let us begin there next week."

She rolled her bike down the Cathedral Close, around the northwest corner of the Cathedral Green, and pulled it up on its stand in front of Tinley's Tea House. She loved this place with its glass case of exotic biscuits and cakes. No blueberry muffins or greasy glazed donuts. Instead they served wonderful short breads and dry, stiff cookies dipped in thick dark chocolate. Tinley's had white linen-topped tables and heavy silverware. She sat at a table in the window and waited for one of the waitresses who fluttered around the room in white pinafores and starched, half-hats pinned on their grandmother heads. Miniature Queen Mothers.

She ordered her usual, Devon Cream Tea. From her seat by the window she could see past the broken remnants of a medieval wall into the wide green park in front of the cathedral. It had taken over three hundred years to build that church. How did they keep at it for so many generations? Where would this world be in three hundred years? But God, she thought, God is infinite. Her eyes traced the outline of the massive building, then softened as she gazed into the sky.

She almost didn't mind being alone, alone with the comfort of tea and scones and thick Devon cream. There were other Americans at Exeter, a whole group from a small college in Minnesota but they didn't like her. She knew them from the English literature lectures for American students, but not one was friendly with her except maybe a goofy guy named Kevin. He smiled at her once in awhile and shrugged his shoulders helplessly when the group turned away from her. Their ring leader was a caustic girl with the appropriate name of Barb, Barb Schneider. She let Alice know she was not one of them and never would be. Why should Alice care? The Americans just buddied around together, gawking and laughing, making fools of themselves, as if they were on a trip to Disneyland. She wanted to get to know the natives anyway, but the British gave her scorning glances too. Like the women at a nearby table who were probably wondering about her black leather jacket and iridescent overalls. She was used to whisperings as people spied her motorcycle helmet or heard the awkward American accent coming from her mouth.

What had she asked the Canon? Did she have God's Spirit? She certainly wasn't a miracle worker. She was more like the medieval wall in the church yard, neither in nor out, crumbling into oblivion.

Chapter 27

"NEXT WEEK WE CONTINUE with Coleridge's poems of the supernatural. Be sure to read his lectures as well." Dr. Burroughs, the English professor in charge of the American students, stretched his lips into a perfunctory smile, folded his reading glasses, and tucked them into his breast pocket. He gave a little tug to the front of his tweed vest, then tilted his head, and looked straight at Alice. She bent down and shoved her notebook into her backpack. It was enough to sit in his lecture room four times a week for class, but she also had to meet with him in his office each week for an hour of private tutorial. The last time he had spent the hour staring at her lace body suit. As she'd stood to leave, he invited her to his house for dinner. "I'll lay a fire in the grate," he said. No way, she blurted in her mind, then quickly thought up an excuse. It made her nauseous to think about him, the thin mustache under his nose and his long brown rodent's teeth. Pipe-stained, she imagined. But no, she didn't want to imagine anything at all about him.

Samuel Taylor Coleridge, on the other hand, did do something for her imagination. She had just finished reading his theory that if you put certain herbs under your pillow at night you would dream about your future. She swung her backpack over her shoulder and headed out to visit the botanical gardens.

A short shower had just ended and the ground was covered with sparkles of rain. Tall clouds rolled away over the hills to the east. It was already November but still warm. Alice loved this weather, temperate and temperamental. Always changing. She scuttled up the path that led behind the science buildings.

"'Scuse me, Yank." A deep voice spoke behind her. "You drop this?"

She turned to find a grinning face chuckling at her. Blue eyes squinted above an untamed beard while ginger-colored hair, thinning on top, sprung in wild curls around the stranger's head. He reminded her of a Greek or Roman bust. Or maybe the head of a satyr. He was dressed in baggy corduroys cinched in at the waist with a long belt. He wore several layers of tee shirts, their colors circling his neck like jewelry below, a stretched out jumper with holes in the elbows. In his hand he held an oval locket on a gold chain.

"That's not mine," she said eyeing him cautiously. She couldn't tell how old he was. Was he a student? Could he be a professor? Maybe he worked in the gardens. But he had a backpack slung over one shoulder. "How did you know where I'm from?"

"I've seen you around. I've 'eard you talk. I know you're not from 'ere." He spoke with a Cockney accent. "But anyone can tell by your plimsolls. They say US Keds on the back."

She lifted her heel and looked down. "And I thought I was incognito."

"No secrets in the West Country," he said. "You'd best be learning that by now." It sounded like a warning. "You sure this isn't yours?" He dangled the locket by its chain, swinging it back and forth like a hypnotist. It glistened in the sun. She followed it with her eyes until she began to feel dizzy. She wondered what was inside.

As if she'd spoken aloud, he pried the locket open. His fingers were strangely elegant for someone so scruffy. "Take a look," he said turning the tiny picture frame toward her. "You sure this doesn't belong to you?"

She stepped closer and peered into his hand. It was a photograph of a girl, a girl who looked just like her. She felt very strange. The sun hid behind a cloud and she smelled something dank and musty.

"Where did you get that?" It took some effort to straighten up and move away from him, as if she was a paper clip and he was a magnet.

"I found it this morning, under the big Redwood. You know the one. They brought it here all the way from California."

She did know that tree. She knew it well. The University had extensive grounds with trees from all over the world, but only one Redwood. Ever since she'd discovered that giant American she had taken to hiding in the sheltered spot at its base when she needed to be comforted. She'd never seen anyone else around there.

"You should have it. Looks just like you. Or your twin."

She thought of Zelda and her claim that Alice had not been alone in the womb. "Take it." He lurched forward and pressed the locket into her hand.

"No!" She pulled her arm away as if she'd been stung. "No, no thanks. But thank you," she flustered. "It's not mine. I've never seen it before."

"There are plenty of things that belong to us, only we don't recognize them. We haven't let them into our imagination, into our dreams." She looked at him. He was staring straight into her face. He wouldn't let go of her gaze. He drew her in. She turned her head away. It scared her that he knew so much about her. He seemed to have a plan. Suddenly the sky let out with a great crackling sound. Soon rain would fall. She turned and ran up the hill to the gardens to pinch a sprig of lavender.

"I will be seeing you, Alice Blankwell," he called out, using her name. Did he know the future too?

That night Alice tucked the bouquet of lavender under her pillow and went to sleep with expectation. In the morning she awoke from a vivid dream: she was walking down the path outside Willoughby when a tall blond boy suddenly appeared in front of her. He held out his hand and as she took hold of it they were stepping into a big bus. He spoke to her in French and told her to look out the window. As she did a great light exploded, like fireworks on the fourth of July.

What a dream. She was glad she hadn't dreamed of the spooky guy with the locket. The boy in her dream was much more appealing. Would something really happen? She was almost afraid to go outside. But later that afternoon on her way to the Grove Hall office to pick up her mail, the dream started coming true. She was walking fast, her usual gait, when she took a shortcut through some bushes and was face to face with the figure from her dream.

"Hello," he said and made a slight bow. "Excusez-moi. I know you are Alice from America. Please allow me to introduce myself. I am Oliver Nicholas Neal." They shook hands formally. Everything about him was formal: immaculately cut blond hair with a straight row of fringe across his forehead, sea-blue ascot tied around his neck, well-ironed shirt, freshly pressed khakis, brightly polished loafers with tassels on the toes. Was he what they called an "odd bird"?

"I know that we British are uncommonly stuffy, not very friendly and all that," he said. "Of course, I, myself, though British, was raised in Belgium. My father's appointment you see. I thought perhaps, since you are not aware of our customs, that you might relish a trip to Ottery St. Mary tonight where the townsfolk will celebrate Guy Fawkes Day with the traditional bonfire." He tipped his head to the side and smiled.

"Oh," was all she could manage.

"I'll be going with my roommate, Tom Mountbatten, and a couple other blokes from my house. We'll be taking the bus. Leaves at eight sharp from outside the main hall. May we have the pleasure of your company?"

"Certainly," she said, entranced. "Thank you!"

"It's a marvelous village," he added. "The birth place of Coleridge."

* * *

On the bus that night, Oliver and his friends reminded her of a big family of older brothers. Their kindness eased her loneliness and helped her forget about herself. The village of Ottery St. Mary sprung right out of a fairy tale. The town green glowed golden with the tallest bonfire she had ever seen, at least forty feet high. Effigies of Guy Fawkes hung on poles before being tossed into the flames. After they'd watched the fire for a while, Oliver took her arm and led their group down a brick-walled lane in search of a pub. Suddenly a gang of burly men stumbled past them carrying barrels of burning tar.

"Isn't that dangerous?" She cowered away from the flames.

"It certainly is!" Oliver raised his jacket to shield her. "About face!" he called to his buddies like a cavalry captain. They turned from the drunken craziness of the night and ran to the safety of the bus. On the way home she curled up on the back seat, her head against the window, and listened as Oliver and Tom and the other boys sang old public school songs.

She kept her dream tucked inside her head.

Chapter 28

THE NEXT DAY WAS FRIDAY, the day Joker had invited Alice to his room. When she stepped inside the vestibule of Bentley House she didn't need to ask directions. Two boys on their way out gave her a nod and pointed down the hall. "Knock three times," said one with a wink. She did and the door was opened.

"Ahh, I was hoping you'd make it. Come right in, Lassie. Meet the lot." Joker was perched on top of his dresser next to a small balance scale. In the dim light from the curtained window she could just make out two ragged fellows, one lounging on the bed, the other sitting on the floor. "Mates, this is Alice. She's one of us," he said by way of introduction. As her eyes grew accustomed to the dark she saw the boy with the pink scarf and withered hand. She was beginning to realize that a campus of 2,000 students was really very small.

"So you're one of the bad girls, huh?" the guy with the scarf asked.

"I prefer to think of myself as experimental," she said.

"Don't take offense," he said. "I'm Seth; this here's Nigel," he nodded toward the boy on the floor.

"Hi," she said and noticed for the first time that the boy named Nigel was sprinkling something in a long, fat joint. A smoky sweetness filled the room.

"Almost ready," he said, noticing her stare.

"What is that?" she said. "Doesn't look like grass to me."

"Ah, grass," the boys sighed together.

"We hardly ever get that here," Seth said. "Too bulky to smuggle in. This is hashish. We heat it up and sprinkle it in with tobacco. It's mighty fine."

"Back home we smoke that in a pipe."

"Yeah, but it goes farther this way."

By now Nigel had licked the edges of the paper and was lighting a match.

"Is it safe to smoke in here?" She was surprised. There was a housemother in Willoughby who kept tabs on the girls. She wouldn't dare smoke in her room. Besides if she did, Rowena would jump at the chance to turn her in.

"Don't worry, Lovie," Joker said. "The good old double standard is still alive and well. Blokes don't have house parents like you birds do. It's perfectly safe."

The cigar-like joint was passed to her and she took in a lung-full of hot smoke. While she held her breath a warm dizziness spread up to her brain. Almost at once the walls of the room grew spongy. As she passed the joint to Seth she watched her hand moving in slow motion. Then slowly, yet immediately, she felt a rumble in her stomach and before she knew what was happening, she vomited all over an academic gown lying on the floor.

"Whoa!" The boys pulled back. She was horrified. She couldn't believe what she had done.

"I'm so sorry," she apologized. "I don't know how that happened!"

Joker jumped off the dresser, rolled up the gown, and stuffed it out the open window. "You don't smoke fags, do you?"

She shook her head. She was so embarrassed.

"That's it," Seth said. "This crappy tobacco can make anyone sick. You feeling all right now?"

"I feel fine," she said. "I never really felt sick, it just happened. In fact, I feel good. This stuff is great."

"Hey, we'd better be off. It's six o'clock. I'll weigh the rest of this later." Joker locked the dope in a drawer in his desk and they all headed to the dining hall.

With her head spinning and her feet feeling like a circus performer's, Alice rushed into the already full dining room. She searched for an empty seat but the only one she saw was right next to Graham. She stepped over the bench and sat down. A girl across the table was giving a long monologue, something about economics and how the government was going to get rid of the old coins and change the value of the pound. Her straight hair hung like a shroud around her thin face. She looks kind of like me, Alice thought. A mummified me. The picture in the locket flitted through her mind. The girl kept talking but Alice couldn't have listened to what she was saying if she'd wanted to. Her whole left side, the one closest to Graham, was on fire. Even though she wasn't touching him, she sensed every move he made. When he reached for the mustard sauce his knee brushed hers. She gasped. She was afraid she would fall backwards off the bench. She couldn't eat the "bubble and squeak." Her stomach was a hard, hot coal. Graham glanced at her once during the meal, studied her face for a few seconds, but said nothing. Did he know? Could he feel what she felt? No, of course not. She was stoned. But when he got up to leave he leaned over and whispered in her ear. "Ten-thirty in the walled garden outside your room."

Chapter 29

ON THE WAY BACK to Willoughby Alice spied her Guy Fawkes friends, Oliver and Tom, along the path. They waved in unison. They looked like a matched pair of book-ends. Tom must have the same haberdasher as Oliver.

"Hold up, Alice," Oliver called. "We've been looking for you. Tom and I are giving a little 'to do' tonight up in Frog Hollow. We'd love for you to come. Music and dancing and a barrel of scrumpy. Bring a friend."

"Oh, well, thanks. What time?"

"Be there by nine." Suddenly her social life was zooming.

Back in her room Alice lay on her bed gazing out into the walled garden. Her eyes rested on the pear tree leaves shrinking from gold to brown. Sundown was moving in fast tingeing the sky over the top of the wall crimson and violet. Deep streaks of red pulsed through the clouds. She couldn't tell if she was excited or afraid. She wished there was someone she could trust, someone she could talk to.

She reached under her bed and pulled out the

fabric-covered box where she kept her special things. She lifted her magic ring from its place in the velvety corner. Her Nana had given it to her, her German grandmother who died while Alice was at boarding school. She held the ring in her palm. Delicate filigree of silver encircled a large jade stone cut into a scarab. That part was beautiful but the real treasure was hidden underneath. She pinched two curly wires together and slid the secret drawer out of its compartment. There, in a bed of silver, lay a tiny emerald Buddha. She slid the ring over her finger. She needed to wear something from someone who loved her.

Next she took out the small fossil fern Bruce had given her before she left Ann Arbor. She unfolded his letters. One had come just today. "You are to me what the imagination was to Coleridge," he had written. How strange they were both studying the same thing from opposite sides of the ocean.

Then she picked up the small yellow envelope that had arrived last week. It had no return address. Her mother had scratched out the Ann Arbor information and written her Exeter address under it, adding more postage. She slipped out the note card with a watercolor of a rainbow on the front. She caught a faint whiff of lemon on the paper. Inside, in tiny cramped writing, it said: You will find shelter at L'Abri. Read Francis Schaeffer's books, they will lead you to the Living Word. Angelina Hightower. Angelina! That was the name Zelda had guessed was hers. But this Angelina had to be the mysterious woman she had met outside Dr. Winston's office last summer. She'd left her address, wanting to know more about L'Abri. But she was confused. Why didn't Angelina give her the address in

Switzerland? She had gone to the bookstore in Exeter and they knew nothing about Francis Schaeffer and couldn't find the names of his books. She'd even asked Canon Shawcross but he'd never heard of the man or the place. And there was no return address on the envelope. What more she could do?

She opened her Band-Aid box of Chigaros and set one on the corner of her desk. For tonight, she thought. Then she put her things back into her treasure box, snuggled under the comforter, and slipped her thumb into her mouth.

Chapter 30

ALICE MUST HAVE DRIFTED OFF to sleep because when she awoke the full moon was shining brightly through the French doors, its light forming a ladder to the sky. She looked at her watch. Eight o'clock. She should get ready. But ready for what? She popped the light brown M&M into her mouth and sucked on it gently letting the thin coating dissolve on its own. She would worry about Graham later, maybe even throw coins for a hexagram and consult the *I Ching* Zelda had given her. But first she had to get ready for the party.

Oliver mentioned dancing so she would wear her red satiny dress with the zipper down the front. She went upstairs to the bathroom and ran a tub. The house was quiet and empty. Where were the other girls? Would they be at the party too? She held her nose and sunk under the hot water, letting her hair float around her like a copper Medusa. Then she lay back and watched steam rise and curl as it seeped out the partially open balcony window. Someone had left a pair of rubber ducks on the windowsill like ones she used to play with when she was a child. Silly rubber duckies. Silly rubber baby buggy bumpers, she said to herself, repeating a childhood tongue twister. She closed her eyes.

Her father loved tongue twisters. Tongue twisters and brainteasers, math games and science problems. He was always bringing home a new puzzle for her to solve. He would set her down at the table in the breakfast nook while he had his cocktail and take out his watch to time her. Tell me the next number in the series, he'd say: eight, five, four, nine, one, seven. That one was easy. The numbers were in alphabetical order. He signed her up for monthly science kits that arrived in the mail. She raised brine shrimp and made a potato clock. She watched thousands of tiny praying mantis hatch out of a cocoon she'd tied to the forsythia bush in the back yard. She even built a computer out of stacks of plastic plates held together with rubber bands. With the pull of a lever she could add or subtract, all on the binary number system.

Her father had big plans for her. She was his darling— as long as she performed. As long as she didn't trip up. Rubber baby buggy bumper. Rubber baby buggy bumper. She said the words faster and faster until they became gibberish. Then she remembered her father's other favorite tongue twister: round the rugged rock the wicked rascal ran.

The water in the tub had turned tepid. She opened the left faucet with her foot and soon simmered in hot water again. She slid down toward the drain to warm her back. A drop of condensation dripped on her nose from the ceiling above. She thought of Graham. Round the rugged rock the wicked rascal ran.

On the way to Oliver's party Alice bumped into Joker and his motley band. He stepped close and slipped an envelope into the pocket of her coat. "To make up for this afternoon," he said. She heard his chuckling as he scurried up the road.

Oliver's dorm, Frog Hollow, had once been a beautiful manor house. Now the grand rooms were divided into student quarters. Oliver and Tom lived in a part of what was once the dining room. Remnants of a chandelier hung from one side of their ceiling. They had two sets of French doors opening onto a stone terrace with a huge waterless fountain in its center. Chinese lanterns dangled from the trees outside. Dozens of students wandered in and out, smoking cigarettes and holding glasses of scrumpy. Abbey Road twirled on a record player. So this is what they do for fun, she thought. Girls wore the tiniest of skirts wrapped around brightly colored legs. They clung to boys like mating dragonflies. They were all skinny and had long straight hair and iridescent eyelids. And they all acted as if she didn't exist.

Alice felt way out of place. Maybe she didn't belong here after all. She scouted out the party rooms but didn't see anyone she knew. Then she noticed the loo. Two vampish girls in matching black dresses with bat wing sleeves came out, lips glowing red in the dim light of the hall. She went in, latched the door, and retrieved Joker's gift. She'd feel more at ease if she got stoned. Luckily she had a pack of matches in her pocket and a safety pin on the hem of her coat. She stood on the seat of the toilet to light one of the small lumps of Joker's hashish in front of the open window.

When she'd smoked it all, the whole cube of resin had turned to ash. She opened the door slowly. The drug made her feel sinewy and sleek, as if she could swim through the air and float near the ceiling, invisible, part of the smoke and music and shadows. She slid down the hallway and back into Oliver's room. Couples were folded together in chairs and on the corners of beds. She hung close to the wall, made her way around to the open door. Then she saw him. Graham. He was sitting with his back to her on the edge of the empty fountain wearing a herringbone jacket. That awful economics girl was standing talking to him, leaning in to him. He was laughing. Alice's competitive spirit sprang into action. How could he like that girl? Boring upon boring. Now the girl had her hand on his shoulder, around his neck. She wasn't going to kiss him, was she? Alice went out the door and made a wide circle around the fountain, letting herself fade into the dark edges of the terrace under the trees. She stopped at a spot directly behind the girl, but directly in front of Graham, and stepped forward just slightly so that the moonlight fell upon her. She waited. He seemed amused. He was drinking a lot of something from a cup. He fiddled with his fingernails. Then he saw her. He twitched just the tiniest bit; no one else would have noticed. He looked back at the girl for only a second, then stared at Alice. She had won. She watched as he stood, spoke to the girl, then turned to go. As he did, he gave her a glance and a flick of his head and she knew she was to follow.

She started toward Graham but bumped into Oliver

instead. "Alice, super. I was hoping you would come." He patted her shoulder. "No sense spending a year in England and not experiencing how the natives live." He was off talking to another guest before she could reply.

She looked around. Where was Graham? She panicked. And then she saw him again, standing in the doorway of another room, watching her with those dark eyes. He curled his finger and she went to him like the tide to the moon.

Colored lights from outside shown into the small room that was covered from ceiling to floor with Aubrey Beardsley posters. She opened her mouth to speak but Graham raised a finger to his lips and shook his head ever so slightly. His long black curls glimmered like oil on waves at midnight. She stood apart from him; they stared at one another. She felt his pull on her again. Without speaking, without touching, he was summoning her to himself. She stood her ground. She felt her feet flow into the floor like roots of a tree. She was on foreign soil, but she belonged to the earth. The pounding of drums and base guitars from outside the door pulsed through her. But in the stillness of the room she could hear her own breathing. With each inhalation she felt herself rise up, away from her roots, up into branches and leaves and flowers. Up and out into fruit. He grabbed her. He pulled her tight and pressed himself against her, mouth and chest and stomach and hips. She felt his leg slip between hers. He was fire and she was going to melt.

Suddenly the door opened and a light flicked on. 'Ho, ho! What have we here?" came a drunken voice as two couples stumbled into the room.

"Graham, honey, what are you doing?" said one of the girls. Without bothering to answer he took hold of Alice's wrist and pulled her out of the room. He wound her through the mash of people and brought her to the table where they were serving drinks. He picked up two glasses, handed her one. "Drink," he said. It was the first word he'd spoken.

"Bossy, aren't you?" she said. A shiver went through her when she saw his long fingernails wrapped around the glass.

"You're getting what you want, aren't you?"

"Am I?" she said meeting his stare.

He drained his glass and held out his hand. "Are you coming?"

The little bit of beer she'd drunk was mixing with the hashish. In the crowd of faces around her, his was the only one she knew. And the music was incessant, *Abbey Road* again. "Something in the way she moves." The guitar crawled up her spine. She stepped forward and put her arm around his waist, inside the dampness of his jacket. She leaned her head against his shoulder and closed her eyes.

The next thing she knew she felt a cool breeze and a door was closing. She was lying on a hard, cold floor, a relief to her feverish skin. Graham covered her mouth with his, his lips softer than she imagined. His hands tugged on the zipper in the front of her dress. She felt something sharp, something warm. His weight came down on top of her as he pushed her against the wall. She heard him cry out. Her own body sparked. He rolled to the side and lay still. A deep, reverberation came from his chest. A hypnotic growl, a satisfied purr. All of a sudden he bit her ear. "Lovely," he whispered. Then he was gone.

The door opened, light from the hall came in for one second, then it was black again. She fumbled around with her hands. She was in the loo! He had brought her to the toilet. She pushed herself up on her knees and pulled herself together as best she could. She had been struck by a tornado, numbed in the eye of a storm. She was undone. She had hunted her prey, but she was the one left lying on the floor. She sat leaning against the wall dumbfounded.

Someone knocked on the door. She opened it a crack. Oliver. "Alice, Alice. Someone said you were with Graham." He extended his impeccable arms and lifted her up, drawing her close. "That wasn't the native I had in mind for you, dear girl. More of a wild boar." She began to sob. "Here, here. Chin up. It's all over now. Come stay with Tom and me. The party's over." She let him guide her around the remaining stragglers and into his room. Tom was busy tidying up.

"Our friend here's had a bad encounter, that Woodsley fellow from Kent." Oliver guided her down onto his bed and covered her with a duvet.

"Graham? Bad luck, that," Tom said. "I wouldn't want to tussle with him."

"I should think not," Oliver said.

She drifted into sleep to the sound of their kind, domestic voices.

Alice awoke the next morning, her head throbbing. She wasn't used to getting drunk. As her eyes took in the room she remembered where she was, and then she felt the warm presence of Oliver lying next to her like a family dog. Silently she crept out of bed, picked up her coat that was neatly folded on a chair, and went to use the loo. She sat down and closed her eyes, held her head in her hands. She couldn't believe what she had done in this room last night. What was she thinking, putting herself in the hands of someone like Graham? She opened her eyes and looked up at the wall across from the toilet. There was a mark on the wall. Three feet above the floor. It was dark red. A hand print. His hand. Her blood. A splintered heart. She broke down and wept.

Chapter 31

As ALICE WALKED BACK TO HER DORM, the early morning air outside Frog Hollow was cold and hard with frost. The sun sneaking up over the eastern hedges stung her eyes with its brightness. She pulled the collar of her flimsy coat around her face. A dog ran by, ignoring her. On the front porch of the private house next to Frog Hollow sat two glass quart bottles of freshly delivered milk. Suddenly Alice felt famished. They wouldn't miss one bottle, would they? They could always get another. She looked around at the silent lane, the blank windows of dawn. She climbed the steps and grabbed the wet, cold neck of one of the bottles and wrapped it inside the folds of her coat and hurried down the road. Just before turning into the road to her dorm, she took out the bottle, peeled off its crimped cardboard cap, and lifted it to her mouth. Cream had risen to the top. She gagged on its thick richness. She sputtered and spit what was left in her mouth into the bushes. Then, in a wild moment, as rage rose above desolation, she flung the bottle, whipping her arm like a lion tamer. The ancient fieldstone wall received her fury in splintering glass. Milk splattered and dripped down stone and moss, over daisies and thistles, and seeped through cobblestones into the earth.

She stayed in her room for three days, venturing out on her motorcycle only to buy coffeecake and oranges at the small grocer's a few blocks away. She did not return to the dining hall. She did not put lavender under her pillow. She spent her class periods soaking in the tub, balcony windows opened wide, steam from the hot water carrying the smoke of her hashish out into the back garden, down to the moors, the western coast lands, the ocean, infinity.

Then she ran out of drugs. She grew tired of her own company. She got dressed late one afternoon and skulked past Graham's dorm over to Joker's room. Even in her despondent state she noticed a big green Triumph motorcycle with a sidecar parked outside Bentley House. A young woman was leaning against the stone wall in the sun, cradling a baby. The woman wore a leather jacket and two helmets rested on the grass near her feet. Alice couldn't speak; she just stared, mesmerized. It looked like a family.

"Hello?" the young woman said. "Need something?"

Everything, Alice thought. She needed everything. A bigger bike. A sidecar. A baby. She needed someone to love her. Tears welled up in her eyes.

"Come and have a seat, love," the woman said. The baby was making quiet little sounds. The woman unzipped her jacket, lifted her wool jumper and began to nurse. She couldn't have been much older than Alice, but she seemed like a different species. She was a mother.

Alice crossed her ankles and sat down. "A boy or a girl?"

"Hannah Elizabeth," the baby's mother said. "I'm Libby."

"You are so lucky."

"It's nothing to do with luck," Libby said. "It's love."

"Love? Where do you find that?"

"It's not something you find; it's something you practice. I guess luck is when you find someone to practice it with you. You're American, aren't you. What's your name?"

She told her and Libby laughed. "You look like a girl lost in another land. Don't worry, you'll find your way home." She took the baby from her breast. "Would you like to hold her?"

"Really?" Alice hesitated. "I don't know how."

"Here, just support her head. The rest will come naturally." Libby settled the baby into Alice's lap and stood up.

"Wait, don't go."

"I'm just going to holler for Simon. We need to get home. We live way out in the country." She opened the door to Bentley House and called his name.

Alice looked down at the perfect human being lying quietly in her arms. A bittersweet pang spread through her body. This is love, Libby had said. Beautiful, fragile, warm, sweet. Needy. Fruit of the womb. The by-product of sex. Potential for pain and fear and death. Alice stiffened and the baby puckered her face and started to cry.

"Here, here, tiny one." Libby came quickly from the doorway. She bent down and took the bundle from Alice.

"She probably has a bubble. And it's time for her nap. She'll sleep on my lap in the sidecar."

Just then the sound of voices came from the dorm and a group of guys sauntered out: Joker, Nigel and Seth, and a handsome man she had never seen before who was zipping up a leather jacket. He strode straight to Libby and gave the baby a kiss.

"So you met Libby?" Joker said when he saw Alice. "This here's Simon. He's The Man." He pointed in Simon's direction and then said to him, "Alice is from the States, not used to our merchandise, but she's adapting. Right girl?"

Alice nodded. She was spellbound by the happy couple with their own little child. That's what she wanted. She watched as Simon settled Libby and Hannah in the sidecar. He turned and waved as they roared down the road.

"Hey Alice." Seth was winding the ends of his pink scarf around both hands now. "Where've you been? We've been looking for you. We've got a rental house down on Old Tiverton Road and we need one more person. Ready to ditch this place?"

"Live somewhere else?" A crack of hope opened.

"It's a row house not far from campus. Three floors, four bedrooms, kitchen, bath, and loo," Seth said.

"And another W.C. outside in the garden," Nigel said. "Great view of the stars."

"We've got me and Nigel, a bloke named Rafe. You would have the third floor room all to yourself. And it costs less than Willoughby. Of course we'd have to fix our own meals. You'll come, won't you?"

"Sounds perfect," she said.

Chapter 32

THE DOWNSTAIRS DOOR of the house banged. Then banged again. Alice had only been living there one week and already she knew the patterns of her housemates' lives. She held her breath and counted. One, two, and before she got to three Nigel had turned on his stereo full throttle. Umpapa, umpapa, um pa pa, the bass came right through the floor, into her mattress, and beat in time with her already throbbing headache.

She had to get some air. She couldn't cope with such insensitive people: Nigel and his blasted Rolling Stones, Seth always flicking around that pink angora scarf like he was Sara Bernhardt, pretending he wore it as an accessory instead of to hide his withered hand. And Rafe with his roomful of pooping puppies. She was just Miss Moneybags from the U.S. to them. That's why they gave her the room with the gas and electric meters. They expected her to reach into her bag of shillings and light up the house. She had to get out of there.

She stayed under the covers while she scrunched into

her jeans and socks, then reached for her jacket and gloves. She pulled on her boots, stuck her coin purse in her pocket, and ran down both flights of stairs, ignoring Nigel's "How are ya?" She scuttled around the dog droppings in their so-called dining room and dashed out the door and into the street where her motorcycle was waiting.

At least she was out of the dorm. She was sure Rowena Bickle hadn't shed a tear when she heard Alice was moving. The bossy American, Barb Schneider, was probably gloating as well. Alice twisted the accelerator on her BSA and gunned her way up the steep hill toward campus. Barb thought she was so smart, so in control. She had invited all the Americans at Exeter to a big Thanksgiving dinner. Everyone but her. They could have their patriotic celebration. She wouldn't want to eat with them anyway. "I'm a freak!" she yelled out loud. "And proud of it!"

She pulled her bike up onto its stand and went into the Student Union to notify the bursar of her change of address. After Oliver's party she'd known something had to change. Nigel and Seth's invitation to Old Tiverton Road was the perfect escape. She was safe in her own room on the third floor. Nigel and Seth were certainly harmless. But she still couldn't shake the eerie feeling she had gotten when she discovered that the downstairs roommate, Rafe MacKenzie, was the ginger-haired guy who had tried to give her the locket the day she went to pick lavender. "Hello again," he had said with a grinning Cockney accent. "I told you I'd be seeing you." So far she rarely saw him, just had to climb over the brood of Border Collies he'd taken in for some gypsy girl who hung around his room. The girl was a whiny puppy herself. *Poor little puppy girl,* she though to herself. *Daddy will take care of you.*

Alice needed something to help her calm down. She wondered about Transcendental Meditation. Seth couldn't stop talking about how fantastic it was, creating inner harmony and world peace. Someone from the upper echelons of TM was coming to Exeter that Saturday to initiate converts. Even though Seth was so strange, with his hidden hand and his elf-ears that stuck out even farther than hers, and even though she had no intention of emulating him, she signed up to be initiated.

There was a hefty fee to pay for the secret of peace, even more than her motorcycle had cost, but everything had its price. Transcendence required seventy-five pounds in cash, a clean white handkerchief, a piece of fruit, and a bouquet of fresh flowers.

She got up early Saturday morning and prepared for her celestial appointment just as she prepared for everything these days: she got stoned. She put on her best flowing Indian dress, collected her offerings, and set off on foot. The natural way. She went the back route to campus, through the narrow lane past Frog Hollow and over a wall into the wide, hilly pasture where wild ponies drank from a stream that cut through the valley. It was an early December morning but the moderate climate made it feel like a Michigan spring. Dew soaked through her open shoes and turned her thin cotton socks cold and stiff. She wasn't used to this end of the morning.

"You are beautiful," she whispered to the trees with their turning leaves. She hoped she was changing too. She hoped her chlorophyll would disappear and reveal her real colors. She felt something wonderful was about to happen. Maybe she would merge with the divine, just like the trees reaching between earth and sky. She was high on the plants she'd breathed into her lungs and the plants beneath her feet.

The initiation ceremony took place inside a classroom that had been transformed into a white tent. A tabernacle. The word made her think of the strange Peter-girl from her patrol. Outward Bound seemed five years ago, not just five months. All that had happened since then made the Alice who flourished in the wilderness feel like a stranger. She entered the tent and found herself in a small, outer room. Gauzy panels draped the walls and ceiling while oriental carpets covered the floor. A Scandinavian man in his mid-twenties greeted her with a solemn "Namaste." He looked like a tent himself, sitting cross-legged on a pillow, draped in a long white robe. His eyes were icy blue and he was all business. She wanted to play.

"First you must answer some questions," he said with a slight accent.

That was easy until he wanted to know when she had last taken drugs.

Oops. She swallowed. "Is there something wrong with taking drugs?" she asked. "I didn't see anything about that in your literature." Was her sex life next? Did they expect celibacy? Seth never brought girls home.

"Maharishi requires that you abstain from all forms of drugs and alcohol for fourteen days before the initiation." He spoke like a robot as he looked straight into her eyes.

Seth, you didn't warn me about this, she swore under

her breath. And what about the Beatles and their trips to see the Maharishi? Did they give up dope in India? She had no choice: she lied.

"Then I'm fine," she told him, hoping her pupils were not too dilated. "I hardly ever drink and I haven't had any drugs for over two weeks."

The man didn't flinch. He didn't pry. He just extended his palm and asked, "Have you brought your offerings?"

She handed him her wad of pound notes.

He stood up and put the money in a hidden pocket in his robe, then motioned to a curtained doorway. "Take off your shoes and follow me."

She entered the inner room and sat down on a pillow as he had done. He added her flowers to a large vase, and her Spanish clementine to a wooden bowl of other fruit on the altar. He showed her how to kneel before the photographs of Maharishi Mahesh Yogi. Was that okay with God? she wondered. Was she worshiping that Indian guy? She'd already broken one commandment; she might as well stick around and see what they were selling.

Alice found it hard to be a good Transcendentalist and practice twenty minutes of meditation every day. She wasn't sure why she couldn't find the time. She only had five hours of class per week. She hardly spent any time studying since she had moved out of the dorm. She never cooked; her housemates were willing to do that for her. But time disappeared. Sometimes she sat in her room in front of the electric space heater on her Indian prayer rug with a stick of incense burning, and tried to keep her mind on the secret mantra the vice-guru had given her. *I-eem,*

I-eem, I-eem, she silently chanted inside her head, breathing slowly and deeply as he had instructed. But soon her thoughts would win out. When were her library books due? What was she going to do for Christmas vacation? Did anyone at home miss her? How many shillings were left in the meter bag? She would find herself scrambling up off the floor and on her way across the room to her dresser to find out before she remembered I-eem, whatever or whoever I-eem was. Could it be a secret name of the Maharishi or some Hindu god? Whatever the case, she was not a good disciple. But she kept trying.

One sunny morning when she went to campus she was drawn to the small stone chapel across the path from the library. She pushed open the heavy door and discovered a narrow room with two rows of pews facing each other and stair stepping up toward high, arched windows. There was no one in sight. She shuddered as she entered; it was colder inside than out. A pocket of sunlight hitting the top row of the pews, up near the altar, promised some warmth. She settled herself in the beam of light and began to focus on her mantra. "I-eem, I-eem, I-eem." She could feel herself beginning to relax. "I-eem, I-eem." The sun pressed warm on her face and made flames of fire dance on her closed eyelids. "I-eem, I-eem, I-em, I-am." With a start she realized she had slipped into a new mantra. *I AM.* She knew what that meant from her Old Testament classes at boarding school. I AM was the name God gave to himself when Moses had asked the burning bush, "Who are you?" "I AM WHO I AM."

You are who You are, she thought. *But who am I?*

Chapter 33

WHEN ALICE FIRST WENT TO ENGLAND she imagined she'd be invited to spend Christmas with the jolly family of one of her many new friends. She would stay at some manor house with a name like "Holly Grove" or "Thistle Croft," ride horses out on the heath, learn to shoot pheasants, eat plum pudding, and pull brightly colored "Christmas crackers" with her friend's handsome older brother. But by the middle of December she had to face the truth: she had no friends; she had nowhere to go; she would have to go home. She humbled herself and approached Barb Schneider one day after a lecture.

"Barb?" The girl was bustling ahead of her down the path toward the library, her short legs pumping with the adrenaline of greed. Professor Burroughs had just told them there was only one library copy of a rare essay Wordsworth had written about *The Prelude*, something about the Socratic principle, "Know thyself." Alice knew who would be the one to check it out.

"Huh?" Barb grunted, not breaking her stride. "Did

you say something?" Her dark brown hair shifted back and forth against her orange parka as she chugged up the steps of the library.

"I wondered how you and the others were getting back home for Christmas."

"Well, we're not swimming." She pulled open the door and went in. "I hope you're not planning to snatch that Wordsworth?"

"No, help yourself," said Alice, "I don't need it. But I do need to find a flight home." She paused. "And I thought you might be able to help me." There, she'd said it. Help me.

"You?" They were in front of the W's. Barb's eyes were scanning fast. "Damn," she said. "It's gone." She turned and searched the aisles for other American students. "Did you see anyone here ahead of us?"

Alice spotted the prize on the top shelf, hidden in the V's. "Here it is," she said and handed the book to Barb.

"Thank you." She tucked it tight under her arm.

"So how are you guys getting back to the States?" Alice said. Maybe one good deed would deserve another. "A special charter flight or something?"

"Don't you have your plans. Isn't it awfully late?" Barb was heading to the check out desk. No nonsense with her.

"I have reservations to go skiing in Switzerland after New Years, but my plane leaves from London. I thought I'd be staying here for Christmas, but…"

Barb cut her off. "Skiing? In the alps? That sounds like fun. I'd like to do that. Where are you staying?"

"Wait a minute. I asked you first."

Barb gave her student ID to the librarian. The precious

book was hers for two weeks. She turned to Alice. "We're all flying together on Icelandic. Great fare. Just one stop on the way to JFK. I've got the airline's number right here in my purse." She patted her bag but didn't make a move to retrieve the number.

"And?" Alice said.

"And I'll give it to you if you tell me where you're staying in Switzerland. I'd love to go. We could be roommates."

Roommates? Alice thought. Why would Barb want to do that? She hates me. This was not what she'd had in mind, but time was running out. "All right," she said and they exchanged pieces of paper, a flimsy contract of temporary friendship.

Alice took the train from Exeter to Heathrow with the other Americans. They stayed mutually clear of one another. Her brief intercourse with Barb was over. She soon discovered the plane was not just a good fare; it was downright cheap, the kind of plane where your knees touched the seat in front of you and you had to bring your own food. Then in the middle of the night, while the plane was refueling in Reykjavik, a fuzzy voice came over the loudspeaker: "Delay...equipment failure," a voice in broken English said. "Take belongings...follow stewardess... thirty-six hours." Thirty-six hours! Could that be possible? A collective groan passed through the airplane. Oh great, she thought. Stuck on an island in the Arctic Ocean. Just perfect. That's what she got for flying home at the last minute on some sub-grade airline. That's what she got for not having any friends.

The plane full of grumbling students slowly dislodged

themselves from the packed-in seats and filed down metal stairs through a bluster of wind and snow. She couldn't believe it when they were led to a cold, empty hangar. Out of the sardine can and into the icebox. She found her over-stuffed suitcase in a big pile at one end of the building and dragged it to a wall. She slumped against it, pulling her coat tight around her body. This was far worse than sitting in the cramped plane. Now they were going nowhere. Her body longed for the prone position. She closed her eyes. She needed sleep. But two obnoxious Southern belles were playing a loud game of cards next to her.

"Hey, you can't take that back!" One of the big-boned blondes squawked.

"Sure as sugar I can," the other said. Alice rolled away from the sound of their rangy vowels and put her head on her backpack. Three months in England had fine-tuned her ears.

She scanned the tangle of marooned travelers. The other Americans from Exeter sat clumped on the opposite side of the room including a sweet but goofy guy named Kevin who was on crutches and had a big cast on his leg. She heard he'd been hit by a lorrie one weekend when he and some other American students were visiting Stratford-on-Avon. She stretched out her legs, thankful she hadn't had any accidents of her own, and closed her eyes.

All of a sudden something jarred her foot.

"Excusez-moi," a low, raspy voice said. Alice looked up at a tall, broad-shouldered girl wrapped in a full-length fur coat. It wasn't a classy leopard like her mother wore, more like a moth-eaten beaver. On her head the girl wore a hat of rainbow-colored feathers sticking out in every direction.

She held a cigarette in a long pearl holder. "Would you happen to have a light?"

Alice leaned over and reached into her bag. "Sure, have a seat." She motioned to her suitcase, then handed the girl a book of matches.

"Merci." The girl lit the cigarette and exhaled a thin stream of smoke. "This is the pits," she said, sweeping the room with her squared-off chin. "Not one good looking guy, not a hippie in sight, not even a soldier in uniform. Just giggly prairie girls and pimply guys with pea jackets." She met Alice's eyes and smiled.

"I love your hat," Alice said. "Where'd you get it?"

"Made it myself from bits of incroyables—odds and ends—from Marché St. Pierre, a discount fabric warehouse down the street from my apartment."

"Your apartment? Where do you live?"

"Montmartre—in Paris. C'est magnifique—the absolute best. My balcony looks out on Sacré Coeur. How about you?"

"Nothing so glamorous. I just moved into a row house with some other students in Exeter. It's cool, I guess. Better than the dorm."

The girl laughed. "So whooo are yooou?" A long finger of smoke wisped out her lips and hung in front of Alice.

"Alice," she said.

"And I'm Victoria, but you can call me the Mad Hatter." The girl pointed to her head.

"Or that caterpillar with the hookah that sits on the magic mushroom."

"Alice, what a great idea." Victoria reached into the satchel hanging from her shoulder and pulled out a fancy wooden box, the kind where you had to shift different pieces of veneer to open the secret drawer. She put something in her fist and said, "We may be stuck in the freezer of the world with a bunch of fish, but come on, bring your matches. We'll thaw dem bones."

Chapter 34

A DAY AND A HALF LATER Alice climbed out of one more airplane. She was running on pure adrenaline. The flights had been a nightmare. No wonder the price of the ticket was so low. She laughed. The price was low, but she was high. She patted the pocket of her jeans that held a cube of hashish wrapped in tinfoil. Victoria had given her a Christmas present and an invitation to Paris for Easter. Meeting the Mad Hatter made up for any inconvenience.

She lugged her bags off the escalator and headed down the long corridor to the shuttle bus. She needed to leave JFK and get all the way to LaGuardia to catch her plane to Detroit. But first she should call her parents and let them know she was finally getting close to home. She readjusted her suitcase and backpack and the bulky box Barb had asked her to carry when they got off the plane. Barb, the self-appointed leader of the Americans at Exeter, had insisted Alice help out and carry a package for Kevin.

Barb Schneider. She pursed her lips in distaste. Why

was she doing favors for that creep? Why did she let Barb boss her around?

"Young lady! Young lady!" squeaked a man's voice behind her but she paid no attention. "Young lady!" The voice rose in a commanding tone. Alice looked over her shoulder and saw a customs agent goose-stepping toward her, his elbows jutting out like a giant bird.

She kept walking down the concourse, extending her stride. He couldn't be after her, could he? She began to panic. The small lump in her pocket grew bigger. She had made it through customs; why would they suspect her now?

"Young lady carrying the big brown package," the man bellowed out close behind her. "Stop!"

Now she knew he was speaking to her. She was trapped. She came to a halt and set down her suitcase. "Were you calling me?" she said as the agent caught up with her. She put on her polite face.

"That package you're carrying, somehow it was over-looked when you went through the inspection station. What is in the package?" He sounded very serious.

"I'm, I'm not sure what it is," she said truthfully. How stupid she was. "One of my classmates asked me to carry this through customs for someone else. I'm going to give it back to the owner when I get out by the bus." She was in big trouble. Were they going to search her? She would go to jail. How could she be so naive?

The agent took hold of her arm and steered her to the side of the hallway where she now noticed three other uni-formed men waiting. "I will ask you once more: what is in here?" He rapped on the package. "Who does it belong to?"

"I don't know what it is." Alice was flustered. "It belongs to Kevin. He's the young man on crutches who was on my flight." She looked down the hallway but didn't see anyone she knew.

"So Kevin gave it to you?" The agent looked over at a pudgy man who was writing something on a clipboard balanced on the shelf of his belly.

"No," she said. "He didn't give it to me, Barb did. She's another girl from our school. Kevin can't carry much. He broke his leg and can barely walk. Barb was carrying it at first, then asked to me to take it through customs." She could see how stupid this all sounded.

"So you brought a box through U.S. customs, the contents of which you are unaware?" He sounded incredulous as he peered at her with scowling eyes.

"I guess so," she said sheepishly. "I was just trying to be nice."

"We will determine that after we open the box." He nodded to the man with the clipboard.

"It's probably a Christmas present." She hoped to high heaven it was. "Something from England."

She watched in suspense as the men unwrapped the box and lifted off its lid. Then she sighed with relief: a plaid wool blanket with long braided fringe on the ends.

The agents methodically shook the blanket and all the wrappings. There was nothing bad, no contraband. She stood still and waited, almost afraid to breathe. Would they search her? Would they let her go?

"All right, young lady. We are finished with you. But let this be a warning. Never take unknown packages from anyone. Be very, very careful what you bring through International customs."

Alice was still shaking inside after the customs agents retreated to their end of the terminal. What a close call. She didn't want to guess what would have happened if she'd been caught smuggling drugs. Even a small amount would change her life forever. She slipped her hand into her pocket and felt the lump, the size of a bouillon cube, wrapped in foil. At least she'd be able to relax when she got home. The magic smoke always lifted her mood.

She leaned against the long wall of the airport corridor, too drained for the moment to tackle her suitcase and the confusion of finding her bus. She watched her co-travelers trickle down the narrow walkway and soon she saw the bobbing of Barb's orange parka bobbing. Alice stood in her path. "Here." She shoved the unwrapped package into the other girl's arms. "I'm done with this. You take it to Kevin."

"Oh." Barb tilted her horsy head. "Is something wrong? You look exasperated, Alice. You didn't have any trouble, did you?" Alice had the odd feeling that Barb knew exactly what had taken place.

"Cut the crap, Barb. I nearly got busted. And if I didn't know better, I'd think you had planned it all out in advance." She wanted to add, you jealous little snot.

"I'm sure I don't know what you mean," purred Barb. "I'm sorry it was so difficult for you to help someone else. I'll be happy to take this to Kevin. Oh, here he comes now, in an airport wheelchair."

Alice walked away, her head spinning.

"See you in Geneva in two weeks," Barb called out. "At the beginning of the new decade. Won't that be fun."

Alice had almost forgotten. That creep was going with her to Zermatt and staying at the same hotel. Even sharing her room. What a nightmare. She went to find a pay phone.

"Hello, Mother?"

"Where have you been?" Nice greeting, Mom, Alice wanted to say. No hello or how are you. No hint of love. Worry always manifested as condemnation.

I'm in New York. At JFK. We got laid over for a day and a half in Iceland. That's why I couldn't call."

"Do you realize how upset we've been? This is too much, Alice. Too much."

"But it's not my fault. There wasn't any way I could reach you. Did you call the airlines? That's what they told us you should do."

"Ha! They told you. Why didn't they tell us?"

"Mother, I've got to run and catch a bus across town to the other airport. Then I'll fly standby into Detroit. I should get there early this evening."

"Well isn't that just fine and dandy? We're going to the Richmond's tonight. Their annual Christmas party. I hope you're not expecting your father or me to meet you at the airport. We'll send Elwood."

Tears filled her eyes. Did she really expect things would be different?

"Why would I think that, Mother?" She laid a heavy sound on the last word—Mother. She couldn't resist making her point.

"Why you little....!" And the receiver went dead.

Her mother hung up on her! Alice laughed a sad, sorry laugh. She'd come all the way across the ocean to have her mother hang up on her. Her eyes blurred with tears. Why was she going home? Home. What a joke. She had no home. She certainly didn't belong in England. And her parents acted like they would much rather have Christmas without her.

Chapter 35

ALICE TRUDGED THROUGH THE AIRPORT in a dark numbness. How fitting that this was the longest night of the year. She hauled her bag outside and climbed onto a grimy bus that said "LaGuardia" in lighted letters above the dirty windshield. She sunk down on the torn vinyl seat as emptiness and fear overwhelmed her with her tears.

A few more people clambered into the cold bus, the driver closed the doors, shifted into gear, and drove off. She felt as if she was in an open boat traveling through the brackish waters of Queens. The peeling roof, the dirty windows, the cheaply padded seats gave her no protection. The storm was inside her. Despair rushed over her in waves. She tasted the saltwater of tears. She wanted to capsize and be done with life forever.

She ruffled through her backpack for a tissue, thankful there were hardly any other passengers on this journey. But just then a hand reached over from the seat behind her and offered a packet of Kleenex. She turned and saw that a girl who had been sitting a few seats away on the other side of the aisle had come forward.

"Thank you," Alice said and blew her nose, wiping the tears from her tired eyes.

"You're welcome," the girl said in a warm, soft voice.

Alice looked up at the stranger. She was just a bit older, with a sweet Shirley Temple face. She wore a periwinkle beret perched on her head and a matching scarf wrapped several times around her neck. She looked like a Christmas present.

"I'm Annie Binghamton. You look as if you could use a friend."

That's putting it kindly, Alice thought. She knew she looked like a complete disaster.

"I'm Alice Blankwell and I guess I've been having a hard day. A hard life." It was a relief to have someone be friendly. It took a move to England for her to realize she liked Americans. They might be loud and brash, but they didn't pretend you were invisible.

"Are you taking the bus all the way to LaGuardia?" Annie said.

"Yes. I've been traveling since the day before yesterday and it feels like I'll never get home."

"Where've you been?"

"At school in England. This is just a quick trip home for Christmas. Then I'm going skiing in Switzerland before the next semester starts."

"Oh." Annie's voice rang like a silver bell. "I'm just coming home from Switzerland. Where abouts are you going?"

"To Zermatt, the Matterhorn. Have you been there?"

"No, but I was near there, high above the Rhône valley, in a little village called Huemoz-sur-Ollon."

"What were you doing?" Alice said. It was better to make conversation than sit alone in despair.

"I was at a sort of school, a study center, called L'Abri."

"L'Abri?" Could it be the same place the funny woman in Ann Arbor told her about? "L'Abri in Switzerland?"

"So you've heard of it?"

Alice couldn't believe the coincidence unfolding before her. She had given up hope of finding out about L'Abri and Francis Schaeffer, but now, on this horrid bus in the middle of New York, on the shortest day of the year, after an angry call with her mother, was a girl who had just been at L'Abri.

"Tell me about it," Alice said. "What did you do there? Did you like it?"

"It was wonderful," Annie said. "So stimulating. People from all over the world asking questions about God. The whole time, when we were studying or doing our chores, and especially at meals, we talked and argued and discussed everything anyone wanted to know about God."

"Like what?" Alice thought of her theology class with Canon Shawcross. He was sweet but the discussions they had in his study were awfully boring.

"Oh, things like, Does God Exist? Can anyone know for sure? Does he communicate with human beings? Is the Bible trustworthy?" Annie rattle off what sounded like just the beginning of a list. "Everyone had their own questions. Questions and opinions."

"So who came up with the answers?" Were there even answers? Alice wondered.

"That's a long story," Annie said. "You have to start with your presuppositions, your worldview. The tutors help you choose what you want to study. If you're interested, you could begin by reading some of Dr. Schaeffer's books."

Annie wrote the book titles on a page in her spiral notebook, along with the address in Switzerland, and handed it to Alice. "Please go. It's very special, way up on top of a mountain. You can see for miles and miles. And the people there are kind."

Like you, Alice thought. You're very kind. Then she said out loud, almost like an oath, "I'm going to go. That's one thing I know for sure. I'm going to go to L'Abri."

"Great. So are you feeling better now?"

"Yes. Some. But it's just that my mother was so mad on the phone when I called from the airport. I hope she'll soften up by the time I get home."

"Just give her a big hug when you see her," Annie said. "I'm sure she'll be happy to see you."

Alice leaned back into her seat. Even the New York potholes couldn't jostle the new sense of peace she had found. In her mind she could see beyond Christmas with her family, she could hear beyond her mother's angry voice. Clear blue sky and the soft sounds of mountain streams rose up inside her head.

Chapter 36

No one was home when Elwood, the family handyman and all-purpose servant, dropped Alice off at her parents' house and carried her bags in the front door. "Watch out for George," he said in his thick Mississippi accent. "His bark is worse than his bite."

"George?"

"Mr. Blankwell's new boxer. Fancy show dog. Too good for the rest of us. Just let him out of his kennel and give him a scrap of meat. He'll settle down."

A frantic barking started as soon as she stepped into the dining room. She found some leftover fried chicken in the refrigerator and split it with the dog and he calmed down. "So you're my replacement," she said as the animal gobbled down the meat and retreated to the living room to make itself comfortable on the goose down sofa. Alice was too wound up to rest and too tired to unpack, so she perched on the kitchen counter top and phoned Yvonne.

"And this detective-like guy came running after me," she told her former roommate. Her legs bridged the double stainless steel sink as she leaned to one side and spotted an apple core hidden behind the Kitchen Aid. It wasn't just turning brown, but completely dried out. Must have lain there for weeks. The tiny compartments holding the seeds were beginning to pull apart from one another.

"…and the dope in my pocket burned like hot coal." She went on with her story. "And I swear, this horrible girl, this witch Barb Schneider, planned the whole thing just to get me in trouble." Yvonne made sympathetic sounds on the other end of the line. "But the worst thing of all was when I called my mom. Can you believe it? Simone hung up on me! When I got to Detroit, Elwood was there. Aren't we lucky to have Elwood," she said in a sing-songy tone, imitating her mother. She loved their handyman; he was kind and safe. Just like one of the family, her mother always said. But not. Not at all. The summer before Alice left for Exeter she had fixed a ham sandwich for Elwood when she was making one for herself, and her mother had a fit. "But Elwood always eats lunch here," she had said. "Not ham," said her mother.

She picked up the apple core and twirled it in her fingers. "Did you know that when you slice an apple horizontally, it makes a star—a secret geometric pattern inside. I wonder if we…." Alice broke off her sentence. "Yikes Yvonne….gotta go….The royal garage door riseth up for her highness. And George, the new number one child, is barking his head off. Call me tomorrow. Not too early." She hung up the phone and jumped down from the counter.

She heard the thunk of one car door, then another. "Alice!" The door between the garage and mudroom opened and her mother swished into the kitchen, leopard coat trailing behind her like the wake of a snazzy powerboat. "Darling. So glad you're safe." She thought her mother was going to hug her, then all of a sudden George charged into the room and jumped on Mrs. Blankwell. "Get down, you brute!" she said to the dog, and then turned back to Alice. "Did Elwood find you? I'm so sorry we couldn't meet you at the airport, but...."

"The Richmond's. I know." Alice fiddled with her hair, waiting to read her mother's mood. "Where's Dad?"

"Where else?" Mrs. Blankwell nodded back toward the garage. "I don't know which he loves more—his new Ferrari or his new dog." Mrs. Blankwell stood at the sink and unscrewed her earrings, dropping them into a silver dish on the windowsill. She reached into a cabinet and got out a bottle and a glass and poured herself two fingers of bourbon. "You don't mind if I go to bed, do you? I'll see you in the morning." She blew her a kiss as she pushed through the kitchen door into the rest of the house. Her mother must have forgotten all about their telephone conversation. Like the apple core. Out of sight, out of mind. Apologies never needed.

The garage door opened and a bank of fluorescent lights lit up the room. "Why can't we have a little light in here? It's dreary as hell," Lincoln Blackwell said.

"Dad!" she said stepping toward him as he came in the room.

"Oh, it's you." He slipped off his topcoat. "We didn't know if we'd ever see you again. We thought you might be lost." He gave her a peck on the cheek and a quick one-armed hug, then bent down to caress the dog. "A beauty, isn't he? Already won best in show."

"Lost?" she said, the word vanishing under the dog's playful growls as her father followed his champion out of the kitchen. She was left alone staring at her reflection in the blackened windows.

Against his mother's wishes, and warnings from the weather man, Bruce drove to Ann Arbor on December 31st to take Alice to a party at his fraternity house. It turned out to be the worst kind of New Year's Eve imaginable. An unnaturally warm wind blew up from the south and turned Michigan snow clouds into freezing rain, coating trees and shrubs and power lines with half an inch of ice. The overburdened branches clinked together in eerie harmony like the ice cubes in Mrs. Blankwell' perpetual cocktail. Weak limbs splintered and fell to the ground. Winter aborted unformed buds from the womb of spring.

"But since he was coming all this way, Alice," her mother tightened the lid on her nail polish, "I invited him to an early supper."

"Mom," she groaned.

"Don't worry. I'm making something light. Poached eggs on little beds of spinach. With my wicked Hollandaise sauce." Mrs. Blankwell blew on her shiny red nails. "And he loves my chocolate soufflé!"

"Isn't that a little heavy on the ovaries, Mom?"

"That's disgusting, Alice. Who taught you to be so vulgar? I don't know what a nice boy like Bruce sees in you, anyway."

Maybe it's you he likes, Mom, she wanted to say.

While she was away in England, Mrs. Blankwell had taken to inviting Bruce over for Sunday dinners. She'd even taught him to make her famous browned gravy. He was the first of her boyfriends her mother approved of, the only one Alice hadn't handpicked herself.

"You could be nicer to him," her mother said as she thumbed through her cookbook. "He says you only wrote him once or twice. Of course that was more than you wrote us."

A few hours later the doorbell rang and the dog went crazy. Dog, with a capital D. George was no ordinary boxer. He was a show dog, a stud, who earned $200 a shot. Female dogs came to the house from neighboring states to be serviced by George. Or he traveled, airfare provided, to far-away females. He was recreating his image all over the country. George resented Alice and the feeling was mutual. The house wasn't big enough for a show dog and a daughter.

The bell rang again. Where was everybody? she grouched as she uncurled from the sofa in the TV room. George stood at the front door, legs splayed in center ring form, barking his head off. Who answers the door when I'm not here? she wondered. She slipped into the guest room adjacent to the front hall and peeked through the curtains. Bruce's beat up Plymouth was parked in the drive. The bell rang a third time. She didn't move. Maybe this wasn't such a good idea. She hadn't seen him for three months and so much had changed.

George kept up his frenetic bellowing. "Shut up," she said as she marched to the door. He growled and put his nose against the doorframe. "Get out of my way." He whipped his head around and snapped at her. "Don't you dare," she growled back and opened the door.

"Bruce."

"Alice."

They both stood still. He'd grown a beard. She couldn't believe it, so out of character. He'd always been clean-shaven and well behaved. His mother must be having conniptions. The December storm had covered his new curly whiskers and the top of his head and shoulders with pellets of ice. He looked like one of those tiny figures inside a glass ball. The wind was blowing bits of ice and snow around his face. He seemed to be standing in another world. Then he stepped forward into the house and George grabbed his leg and began to hump.

"Disgusting dog!" she yelled. "Get off!"

"It's okay," Bruce said as he calmly disentangled the animal from his leg. "He just wants me to know he's boss." George sat as Bruce scratched him behind the ears. Bruce took off his gloves and rubbed the dog's sides. George rolled on his back and Bruce huddled over the tawny muscular mass.

"I didn't know you two were on such good terms."

"Get up, boy," Bruce commanded. "Go get your ball." The dog ran off toward the kitchen. Bruce stood and faced her. "You look, umm...."

"Let me take your coat." She jumped in at his hesitation. She knew she was a wreck. Skinnier than ever. Dark circles under her eyes. Her British clothes felt weird and out of place now that she was back in the States. What was it about color? Her green sweater looked great over there.

Here it looked like some kind of mucky moss growing around her body. Maybe it was the angle of the sun.

Bruce's coat was warm and musky with his body heat and felt heavy in her arms. She was startled by the familiarity of his smell. She hung his coat on the back of a chair in the tiled front hall, near a heat vent where the ice and snow would melt and dry.

"New clothes?" he asked, his hands awkward behind his back.

"I got this jumper—that's what they call sweaters—at a jumble sale over there, a flea market. Only two pounds. That's like five dollars."

"Oh," he said.

"I know I look horrible."

"No, no." He took a step toward her, reaching for her hand, and started to hug her.

She made a sound like she was hurt and twisted away from him. They looked at each other; it was as if there was a glass wall between them.

"Your beard...." she started to say, but he cut her off.

"I know it's ridiculous. I haven't shaved since the day you left."

What was that supposed to mean? Had he done that for her? Some John-the-Baptist sacrifice or Samson initiative? Some fasting from shaving in memory of her?

At the other end of the house the kitchen door swung open. George bounded through the dining room, living room, and into the hall. He jumped up on Bruce's thighs, ball in mouth. "Hello?" Mrs. Blankwell chirped. "Is that you, Bruce?" Alice caught a glimpse of her mother in the dining room, setting down her cocktail, then untying her apron and draping it over a chair. She smoothed her wool skirt and cashmere sweater set as she headed toward the hall. While her mother disappeared from view for a moment, on her way through the living room, Alice darted into the guest room, leaving Bruce to deal with Mrs. Blankwell alone.

Through the door she could hear her mother give him a hug. "Was your drive just terrible in this awful, awful weather?"

"It took over four hours. The roads are covered with ice. But now it's beginning to snow."

"New Year's Eve is so capricious. Why is that? And where is Alice? Didn't she let you in?"

"I think she may have gone to change her clothes," he fumbled.

"Oh, I hope so. She looks ghastly, doesn't she?" He didn't reply. "Well, we won't let anything spoil our evening. Come back to the kitchen with me. I'm making a Julia Child's chocolate soufflé just for you."

Alice peeked out from a crack in the guestroom door and saw her mother loop her arm through his. Bruce glanced over his shoulder at her but she turned quickly away. She didn't want him to see her tears. When she heard the swing of the kitchen door she slid silently across the hall and upstairs to her own room. I'll show her, she thought and rummaged through her still-packed suitcase. She pulled out her shortest dress, the stretchy red one with the big zipper down the front.

Alice hated Bruce's fraternity house even more since she'd been to England and seen what fine old houses were really like. This was a big gothic building more suited to Halloween than New Year's Eve. She didn't like most of Bruce's brothers either. They were boozy business school students who spent their weeknights playing bridge and their weekends passing around sorority girls. They were going to turn out just like their fathers and produce an endless chain of more of the same.

"This place reeks worse than ever," she complained as Bruce led her up the curving stone staircase to his room. "I swear they wash the floor with beer and urine. With a little vomit thrown in on Saturday night."

"Don't be so crude."

"You sound just like my mother. Isn't that strange?" She twisted her hair into a knot and then let it fall back over her shoulders. "Did you notice the sweet little coeds on the dance floor? Every single one of them was staring at me. Prissy sorority sisters. They're cookie cutter copies of my mother's friends. How can you stand to live here?"

"Not everyone's as sophisticated as you." He gave a little yank to the top of her zipper, then grabbed her waist, and pulled her close for a kiss. She was shocked by the scrub of his strange whiskers. She stiffened and turned her face away.

"Don't be so rough!" She pulled up the zipper and had a flash memory of Graham and what happened the last time she wore that dress.

"I'm sorry." He squinted his brown eyes at her rebuff. "I didn't mean to hurt you." He reached for the handle to the door of his room but it was locked. He knocked loudly. "Hey, open up."

"Tough luck, Bruce," said a deep voice. They heard a giggle, then a shriek.

"Hank!" He kicked at the door. "It's my room too. This is my only night with Alice."

There was silence.

He kicked again and struggled with the handle. "I'm getting the key," he yelled at his roommate through the door.

"Forget it," Alice said, tugging on his arm. "I'm not in the mood anyway."

"Well, that's obvious. What's the matter with you? I've been waiting to see you for three months, and you tell me to forget it?" His eyes narrowed and his face grew red behind the beard. "What's with you, anyway?" He shrugged away from her hand and stood with his elbow cocked, his fist clenched in anger. "You've hardly let me touch you all night. And what about the letters you were going to write me? What's going on?"

She fumbled around for words. She felt so lost and out of place. They were two puzzle pieces that no longer fit. What was wrong with her? Why couldn't she be kind?

"Your mother said that you...."

"My mother? What does she have to do with anything? We're not married, you know. Not engaged. For your information, it's lonely over there. The British aren't known for their friendliness." She started down the stairs.

"Come back!" He grabbed her arm, hard.

"Stop! You're hurting me. Bruce, you're hurting me!" She began to sob.

"Alice, I'm sorry! I didn't mean it. You know I would

never hurt you." He reached out to hold her but she pushed him away.

"Just leave me alone," she said. "Take me back to the house."

"But it isn't even midnight yet. I'm sorry, Alice. Please forgive me."

"I need to pack. I leave for Switzerland tomorrow."

"Please Alice. Can't we spend just a little more time together. I'm really sorry."

Maybe if she kept him apologizing she could convince herself he was the one who was in the wrong.

Chapter 37

"IT'S A FAIRYLAND," Alice said peering out the window as the Swiss shuttle train pulled to a stop. "Look, that boy skating is straight out of Hans Christian Andersen." She and Barb Schneider got off the train that had carried them up the mountain to the carless village of Zermatt. All around them steep-roofed chalets and split-beam shops lined the narrow streets. A sleigh pulled by two bell-laden horses jangled in front of them. "Need a lift to your hotel?" a man called in a thick German accent, his face as round and red as a cabbage.

Alice rose on her toes with excitement. "Danke." She looked over at Barb with a grin, but her companion's face was pale. Her usually stiff shoulders were hunched and her eyes jumped furtively from the edge of town to the mountain that loomed close beyond the buildings. Strange. At Exeter Barb was always in charge.

The man loaded their suitcases in the sleigh and helped the girls onto the bench seat. He covered their knees with a heavy fur rug and asked for the name of their hotel.

"The Bergruh," Alice said.

"A lovely spot." He shook the reins and headed the horses down the street. "*Bergruh* means mountain of rest."

Alice grew and more entranced as they passed through the village. Every rooftop and window ledge was frosted with snow. It was a Hanzel and Gretel gingerbread town. People bustled from building to building and skied down the middle of the road. Candy-colored skis and poles leaned outside every door like giant pick-up-sticks.

"Isn't this great?" she said to Barb. "We can go everywhere on our skis."

"Great?" Barb's eyes stabbed at hers. "Maybe for you, Miss Winter Olympics. But I don't know how to ski."

"Really?" Alice was shocked. Zermatt was hardly the place for an inexperienced skier. "You signed up for lessons, right? I'm sure you'll learn fast. It's practically 24-hour skiing here. I bet you'll be going down the mountain with me in just a few days."

"What do you mean, 'going down the mountain?' Where else would I go?"

She decided to let Barb discover the bunny hill on her own.

The sleigh driver edged his horses round a corner and pulled up to a small chalet with a carved wooden sign hanging above the door. Bergruh. "Here you are, frauleins." He jumped from his seat and went to the back to unload their luggage. "Just leave that robe on the bench."

Alice and Barb climbed down and went into a small lobby, though leaving the afternoon sun and entering the dark room was like walking into a cave. A cluster of young men in ski sweaters and knickers sat together in front of the fire. "Après ski," she whispered to Barb. "Probably hot chocolate and cookies. I wonder what they do at night?"

The girls took care of their reservations with the clerk behind a carved desk. He helped them carry their bags up a narrow winding staircase to their room on the second floor. "Towels on your beds." He gestured toward a slim pile of well-worn towels neatly folded on top of the duvets. "Bathroom is third door on the left. Please limit your time to ten minutes. Dinner is served at seven."

"Not exactly five-star hospitality," Alice said after he left.

Barb went straight to the bed in the corner and began unpacking her suitcase. "You take the bottom drawers; I'll take the top. You take the right side of the wardrobe; I'll take the left."

"Yes, Ma'am!" Alice clicked her heels together and saluted. Barb wasn't going to spoil her fun.

Barb put down an armful of sweaters and turned slowly to Alice. "Very funny. You think you're so very funny. So smart. So cool. Well, you don't know everything. Just wait."

"What?" Alice said. "I'm sorry. I wasn't making fun of you. It's just that you sound so serious, so in control."

"In control? I don't have to use words to be in control. You're the one who's always going on, oohing and aahing about how wonderful everything is, using your cute little phrases to get what you want. Just wait and see."

Alice didn't know what Barb was talking about, but she didn't like it. She had to get out of the room. She grabbed her jacket. "I'll be back for dinner," she said, and as she headed out the door she heard a strange sound, almost a growl. Goose bumps stood out on the back of her neck.

That girl was weird. Something sinister lived inside her. Something ugly. Barb wasn't ugly herself, though her hair grew low on her forehead, a wide mane of dark brown that made her look like a horse. No, not a horse, a pony. Like the wild ponies that roamed the moor on the edge of the Exeter. That was it. She was like a Dartmoor pony: they seemed harmless from a distance with their short legs and bushy tails, but up close they were fierce, as eager and likely to bite your hand as to take an apple.

Dinner at the Bergruh Hotel was bland: unidentifiable roasted meat, boiled potatoes, and boiled vegetables. Boiled custard for dessert. The young men who had been by the fire when they arrived were from Czechoslovakia and didn't speak English. They didn't seem to care for female company either. The other guests at the small hotel were two families from Austria with a bunch of young kids. They spent the meal disciplining the children and barking German at one another. So Alice and Barb were alone. They finished quickly and went to their room, tired from the flight and the altitude and the change in time zones.

"Do you know what happened to Kevin?" Barb said as she climbed into bed.

"You mean Kevin who broke his leg in that accident at Stratford?" The one whose package you made me carry, she wanted to say, so I nearly got busted at customs.

"Mind if I turn out the light?" Barb reached to the night-stand between them. At least she was being more congenial since their afternoon skirmish. "What I mean is…." The room was suddenly pitch dark. "Do you know how Kevin got in the accident? *Why* he got hit by the truck?"

"I heard he was driving back from Stratford. That's all I know. Some kind of traffic accident."

"Exactly." Barb sounded like a schoolteacher. "A well-planned traffic accident." There was a pause, then she said, "I planned it."

"What?" Alice was horrified. "What are you talking about? How could you think you planned such a thing. He nearly lost his leg."

"Nearly," Barb said.

Alice shuddered under the thick down duvet covering her body. "You're not responsible. That's impossible." She opened her eyes wide and tried to see in the darkened room.

"I made it happen," said Barb. "I wished it to happen." She sounded oddly smug. It didn't make sense. How could she be happy, even proud, to imagine she caused a heavy lorry to smash into the side of Kevin's Mini, breaking his leg through the thighbone? A clammy feeling slid over Alice's skin. She pulled the puff close round her neck.

"You see, Alice." There was a trace of a hiss as Barb held her name a bit too long. "I have powers, psychic powers. My father had them too. He passed them on to me."

Alice stared at the other twin bed. A sliver of moonlight escaped past the shade creating an eerie gleam on Barb's face and revealing her stretched out hands, fingers curled claw-like in the cold night air.

"My father and I have the same hands, the same eyes. Cat eyes. We see things." Another shiver ran through Alice. She wanted to sit up and turn on the light, but she felt frozen, almost paralyzed in her bed.

"When someone is unkind to us, we retaliate." Barb said the word slowly. "All I have to do is meditate. I imagine every detail, and it happens."

"So you are saying you wanted Kevin to have an accident?" Alice was incredulous. She was starting to get mad. "That's crazy, Barb. What did he ever do to you?"

"What did he do?" Her voice spiked. "He went to Stratford-on-Avon for that Shakespeare festival and didn't invite me. He took Doug and Mary and Joanne and left me all alone. After all the trouble I went to planning Thanksgiving dinner. That's what he did. He should have taken me." She ended with a pout.

Alice propped herself up on her elbows, feeling a bit more courageous because this girl was obviously sick in the head. "I don't believe you could control his car, or a truck. People's minds don't have that kind of power."

"Ha!" Barb laughed. "You don't believe me? You, the great Experienced One. You don't know anything. Just wait and see." With that Barb rolled over toward the wall and pulled the covers over her head.

Alice lay down but her body was tense. Fear filled the room. The German prayer Nana had taught her as a child rose in her consciousness like a song coming from another room and circled in her head. *Ich bin klein, mein Herz ist rein, soll niemand d'rin wohnen als Jesus allein.* "I am a little child, my heart is pure, no one shall live there but Jesus alone." It was going to be a long ten days with Barb.

On Sunday Alice woke up for the sixth morning in a row in a cold sweat. Her flannel nightgown was bunched under her arms; her heart was pounding. All her muscles ached. She peeked across at the other bed. Good, Barb wasn't there. She was probably in the bathroom. Quickly Alice flung the covers back and sat up, determined to rid herself once and for all of the terrible nightmare that clamped onto her every night, and the terrible reality of sharing a room with a wicked person.

In her sleep that night, just as every night since they had arrived in Zermatt, she dreamed that she skied off the side of the mountain, down a precipice, and into an icy crevasse that ended in darkness. Every morning she woke up terrified. "No more," she said out loud as she stood and stripped off her nightgown. No more voodoo. No more crazy jealousy. No more small-minded girl from Minnesota with cat's eyes and a witch's heart.

She hurried and pulled on long underwear and ski clothes and went down to the lobby to change her plane reservations. She was going to go back to England tomorrow. Then she called the ski school to arrange for a private lesson with her instructor, Karl, since there were no group lessons on Sundays. She had one more day to ski. She might as well learn as much as she could.

Karl met her at the base of the gondola. "Hello Carol," he called out. During their regular lessons Karl had christened her Carol because she whooped and sang her way down the slope. They put their skis on the rack and stepped inside the hanging tram that would carry them to the mountaintop. "It's a perfect day to ski," he said.

"Thanks for the private lesson." She smiled at the kindly old man who had been a ski instructor for forty years. The crags and slopes of the mountain were worn right into his face. His blue eyes held the same infinity as the sky, softened by the clouds of his white beard.

"I don't mind missing church on a day like this," he said. "I get a better look at the good Lord when I stand close to the heavens than when I'm under a timber roof." He laughed. "You should see these hills in summer, Carol, when wild flowers turn them into a crown of jewels. I swear this is one of the twelve gates into the City."

"The city?" she asked. "Which city?"

"Why, the New Jerusalem. Haven't you read your Bible?" He gave her a wink and she knew there was no condemnation in his words.

"I'm studying theology," she told him. "My major in college is religion, but I'm afraid there's a lot I don't know." And a lot she didn't understand. "Have you ever heard of a place called L'Abri? It's somewhere in Switzerland."

"The shelter? No. But don't worry," he said. "The good Lord has safe places all over the world. Just keep following the road. He'll lead you."

She felt safe with Karl. She trusted him and his confidence on the mountain, with his bright red jacket and its big white cross on the back. She wished she could confide in him, in someone. But who would believe her if she said her roommate was evil and had dangerous powers. Wasn't everyone basically good? Maybe she was the crazy one. Maybe the nightmares were her own imagination gone wild.

After half an hour they reached the summit. There weren't many skiers out that day. Perhaps all the Swiss went to church. It felt wonderful to stand on the top of the mountain. The menacing Matterhorn was across the next valley, and they looked down on pure, white, new-fallen powder from the night before. No ski tracks marred the flawless surface.

"You've already learned what I was teaching the class last week," Karl said. He slipped into his bindings and buckled the straps. "Today why don't you just follow me down the mountain. I'll show you where to turn. Keep your eyes on me." They took off into a wide bowl, making rhythmic, sweeping turns. Then the terrain changed: they came to a steep face littered with moguls. "Keep to my tracks," he called over his shoulder. The thick powder absorbed any sound. They were alone with the whiteness of the snow, the blue of the sky. She loved the way her body carried her, muscles stretching and contracting, her weight leaning into the hill. It almost seemed like magic the way the elements—the wind, the snow, the sun, and the earth beneath—all worked together and propelled her along.

After a while she followed him down a narrow trail banked on either side by tall fir trees. Their branches nearly blocked the sun. Her skis whispered to one another as she made smaller and tighter turns. "Whooop!" she sang out when she hit a patch of ice. Last night's new snow had not penetrated through the thick cover of trees.

Then, all at once, the woods ended. And so did everything else. The sky was gone. She was surrounded by snow, assaulted by cold. Wet wind blew at her from every direction. "Karl!" she yelled. The tiny spot of his red jacket disappeared into the white. "Karl!" She skied faster toward the area where she thought he had disappeared. He wasn't there. "Karl!!" she screamed and then suddenly dug her edges into the snow and came to an abrupt stop. She'd better be careful, she told herself. She pulled the hood of her parka up over her hat and tightened it around her face. Snow pelted her body, closed in around her goggles. All she could do was wait. Wait and pray.

"O God," she said, "whoever you are." She closed her eyes and tucked in her chin. "Please help me. Please protect me, please keep me safe." She wasn't used to making up her own prayers. At church they always read from the Book of Common Prayer. But this was an emergency.

She opened her eyes. The snow was letting up. Blue was breaking through. She looked around her and then down at the place where she was standing. Just a foot beyond where she had come to a stop, the mountain opened into a deep crevasse, just like in her dream. She felt her heart rise in her chest. How close, how close, how close she had come. She sobbed and shuddered with waves of fear and relief.

"Alice!" It was Karl. He skied out from behind a big boulder, a few yards back from the crack in the earth. "Thank God you are safe." He wrapped her in his big arms. "That blizzard came out of nowhere. I didn't see a cloud in the sky. But these mountains, sometimes they are treacherous. They seem to twist and bend to dark, destructive forces." He took a step away from her and lifted up her chin. "You are all right, little Carol?"

"Yes, I am. But I couldn't see you. I was so scared. I almost went over the edge."

"But you didn't. The good Lord was there. *Der Herr seiht*. He sees you."

He surveyed the sky. "It looks clear again. We will go slowly and stay together. Why don't you sing a song? Then I will know you are right behind me." He led her away from the edge. She followed, her eyes focused on the white cross on the back of his red jacket.

Chapter 38

THE UNIVERSITY CAMPUS was nearly deserted when Alice arrived back in Exeter. There were still three days left of Christmas vacation. Who would return to school early? Only someone who feared for her life.

She rode her motorcycle up to the Student Union to collect her mail. Four people had written to her: Bruce, Will Fowler—she'd barely thought of him since their trip to Chicago—Yvonne her old roommate, and something odd. She opened that one first. It was a strange, folded-over postcard with a governmental return address: "Got busted. I'm in Tower Street jail for thirty days. Please come see me. Luke." It took her a moment to realize who it was from. Luke! The boy she'd met her first night in England, who'd been so kind and welcoming, who'd spoken truth to her, words she'd written down in her spiral book: "If I am a purist, why do I need to smoke dope?" Now he was in trouble, caught with drugs. He'd probably been in jail over Christmas; how awful. But what could she do? London was a long train ride from Exeter.

She turned to the letter from Will. He was an ocean away, just a distant memory. Yvonne must have given him her address. He had dropped out of school and was driving a cab in Ann Arbor—just like a New Yorker, she thought. He was planning to travel through Africa, hitchhiking across the Sahara, and he wanted her to come with him. He claimed she was his muse, his music. She shook her head. Poor guy, he was so confused.

Next she took Bruce's letter and held it to her heart. She had been so mean to him on New Year's Eve. Why hadn't she let him hold her? Why hadn't she told him the truth? His devotion to her scared her. She needed to be free. Yet she longed to feel the closeness they used to have.

His letter was sweet, like him. He said he was sorry. Sorry for what? For humoring her silly mother? He took all the blame. He said he's been too rough. He said he missed the moonlight on her silver skin. An ache rose up inside her. I'm sorry, she sobbed. I'm the one who's bad, not you. I'm sorry. But she couldn't do everything. She couldn't be everywhere. She couldn't take care of everyone. She could barely take care of herself.

Then she ripped open the letter from Yvonne, a girl-friend. Surely her news would cheer her up.

"What?" Alice said aloud to the empty lounge area as she looked at the typed words on paper. "A chain letter!" There was no personal note from Yvonne, just her name and address added to a list of other people who had put their lives into the hands of fate. Fate or something worse. Something like Barb Schneider.

"This is a letter of luck," it read. "If you send out seven copies of this letter within seven days of the postmark on your envelope, you will receive something in the mail that will thrill you beyond your wildest dreams. But beware. If you do not follow these instructions, something terrible will soon arrive through the mail." The letter went on to give testimonies of people who had gotten checks for thousands of dollars, free cars, trips to Florida. But some unlucky, unresponsive people had gotten news of death and imprisonment. Whoa! she shuddered. Death? Imprisonment? Luke was in prison. Quickly she looked at the envelope. It was fourteen days old! It had been sitting in her mailbox the whole time she had been risking her life on the slopes of Zermatt.

She reread the letter, looking for a way out. The curse was clear. No exceptions for Christmas vacation. She crumpled up the letter and the envelope and shook her head. Thanks a lot Yvonne. Just like her to forget Alice wouldn't be home to get her mail. Alice tossed the paper into a waste bin on her way out the door. She was anxious to get back to her room at the top of the house and curl up under her quilt. But just as she was leaving the Student Union she noticed a piece of paper posted inside the glass-encased message board that said, in bold letters, "ALICE from ANN ARBOR, a package is being held for you at the bursar's office." She went to the case to have a closer look. Alice from Ann Arbor. Who else could it be but her? There was no Ann Arbor in England.

Her stomach knotted. Could this be the bad news predicted by that stupid, stupid, stupid letter? Could it be a trap? Should she even claim the package?

When she knocked on the door and explained herself, the bursar, an apple-faced man with tiny seed eyes, and a cowlick that stood up like a stem said, "So you are Alice. We thought you might be, me mates and me. Never seen anything like it. No surname, no return address. And all the way from the United States of America. Well, it must be yours." He handed over a small package wrapped in a paper bag and tied with a string. No return address. The handwriting was unfamiliar.

She didn't dare open the package at the Student Union, even though she could tell the bursar's curiosity was piqued. She shoved it to the bottom of her backpack and hurried out to her bike, thankful no alarm sounded and no policemen swarmed her when she took possession of the mysterious item. Somehow she knew she was holding something dangerous.

She set her helmet on her head with an angry jerk. Its wide, plastic visor dropped down over her face. Stupid thing was too loose and falling apart. Just like her. She pushed it up away from her face and rocked the bike off its stand and opened the air vent. Who could she trust? Who were her friends? She got all excited by a stranger on a bus in New York, but then pushed away the one person who was loyal to her. Her best friend sent her bad news, then some mystery person sent her a package. And a cat-eyed girl who hated her guts tried to put a spell on her. She gunned the engine and took off. The sun was going down and the winter mist blowing in from the west made the pavement glisten as she coasted down the steep street toward her house.

There was a roundabout at the bottom of the hill. She squeezed the brake levers to slow herself down, but the brakes slipped against the wheels. The tires must be wet.

At least there were no cars coming. She squeezed again. Neither brake would hold until all of a sudden, the one on the front wheel grabbed tight and stopped instantly. The rear tire kept spinning. The bike reared up like an angry mare on its forelegs. Alice flew forward over the handlebars, stretching out her right hand to break her fall. She spun headfirst in slow motion and saw herself as a tiny insect, a butterfly still wrapped in a cocoon. Just before she hit the pavement the visor dropped again, covering her face. She made a three-point landing: heel of her right hand, hard cartilage of her right knee, and the visor-covered surface of her right temple. She rolled over in the street, doing a somersault. The leather scraped off her glove, the skin tore on her knee through her pant leg, and the edge of the visor made a small nick in her cheek, just above the corner of her mouth where its protection ended.

She lay on the ground near the curb, stunned and afraid. An angry sound roared behind her. She lifted her head to see her bike, spinning on its side, handlebars bent at an awkward angle. Someone should shoot it, she thought. Someone should shoot me. Was she all right? She couldn't tell. Her knee was bleeding. Her hand hurt. A Mini pulled up behind her and the apple-cheeked bursar ran to her side.

"Dear, dear," he called out. "Are you hurt? What a catastrophe. I saw the whole thing. One moment you were riding free, the next you flew through the air like an acrobat from the circus."

He took hold of her arm as she righted herself. She felt stiff, but all her body parts seemed to be working. "Cut that motor, would you?" she said. Her voice came from far away as if she was under water, as if the ground, before it hit her, turned into a tidal wave and was sending her into a subterranean sea.

"I left the Union just after you, Miss. Short hours since everyone's gone for the hols. I can load the bike in the back of my van, drop you off where you want."

She looked at him; he was a grandfatherly sort. "Thank you. That would be wonderful."

He helped her into the front seat of his car, loaded the bike, and drove her home.

The house was dark when they pulled up to the curb on Old Tiverton Road. All her roommates were still away, of course. The bursar wheeled the bike down the narrow alley behind the row houses and parked it in their small back garden. She went right to the hot water tank and put in some shillings so she could run a bath. She fixed a bowl of muesli with a handful of almonds and dates and went up to her room to wait for the water to heat. She turned on the space heater, then peeled off her clothes and put on her robe. Her skin and muscles were numb and her body had a strange odor. Not sweat, exactly, maybe fear. Fear mixed with thankfulness. Little chunks of gravel were stuck in her knee. She would let the water coax them out. She peered at her face in the mirror, at the small horizontal cut made by the visor, the unruly visor, the one she had cursed, the one that saved her life.

She remembered the mystery package and told herself she should leave it alone, wait until morning. She should at least wait until she had taken her bath. But curiosity trumped self-control. She went to her backpack and dug out the package. Crouching before the heater, she slowly unwrapped it. Inside, hidden under layers of colored tissue paper, were two tabs of acid. She knew the small green pills were LSD because there was a tiny note: "Thanks for the book. Have a great trip. LUCY."

Lucy. That wasn't a real name, just a code. Lucy in the Sky with Diamonds. She puzzled for a moment—Thanks for the book—and then she knew. The drugs were from Zelda, her next door neighbor at the co-op. She'd asked Alice to send her a copy of *The White Goddess* that was only available in the England. Alice had bought it and mailed it to her back in October and this was Zelda's thank you. Without warning the electric meter that controlled the lights and the heater ran out of shillings. The room went dark and the heat went off. Alice curled into a ball and sobbed.

Chapter 39

ALICE'S ALIENATION GREW. Any healthy shoots remaining from her roots were crowded out by the weeds of her new environment. Their off-campus house was one continual haze of hashish. People collected in the front room on the second floor where Nigel had hooked up his stereo system and his experimental light-show equipment that was part of a project for the drama department. He fancied himself a movie producer. Exeter's small population of druggies drifted in and out, day and night. Someone was always lighting a joint and passing it around. Alice never refused. Day and night, weekday and weekend all seemed the same to her. With only five hours of class a week, she had little reason to go on campus. She was so out of touch with the order of life, she even missed some of her lectures and tutorials.

One day she noticed Simon's big green Triumph and sidecar parked outside the house, but Libby and the baby weren't with him. Alice was too shy to talk to him and she doubted he would he remember her anyway. She fled to her third floor room and watched his motorcycle until he came out and drove away. That tiny sidecar, like a beautiful shell washed up on the beach, filled her with longing. Simon had someone to fill it, two someones. She didn't even have a shell.

On the first day of February there was a knock on her door. "Just a minute," she called as she unwound from the lotus position where she had been basking in front of the space heater, and slipped on her bathrobe. "Come in."

"Ah ha. We've tracked you down." It was Oliver and Tom from Frog Hollow. "We haven't seen you for eons, maybe not since our party. We've come to take you on an adventure."

She gave them each a hug. "Sorry I disappeared. I had to." Then she roused a weak smile. "What kind of adventure?"

"My family has a house, a summer spot by the shore," Tom said, "down near Teignmouth. There are ruins of an old castle—Abaddon—on the edge of the property. Super spot for a picnic. And it's a splendid day. Sunshine called for all afternoon. We've packed a picnic and would be ever so honored if you'd come exploring with us."

"Yes," said Oliver. "Tom brought up his motor car after Christmas. Convertible and all that. Will be a smashing day."

"You two are so sweet to think of me. Just wait outside the door while I slip into some clothes." She dressed in her favorite pink overalls and red lizard-print socks. "What did you say the name of the castle was?" she called through the door. "Avalon?" As she brushed her hair, she remembered something Professor Burroughs said about Avalon being from the Welsh word afallen meaning apple tree. Like the garden of Eden before Eve picked the fruit. Before the human race was fallen. Afallen.

"Not Avalon," Tom called back. "Abaddon." He spelled out the name. "Some Hebrew word; something from the Bible."

She knew Abba meant daddy in Hebrew, except with two b's. She opened her top drawer to pick out earrings and her eyes fell on her covered Bandaid treasure box. As if the top were transparent she saw exactly what was inside next to the Chigaro M&Ms: Zelda's payment. Did she dare? What would the boys think? She looked out the window. It was a beautiful beginning to February, the shortest month of the year. All at once she felt the shortness of her own life. She wanted to experience it all. She flipped open the top and withdrew one green pill. Staring straight into her own eyes in the mirror, she gathered a mouthful of saliva and swallowed the magic potion. Then, for good luck, she ate a Chigaro too.

The ride to Teignmouth was exhilarating. Tom and Oliver sang old RAF songs they'd learned from their fathers. The closer they got to the southern shore, the greener the trees. Buds that were still hard and grey in Exeter gradually grew yellow, then chartreuse, then emerald, then jade. She slid her hidden Buddha out of its secret compartment in her ring. See, she assured herself, life isn't so bad. Her stomach was beginning to feel a bit queasy; her hands and feet pulsed with jolts of buzzy energy.

"Close your eyes, Alice," Oliver ordered as they drove up a steep hill. She could feel the car reach a summit, then stop. "Now look!"

Far below lay the grey green of the winter ocean. To her acid-laced mind the waves looked like millions of fish dancing and diving over one another. She moved her gaze back to the shoreline spreading out from the base of the cliff before them. Palm trees! "Where have you taken me?" she said. "Spain?"

The boys laughed. "Isn't England marvelous?"

It was only a few more miles to the castle. The effects of the LSD grew stronger. When she looked down at her hands, she could see veins pulsing under the skin. They parked the car and carried the picnic basket and a bundle of blankets through vine-laden trees and into a clearing that led to the remains of the castle walls.

"I need to pee," she said.

"Pop round some bushes," Oliver said. "We'll lay out the meal."

She headed off toward a stand of rhododendron and did her busines. Just beyond her was an old stone stairway partially buried under the brush that led up to a plateau. She had to explore. She ducked her head and began to climb. At the top a gnarly old oak nearly five feet in diameter lay on its side and hung out over a dip in the landscape. It was the opposite of the lodgepole pine that sheltered her on her solo at Outward Bound. She held onto the vertically growing branches and inched her way out to the end of the tree. She began to feel her confidence return. She believed her body could do anything, just like at Outward Bound. She peered over the side of the tree and found she was suspended directly above a picnic table. But this was no ordinary picnic. The table was covered with a white linen cloth embroidered with pink and blue flowers. Wine goblets and bone china were set out, along with gleaming silverware and matching cloth napkins. Great platters of food marched down the center. But most extraordinary of all were the people sitting around the table. They looked like characters out of *Through the Looking Glass*: two tiny men with long, pointed noses; a tall man in a dunce hat; two pudgy Tweedle Dum girls with horrid piggy faces; and a huge, fleshy woman in a gauzy pink dress that seemed to have wings.

Alice swooned and held tight to the tree. Was she in a Fellini movie? Could this be the final banquet at the end of the world? Quickly she backed off the horizontal oak and retraced her steps down the hillock to where Oliver and Tom were waiting. The LSD turned branches of ivy into fingers that reached out and plucked at her body as she passed.

"We were beginning to worry," Oliver said. "Were you lost?" He tucked a napkin under his chin.

"No, but I saw the strangest people on the other side of that hill." She tried to explain the odd picnic. "It was another world. Like a movie. I thought I was watching a movie while hanging above another world. An unreal world. The end of the world." Her words circled back around each other. She wasn't making sense.

"Abaddon's a popular spot," said Tom. "The public often stops by." She saw them exchange a look. "All quite normal, I'm sure."

"Normal?" she said. A flood of dizziness overcame her and she sunk to her knees on the blanket.

"We just need to deposit some nourishment in your

account," Oliver said, always ready to come to her rescue. He handed her a cucumber sandwich.

She stared at his offering, them lifted the crust-trimmed bread and peeked inside. "What is this?" she said. To her the thin white circles looked like silver coins. Did they expect her to eat money?

"Cucumber. Very good for you. Trace vitamins," Tom said, pronouncing vitamin the British way with a short *i*.

"And this green stuff?" She sniffed but could only smell mayonnaise. Could it be shredded pound notes? Oliver and Tom were both so wealthy, maybe they ate money for lunch.

"That's watercress. Don't you have that in America?"

"I've seen it in the creek on the golf course, but I've never eaten it."

"Well, go ahead and try it. It won't bite you."

With the word "bite" she looked at Oliver and Tom. They seemed to have grown long, sharp teeth and their noses protruded way out from their faces. Grandmother, what big teeth you have. She shook her head. These were her friends. When she looked again, their rodent-ness was gone.

After sandwiches they had strawberries and crumpets and even a pot of tea made with hot water from a thermos. Oliver and Tom lay back, hands behind their heads, and announced it was time for a nap. "I'm going to walk around," she said. She felt much too jittery to sit still. Every muscle in her body was demanding movement.

"You go on. We'll catch up later," Tom said. "There's a diagram on a post over there." He pointed to a tall gate. "It explains the different areas: the merlons and embrasures, and the slits in the towers where they shot their arrows. But careful—remember these are ruins."

"I'll be fine," she said as she raced toward a tower with three crosses on its top. She felt like a horse and galloped over the springy grass that looked as if it hadn't been mowed for years. Dry brown strands lay matted under the new green growth creating a trampoline under her feet. She was tempted to bounce down on her knees, but part of her mind warned her there was hard ground underneath. Birds sang to one another from tree branches and nests in the crags of the stone walls. She thought she could hear them singing out words. "Abaddon," sang one. "The prince is here," sang another. "To the top," sang a third. Or could it be those strange picnic people talking? Were they trying to trick her? She pressed her fingers against her ears. When she released them the voices had faded.

A portion of the outer wall was low enough to climb up on. The wall was nearly three feet wide, easy for her to balance. She began to walk the perimeter of the castle. Every few feet or so, the wall went higher, almost in steps. She climbed over loose stones and spanned broken window openings. Her heart thumped hard in her chest. "To the top, to the top," sang a voice. She shook her head at its insistence. "The prince is here. The prince is here." The voice seemed to push her ahead. She was getting quite high, above the trees, nearly to the top, when she heard Oliver call out from below.

"Alice," he said in his friendly, big brother manner.

"Hey!" she waved. "I'm almost at the top." He looked tiny from where she was. A tiny golden mouse in a blue velvet vest.

"Say Alice, I think it would be good if you came down now."

"Down? Why? I've only got one more section to go."

"Tom," Oliver said as his friend came up beside him, "don't you think Alice should come back down?"

Tom looked up at her, nodding vigorously. "Oh yes, very good idea. Come down Alice. We really need you to."

"But I want to finish my climb," she protested. "Maybe I'll see the ocean from up here."

"Maybe," Oliver said. "But how about this? Come down for a moment and stand with us. Then you can go back up if you want."

"Yes," Tom said. "Please come down with us. Then you can decide. Please do this for us."

Something in their voices, their real voices, made her stop and consider. Now they looked like two little kittens in their fuzzy blue jumpers, two little kittens mewing at her. They needed her. She turned and made her way down the wall, leaping off at the end and running to where they waited.

"Thank God you're safe," Oliver said. "Look."

She followed their fingers as they pointed up to the place where she had been standing. She had been about to step onto a part of the wall that had appeared to be solid stone from above, but now, from below, she could see that the narrow row of stones was held up only by ivy. The rest of the wall was gone.

She dropped her head into her hands. "O God!" she cried. "I would have fallen thirty feet to the ground. I could have died." She looked at her friends. How did she get so close to the edge without knowing it?

Oliver reached out and drew her close. "Alice," he whispered. "There are so many dangers in the world."

"And you rescued me," she said into his shoulder.

"Come on," said Tom with a bright smile. "All's well that ends well. I know a lookout that faces west. We can watch the sunset before we drive home."

She sat in the backseat of the convertible, shivering in her thin coat as the sun withdrew its warmth, while Tom ferried them to a craggy spot at the top of a cliff. They got out of the car and stood watching the day end. The boys each held one of her hands—probably to be sure she didn't fall. "Don't those clouds look like mountains?" Tom said.

Red and purple from the setting sun reflected off their faces like the glow from a fading fire. By now the LSD was wearing off. It had puffed her up with imaginings but now she felt like a dry husk, a chaff of wheat. She was afraid she might blow away if Oliver and Tom let go.

"Like Kilimanjaro. At least as my father describes it," Oliver agreed. "What do you think, Alice? What do those clouds look like to you? The Rockies?"

Her eyes faded inward and her senses withdrew deep inside her bones. The castle wall, the crevasse in Zermatt, the terrible chain letter, the LSD. All her adventures led to the edge of a cliff. She was afraid to take another step.

Oliver waved his hand in front of her face trying to get her attention. She saw it again: the bloody hand print on the wall. The shattered heart. A tremor passed through her body, as if her soul were leaving. With a great sigh she opened her mouth, but words fled like a flock of birds, a murder of crows. "They're only clouds," she said as ahe released their hands and climbed back into the car.

Chapter 40

TOM AND OLIVER DROPPED Alice off in front of the house on Old Tiverton Road. With great effort she pushed open the door and stepped inside, then slid down to the floor, her back against the wall, her eyes blinded with tears. I can't, she cried, I can't. I can't go on. She leaned her head against the wall and tried to stifle back the low moans that rose out of her belly. Her body shook with a numbing pain, like a barren woman panting through a fruitless labor. I don't want to live. I don't, I don't, I DON'T.

She heard a door open. "Alice?" She looked up, too lost in sorrow to worry about shame. It was Rafe. She didn't know him well even though they'd been living in the same house for almost a month. She avoided him as much as she could, still spooked by the time he approached her on campus and showed her that locket. But now he looked almost safe, like an old uncle, with his ginger hair and a glint in his blue eyes.

"What is it, dear?" he asked. He sounded as if he was from another generation even though he was only two years older than she was. As he came out into the hall, a train of puppies followed him and ran to her, crawling on her lap and licking her cheeks. She pushed them down. "Off of 'er boys!" Rafe commanded and scooped the little animals into his arms. "Just a second," he said, "I'll put 'em in their box." He was good to the dogs.

She wiped her face with her sleeve and tried to stand up.

When he returned he gently took her shoulders and held her at a distance. "Something 'orrible 'appened," he said knowingly. His Cockney accent almost made her smile.

She'd never really looked at him before. Everyone said he was "experienced," "worldly," that he knew all about drugs and politics and music, and women. He'd even been in jail. But he seemed kind. He took good care of the puppies; maybe he would take care of her. She began to sob again.

"There, there, girl," he comforted. "It won't last forever. I'll help you to your room, and make you a spot of tea. And when you're ready, you can tell me all about it." He put his arm around her and she caught a familiar smell, like an old Halloween costume.

Alice cried for three days. Rafe brought her soft boiled eggs with toast "soldiers" as he called them. He went to the bakery and got her favorite crumble cake. He brought up puppies, one at a time, for her to hug and cuddle. He sat at the foot of her bed and rubbed her feet. He brought his record player up and played Ritchie Havens for her, "Let the River Rock You like a Cradle." She still cried.

"Can you try to talk about it?" he said. "I'm sure that will help."

"I don't have any words. I'm not really alive."

"What happened? Did someone hurt you?"

"I did. I always do. It's all my fault." She felt a shift inside, the close of a door. Her tears were over and a dry hard took their place, as if she were a vacant lot where once a building had stood. Self-pity sunk into self-hate.

"What did you do?"

"What haven't I done?" She stared out the window, seeing nothing.

"Well, what was the last thing you did, you know, before I found you in the hall?"

"I guess you could say I went on a bad trip. An acid trip. I went away and never returned."

"Oh." He rested his hand on her knee. "One of those."

She looked at him with stony eyes. "Any cure?"

"I've seen a lot of cases. It's not easy. But first I prescribe a fast ride through the countryside. I'll sort the puppies while you get dressed."

He spoke with such authority that she obeyed. Mechanically she pulled on her jeans and a jumper, zipped up her leather jacket and gathered her helmet and gloves. She had done this a hundred times before. She could do it again.

She rocked the bike off its stand. It had never felt quite safe to her since the accident. She straddled the seat and pushed down on the kick-start with her desert boot. The rubber sole was beginning to wear thin from the sharp end of the starter. Rafe climbed on behind and circled her waist with his arms. "Down to the roundabout," he said, "then we'll head north to Tiverton." His beard scratched against her neck as he pressed his lips close to her ear.

Slowly they climbed the sloping streets of the city until they reached the open road. The bike labored under the extra weight. Rafe leaned with the curves, his hands clasped in front of her. When the ground leveled she opened the throttle and they sped fast along the road, engine whirring loudly. The directions he yelled were lost in the wind so he reached in front of her and pointed where to turn. Tall hedges, locked together like barbed wire on either side of the road, blocked her view. Every so often they passed a small gate, but they were moving so fast she couldn't see anything but the narrow trail that stretched out before her. Did the road ever stop? Would there ever be a place where she could rest?

It felt strange to have someone on the bike with her, especially someone heavier than her. The Bantam's meager 175 cc's meant she had to shift into second or even first to climb a hill. She felt embarrassed with Rafe's cumbersome body behind her. Yet he made her feel weighted down, anchored. And his breath in her ear, his body pressing against her back, seemed like the only thing keeping her from disappearing altogether.

As the sun set they rode into a small village. "Pull up at that pub," he told her.

An onion-faced man at the bar whistled when they walked in. "Git a load a that," she heard him say to the barmaid. "Look who wears the pants in the family!"

"And looky at that the long hair!" said a bloke next to him.

Rafe took hold of her arm and directed her to a corner

table next to the fireplace. "I'll get us some scrumpy and a couple of Ploughman's lunches. Have you got a quid?" She reached into her pocket and took out her leather coin purse, another gift from Nana.

"Here," she said. One syllable was all she could manage. She stared at the fire. The crackling and snapping of the wood sounded far away. The smell of the smoke hardly reached her. Everything burns up, she thought. Fire next time, isn't that what they say? Dust to dust, ashes to ashes. All this, she looked around the room, is just carbon.

Rafe attached himself to her like a shadow. He rode with her when she went to class and she took him to campus when he had class or wanted to practice piano. He was reading Classics, Latin and Greek. He must have been some kind of a genius because he hardly studied, just sat down and went straight through his texts before a test. He was a natural musician too. He could hear something once and then play it on the piano. When a symphony was broadcast over the BBC he could name the orchestra and the conductor. Sometimes he jammed with other musicians and played at student parties. He'd joined the Communist Party at age twelve and lost his virginity at thirteen, an age when Alice barely knew what sex was. He looked like an old man, a Cockney Father Time. The only thing he regretted about himself, he said, was his weak chin. And she never saw that, except for faint hints when his beard was wet. He seemed strong all over to her.

She needed somebody strong; she needed him. She had lost her voice, lost her footing. When she dropped that tab of acid the universe slipped away and took color and life with it. Words, her old friends, became hollow, mere vibrations of air.

At first Rafe kept some distance. He only touched her when they rode on the bike. But then, slowly, almost imperceptibly, he moved in. With his room by the front door and mail slot, he appointed himself mailman. He delivered the morning mail to her room while she lay on her stomach, pretending to be asleep. Gradually he took to rubbing her back. Then more. He never spoke. One day she found the golden locket lying beside her pillow. A sprig of lavender was tucked inside. She let him enter her dream.

Chapter 41

"COME WITH ME TO LONDON for the weekend," Rafe said one day in his fatherly tone. "Some of me old mates are having a house party up in Nottinghill Gate. We'll spend the night in their huge flat."

"I don't know," she said. Even parties didn't excite her anymore. Nothing moved her, not since she'd dropped that acid at Abaddon.

"You won't want to miss this," he coaxed. "We can stop by a fantastic dealer-friend of mine and score something special. I'll even take you round to meet me mum and da in East Ham. Mum'll make you the best cup of tea you've ever had."

"I don't know, Rafe. I don't want to be around lots of people."

"You don't have to talk, Alice, just look pretty. Come on." He reached out and massaged her shoulders. "Please, baby. I promise you'll have fun."

"Why not," she said, giving in. She didn't want to stay home alone.

"Brilliant!" he said and grinned. "Say, have you got enough money for the train? I'm a little short this month."

"Sure," she said. Money was the one thing she still had.

That Friday afternoon she slouched in a private car on the train as it cut through the green-hedged hills of southwestern England. Sheep dotted the open fields like clouds that had lost their way. The small rhythmic motions of the train, the chungling chug of the wheels, dislodged words and phrases from her mind. *The future is endless and so is the past. The starlings lie empty, dead on the grass.* She scratched her thoughts in her small spiral notebook, just the right size for her small, spiraling thoughts.

The apartment in Nottinghill Gate was immense, the whole bottom floor of a big house, with tall windows facing every direction. Three couples lived there, none of them married. All six worked at London jobs. The women came home in short-skirted suits and high platform heels; the men wore ties and jackets. Square bank tellers, she thought at first until they changed into their party clothes and brought out the booze and drugs. Rafe sat on a sofa with one of his friends, looking through a photo album.

"Come 'ere, Alice," Rafe said patting the couch, "I want you to get to know Dick." His friend was handsome with heavy brows shading dark, intense eyes. "And Dick to know you." They both laughed. An inside joke. She sat down between them.

"Glad you could come for the weekend," said Dick, his eyes hooded as he looked at her. "Rafe's told me a bit about you." A rumbly sound came from his throat, like a large cat, a puma or a leopard.

While he was talking Alice's eyes wandered to the photographs in Dick's lap. What is that? she wondered. She was legs and arms and body parts, but something was odd, very odd. All of a sudden she flushed red from head to toe. She was looking at pornography. Homemade pornography. She dropped her eyes and tried not to move or flinch. She didn't want to touch either of the men sitting next to her. She wanted to get up, throw up, run away.

"Dick took those 'imself," Rafe was saying from somewhere far away. "Somefin, ain't it?" His Cockney accent grew stronger now that he was in London.

Something? Something sick! she wanted to shout, but she sat paralyzed, almost hypnotized, as if the photo album were a snake charmer's basket and the twisted limbs were a writhing snake. She turned hard as stone, hard as a pillar of salt.

Over the next few hours dozens of fancy young Londoners filled the flat. Stacks of LP's took turns dropping on the turntable. Dr. John the Night Tripper. Frank Zappa and the Mothers of Invention. The ever-present Rolling Stones. People danced on the hardwood floor of the dining room where the rug had been rolled to one side. Couples slithered together on sofas and chairs. The bedroom doors opened and shut again. She huddled alone in a corner of the kitchen, next to the back door. Rafe came up to her every so often, but she flinched at his touch. He didn't care. He was happy to be with his old friends. Probably old lovers.

As the night progressed into the early morning, people

began clearing out, and Alice found her coat and curled up on a love seat in the living room for the night.

"You can crash on one of the beds," Rafe said. "There's plenty of space. A king-size bed in every room."

"No," she was emphatic. "I'm staying here—by myself." At least she could still draw the line somewhere. "You do what you want."

"Fine," he said and left.

She pulled her collar around her face and prayed for morning to come.

Chapter 42

AFTER A FITFUL NIGHT of murmuring voices and sudden sharp laughter, doors opening and closing, water running, footsteps passing close by, she slowly rose into consciousness. She smelled coffee. Cups and saucers clinked in another room. She wanted to keep her eyes closed and her head under her coat but she ached all over. Her legs were cramped from being curled up all night on the short love seat. Cautiously she stretched them out, then lifted her arms above her head and twisted into a sitting position.

"Good Morning, Suzie Cream Cheese," said a voice. Sitting cross-legged yogi-style across the room from her was a black man she'd never seen before. His hair hung down to his shoulders in long, twisted clumps, with beads and ribbons attached to the ends of his strange braids. In his hand was the mouthpiece of a big water pipe that sat on the table in the middle of the room. Smoke circled him in a lazy cloud.

"Who are you?" she asked, thinking he looked like a combination of characters from Alice in Wonderland.

He shook his head and grinned, then exhaled and said with a West Indian accent, "Hey Suzie Sunshine, want a hit? Moroccan Gold. Just like the color of your hair. The most excellent ganja Jah ever created."

Why not? she thought. It was morning. The sun was up. How else was she going to get through this day? She crawled over to the coffee table and sucked in a deep breath, creating bubbles through the water in the glass bowl. It was becoming harder and harder for her to get stoned these days. She wondered if the drugs were losing their potency or if she had reached some kind of dry plateau. But this Moroccan Gold, it was good. She held her breath as long as she could and felt the reassuring buzz behind her eyes. She handed the pipe back across the table. "How did you do that to your hair?"

"Aaahh. Dreadlocks." He tossed the long braids from side to side. They made a soft tinkling sound. "I didn't do anything except tie on the bells and beads. I was born like this, a mark of my people. Rastafarians."

"Rasta...." This was something new.

"Rastafarians. We follow Haile Selassie. But don't worry. I'm not of the violent strain. Besides, I can see you're a lost lamb. Here," he leaned toward her, "you want to touch my dreadlocks, don't you?"

She reached out her fingers. The hair was soft and springy, like a lamb itself.

"Now, Suzie Sunshine," he said with a smile. "Tell me we're friends."

"But who are you?"

"Othello. Call me Othello." He said the name as if there was no *h*.

"All right," she said. "As long as I'm not Desdemona." Her sluggish brain still remembered some Shakespeare.

"No chance of that, my girl. Do I detect a Yankee in our midst?"

She nodded.

"And a sad one at that?"

She nodded again and took another drag from the water pipe.

"Have you been to the London zoo?" he asked.

"No. I love zoos."

"Then let's go. It's a perfect day. Leave these sods to clean up their mess."

She noticed for the first time the squalor around her. Cigarette boxes, butts and ashes, sticky pools of spilled drinks. Nylon stockings, stray earrings, dirty plates, and half empty glasses. One of the curtains was torn from the window. Record album covers were strewn on the floor. And over on the windowsill she spied the cover of that awful photo album. She wanted to get out into the sunshine.

"Did you come with someone?" Othello asked her.

"Oh, yes." She had almost forgotten. "Rafe. Do you know him?"

"Who doesn't," he said with a smirk. "And who hasn't he known. I'm sure he wouldn't mind if I borrowed you for a couple of hours. I'll leave him a note."

"Maybe we should ask him first."

"You can if you want," he said. "But I'll bet you a quid he's in Dick and Theresa's room with Molly."

Molly? A queasy feeling lurched in her stomach. "Let's

just go," she said. "I need to see some creatures besides human beings."

They caught a double decker bus to Regent's Park. Othello motioned her up the stairs to the top. "This is the way to see London," he said with his musical accent. "So how long have you been in this 'green and pleasant land'?"

Alice noticed the allusion to Blake's poem because the words were in "Jerusalem," her favorite hymn from boarding school. "That's just what I was going to ask you."

"I've been here since I was eight. My da's dead; my mother's clairvoyant."

"Like a fortune teller with a crystal ball?" The crisp cool air was reviving her a little.

"She does everything. Crystal ball, tea leaves, seances, reads palms. I can do that too."

"You can read palms?" Involuntarily she tightened her two fists in the pockets of her coat.

"Give us a look," he said and held out his toffee-colored hands.

"I don't know," she said but brought out her hands anyway.

"But I do," he assured her and warmed her skin between his fingers.

"Hmmm," he said as studied her palms. His forehead knotted and the bells on the ends of his braids jingled as he slowly shook his head. "I'll have to ask my mother about this. Strange, very strange."

"What is it? Am I going to die soon?"

"No, I don't think so, though the lifeline on your left hand is very short. But you're right-handed, correct?"

She nodded.

"Then your left hand is what you were born with; your right hand is what you do with your life."

"And what does the right hand say?"

"Here," he pointed to a crease, "your life line merges with your imagination. And then it never ends."

"What does it mean?" She felt a surge of fear and excitement.

"I don't know, Suzy Q. But I'm sure it's good." He sat up straight and looked her in the eye. "Listen up, girl. Don't let anyone manhandle you. Your life is within you. Your life is with Jah." The bus slowed to a stop. Before she could ask who Jah was, he stood up.

"Here's the zoo! Let me show you the monkey house. The best in the world."

Chapter 43

RAFE WAS SPUTTERING WITH ANGER when she got back to Nottinghill Gate that afternoon. "What did you think you were doing, Alice? How could you go off with Tony and not even tell me?" Now they were hurrying to get the train to East Ham to spend the night at his parents' house.

"He told me his name was Othello."

"So you thought he was a nobleman?" Rafe curled his lips with disgust. "He's a liar."

"He seemed nice." She didn't know who to believe anymore.

"Nice? And who didn't seem nice?"

"I wasn't comfortable with those, you know," she couldn't make herself say the word. "At Dick's."

"What about Dick?" He sneered. "Oh, the photos? Come on, Alice, I thought you were hip."

"Yeah, and I thought you were nice."

"What's this nice business? Who do you think you are, poor little rich girl from the big US of A? How nice are you with the World Bank and IMF and all your multi-national stock options putting the rest of the world in poverty. You think that's nice?" She'd never heard him talk like this. She didn't know what to say.

"I can't help it that I'm an American, and my family's rich." She wanted to cry.

"Well now you're going to see how the other half lives." He jerked her arm and pulled her down the stairs to the entrance of the tube station.

Rafe led Alice through a neighborhood of small, rundown houses with tiny fenced gardens in front. They passed a green grocer and a fish-and-chips take away, a cobbler's shop, a garage specializing in brake repair, and *The Barking Dog*, the local pub. Rafe paused in front of a brown brick house with green shutters. The garden was crowded with upturned terra cotta pots like round tombstones. "Me da loves roses," Mick said pointing at the containers, his Cockney accent growing stronger. "He's still at work, works six days a week repairing mail trucks and what not. Government keeps him busy." He opened the wooden gate and they walked up to the door. "Me ma takes in washing and a bit of mending," he said. "She's not much for words." He opened the front door and ushered Alice in.

She found herself in a small dark vestibule with two closed doors and a steep set of stairs. "Here's the parlor," he said and opened the door just a crack. "Only used for weddings and funerals." The cold, stale air escaping the unused room seemed to come from an abandoned mine. The second door opened into the kitchen where Rafe's mother sat in a faded paisley-covered chair, a pincushion around her wrist and a needle in her hand. She didn't get up when Rafe approached, just grunted a little and let him peck her cheek.

"Ma, this is Alice. An American."

His mother was a glum bowl of cold porridge, her face nearly formless except for a jutting chin. She hardly opened her mouth but sat looking at Alice through small black eyes. I bet she's seen plenty of Rafe's girlfriends come and go over the years, Alice thought. She was relieved when Rafe's father bustled in, all cheerful and friendly. He smiled and chatted with Alice over tea. She could see Rafe got his charm from his dad.

"Rafe says you've got a BSA 175—Birmingham Small Arms Company—like we used to 'ave at the postal service." His fingers were permanently stained and looked like his own attached set of tools. "What year's it? Could very well be one of the ones I worked on wit me own 'ands."

After a light supper of steak and kidney pie Rafe took Alice upstairs where there were three tiny bedrooms, each barely big enough for a bed, and a separate water closet, and a bath. She felt grungy from her night on the love seat and her day at the zoo, so she asked if she could take a bath before bed. Rafe went downstairs to check with his mother. He came back up and without speaking started scrubbing the tub. She had a terrible feeling she'd made an extravagant request, so when Rafe left the room she filled the tub with less than two inches of water and sponged herself clean with a washcloth. She dried herself with a small scratchy towel and crawled into Rafe's married sister's bed where she sunk into the hollow center of the mattress that gripped her body like a hand and felt as if she were lying where bodies had lain for hundreds of years before.

Chapter 44

"So," RAFE LOOKED UP from his Virgil. He and Alice had hardly spoken since they got on the train to Exeter that next morning. "How did you like hobnobbing with the hoi polloi?"

"If you mean your parents," she said, "fine. I thought your dad was sweet."

"But me mum?" Rafe made a contemptuous face just like his mother's.

"I don't think she liked me either." Alice turned her back toward him and stared at the scenes darting by out the window.

"Didn't give her a chance, did you? Flashing your fancy ring around, making your uppity demands."

"You could have told me about the bath. How should I know?"

"Are you going to show me your parents' house this summer when I come to the States?"

"Are you sure you want to associate with capitalist pigs?" She couldn't understand why he liked her anyway.

"Of course, lovey," he said and grabbed her fingers. "I never bite the hand that feeds me."

Two weeks later Rafe came up to her room to tell her he was going back to London for the weekend. "Some unfinished business. You'd be bored. Besides I'll be staying in East Ham with my parents."

"Fine," she said, hiding her surprise. "That's fine with me. I'll just hang around here. Visit some friends, maybe Oliver and Tom."

"Those two queens who took you to Teignmouth?"

"That's not nice, Rafe. You don't even know them. Besides, Tom had a girlfriend last semester."

"Wake up, Alice." He shook his head at her. "Homosexual. Bisexual. What's the difference? I'll be back late Sunday." He was gone.

She unplugged the electric kettle and sat on the corner of her rug with a pot of tea and a package of chocolate-covered digestives. Her eyes fell upon some books she'd stacked under the bed when she'd gotten back after Christmas. They were the ones by Francis Schaeffer that Annie, the girl on the bus in New York, had recommended. She'd bought them right away in Ann Arbor and had even written to L'Abri and made arrangements to visit in the summer when the semester was over. She really should try to read them if she was going to go there in July. But ever since her trip on LSD she had a hard time reading a whole page of anything. Her mind just couldn't concentrate.

She picked up *The God who is There* and held it with one hand while she dipped a digestive into her cup with the other. She flipped to the middle. "The First Step in the Line of Despair: Philosophy." What a depressing chapter title. Another section was called "Philosophic Homosexuality." This guy is strange. What could he be talking about? "The Anti-philosophy of the Anglo-Saxon World." She squeezed her eyes tight. She'd never really liked philosophy, that class she'd taken with Will. She didn't get this Existential/Logical Positivism stuff. She scanned the pages and finally found something she could relate to: "The Use of Drugs. Whether it is the existentialist speaking, or Aldous Huxley, or Eastern mysticism, we find a uniform need for an irrational experience to make some sense of life." Now that made sense to her. Maybe what she needed was another irrational experience. She closed the book and sprang to her feet. There was one more tab of acid in her treasure box. While Rafe was having fun, she'd have fun too.

She swallowed the pill with lukewarm tea, ate another biscuit, then went to stand in front of her wardrobe. She needed something special for today. As she put on a puffy sleeved blouse and her blue velvet overalls she felt the familiar pre-hallucinogenic flutter in her stomach. The LSD had made it that far. Soon she would see what was hidden from the naked eye. Soon she would have one of those "irrational experiences." Maybe this time she would be able to make some sense out of life. Like the Jefferson Airplane sang, "*One pill makes you larger and one pill makes you small.*" Maybe this trip would bring her out of the dark hole she'd been in. She slid into a skinny purple jumper and a pair of gold socks with paisleys running up the sides like yin and yang symbols. She was almost ready to go.

On the corner of the table next to her bed was a white

porcelain egg with pink and red rosebuds on top that Yvonne had given her as a going away gift. Carefully she lifted the lid and took out the three special shillings she kept inside. She sat back down on the floor, pushing aside *The God who is There* to make room for her ritual with the *I Ching*. She loved this book Zelda had given her, with its beautiful poetic images. It was like a diary that spoke back to her, that told her which way to turn. She closed her eyes and tried to make her mind into a blank page. She invited the forces of the universe to take control of her life. Paint me a picture, she whispered, sing me a song, tell me your secrets. She opened her palm and let the coins drop. Two heads and a tail—uneven. She drew a broken line. Next she threw three tails—even. A solid line. She did it four more times and recorded the hexagram on the card she used as a bookmark. She looked up the diagram's passage in the index. "Wind over water. No safe destination. The King withdraws to his chambers." All of a sudden her vision blurred. The letters began to move on the page like boats on an ocean. Oh, that's right, she said, closing the book and getting up on her knees. I'm tripping.

She pulled the diagonal zipper up to her chin and snapped down the flaps of her leather jacket. The sun would soon set and the night would turn cold. Better not take her bike this time, she quickly decided as the sidewalk undulated under her feet like waves of grey cement. Wind over water. Walking on water. Did Jesus really do that? Beeeep!! A blue Mini honked at her as she stepped off the curb. She watched it stretch into a long blue streak, an elongated rubber band, then snap out of sight when it turned the corner. Wow, this stuff is visual. *Vis-u-well, hid-din-hell.* A sing-songy voice played through her mind. "Stop that!" she said. *Vis-u-well, hid-din-hell.* "No!" She had to find a way to silence the voice. She started to sing, *"The water is wide, I can't get o'er. Neither have I the wings to fly. Build me a ship that can carry two, and both shall row, my love and I."*

She sang on and on, through all the verses twice, then three times. She had to keep the Voice away. Her legs became wooden oars and skimmed the watery sidewalk toward the university. Up, up she climbed. The school buildings looked like ocean liners bobbing atop huge waves. Her breath surged loud and heavy, an engine chugging in her chest. She could hear her heart beating, banging, bludgeoning. She ran to her favorite bench in the garden outside the library and sat down to catch her breath. The bench was tucked away in a covered alcove built right into the side of the hill. Soon, when spring came, the web of vines would uncurl green fingers and seal it up into a secret tomb. When she lived on campus in the fall, she used to come here sometimes to get stoned. Stoned on the stone, she laughed. Maybe that's a poem. It was almost dark, the grounds were deserted except for some hurrying shapes in the parking lot. She lay back on the bench to look at the sky. No stars. Not yet. The stars don't appear until the sun goes down. The marble bench felt smooth and cold under her. She thought of the prostrate statues of lords and ladies laid out life-size above their crypts in the cathedral. She felt the heat of her body seep into the stone. It was stealing her life. She was turning into stone. Fear rollercoastered through her. She stood up in panic. She had to get home.

Now it was really dark. The waxing moon, awkward in its fat gibbous shape, was already on its way to the west. She stumbled along the lush paths of the garden. Something hooted, she glanced at the branches above her. They looked like a jumble of slithering eels. She ran. The leaves under foot became insects. Pinchers stretched out to grab her. She was an alien. This was not her universe. The tiny thread that had linked her to the earth had been snapped in two. The fragile helium balloon of her life was drifting farther and farther away from reality. Help, she called into the black vacuum of the sky. Help me find the way. Almost at once she stepped through the woods and onto the familiar sidewalk. The darkness fled. She was under a street lamp. She stood still and the world hushed back to normal. The hallucinations stopped. The road before her became flat and solid. "Thank you," she breathed into the night.

Chapter 45

ALICE FOUND HER WAY through the streets of Exeter and back to her house on Old Tiverton Road. She opened the gate and walked through their neglected garden. The music blaring from inside the house seemed louder than normal. As she opened the front door cigarette smoke and the chatter of dozens of people fell out into the night like a mist of dry ice. Brightly colored paper lanterns covered the bare light bulbs in the hall, beads hung in doorways, lamps were draped with fringed shawls. She stood still and looked around. This was her house, wasn't it? Was she still tripping?

"Alice, darling!" Seth loped up to her dressed in a long black cape, a top hat on his head. Even with the colored lights she could see he'd put some kind of white powder on his skin. He leaned over and nipped her neck.

"Stop that, Seth!" she said and pushed him away. Then she noticed the fake fangs he was wearing over his teeth. "What's going on here?"

"I'm Count Dracula. Who are you supposed to be?"

Then she remembered. This was the night Nigel was

hosting a party for the drama department. He must have raided the prop room at the theatre building for decorations. A tall willowy girl appeared from nowhere and wrapped her limbs around Seth. She nibbled on his ear and gave Alice a get-out-of-here look. Seth peeled her off and said, "You haven't met Alice, have you?"

"Enchantée, I'm sure," the girl said and extended a hand of long pointed fingers covered with half a dozen rings. "Vancheska Beroyska." Seth had a girl friend? Alice was so out of touch.

"Nice to meet you."

"Of course," the girl said and latched her arm through Seth's. "Let's go see Nigel's light show again. Absolutely fantastic." Seth gave Alice a wink over his shoulder as Vancheska led him from the room.

Light show. The pieces were falling into place. Nigel had been working on it for days, dropping bits of colored oil onto a slide in his projector. Somehow he got the colors to mix and divide in time to the beat of the music and projected the images on his wall. He must have been planning for this party.

She wandered through a mash of dancing bodies and into the kitchen at the back of the house. She was surprised to see Simon the sidecar man standing in front of the stove stirring carrots and shallots and pieces of broccoli together in a huge pan. She hadn't noticed his bike and sidecar on the street. He was wearing a fringed leather vest and had a bandana tied around his neck. A cowboy?

"Hello," he said. "You're Alice, right?"

She nodded as she leaned against the end of the counter and watched while he added a few cups of cooked brown rice. He broke some eggs into a bowl and beat them together with soy sauce. She knew what she was looking at—he was fixing dinner, vegetable fried rice—but was it real? What about the things she saw when she was hallucinating? Were they really there, only no one saw them?

"Libby's upstairs with the baby. Trying to put her to sleep."

Alice looked at Simon. He was so calm. Tall. Six-foot-four or more even without the cowboy boots he was wearing tonight. He had a great mane of blond hair he swept back from his forehead with a shake of his neck. She heard he'd graduated from the drama department the year before. She could picture him as Hamlet or even King Lear. He dribbled the egg mixture into the fried rice, his movements slow and sure. He gave her a smile.

"What is food?" she asked.

He looked over at her. "Food? Did you say 'What is food?'"

"Yes. What is it? How do you know what to eat? Which plants are food, which plants are poison? Who figured out carrots were good? And what is rice?"

"Are you feeling okay? Have you eaten?" He put a hand on her forehead.

"Squirrels eat acorns, but in *Elvira Madigan* the people died when they ate acorns. Acorns and grass."

"That was a movie," he said. "Sit here at the table and I'll give you some dinner." He spoke like a big brother. "Then you'll know the answer." She sat down and buried her head in the nest of her arms while eels and insects and kernels of rice writhed on a stone altar in time to the pulsing music. Her trip hadn't ended. She wanted to cry.

"It's Molly, isn't it," she said to the back of his head.

"What? In the picture? Nah, just looks like her."

"I mean Molly is the reason you're staying home, the reason you went to London last week." Anger was the one emotion that put words in her mouth.

"What makes you think that?" He turned in his chair to look at her.

"You're not answering me."

"I told you." He snapped his words. "I had business to attend to."

"Did you see Molly in London last week?" She glared at him.

"What if I did? She's been having some problems. She's an old friend. Nothing wrong with helping out an old friend, is there?"

"Did you sleep with her?"

"I told you, I stayed at me mum's."

"Come on Rafe, you know what I mean." The anger felt good, at least she could feel something.

"Molly's had some bad times and she needed me."

She turned and left his room, slamming the door behind her. Poor Molly's had some bad times. What did she care? Rafe was a jerk.

But Alice did care. She needed Rafe. He was the thin cord that kept her tethered to herself. Now he was fraying away. Well, she would show him. She would go to the dance by herself. She gunned her bike up the hill to the university, raising her visor to let the fresh, cold air rush against her face. The stars were out. Their faithfulness calmed her. She told herself it was okay to be alone. Like the stars. Alone and far away.

She parked her bike, hung her helmet from the handle bar and went into the steamy auditorium where one of the student bands was playing a poor imitation of The Who. She spotted Simon and Libby standing by the stage.

"Hi," said Libby.

"Where's the baby?" Alice said.

"Simon's mother has her for the weekend. We're pretending we're students again. What about Rafe? Aren't you usually with him?"

"He's...." She felt a lump in her throat. "He's got something else to do. I came on my own."

"I thought he might be playing piano with one of the groups," said Simon. "He's terrific."

"I don't know," Alice said. "He doesn't tell me everything." It was hard to keep her emotions from spilling out.

Libby whispered something in Simon's ear and he nodded. The band was starting a slow song. "Would you like to dance, Alice," he said. She looked over at Libby who smiled.

"Thanks. That would be nice."

Simon glided her around the floor. His hand was firm against the middle of her back. She was wearing the cut-off top of an old dress of her Nana's, a black peasant-style blouse encrusted with fake jewels. Simon looked down at her and said, "Very pretty."

"Thanks," she said. She told him how she'd found the blouse in her grandmother's closet after she died. "Way up on a shelf," she said. "A tidbit overlooked by my vulterous mother."

"No," he said, "not the blouse. Your shoulders."

She felt a warm flush, but knew he was just being kind. Lucky Libby: she must have done something right that Alice was doing wrong. No one treated her so kindly. No one was a gentleman. No one except Bruce. And she had ruined that.

She thanked Simon for the dance and, still floating on the compliment, went off to listen to another band. In the activities room, now transformed by pulsing red lights, a group was playing rhythm and blues. She saw an empty seat next to a friend of Graham's. She'd seen him around at parties and he'd been over to their house a few times for the smoky festivities. They called him Black Steve since he only wore black, like he fancied himself a Keith Richards.

"Hey," she said. "Mind if I sit down?" She learned she had to make the first move to be friends with the British.

"Sure," he said. "But where's Rafe?" The campus was so small that everybody knew her business.

"Who cares," she said.

Then all he did was put his hand on her knee and the next thing she knew they were outside smoking a joint and she was following him to his flat. Why did she go with him? She knew he had a girl back home. She'd never been attracted to him until he touched her. Was it a careless gesture on his part? Or a dare? Just how far would the crazy American girl go? To the edge, she thought. To the edge and over. Let Rafe worry. Let him see how it feels to be thrown away.

Chapter 47

THE NEXT MONDAY Alice forced herself to the library. She was way behind in her studies. She had no motivation. Nothing seemed to matter. She waded into the stacks and over to a study area where stringy haired boys and skinny legged girls sat hunched around tables, their unkempt heads resting at various angles on elbowed arms. They looked like the flamingos she and Othello had seen at the London zoo. Only drab, featherless, dull.

She unwound the scarf from her neck and peeled off her thick wool jumper. Why was this building always so warm? Her room was frigid. She unhitched her backpack and dug out the heavy books that had cloistered in there for weeks. *Ontological Questions and the Incarnation* by R.T.S.Harmsworth. *The Sufficiency of Sacrifice* by C. Dole. And a bunch of other theological treatises that made no sense to her at all.

She pulled out a chair and sank down like the other students, resting her cheek on her stack of books. Her eyes scanned the walls of the room: rows and rows of books.

Hundreds and thousands of titles. Millions and billions of words. What could they possibly say? What could they mean? Just mark upon mark and noise upon noise. Dust, ashes, all will disappear. "O God," she murmured. "O God, what am I doing here?" Her mind went blank, retreating into its familiar black hole. She closed her eyes. If only she would cease.

A twitter of laughter a few tables away startled her out of her haze. Two male students were strutting and clowning with an old knit cap, trying to win the attentions of a group of females at the next table.

"Eh Lassie," one boy said as he yanked the cap down over the other boy's face. "Give us a kiss, give us a kiss."

"Cut that out, you ninny," the boy squawked back and grabbed his opponent by the collar of his shirt.

The girls laughed. Alice shook her head. It was all so stupid. Meaningless. She wished she could disappear through the floor. Or float, corpse-like, out through the window. Or vanish like heat rising through the roof. She was not there. She was not one of them. She did not belong on the planet.

She worked her wool jumper back over her head and hung her scarf around her neck, then gathered her lug of theology books and dumped them on the check-in cart by the desk. "I don't need these," she said to no one as she bullied her shoulder into the door and set her face toward the damp drizzle of the afternoon.

It was early spring. March daffodils covered the grounds between the buildings. Violet starflowers huddled at the foot of flowering crabs. A brook ran through the middle of campus. A sudden break in the clouds parted the drizzle and presented a faint but perfect rainbow, like an old actress appearing for her final curtain call.

She saw all this, the flowers, the rainbow. She heard the sound of the brook, the birds. She smelled the new grass, the wormy soil. She felt the mist, the soft breeze against her skin. But nothing penetrated. She was grey. She was winter. The rainbow was just some trick of the light. Refraction. Big deal. Who cares. Only fools think there's a pot of gold waiting somewhere.

Fools, she thought. All these people are fools. And me? I don't exist.

Chapter 48

ALICE SETTLED into the big back seat of the Paris taxi. "Orly," she told the driver and he sped off toward the airport. Her cloud of depression had thinned a little since she'd arrived in Paris. Wasn't it called the City of Lights? She was feeling almost happy. She hugged her leather bag to her chest. Inside was a quarter ounce of Moroccan Gold—just like she'd smoked with Othello in London. Her very own quarter ounce of marijuana. It should last all the way through her two weeks of skiing in Norway. She could stay high all the time. She didn't even mind now what she'd had to do to get it. Everything was going to be fine.

She laughed to herself. This trip had not been what she'd imagined. When she met Victoria in the airplane hangar in Iceland before Christmas and was invited to Paris for Easter, she had assumed her friend would be well-stocked and well-connected. She'd been wrong. Victoria's bidet was filled with dirty underwear, her extra bed was a lumpy couch, and the *café au lait* she served in big flowered bowls was hot milk with Nescafé. But true to her nickname, the Mad Hatter, a dozen outlandish hats hung from hooks around the ceiling in the small apartment. The two of them had ridden around the streets of Montmartre at ten miles an hour, both squeezed on Victoria's rusty moped, searching for a French dress for Alice and—more importantly—marijuana.

Finally, on the day before Alice left for Norway, they found a dress in a *dépôt-ventes*, a store selling last season's haute-couture at discounted prices. Alice picked out a sumac-colored midi-length knitted dress and matching jacket. Victoria said it looked great with her coppery hair. She had handed the sales girl a wad of francs—Alice had learned how to convert dollars into pounds, but got confused changing pounds into francs—and was shocked to discover, when they got back to Victoria's apartment, that she only had enough money for dinner that night and a taxi to the airport.

"Now what?" she said to Victoria. "I've got the dress but not the dope. I can't spend two weeks in Norway without getting high."

"Too bad you're not going to Sweden or Amsterdam. I hear Norway's still in the nineteenth century. You won't score there. All I've got left is this." She pulled a carefully wrapped joint out the drawer in her coffee table.

"There must be something we can do? Trade some clothes for a little grass? My Levi's or my Boy Scout shirt?" It scared Alice to think of being totally straight in a strange country where she didn't speak the language.

A deep, serious church bell began tolling outside the flat. "There goes old Savoyarde again," Victoria said. "They say that bell weighs nineteen tons. I say it sounds like Judgment Day." She was still fingering her one last joint.

"Hey. Let's get stoned and go visit the bell. You can see the whole city from there. It's like standing on the balcony of Paris. Maybe if we climb all the steps of Sacré Coeur God will answer your prayers. Drop down some grass like manna from heaven."

Victoria lit the joint and passed it to Alice. The smoke blended with her breath like a lover. But could she really ask God to give her marijuana? She knew God had protected her: on the mountain in Switzerland when Barb had put that curse on her, and when she had her motorcycle accident, and on the wall of Abaddon when the wicked voices were calling her higher and higher. Maybe he did answer prayers, at least some of them. She thought of the long months after Nana's stroke when she lay in a bed in a nursing home in Ann Arbor slowly dying. Nana didn't recognize anyone, not even her granddaughter. Alice had sat by her bed, holding the spidery hand, asking God to bring her back so they could talk. So they could laugh. So she could tell her how much she loved her. One night she had even gone into her father's study and pecked at his typewriter: "Dear God, Please don't let Nana die." But then she had added the words she had learned from Sunday school, "Not my will but Yours be done." So maybe he had answered that prayer after all. How could she ever know what God's will was, anyway?

When the joint was done they each grabbed a hat and left the apartment on foot, headed toward the Basilique, the famous wedding-cake church on the pinnacle of Montmartre. "Why do they call this area Montmartre?" Alice asked when they stopped part way up the steps. There were two hundred sixty-six altogether.

"Most people say it's named for the martyrdom of St. Denis, the first bishop of Paris," said Victoria. "Tradition says that after the Romans decapitated him, he picked up his head and carried it over the hill."

"Spooky," said Alice. They started to climb again.

"But there also used to be a Roman temple to Mercury somewhere on top of the Butte." She pointed above the buildings to their left.

"Mercury, like quicksilver," said Alice. She began to sing, "*She's a quicksilver girl, a lover of the world.*" Victoria joined in, "*She spreads her wings and she's free.*" They both lifted their arms like they were flying. "*She's a quicksilver girl, a lover of the world. She's seen every branch on the tree.*" What did that mean, every branch on the tree?

They reached the top and joined a smattering of tourists going into the church. As her eyes adjusted to the darkness, Alice was sobered by a gigantic mosaic on one wall portraying Jesus with outstretched arms. Sunday school verses rose from her subconscious. "He bore our sins in his body on the tree.... Cursed is everyone who is hung on a tree.... In the middle of the garden were the tree of life and the tree of the knowledge of good and evil....To him who overcomes I will give the right to eat from the tree of life."

The Savoyard began again its deep, long song. It sounded like the voice of God. Steady, strong, and frightening.

The walk down the steps was much easier. The lower they went, the farther the sun sank behind the city. Alice was quiet the whole way. It was nearly dark when they got to the door outside Victoria's apartment.

"This is your last night," Victoria said, "and you can't be in a frump. Let's go to the Moulin Rouge and peek at the cancan girls."

"Cancan girls?" The image on her parents' powder room wallpaper snared her like a web. "No! I can't."

"Can't?" Victoria turned on the stairs and looked down at her.

Alice brushed her fingers across her face, feeling for imaginary threads. "Won't," she said.

"Whatever. Let's go eat at the café around the corner. They sat on slatted folding chairs at a sidewalk table at the café and ordered *croque-monsieurs*, the French version of grilled ham and cheese. Victoria suddenly sprang up and waved to a man on the other side of the street. "Your prayers have been answered!" she said to Alice, then yelled, "Eduard! *Viens ici.*"

A small-boned man with a thin mustache and bright purple beret crossed the street at her greeting. He was carrying a large flat package wrapped in brown paper. After he and Victoria kissed cheek to cheek she introduced him to Alice.

"*Enchanté de faire vôtre connaissance*," he said kissing her hand. Victoria invited Eduard to pull up a chair and the two of them dove into a torrent of rapid French. Alice could only pick out a word or two: "*Très belle...*" "*C'est possible...*"

Eduard kept glancing over at Alice, not with a smile or any discernible expression, but as if he were studying her.

Victoria looked at her too, then gave a shrug. "*Peut-être*," she said. Alice wished her French was better.

Eduard looked at his watch. "*Merde*," he said, grabbing

his package. He rushed across the street and disappeared around a corner.

"What was that all about?"

"Eduard's your guardian angel."

"That guy?"

"Listen to this. He wants you to model for him."

"Model, you mean pose?"

"Something like that. He's a typical starving artist. I see him around here all the time, sketching in cafés. He lives mostly by bartering."

"So?"

"So when he asked if you would model nude for him, I told him you probably would if he could score some grass for us, some really good stuff."

"Victoria!"

"He's harmless. He just wants to take some photos. Then he'll paint from them. He's gone to deliver a painting right now and he'll see what sort of goodies he can get for it. Your prayers are being answered!"

"I don't know. He's a total stranger."

"It's up to you. You're the one with the habit."

Habit? The word stung. She shook it off with a shudder and repressed the comments Luke had made to her months ago on her first night in London. How ridiculous. Her mother was the one with the habit. She just liked to get stoned once in awhile.

Alice glanced at the taxi driver, a dark Middle Eastern man, busy dodging traffic and not paying attention to her. Did she dare? Why not? While the taxi left the twisting city streets of Paris and entered the highway to the airport, she fumbled in her bag and pulled out a packet of bright yellow cigarette papers. She retrieved the precious tin of marijuana from her purse that Eduard had found for her the night before and balanced it gingerly on her knees. She sprinkled leaves in the center of the creased paper but the ride was bumpy and she was nervous, so the joint ended up with one end open too wide. She stashed it in the pocket of her ski jacket for safekeeping, hoping not too many of the brown flakes would spill out.

She checked her bags for the flight to Norway and since she had half an hour until departure, she went outside to get high. The early April air was as brisk and cold as the passengers who hurried in and out of the terminal, but she found a sheltered spot in an elbow of the building where she could light up. She crouched over and held the misshapen joint between her lips and tried to light a match. One, two, three matches went out. She couldn't get the thing lit. She tried huddling closer, out of the wind, when she heard footsteps coming her way.

She peeked over her shoulder, then instantly stood up and dropped the joint to the pavement, covering it with her foot. A gendarme stopped directly in front of her, cornering her against the building. *"Mademoiselle, Qu'est-ce que vous faites?"* he demanded.

"Moi?" she said. *"Je ne comprend pas.* I don't speak French."

"Aaah." He lifted his mustached nose as if he were smelling the salt air of the English Channel. "British."

She didn't correct him.

"Qu'est-ce que vous faites? What are you doing? *Qu'est-ce*

que c'est dans votre mains? What is that in your hands?" he said with a thick French accent.

"My hands?" She fumbled and looked down at the book of matches still clenched in her fist. *Oak and Acorn* was imprinted on the dirty white cover of the matchbook. Might as well read *Ball and Chain* she thought as she showed it to the menacing man.

"And where are your cigarettes, Mademoiselle?" barked the policeman.

"I, I don't have any cigarettes....I, I just found these matches in my coat pocket. I'm going skiing, you see, in Norway, and I haven't worn this jacket since Christmas and I was just wondering if the matches would still light and so I've just been striking the matches. That's all." She fumbled on in accelerating phrases. Fear loosed her tongue. "Now, *excusez-moi*, I must go catch my plane."

"Non." The gendarme threw back his shoulders and snapped his heels together like a Gestapo. "*Une minute*, Mademoiselle. I must see your passport. Give me your passport." The last four words came out in slow, clear English.

She had no choice.

She dug into her leather bag, reaching past wallet and coin purse and hand lotion and the hard round candy tin that now held an enormously dangerous half ounce of marijuana. She pulled her passport out of its brown case and handed it over to the gendarme. He sputtered and nearly choked with joy when he saw the dark blue cover. "*Américane? Américaine! Vous êtes Américaine!*"

She looked around nervously. This man, this policeman, now had her passport. And she had half an ounce of an illegal substance in her purse and was preparing to cross international borders.

"I must go catch my plane now." She reached her hand toward the passport. "*S'il vous plaît*. I must go now."

Her heart thundered loud in her ears as she stepped away from the man, toward the busy door of the terminal, her hand still outstretched and pleading. Please God, help me!

As she moved away from the spot where she was standing, the gendarme spied the crumpled yellow joint. He bent over at the waist like a courtier, stretched out his fingers, and retrieved his prize. He held the cigarette to his nose and sniffed. "Ah ha!" he shouted in victory. "What is this?" His voice was stern and commanding.

"I don't know," she squeaked, making a desperate, tiny noise like a mouse caught in a trap. "It's not mine," she lied. Principles be damned; this was serious.

In a flash the policeman reached forward and locked his fingers around her left arm above her elbow and trapped her with a vise grip.

Time, that before had seemed to be standing still, went into fast forward.

"Come with me," the policeman ordered, knowing she had no choice. He led the way to the airport police station with her in tow and the golden cigarette held out high in front of him, a blazing torch of victory over Yankees.

Her life became a movie. She watched from somewhere else as actors formed a curious crowd of onlookers, stopping to gawk at the procession of justice. Gendarmes appeared every few feet, their navy uniforms and flat brimless hats now standing out from the throng of travelers.

The airport was crawling with police. How could she be so stupid? As the scene unfolded her captor led her past the departure area, her mind feverishly clicked ahead. The tin in her purse was full of a quarter ounce of pot. What was she going to do? She had to get rid of that tin. With her free right arm she ever so slowly reached into the bag hanging from her shoulder and palmed the small box that contained the evidence of her guilt. Did she dare drop it? Would he notice? She looked at the policeman, so arrogant in his role as victor. He had his fish on the line and his hand was the hook. She could tell he was thinking only of how powerful he appeared to the international audience of Orly, anticipating the praise he was about to receive as he reeled in the prize. He was not paying attention to her.

She waited for her chance. As the policeman whirled her sharply to the left to enter the police entrance of the airport, she opened her fingers and let the tin drop into the gutter. It clanged loudly in her ears as it hit the cement, but buses and taxies and the multilingual announcements coming from the loud speaker covered the sound. The gendarme just kept goose-stepping ahead, straight into the building.

Her mind raced as fast as her pounding heart. Had she done it? Did she fool him? She had no thought for the future, only for the immediate fate that awaited her inside the building. Captor and captive passed quickly through the doors. She heard murmurs of surprise and congratulations as the policeman was greeted by his comrades. He propelled her into a small room with a table and plastic chairs with wide arm rests, like the desks they had back home at the driver's license bureau. "Sit down," he commanded. Soon two other officers entered the room.

They began their interrogation in French. *"Vôtre nom?...Où allez-vous?...Qu'est-ce que vous faites?"* All the French she had learned since fourth grade rose to the surface on the surge of adrenaline flooding her body. She had never been so fluent. One man took her purse over to a table and dumped out the contents, examining them closely.

"Empty your pockets," the man in charge said in English. She reached in and pulled out the matchbook, a tube of lip gloss, a half eaten roll of peppermints, an unused token for the Paris subway, her taxi receipt, and a crumpled tissue. To her horror, every item was peppered with fragments of little brown leaves that screamed "guilty" at her like wagging tongues. But the policeman took no notice.

"And what is this?" he asked, as he brought over the abandoned "cigarette" and held it in front of her nose.

"I don't know; I don't know. It's not mine!" she lied again in French. She clenched her muscles to keep from crying.

"And what exactly were you doing when Officer Pajou approached you?"

What could she say? Looking at her matchbook? It sounded ridiculous. "I need a lawyer," she said. "I'm an American citizen." And then to protect herself she said, "I don't speak French."

The officers laughed and winked at one another. "We are sending this 'cigarette' to our lab upstairs," said the man in charge. "Soon we will know the truth." Alice thought her life was over, but then he said, "Mademoiselle, follow me."

He led her out of the room, through a series of doors and hallways, then down a long staircase and out the building. "Get in," he said as he pointed to a police car and handed over her red bag. Suddenly he was driving out on the tarmac to a waiting plane, her plane to Stavanger, Norway. She found a seat and sat trembling as the engines roared and carried her up, away from Paris, away from France, and into an even more foreign country where she had no money, no language skills, and no friends.

Chapter 49

ALICE TOOK A DEEP, SHAKY BREATH as the plane touched down on the Norwegian runway. Had she escaped? Would the French police come after her when the lab confirmed the joint was marijuana? How could she have been so stupid? Cautiously she got off the plane in Stavanger, but there was no sign of police. No one paid any attention to her. All the voices sounded like gibberish. She was an alien in an unknown land. She looked at the strange signs around her. *Parkeringsplass.* She could guess what that meant, a place to park cars. But where was the place for her?

An hour later she somehow found the dock where a boat was scheduled to take her to the skiing village where she had a two-week reservation. A burly man in a knit cap swung her bags into the back of the small hydroplane and held her hand as she climbed on board. "Thank you," she said. "Ta. *Merci.*" She was at a loss of what to say. She knew no Norwegian.

"*Ingen årsak,*" came his reply and he pointed her in the direction of the narrow, window-lined cabin. Only three or four of the twenty seats were taken. She slumped down, still shaken by her near catastrophe at Orly. Now she had no drugs or money, just a confirmed reservation at a hotel in a country where no one seemed to speak English.

"Hallo!" She jumped when a man's voice addressed her. She turned as a stylish young man took the seat across the aisle from her. He was strikingly handsome, with prominent cheekbones and a perfectly balanced face. He looked like a model. His charcoal grey topcoat matched the color of his eyes and his blond hair was set off by the red silk scarf wrapped around his neck, ascot fashion. He wasn't like any of the Norwegians she had seen so far.

"Speak *Engelsk*?" he said and revealed a bright, straight-toothed grin.

"Hello," she answered, barely able to be polite. She was exhausted and not up for any more adventures today, and definitely not stirred by any hint of romance.

"Where you go?" he asked in broken English.

"Hardanger, to ski," she replied, not sure at all how to pronounce the name.

"Hardanger!" He raised his voice and pointed at his chest. "My home, my home." He extended his hand and said, "I Bernt Johans. I welcome you my country."

"Thank you, Bernt." She tried to mimic his pronunciation. "I'm Alice, from the United States."

"United States!" He grew more excited. "Home of Hollywood! I hope to go there some day—I am actor."

She wasn't sure she had understood him correctly. "An actor, did you say?"

"Yes! yes!" he said, fully animated now. "An actor. In movies. You know movies?"

"Really?" she said thinking this was more than a little hard to believe. "You've been in movies?" She spoke slowly, watching his face as he concentrated on her words.

"You know Ingmar Bergman? *Persona*?"

"Of course," she said, amazed. "Were you in that?"

"Just little part." He gestured with his thumb and forefinger. "But I hope I do big." He continued to smile. "I go home to Hardanger for interview with famous magazine. Reporter from Oslo there. Take photographs of my family, my home."

Was she dreaming? She could be, she was so tired and disoriented. "Perhaps you can help me..." she began. He interrupted her right away.

"*Hjelp* you? You need help? I help!" He was effusive. Help was an English word he understood.

She began to explain, in as simple words as possible, that she had run out of money in Paris and had to find a way to get some sent to her from her father. He reassured her that everything would be fine. He would take her to his parents' house—his brother was studying to be a Lutheran minister. He would talk to the hotel manager—the reporter from Oslo was also staying there. He would introduce her at the bank—it would only take a few days to have money wired from the States. He was her guardian angel with a Norwegian accent, and looked like one too. But then she remembered that's what she had thought about Graham. She wasn't sure of anything or anyone anymore.

Alice spent a long hour at the Johans' house, sipping bitter coffee and looking politely through the family collection of postcards, while Bernt's mother, a small greying woman with a ramrod straight back and incessant scowl, hovered in the background. She spoke no English, which was probably a good thing. But Alice could tell by the way his mother looked at her that she didn't approve of this female her son had brought home. She behaved as ladylike as possible and wondered how Bernt was explaining her to his mother.

Then he drove her to the hotel—the only one in the small village—and left after a quick word with the hotel manager. She surveyed her surroundings; it was unlike any hotel she'd ever been in before: stark, cold, and worst of all, empty of people, except for Mr. Krone, the weasel-eyed man behind the desk. He scanned her up and down and shook his head. I don't like the looks of you either, she said to herself, then took a deep breath and put on a smile. She needed him to be her ally.

"I'm Alice Blankwell. I have a...."

"Yes, I know. We have your reservation." At least he spoke some English. "You are friend of Bernt Johans?" he asked abruptly.

"Well," she spoke hesitantly, "I just met him on the hydroplane. He's offered to help me."

"*Sannsynlig.*" A loud ugly snarl came from the man's lips. "You know what he is?" He didn't give her a chance to reply. "He is a *skuespiller*—an actor!" His eyes grew wide and his face turned red as if he had just named the worst profession in the world.

"He told me he's been in a movie."

"A film! On stage! Who knows what else he has been doing. He lives in Stockholm!" The man's face looked as if he had just eaten something awful. "I will tell you something—for your own good. He is a black, black sheep. Have nothing to do with him."

She didn't know what to say. "Thank you" seemed not quite right. She felt as if reality was tipping over on its side and she didn't know which way to turn. She changed the subject.

"I have a problem, Mr. Krone. I don't have enough money with me so I need to call home and have my parents wire some to me. Will it be all right for me to stay here until the money comes?" Or will you cast me off to wander with the black sheep? she wanted to add.

The manager agreed. She understood why he wanted her to stay when he told her that the only other guests at the hotel were the reporter from Oslo and a newlywed couple on their honeymoon. Then she asked about paying for the ski lifts and rental equipment.

"That will not be a problem for your money," he said. "The ski lift stopped running after Easter. All we have is cross-country now."

"Cross-country?" She'd never done it.

"Perhaps the newlyweds will take you with them," he said. "But they don't speak any English."

Alice couldn't believe what was happening to her. No money. No skiing. No way to get high. Nothing to do. And whom could she trust? "What about the reporter?" she asked. "Does he speak English?"

"That I do not know," he replied, "but you will see him at dinner. Six p.m. sharp. I hope you like cod."

She lay on the cot-like bed in her hotel room and stared out the window as light drained from the grey afternoon.

What had gone wrong? When she left America six months ago she had felt so free and full of hope, like a giant balloon, untethered, full of excitement, about to find her true place in the world. Now she was heavy with dread, an anonymous rock dropped into the ocean, sinking to the bottom.

A jarring sequence of bells sounded outside her room. She counted six—six o'clock on the dot. She rolled onto her side and sat up. Maybe the reporter from Oslo would fill her in on the truth about Bernt. She sighed as she got up to wash her hands and face in cold water from the sink behind her door.

In the dingy dining room it wasn't hard to find the man she wanted to talk to since there were only three people, and two of them were sitting together with their hands knotted across the table staring into each other's eyes. She put a few unidentifiable bits of food from the skimpy buffet table on her plate and went up to the single man. "Excuse me," she said to a glum face set in an oversized head. "Would you mind if I joined you?"

He looked up and scrutinized her for a moment, then said, "You must be the American Bernt's been chattering about. *Sett deg.* Sit down."

"Thanks," she said, eyeing the wisps of blond hair that stuck out in odd places from his egg-like skull. "I hope you don't mind, but I'd like to ask you a few questions about Bernt."

He laughed. "That's what I'm here to do."

"I know. But you see, I'm confused. I just met Bernt on the boat. He seems very nice but the hotel manager says I should watch out. What do you think?"

"Well, just what do you have in mind?" He narrowed his eyes into tiny slits.

"Nothing." She was defensive. "But he invited me to go on your excursion tomorrow. I just wondered if he's a nice person, if I can trust him. Why does the manager hate him so much?"

He laughed again, not a pleasant sound. "Do you understand where you are, Miss? Me, I'm from Oslo. The capital. But here in what we call the "*bibelbelte*," things are not the same. No drinking, no dancing, no card playing, and definitely no acting. An actor is a very bad fellow—a heretic, a heathen, *en hedning*."

"Really?" She had never heard of such things—or had she? It sounded like the college where Peter, her Outward Bound teammate, went to school. "So that's why...."

"That's why a girl like you, all on her own, who comes in with a man like Bernt...." He shook his head.

"But it's not like that at all. I don't even know him."

"That's not what it looks like." He made a cynical sound again and pushed his chair away from the table. "We'll see you in the morning, no doubt."

After breakfast Alice sat in the small sitting room off the hotel lobby, over in a corner lined with shelves of books. But all the books were in Norwegian. Snow veiled the windows. She shifted her legs and sank deeper into the scratchy arm chair. Nothing felt inviting here in this land of strangers. Her room was even more stark than her dorm room at boarding school—only a stiff mattress and a straight-back chair. Bruce's mother would love it. And the food, the food was inhospitable: cold fish for breakfast with their poor, dead eyes peering up from the platter. Stacks of dry brown bread, rows of bitter cheeses, grilled green tomatoes, and soupy Welsh rarebit. Who were these Norwegians?

But she wasn't hungry anyway. Two days ago she'd been at Victoria's apartment in Paris, sipping café au lait and eating fresh baguettes with jam and butter. Why had she spent all her money on that stupid French dress? Now she was like one of those dead fish at breakfast, lying on some forgotten shore of nowhere. Nothing to do. Nothing to read except her copy of T.S. Eliot's *The Four Quartets*. She didn't even have four quarters.

She tried to read the T.S. Eliot poem but her mind, in a wasteland of withdrawal from drugs, could only pick words from the page one by one, like broken shards washed up on the beach. The letters were empty shells that used to hold life, but now held only a distant whisper of icy waves. Any meaning implanted by Mr. Eliot had dried up for her.

Poor T.S., she thought, and a bullet of shame shot through her as she remembered the chapel service at boarding school given *in memoriam* to the poet. All during the tribute to "one of our greatest men of letters" she had giggled uncontrollably at the thought: T.S., Eliot. Tough shit, Eliot.

She was so juvenile, so self-absorbed. Well, now it was T.S. Alice, you beached whale, you lost Jonah, you criminal, you liar, you sad, lonely girl.

She took her pen out of the back pocket of her jeans and wrote on the inside cover of *Four Quartets*:

"Four quarters clog my heart
Twin arteries lined with tin
One to buy a kiss of gold
One to pay for all my sin...."

The heavy front door of the hotel opened with a bang and she heard two sets of winter boots stomping off snow. Then there were guttural greetings with the horrid hotel manager. It had to be Bernt and that reporter, she thought as she tried to disappear into the big chair. Maybe they wouldn't see her. But no, almost immediately she heard Bernt's broken accent, "Hallo—Aleece—is that you in chair?" His blond face bent over her shoulder and gave her a wide, perfect smile. "Are you ready for wonderful day?"

Was this all an act? she wondered. He seemed so sincere.

The Oslo egghead appeared at his side. "Tell her, Sven," urged Bernt. "Tell her she must come with us."

But the other man just lifted his arm and looked at his watch. "We're going to be late."

She kept her eyes from the imploring look on the actor's face. Snow from his cuffs was running down his boots and puddling on the floor. "Thank you Bernt, for the invitation," she said. "But I came here to ski and so that's what I should do. And I have to go to the bank this afternoon to see if my money has arrived."

"Too bad, too bad," Bernt frowned. "But it's okay. We will see you tomorrow night when we return, yes? We escort you to...disco." He leaned close and whispered the last word. A forbidden dance here in Harbangar? "At eight.

På gjensyn. See you then." He reached down to squeeze her arm. Alice froze at his touch and he quickly retreated.

"At eight tomorrow," she said and turned to stare out the window at the snow blocking her view.

Chapter 50

THE NEXT DAY Alice slowed her skis to a stop and peered out to the Norwegian Sea. She and the newlyweds from the hotel had spent the last three hours following a gentle twisting path through the woods until they reached the top of the fjord. The furry-bottomed cross-country skis she borrowed from the hotel enabled her to practically walk on top of the snow without sliding backward. Now, at the sight of open water, she moved away from the couple and gazed at the grey expanse far below. Over there lay England, she thought. And beyond that—home. A lump formed in her throat.

She inched sideways a little closer to the edge. Changing direction on the strange skis was awkward with only her toes held in the bindings. The tip of one of her skis clunked against something hard. She looked down and gasped. There was a hollow rectangular shape under the snow that looked like an open tomb. Then she realized it must be a bunker from World War II, a concrete foxhole without its canons. She shivered as the wind wailed around her and wondered if she was hearing the cries of the dead.

"Hallo, hallo." Alice jumped at the voices of her companions. They lifted their poles in greeting and skied up beside her. "*Vakker utskit.*" She had no idea what the words meant as the two skiers pointed to the sea, then gestured toward the bunker. They sputtered sounds to each other and smiled at her. Then the husband broke off a pine bough and brushed snow from a fallen tree trunk. His wife sat down and unzipped her backpack. She pointed to the wrapped sandwiches and packets of dried fruit prepared by the hotel kitchen and said, "*Formiddagsmat.*" Then the man produced a thermos out of his backpack and poured three cups of steaming black coffee. "*Kaffe.*" They motioned for her to sit with them.

"Thank you so much," she said and tried to look happy. "You are both so sweet to spend part of your honeymoon with me. I don't deserve this at all." They nodded and smiled and exchanged a few words with one another. The wife patted Alice on the arm.

What a strange trio they made. The newlyweds didn't seem much older than her. She wished they spoke a common language. But what would they say? The two of them looked like an ad for a vacation brochure with their matching red parkas and their Scandinavian knit hats and scarves. Two peas in a pod, two bugs in a bed. They were picture postcard perfect and she was a blank page. They were starting a new life together and she was alone. A dead end. An abandoned bunker. She had no more ammunition.

She couldn't hold her line of defense. The enemy had taken her captive. She was in exile from herself.

After they finished eating, the young man—she didn't even know his name—signaled for her to follow them away from the edge of the fjord. They led her a short distance over flat terrain, then stopped at the top of a steep downhill ski slope. The towers of the defunct chair lift stood strung together down the side of the mountain, growing smaller and smaller until they ended at a hut at the bottom of the hill. The couple held her attention and made zigzag lines in the air with their poles. She realized with horror that they were telling her to traverse the slope. She nodded her head in understanding but her stomach shook with fear. How was she going to make the turns without a binding holding her boots to her skis?

The two of them headed down, first the woman, then her husband. They bent in a strange kneeling motion as they went into their turns. Alice had no idea how to ski like that. She was used to heel and toe bindings that gave her control over her edges when she shifted her weight and leaned with her knees. After several traverses the Norwegians stopped and looked up at her and waved, motioning her to follow.

There was no other way down. She had to try. She pushed off at an angle to the hill, hoping not to gain too much speed. Then, just before she came to the line of firs edging the slope, she tried to turn. "*Ow!*" she yelled as she wrenched her toe out of the binding and landed hard on her left side, sliding several feet down hill on her hip.

Concerned noises came from below. She lifted a hand to let them know she was okay, then got up, brushed the snow off her body and replaced her boot in the binding. Then again, from the other direction, she skied across the face of the hill, failed to turn, bruised the other toe, and lost her ski. Back and forth, time after time, she made her way down the mountain, not knowing what she was doing wrong, not being able to ask for help, knowing with each new attempt that she would feel more pain. Tears smeared her cheeks. Snow wedged its way into her boots, under the cuffs of her mittens, down the back of her neck. Just four more turns, just three more, just two, one. The Norwegians skied over and pulled her up from her final fall. The young woman shyly patted Alice's cheek. The young man handed her a handkerchief. Their foreign words were soft and cooing, the sounds of compassion in any language. She blew her nose and wiped her eyes and numbly skied behind them to the hotel.

When Alice got back to her room she took a bath and soaked her bruises, then curled on her bed and covered her head with the quilt to keep out the afternoon sun. She fell into a deep sleep until a loud knocking on the door jarred her awake. "Who is it?" she called out weakly.

"Alice, you there?" It was Bernt.

She sat up with a start and looked at her watch. Already twenty past eight—at night. "Just a minute," she said through the door and pulled on her bathrobe. "I'm really sorry, Bernt," she apologized as she opened the door. "I was so tired from skiing I went to sleep."

He looked down at her robe and back at her face. "You want sleep?" he asked. "Not go to disco?"

"No, I fell asleep. Now I'm going to get up." It was so hard to communicate.

"You want to get high?"

Didn't she wish, but according to the Oslo reporter they didn't even have alcohol in this part of the country. "I'll go to the disco with you," she said slowly. "Can you wait while I get dressed?"

Bernt surveyed her room, the narrow bed, the straight-back chair. He walked over and examined the sink when another knock rattled the half-closed door. She opened it and found the hotel manager standing there with an arm full of fresh towels.

"*Motbydelig!*" he said, looking at Bernt. "Just as I thought." He gave her a hooded stare. "I will have to charge you for two." He handed her the towels and left without another word.

"What a creep," she said.

"Creep?" asked Bernt.

"Creep, crud, jerk, idiot."

"Oh, idiot," said Bernt, nodding his head. Apparently that was part of his English vocabulary.

"You'd better go. I'll meet you in the lobby in ten minutes. Understand?"

"Yes," he said, "Understand." He left with a nod and a wave.

Red and blue lights pulsed from the second story windows of a small drab building in the middle of downtown Hardanger. Alice could hear the monotonous drone of a bass guitar. The "disco" club was above what looked like a hardware store, across the street from the bank where she'd made arrangements to receive the wired money from home. Bernt led the way up the steep steps with the reporter bringing up the rear. A thick-necked man sat on a stool in front of a cash box at the landing. He jumped up when he saw Bernt and showered him in a flurry of words. He kept bobbing in little bows from the waist as he shook Bernt's hand over and over. He obviously recognized the local celebrity. Apparently Bernt wasn't on everyone's black list. The bouncer, if that's what he was, smiled broadly at Alice and the reporter and welcomed them in, then shook his head when Bernt pulled out his wallet. Their tickets were on the house.

They stepped inside the dark room. Through thick smoke and the alternating blue and red lights she made out the band in the front corner by the windows. A bar was set up along the opposite wall and a scattering of round tables and chairs dotted the room. Two girls danced together on a small black and white linoleum dance floor. She looked around again. Something was strange. What year was it? Wasn't it still 1970? The two dancers wore poodle skirts and saddle shoes with bobby socks. The band members had slicked-back ducktails. The music was early Elvis. American Bandstand of the 50s all over again.

Bernt took her elbow and led her to an empty table. "Groovy, yes?" he said. She forced a nod. The reporter pulled up a chair for himself, took out his notebook and began making notes. She felt the eyes of the room focused on them. "This is—how do you say—hot place in Harbanger," said Bernt. *"Når begynner moro?"* the reporter asked. Bernt said something back. The two men laughed.

"What? What did you say?" she asked the reporter.

"Just some predictions about the lead story in next week's local paper," the reporter smirked. He was no help at all.

Two more couples took to the dance floor.

"Come on." Bernt pulled at her arm. "Dance."

"No!" she snapped. She was horrified. She didn't know how to do the jitterbug. It was way before her time.

"Please, Alice, please," Bernt begged.

"I can't," she said. "My feet are too sore from skiing." At least that much was true. Her toes ached from being wrenched out of the cross country bindings over and over.

A waitress approached their table. Her hair flipped up at the edges like Alice had worn in junior high. The girl could barely look at Bernt when she talked. Even under the colored lights Alice saw she was blushing. The waitress hid her chin behind her shoulder and peeked out at him.

"She wants to know if you are famous movie star too," Bernt whispered, draping his arm around the back of her chair.

"Tell her I'm Marianne Faithfull. Or Jane Fonda." Alice slouched in her chair. She was in the Twilight Zone. Not one girl had a skirt above her knees. Every male except Bernt and the reporter wore long sideburns and pointed shoes. The music was vaguely familiar, but the words were in Norwegian.

A group of poofed-hair girls walked by their table, noses in the air, little organza scarves knotted around their necks. She recognized the teller from the bank. "How many people live in Harbanger?" she asked Bernt.

"Oh, five or six hundred," he answered. "Many farms nearby." He went to buy her a Coke between sets and stopped on his way back to talk to the lead singer in the band. "I have surprise for you, my Alice," he said, setting down her drink.

I'm not your Alice, she muttered to herself. I'm not anybody's Alice.

The band began a new song. Same old one-four-five chords, same old four-four time. Same old—she perked up her ears. What were they singing? It sounded almost like English. Simon and Garfunkel. "Michigan seems like a dream to me now...." Could she have heard that right? The band came to the end of the song. "They've all come to look for America." She looked at Bernt. He was beaming. She looked at the reporter. Same snide grin. She looked down at her coca cola and began to cry. Somewhere on the other side of the world was a place where she had once belonged.

Chapter 51

WHEN ALICE RETURNED to Exeter after spring break in Paris and Norway, Rafe announced he was leaving Old Tiverton Road and wanted her to come with him. They could share a room and it would be cheaper by more than half. He'd found a house on Streatham Hill, adjacent to Blackmoor Prison, and made arrangements with three blokes who had become regulars in their Old Tiverton party room.

"Those guys?" she said. "They aren't even students. They just sit around all day smoking dope and live off the dole." She didn't want to move into another strange situation.

"How are they any different from you? Except your check comes from big daddy."

"I don't want to move, Rafe. Can't we stay here?"

"You can if you want. I'm going."

Who else could she turn to? She didn't want to be alone. So she went.

* * *

Her new room—her room and Rafe's room—was on the third floor of the house that was at the dead end of Blackmoor Street. Their one window, above the sink, looked out over the county prison and the valley below. The prison, dark brick with narrow vertical slots for windows, was surrounded by a tall brick wall topped with knots of barbed wire. Alice felt as if she were living in a DMZ. If she stood on tiptoes, or crouched on the rim of the sink, she could just see over the wall and into the prison yard. She never actually saw prisoners moving around—maybe they had a courtyard inside—but she did see the slow movement of cows and the darting of wild ponies that roamed free in the grassy field beyond the prison. The field ended at a creek with a narrow woods at the other side. Far beyond the woods she could see the tops of the university buildings, high up on Streatham Hill.

Life moved slowly at the Blackmoor house. Jeremy, Alan, and Zach, her new housemates, were longtime friends of each other from the north of England. They'd come to Exeter in search of an easier—and warmer—life, but they didn't seem to be searching too hard. No one's day started before noon. Even then, it began in a cloud of tobacco smoke laced with hashish. The boys would shuffle down to the worn out couches in the living room and sit quietly, holding in their thoughts with their inhalations. Alice settled into the slow drift of their lives. She was going nowhere. Not forward. Not even up. Drugs had lost their power. No matter what she tried, she couldn't get high. She never felt a rush of excitement anymore, just a numbing

heaviness, as if she was swimming through seaweed, and the university was a distant shore too far to reach.

At night the five of them would go to The Three-legged Dog, the local pub, to drink a few pints of scrumpy and revive the lagging buzz of hashish. The three boys threw darts or played a complicated game that looked like skittles. Rafe bantered politics with the locals standing at the bar, and gave a nod to Glover and Peacock, the local drug squad, when they came in to enjoy a pint or two. Alice would sit at a table with a bag of crisps and a package of Rolo's, alternately feeding herself sugar and salt, sorrow and pity.

In May Rafe confirmed the dates for his summer trip to the States. He had a friend in Los Angeles and was flying to California when exams were finished at the end of June. Months earlier, after she had met Annie on the bus between JFK and LaGuardia in New York, she had written L'Abri and arranged to visit the first two weeks in July.

"Forget your trip to Switzerland," Rafe insisted. "Come with me. We'll have a grand old time."

She didn't know what to do. She was a bruised reed. She needed someone to prop her up. She was a dimly burning wick. She needed Rafe to keep her flame from blowing out. Why did she want to go to that religious place anyway? No one she met had ever heard of Francis Schaeffer except for Annie on the bus and Angelina, that mysterious woman in the office in Ann Arbor who seemed more like an apparition than a real person. Maybe she'd made them both up. Besides, she couldn't understand Schaeffer's books. Why should she go all by herself to some weird spiritual school in the mountains? When Rafe told her there was one seat left on his charter flight to LA she agreed to go.

She wrote a check to reserve her seat and hurried to the post office to mail it. She felt relieved to have made a decision. She would put herself in Rafe's hands and he would take care of her. But when she got back home, Simon's motorcycle with the sidecar were parked outside the Blackmoor house. Maybe Libby and Hannah would be inside. Maybe this was a sign her life was going to look like theirs.

"Hey," she called to Simon as she came in the back door. "Are Libby and the baby here?"

"Nope, just me. I brought you and the blokes a bushel of potatoes—barter for some tabs of acid." He spoke in his slow, deliberate way. Did he drop acid or sell it? She couldn't tell, but he seemed sane. "And you, Alice? You look happy today." He smiled.

"I guess am. Relieved at least. I finally decided not to go to that convent in Switzerland."

"Switzerland?" he said perking up. "What place?"

"Oh, you wouldn't know." She kicked off her boots and sat down. "Some weird religious place no one's ever heard of."

"Tell me." He actually seemed interested.

"Just some crazy place I was supposed to go to in July. I really don't know much about it. It's called L'Abri."

"L'Abri!" he said. "L'Abri in Switzerland. I know L'Abri. My little brother just got back from there."

"What? Your brother went to L'Abri?"

"Julian was there for six months. Just got back."

"Six months! Is he okay?"

"Super. Better than ever, in fact. He loved it."

"What was it like? Did he tell you about it?" She couldn't believe this was happening. "Have you seen those books by Francis Schaeffer?"

"Julian gave some to me but I haven't read them yet. But Calvin Schaeffer, that's the son, is my brother's mate. Julian's going to be in his wedding." He patted the top of her head on his way to the door. "Got to get home." Then he rested a hand on her shoulder and said, "You should go to Switzerland."

Alice's heart leaped then sank. What should she do? She'd just sent in her money for the flight to the US with Rafe. Was that a mistake? Could crossing paths with Simon be like meeting Annie on the bus? Was it a sign? She should reconsider, but who could help her decide? She rushed up to her room, thankful Rafe was gone, and pulled out the *I Ching*. What should I do? she asked the book. Tell me about L'Abri, she pleaded as she threw three coins on the floor until she had a hexagram. She looked up pattern number four titled "Youthful Folly / Inexperience" and read:

> The image is a fresh Spring at the foot of the Mountain. The Superior Person refines his character by being thorough in every activity. The Sage does not recruit students; the students seek him. He asks nothing but a sincere desire to learn. This is a time of interchange between a mentor and pupil and we are reminded of youth and folly. The youth himself must be conscious of his lack of experience and must seek out the teacher.

Then she threw the coins six more times, focusing

on Rafe, and got number forty-four: "Coming to Meet / Compulsion."

The image is a playful Zephyr dancing and delighting beneath an indulgent Heaven. A Prince who shouts orders but will not walk among his people may as well try to command the four winds. A strong, addictive temptation, much more dangerous than it seems. You are ignoring a clear and present danger to your well-being. If this threat emanated from a heavy-handed oppressor, you would see it coming. But this danger comes to you in the form of a seduction, an amusement, a diversion, an indulgence that is eating away at the fiber of your secure little world. You under-estimate the tribute this dalliance will demand. This hexagram indicates a situation in which the principle of darkness, after having been eliminated, furtively and unexpectedly obtrudes again from within and below. It is an unfavorable and dangerous situation, and we must understand and promptly prevent the possible consequences.

The message was clear even to her drug-dulled mind. Without stopping to talk to anyone, she ran to the phone box around the corner by the pub and called the airline. "I've changed my mind," she told them. "I made a mistake. Tear up my check. I'm not going back to America yet."

Chapter 52

RAFE WAS FURIOUS when he found out that Alice had defied him and was going to L'Abri, but she knew he didn't really care. He'd find a new meal ticket soon enough. A few weeks later he left Exeter for his summer in the States and she was relieved to have the last week of June on her own in the house. Not exactly alone since Jeremy, Alan, and Zach were there, but she had her room to herself. Early one evening near the end of the week, as the sunset spread coppery-red across the sky, a restlessness rose in her so she decided to go for a walk. At the weedy dead end of their street she slid through a break in the fence and stepped into the corner of the field. The great hulk of the prison loomed dark behind her to the west like a menacing ship riding low in the sunset ocean. Ahead of her, across the field, stood the woods, and beyond that the promise of familiar university grounds.

She walked through the field picking her feet between cow pies and humming a little tune, aware of the black-slitted eyes of the prison behind her. All of a sudden she heard a deep lowing sound to her left. From behind a small rise in the field a string of mottled cows came into view. Moooo, mooo, they chanted. Soon more cows joined in on her other side. Slowly, almost imperceptibly, they closed rank around her. She was encircled by the huge beasts.

"Good cows, good cows," she tried to soothe them with a sing-songy voice while she made her way toward the woods and the fence beyond it. A few of the cows were close enough that she could stare into their eyes, full moons of white with wild glints of brown in the center. She felt a jolt of fear and held her breath. She shouldn't be afraid of these cows, should she? They were domesticated animals, right? The cows, lowing their sad, plaintive song, moved in closer. If she reached out her hand she could touch one.

This must be the spirit of Pan, she thought looking into the great pie eyes. These creatures were filled with with some strange power. The power of the universe. Weren't she and the cows all one? Then, as if in defiance of her thoughts, a cow stepped in front of her, right in her path. Instinctively she held up her hand, like she had done when she was a traffic safety guard in elementary school. "Mooove", she commanded with her deepest, loudest voice. The cow in front and the ones on the sides of her twisted their ears and flicked their tails and turned theirs necks away from her in one synchronized movement, like a flock of sea birds veering in the wind. "Mooove!" she said again, feeling empowered. The cows slowly picked up their heavy feet and trotted away.

She couldn't believe it. They obeyed her. They honored her power—or respected her fear. She ran and leapt over a small creek and headed into the woods. There was just enough light to make her way through the trees and up to the base of Streatham Hill. She followed sidewalks and street lamps and wound back to her house, her restlessness replaced with the tingly mixture of triumph over fear.

When she got back to the Blackmoor house Alice entered through the back gate and walked up to the kitchen door, but stopped before going in. Through the window she could see some kind of commotion in the kitchen. Two strange men stood talking to her housemates and passing around a fat joint. She stayed outside in the darkness watching. The new guys must have brought the dope because she knew their cupboards were bare and their bank accounts empty. They'd been having lots of potato meals since Simon brought them the bushel.

Sounds of laughter escaped through the window but she could tell by Zach and Jeremy's body language that they weren't comfortable. Zach pulled on his earlobe and fussed with his bald head as he always did when he was nervous. And Alan looked jumpy, pacing back and forth in front of the sink, shaking his head.

Who were those guys? They weren't from the university and she'd never seen them at the pub or downtown. They had a sinister look. One was tall and sickly thin with stringy dark hair hanging down past his shoulders. He had a scraggly goatee and wore a tight black suit coat. When he laughed she could see that one of his front teeth was gold. The other bloke was shorter, squatter, and blond, with a tired, wrinkled face. He couldn't be more than twenty-five, she guessed, but he looked like an old man. An ugly purple scar jogged down the left side of his face from his ear to his neck.

Suddenly shivers ran down her spine as the blond guy's gaze shifted out the window of the kitchen door and locked eyes with her. She looked away from him, down at the door handle, and reminded herself that this was her house. They were the intruders. She belonged here. She took a deep breath and opened the door.

"Hi guys," she said, looking at her housemates. "You'll never believe what just happened out in the meadow."

"Wish I'd been there," the dark, greasy guy smirked. She ignored him. He reeked of dirty laundry.

"Hey, Alice," Jeremy said and lifted a hand in greeting. He was a sweet boy, though not too smart. Like an old dog, she always thought whenever Jeremy plopped down near her. He just needed a safe home and someone to pet him.

The dark newcomer spoke up again. "You must be Rafe's bird. Nice to meet ya. I'm Eddie, an old mate of Rafe's from East Ham. This here's Jake." He motioned to the scarred fellow. "We're old school chums, knew Rafe back when, before he got so ed-u-ca-ted and high faluting. Too bad we missed him."

"Yeah, well, he's in the States for the summer," she said, her antennae buzzing with danger. These losers were not to be trusted. "Guess you'll have to catch up with him in the fall." She narrowed her eyes and gave him her "get lost" look, trying to sound authoritative like she had with the cows.

"Well, umm." Now Alan spoke. He was the decision maker of the three friends and steered their little ship through the choppy waters of unemployment. He addressed her. "If it's okay with you, we told Eddie and Jake they could crash in my room for a few days. I'll move in with Zach. They've come all the way from London and have business to do." Alan shifted his eyes to the counter where she now saw a big chunk of hashish sitting next to a scale. She shook her head.

"Have a sample." Eddie stuck out his hand and waved the still-burning joint under her nose. Its smoke wavered in front of her like a hypnotist's watch. "This is the greatest stuff to cross the Channel in years. Right boys?" Her friends made half-hearted sounds of assent.

She had to admit it smelled good, really good. Maybe this stuff could get her high. She'd been blaming her inability to get stoned on the poor quality of dope, not letting herself believe she'd reached a level of tolerance. Maybe she should try this.

Eddie took a hit from the joint and leaned close, exhaling right in her face. He swayed his hips and stared into her eyes. "No!" she said suddenly before she could even think. "I'm not feeling so good. I just had a run-in with a bunch of wild cows. I'm going to bed." She couldn't believe she was refusing free drugs.

"Hey, don't go," Eddie said. "This stuff will cure your ills. Besides the night's still young. The party hasn't even started yet. We've got a whole bag of tricks." He nodded toward a carpetbag on the floor. "I know I can find something that'll make you quiver and purr."

She heard a low, grizzly sound coming out of Jake and he began to laugh. He was staring straight at her. Or rather at her body. "Give her time, Eddie. Give her time. She hasn't met the candyman yet."

Get me out of here, God, Alice prayed silently. These were the creepiest guys she'd ever met, worse than the man in the Kalamazoo train station. They made Rafe's friends at Nottinghill Gate look like innocents. Why were these scumbags coming into her life? "No thanks," she said. "I've got a lot of packing to do."

"But Alice," Zach said, almost pleading. "You haven't told us about the cows."

"No bedtime stories tonight, Zach." She darted out of the room and toward the stairs. On her way up she heard Eddie say something about bedtime stories. Jake's repulsive laugh was cut off as she shut her door. She leaned all her weight on her dresser and pushed it across the room, blocking the door.

Chapter 53

TWO MORNINGS LATER was the first of July, Alice's last day in England. She had shipped her big trunk home and now she managed to stuff the rest of her belongings into her huge leather suitcases with her initials stamped in gold near the handles. She gave token gifts to her housemates: her Boy Scouts of America shirt to Alan since he was their leader, her cozy chartreuse-striped knit shirt for Jeremy, and a hooded University of Michigan sweatshirt for Zach, to keep his bald head warm. Rafe had already left with her favorite dress—the purple Mexican cotton one embroidered with turquoise, the one she'd worn on her blind date with Bruce. Rafe liked to wear it over white bell-bottoms when he played piano with a band. One more part of her he'd confiscated. She doubted she'd ever see it again.

She surveyed her third-floor room one last time: dust balls, candy wrappers, rumpled tissues, empty matchbooks, and a lot of butts from smoked-up joints littered the floor. It was a pigpen and she didn't care. She bequeathed it all to the next renter. Maybe those creepy dealers from

London would decide to stay. But not her, she was out of here. She shut the door with a bang and lugged the first of her heavy bags down the stairs.

What a load she was carrying; she had way too much stuff. She didn't even really know where she was going, just some crazy place in Switzerland. Back in January when she went skiing in Zermatt, Switzerland, the country had seemed almost too pure—the trains too clean, the air too thin, the mountains too high, the snow too white. The prospect of going there again frightened her. But at least Barb Schneider wouldn't be there this time. Alice had hardly seen her since they'd been to Zermatt. Barb must be casting her spells on someone else these days.

She thumped her suitcase down the steep staircase and wondered what kind of religious jargon was going to get shoved down her throat this time? At least L'Abri didn't charge a huge fee to dole out a phony mantra like TM. In fact they didn't ask for any money at all, only a donation of your own choosing. But not one page of Francis Schaeffer's books had made sense to her. Not even the titles. What did he mean by *Escape from Reason* and *The God who is There*? Were there gods who weren't there? But words and ideas weren't making much sense to her lately. Ever since tripping in Abaddon she'd had trouble reading a whole page of anything. It was even hard to finish a sentence when she talked.

"Can I give you a hand?" Zach asked as she bumped her bag at the bottom of the stairs.

"Thanks." She smiled at his peach-fuzz head and neatly trimmed goatee. "The monster bag is still up by my door."

She dragged the suitcase through the front room

where Jeremy was lumped on the raggedy couch, flipping through a tabloid newspaper. "Those slime bags still here?" she whispered, motioning her head in the direction of the back bedroom.

"Nope, they've gone out for the day to 'take care of business.' Alan went with them." He folded the paper and sat up. "Too bad Rafe had to go to the States before you left. I'm surprised you didn't go with him. You sure you're up for that place in Switzerland?" He might be lazy, but he was kind.

"I hope so." She left her bag on the floor and bent over to give him a hug. "What can it hurt? It's only for two weeks. They can't do much to me in that time, can they? Besides, I'll see Rafe when I get back to the States."

Zach lumbered into the room with her other bag and set it down in the hall. "We wanted to ask you something, Alice." His eyes darted over to Jeremy who made some undecipherable movement with his head.

Jeremy pushed himself up off the sofa and went to stand by Zach's side. "Yeah," he said and looked back at Zach.

"Umm, Alice...." They were clearly nervous. What was wrong?

"Just say it, it's okay." She looked at her watch. The taxi should be there soon.

"We were wondering, that is Jeremy and Alan and me, if you've got any blank cheques left from your bank account?"

"Probably." She wasn't sure what he was getting at. "My cheque book's up in my room somewhere. But I closed my account already; there's no money. "

"We figured it was closed," Zach said and rubbed the top of his head. "But you've got a cheque cashing card, right? And with that and your blank cheques, since you're leaving the country and all...."

She could see he was embarrassed, but not too embarrassed to ask her to help him cheat and steal. A horn beeped. "There's my taxi." Jeremy and Zach exchanged another panicky glance. They looked so sad and pathetic. Their lives were just like the dead end street outside. What did it matter, she thought. She was leaving all this behind. It was over now. She opened her wallet and took out the pictureless ID card. "Which one of you will be me?" She handed the card to Zach.

The horn beeped again. Each of the boys, now smiling, grabbed one of her heavy bags and headed for the door.

"You the one going to the train station, Miss?" called a dark, thin Indian with a turban wrapped around his head. Another Sikh. She nodded and asked him to wait while she said her goodbyes.

He got out of the car to load her luggage. "I wait, but the meter runs. Take your time."

She followed the boys inside.

"Be good," Jeremy said and gave her a hug.

"Come visit me anytime," she offered, knowing it would never happen.

"We've had some fun times, eh?" Zach grinned, but there was a choke in his voice. "We won't forget you, Alice. And thanks a lot for this." He patted his back pocket where he'd stashed the bank card.

"I won't forget you guys either. Tell Alan goodbye for

me. And get rid of those creeps before something really bad happens." She reached behind her for the door handle.

Just at that moment, as she turned and swung the door open, the doorbell rang and she was face to face with half a dozen uniformed policemen—and a policewoman.

Oh God! It was Glover and Peacock, the local drug squad, and a bunch of their lackeys. They were a famous duo in Exeter. She and her friends had seen them before, peering at them through the smoky room of one pub or another. The drug users in Exeter were a small and chummy group. So were the police.

"Miss Blankwell?" Sgt. Glover knew her name. "Are those your bags?" he asked, pointing to the open boot of the taxi.

"Yes, sir, yes. But, sir, I'm leaving the country," she pleaded, "I'm off to the train right now. I'm leaving England. I won't be back."

"Hanson, bring the lady's bags inside," barked Glover to a bulky young man with a lumpy face.

From the corner of her eye she saw the taxi driver grin and look at his watch. But she didn't have time to think about money or the train or the plane. A shade snapped up in the dark room of her heart. The glare of reality blinded her. This could be the end.

"Follow me," Glover ordered as he grabbed her arm in the all-too-familiar vise grip of a policeman and took her deeper into the house.

"But I'm leaving Exeter. My train goes in an hour. Then I catch a plane to Lausanne." Anger rose through her panic. Glover ignored her.

"Miss Stalward, take Miss Blankwell into a private

room and search her. Leave her purse here. Hansen, you open her bags. We'll deal with her first since she's in such a hurry to get away." The police swarmed the house like termites in soft wood.

Alice followed the skirted uniform into the small pantry off the kitchen. She felt as if she was in a dream, her own personal nightmare.

"Everything off, Missy," the policewoman said with a snap.

Alice pulled her dress over her head and stepped out of her underpants.

"All right, put 'em back on." The policewoman sounded disappointed Alice didn't have drugs taped to her body.

Back in the living room she watched as the police manhandled every object from her suitcase, felt along every hem and seam, opened every toiletry bottle, flipped through the pages of her diary, her address book, inspected all the surfaces of her luggage for hidden compartments.

Thank God I ran out of dope, she thought. Thank God I didn't buy any from those creeps. Oh God, if you are there, get me out of here. Please, please get me out of here. Out of this house, out of this country, out of this life.

Time felt heavy and slow as she watched the police do their job. Every second weighed upon her as she fought against panic. Then, just as suddenly as they appeared, Sgt. Glover pronounced her clean. "You're very lucky Miss Blankwell," he growled. "I advise you to change your ways if you know what's good for you. A girl like you living here with...."

"Glover!" Inspector Peacock, the silent one in charge, called his sergeant to order. Then he addressed her. "We found no illegal substance in your possession. You are free to go."

Numbly she walked out the door and climbed into the back seat of the waiting cab. She didn't say thank you. She didn't look back to see what was happening to Jeremy and Zach. She only managed a slight nod when the Sikh grinned and told her they might still have time to make the train.

Chapter 54

THREE COUNTRIES and several hours later Alice knocked tentatively on the Dutch door of a Swiss chalet.

"I'm Alice," she said as a petite woman with pale blue eyes and a blonde ponytail opened the top half of the door.

The woman glared at her and said, "Alice Blankwell." It was a statement, not a question. "Finally. We've been waiting." She spoke with a rat-a-tat-tat like a machine gun. "I'm Gwendolyn. Wentworth. This is Sam's and my home." She dusted flour from her hands onto the front of her apron and opened the rest of the door. "I'm in the middle of making dinner. Everyone else is gone. Except your roommate." She pointed to a hole in the ceiling of the hallway where a ladder leaned. "She's up there supposedly making your bed. Get her to help you with your bags."

Gwendolyn's eyebrows, what Alice could see of them in their translucent blondeness, went up in sharp judgment as she glanced at Alice's bulging luggage. Gwendolyn could hardly be older than thirty. She was fierce for such a small, light thing. Alice began to explain that she had so much stuff because she'd spent the whole year at school in England, but Gwendolyn had already turned on her heels and disappeared into another room.

Welcome, welcome. So glad you're here, sang a mocking voice in Alice's head. What had she gotten herself into? She lugged her heavy bags inside the door and began to climb the crude pine ladder to the floor above.

When she reached the top she could see the blue-jeaned-backside of a young woman bent over a low bed in the corner of the peaked-roof room. "Ah hem." She cleared her throat but the girl kept at her task. She was short-legged. Boxy. The grunts she made as she struggled with the sheets and blanket reminded her of George, her father's dog, when he tugged on a rope or someone's pant leg. She stepped over the top of the ladder and leaned her shoulder against the doorframe.

"Howdy." She tried again to get the girl's attention. "Cheerio? Bonjour?" Nothing was working. Was she deaf? From the way she was yanking at the sheets and kneeing the mattress, the girl didn't seem too keen on sharing her room. Alice took another approach.

"Hey there, slave woman, need some help?"

The girl swung around, a smirk on her sulky face. "Who are you calling a—Alice?"

"Peter!"

"What are you doing here?" they said at the same time as they rushed together in an awkward hug. She couldn't believe it. It was Peter from Outward Bound. She knew Peter'd gone to some weird religious college in Illinois, but that was about it. Peter had kept to herself and didn't join in their chatter. She was always aloof, reading from a little leather-bound French New Testament she carried in her backpack. Alice had classified her as strange in an unappealing way.

"I'm not Peter anymore," the girl said. "I'm Helen now."

"Helen?" At Outward Bound she and Audrey had never been able to find out Peter's real name. Helen, like Helen of Troy? The most beautiful woman in the world? No wonder she had trouble with her identity.

"I'm one of the workers here, a *doulos*. That's slave in Greek. And I have been slaving away for six weeks. But you—my God, you look awful, Alice. Where's your golden-girl glimmer? You look like you just crawled out of a cave."

Alice stuck out her tongue. "Thanks a lot, Peter."

"I didn't mean to insult you. It's just that you've changed. But I'm glad you're here. Why are you here? You've come as a student, right?"

Alice sunk down on the newly made bed and started to laugh. "Mind if I go insane for a minute or two?" She kicked off her sandals and flopped on her back. "What a day. What a year. You're right. I've been living in a cave. But wow, can you believe this? You and me here in some albino's attic in the Alps? Have I entered a time warp?"

She gave Helen a brief history of her year in England, her chance meeting with a girl from L'Abri, the *I Ching*, and the Exeter police just that morning. Helen's story was different. She had been getting more and more unhappy too, but she was totally repressed. Her college was its own form of prison and she was almost ready to throw Christianity out altogether.

"This summer is God's last chance to prove if He's real or not," Helen said with a sudden hard set to her jaw.

"Whoa," Alice said. "The God who is or isn't there! But how come you changed your name?"

"I was petrified last summer when my parents forced me to go to Outward Bound. I thought it might help to have a stronger persona. You know, something macho, something solid. Peter means rock in Greek."

Weird. Something macho? No wonder Alice hadn't liked her. No wonder Helen had been so standoffish and square. She couldn't be bothered with Helen back then. But now, after ten months of living with strangers, she was happy to see a familiar face. Helen looked like home.

Alice slept through dinner that night. The arrest in Exeter and the long journey to Switzerland had exhausted her. When she finally woke up, it was late evening and she was hungry.

She climbed down the ladder and found her way into the kitchen. No leftovers in sight, but a sign on the tiny refrigerator said to help yourself to yogurt. Yuck. One more sour, unwelcoming thing.

She wandered through the kitchen and dining area into the living room where eight or ten young people were seated in an informal circle in front of the fireplace. Tchaikovsky was playing softly from a record player in the corner. Helen wasn't in the group so Alice stood off in the corner, eating her yogurt and trying to follow their conversation.

"Well, I was I-V chapter president last semester," said a large blonde girl with thick glasses and lips that didn't quite close under her piggy nose. "We put flyers into all the SDS mailboxes, but I don't think it did any good."

"Of course not, Sally," said a greasy-haired boy in a professorial tone. "Friendship Evangelism. That's what you've got to do. Flesh out the message. Let your light shine."

She wasn't sure she was hearing right. Clearly those two kids were Americans, but what in the world were they talking about?

Another boy spoke: "Our I-V group created a counter-classroom when the campus shut down in May, right after Nixon sent troops into Cambodia and those students were killed at Kent State. We set up a projector outside in the quad, in front of the bio lab and showed an MBI filmstrip on the fallacy of evolution. It was cool. We got a lot of boo's but I know it made some kids think. Two new girls came to our next meeting."

I-V? she puzzled. Intravenous? These guys were far too straight to be shooting up. Booze? She doubted they smoked cigarettes. And what was he saying about evolution?

"Yeah, that's the big issue," added a cute boy with what sounded like an Australian accent. "That's where we've got to hit 'em, right where it all begins. If people really thought about Darwin—a self-proclaimed descendant of apes—they'd see his theory is just a bunch of monkey business."

Chuckles spread around the circle and Alice could hold herself back no longer. She took a few steps forward, leaned toward the group and said, "Do you mean you don't believe in evolution?"

Every head turned in her direction and with one voice they said, "You do?"

Alice shook her head, not to reply, but out of sheer

disbelief. Who were these people? Was this still the 20th century? What kind of troglodytes were they?

She fled the room and climbed the ladder back to her nest. O God, where am I? she said into her pillow. A tear crept out of the corner of her eye. Helen, Peter, whoever you are, come back and tell me this isn't for real. Let me wake up tomorrow and be—where?

Where did she belong? Where could she fit in? She felt like a stranger in the universe. England was a closed door now that the drug squad had raided their house. Her parents, what did they care? Her friends back home? She hadn't heard from Bruce for months. What about Rafe? He'd probably hooked up with some California beach babe by now—or two.

Why had she come here, this little perch on the side of a mountain where people didn't even acknowledge the truth of science? She reached over and brought the *I Ching* up to her chest. You sent me here, she whispered into its smoky pages. Show me your secrets again. But before she had a chance to toss her magic coins and look up a hexagram, she fell asleep.

Chapter 55

BELLS CLANGED and Alice stirred from her sleep. A sweet grassy smell came in through the open window. Beyond the red and white checked curtains she could see the morning sun lit up the mountainside. L'Abri, she thought, the shelter. Helen was still asleep on the bed across the room. Alice sat on her knees and leaned out the window. Below her a dozen cows crowded around a watering trough, each with a bell hanging around its light brown neck. They looked like a bovine church, much tamer than the cows in the field at Exeter. She spotted Gwendolyn with a man who must have been her husband, Sam, sitting on a bench under an apple tree. He was holding an open book and Gwendolyn sat with her hands folded, her loose hair falling like a lacy veil around her face. Alice guessed they were praying.

"Alice, you're still here." Helen was awake.

"Where were you last night when I needed you? This place is haunted with weirdoes."

"Tell me about it. But I've got good news for you. I was

over at another chalet last night when some really far out dudes from the US arrived. You'd like them a lot; they're just your type."

"My type?" It was strange to hear the word "dude" come out of Helen's mouth.

"Yeah, there's this guy, Mick, and his girl friend, and another guy, Will, who's totally groovy. They were hitch-hiking to see some Sufi guru over on the next mountain. But the Sai Baba guy, or whatever his name is, won't be there until next week. So the three of them are crashing at L'Abri. Cool, huh?"

"I thought Sufis were some sort of Muslims."

"They are. They're the ones who dance all the time."

"Whirling dervishes?"

"I don't know. You can ask Mick and Will about it. In fact tonight after dinner is the big weekly meeting with Dr. Schaeffer. That should be interesting. Mick says he's got some questions for him."

There was a knock on the door and then Gwendolyn's blonde head peeked in. "Time to get up, girls. Alice, you're to meet with Milton in his office at the study center at eight-thirty. He'll be your tutor while you're here. Have you filled her in yet, Helen?"

"Just about to, Gwendolyn," she answered, giving Alice a wink.

"Good. Breakfast is in twenty minutes." She shut the door and was gone.

"Not exactly a fount of friendliness, is she?" Alice said.

"A bit harsh, it's true. But she's got all us atheists and agnostics crowding in on her, and no kids of her own.

Must be tough." Helen pulled on blue jean overalls and laced up a pair of high top Converse All Stars.

"You're different than you were at Outward Bound," Alice said. "What else have you changed besides your name?"

"Oh, I've been doing a little experimentation, taking some weekends away from college. Sneaking to movies. Testing the four spiritual laws."

"Never heard of them, but from the way the kids were talking downstairs last night, there are lots of things here I've never heard of. What's I-V?"

"InterVarsity. InterVarsity Christian Fellowship. Big-time evangelical group on college campuses. I used to belong. I tried everything. I-V, Navigators, Campus Crusade for Christ. But I'm sick of meetings and all the rules on campus. No smoking, no drinking, no dancing, no playing cards."

"No dancing? No playing cards? You've got to be kidding. That's even worse than the hokey Norwegian village where I stayed after Easter. Sorry, Helen, no Sufis for you." She laughed and gave her a little shove.

"That's why I'm glad Mick and Will showed up. Divine Providence, maybe. I might ditch this place and go with them next week." Helen jammed some books into a small backpack.

"You mean if God doesn't reveal himself before then?"

Helen gave her a playful bash on the head. "You'd better get dressed, lady. And I'd better tell you the way things work around here. If you don't show up when Gwendolyn rings the breakfast bell, there are no second chances."

* * *

After breakfast Alice gathered a notebook and her *I Ching* and started out to find the study center. Gwendolyn was supervising a group of students bent over at various angles in the garden pulling weeds and picking beans.

"Where can I find Milton's office?" she asked, stopping to admire the tidy rows of raised beds that mingled vegetables and flowers like an Impressionist's canvas.

"The study center is below the chapel, about half a mile up on your—Alice!! What are you doing with that book?!" Gwendolyn's pale face turned red under her straw hat.

Alice followed the pointing finger down to her hands. "This?" she said, holding up the *I Ching*. Gwendolyn took a step backwards, as if the book were a poisonous snake.

"That should be burned!" she thundered.

"Well I like it," Alice muttered under her breath and headed up the path toward the road. It told me to come here, Miss Fancy Pants, she thought to herself, though why it should have I don't know. These people are crazy. Perhaps the air is too thin. The yogurt too sour. Oh, well, she was only here for two weeks. Maybe she could find those Sufi guys. They might have some grass.

She stopped as the road jack-knifed upon itself and looked out over the valley. Multi-storied chalets with gingerbread trim dotted the crumpled quilt of the hillside. There was such an economy of land and space here. Houses stacked their rooms one on top of another, like little mountains. Every open bit of ground was put to good use: flowers, vegetables, a chicken pen. In the distance a stream flashed bright as it wound down a hillside. And the sky, it was so blue, so clear, so forgiving.

A chiseled wooden sign on a short post read "Study

Center" with an arrow pointing down a curving stairway around a split log building. This must be the chapel, she thought, as she wove her way through a group of young people standing in the sunshine outside rustic double doors. She walked down the stairs and went inside a door marked "Milton Hunsburger".

"Come in," a German-accented voice responded to her knock. "Welcome. You must be Alice Blankwell." He extended his hand. He was a tall, slender man with a finely pointed face—long nose, straight hair, but happy lips. He held his head at a slight angle, looking at her through one eye. The other eye was wide and motionless. "I hope you didn't have trouble on your way here," he said, directing her to a seat next to his desk.

She shook her head. Trouble? Was almost getting arrested for drugs considered trouble? This wasn't the time to tell him about her life. Did that really happen to her just yesterday? She felt as if she had been transported into a completely different world, a parallel universe. Yesterday was someone else's life.

"I'm here to help you plan your course of study." He cocked his head like a cockatiel. "I'll meet with you every other day. Have you decided what subjects you want to pursue?" He was friendly, but she could tell he'd been through this speech a hundred times before.

"Subjects?" she said. "Umm, I don't really know." She was suddenly nervous. What had she thought would happen here? Was this a school?

"Let me ask you," he went on gently. "Have you read Dr. Schaeffer's books?"

"I've got some of them, but I wasn't able to read very

much." I can hardly read anything, she wanted to say, since I fried my brain on LSD.

"Oh," he looked down. "The *I Ching*. Do you read that?"

She tensed. Was he going to flip out like Gwendolyn? "Yes," she said. Something about his one soft eye made her want to trust him. "I do. In fact this book told me to come here." We'll see what he says about that, she thought.

"That doesn't surprise me," he nodded. "You know, the One who created all things has no problem controlling the fall of a coin."

"So you know about hexagrams?"

"Sure. Here at L'Abri we look at all aspects of philosophy and religion, science and art. Maybe you'd like to study something related to the *I Ching*."

"Can I do that here?"

"Are you familiar with John Cage?" Milton asked. "We've got some tapes that discuss his music."

"Sort of," she said. She knew Cage was the composer who made strange music out of groups of radios or by putting nuts and bolts on piano strings.

"He liked the *I Ching*. His music is called 'aleatoric'— random or chance. He composed some of his music by tossing coins, just like you do to get a hexagram."

"But the little I've heard of his music, it doesn't make sense," she said.

"I agree." Milton bobbed his head forward. His thin bangs fluttered above his eyes. "Cage says that the truth about the universe is all up to chance. But you know, Alice, he couldn't live his life by that principle."

"What do you mean?"

"He's an avid mycologist."

"What?" All these big words.

"Someone who studies mushrooms. It's a perfect hobby for him. Finding mushrooms is chancy and indeterminate. But eating what you find is another matter. He himself said that if he approached mushrooms like he did music, he would soon be dead."

She thought a minute. "You mean he has to trust his knowledge about mushrooms to know which ones he can eat and which ones are poisonous?"

"Exactly. Everyone lives most of their life on the assumption that the universe has order and purpose, that all morels are edible, so to speak. The challenge is to find the source of truth."

"You talk as if that's possible, to really know truth. I'm not so sure." She wasn't used to people who were so certain in their beliefs. She told him about the kids in her chalet who didn't believe in evolution. "And then they all turned and looked at me like I was the weird one. I don't get it."

"Evolution is a key question. We've got a series of tapes on Darwin. Would you like to start with those? We can talk again tomorrow."

Milton signed her up for a lab space in the study center and she began to listen to the odd, high-pitched voice of the yet-to-be-seen Francis Schaeffer.

Chapter 56

A LOUD BELL CLANGED over and over and Alice watched as the students in the carrel spaces around hers took off their headphones and pushed their chairs back from their desks. She leaned around the partition wall and spoke to the girl next to her.

"Why are they ringing that bell?"

"Lunchtime," the girl said. "You're new here." Why did everyone make statements when they should be asking questions? She looked at the girl, her navy blue Bermuda shorts and seersucker shirt bunched around her wide waist. Her hair was cut like a Dutch boy—heavy bangs across the front that rested on her thick glasses, and then straight back just below her ears. There was something familiar about her, but she couldn't quite place her.

"Aren't you that new girl rooming with Helen Visser?"

Now she remembered. This girl with the permanently parted lips was one of the ones she had overheard in the living room the night before. "That's right," she answered cautiously.

"I'm Sally Rembrandt," she smiled and suddenly her mouth didn't look so bad. "You know your lunch assignment?"

"I think Helen said Chalet les Malaise," she said, malaise being the French word for sickness. "It sounds like a hospital!"

"Oh, that's Mélèzes," Sally laughed. "That's where the Schaeffer's live. I'm going there too. Walk with me. I've been here since May and I never want to leave. I love all the discussions about things that really matter. How about you, what brought you here?" Sally led her up past the chapel and across the road to the beginning of another set of stairs cut into the side of the hill.

"I don't know why I'm here. I just knew I was supposed to come. It's a long story."

"I'd love to hear it," Sally said and nodded to various people they passed on their way. She seemed more normal than she had the night before. "L'Abri's like that. People are drawn here and then their lives are changed."

"Were you changed?"

"Sit with me at lunch and I'll tell you about it."

Two long tables were set up in the dining room. She was surprised to see tablecloths and cloth napkins, vases of fresh flowers, candlesticks, and baskets of homemade poppy seed rolls. An aproned woman was laying out real china plates at the place settings. Each plate was arranged with a stuffed tomato, a mound of brightly colored coleslaw, and two deviled eggs. They looked like an artist's still life.

"It's so pretty in here," she said. "I didn't expect such a formal meal."

"It's always like this," Sally said. "Edith Schaeffer believes everything we do should be a work of art. Fellowship around the table is a high point in the day."

She and Sally found places and stood behind their chairs like the rest of the gathering group. A wizened-looking man with a white goatee and knicker-like pants was standing at the end of the other table. When everyone quieted down he began to say grace. At least she thought it was going to be grace, like the memorized lines her mother had made her say at home when she was little. But he went on and on, talking to God as if God was right there in the room with them. Thank you for this, help them with that, somebody's plane trip, somebody's brother. Lots of specific names and dates and details. She didn't know what to think. She was glad they were having a cold lunch. Finally the Amen came and they sat down.

"Francis Schaeffer?" she whispered to Sally as the woman sitting at the head of their table began passing the rolls and jam. "I recognize his voice from the tapes. It's almost as strange as his outfit."

Sally nodded. "Creativity, that's the key word here. Dr. Schaeffer says a Christian is the one whose imagination should fly beyond the stars."

Creativity, she mused. Creation. Creator. She chewed the word over as she took bites of the delicious roll. She thought about the lecture she had just listened to on Darwin at the end of his life. He had been creative in his theories, hadn't he? But somewhere he lost the joy of living. He lost his interest in music and literature and even nature. The way he described himself was just how she felt: empty. Her imagination was dead.

She looked at the plate in front of her. Red tomato, fluffy stem of parsley, apple green cabbage, oranges bursting with tiny sacks of juice, eggs with perfect yellow yolks balanced in a boat of white. She rubbed her eyes. She felt as if she were waking up from a long sleep. She thought about the rolls in the linen-lined basket in front of her. They started out as just flour and water, probably some sugar and salt. Flat, sticky, formless. But when yeast was added, the mixture grew and multiplied, creating tiny pockets of air and raising the whole lump. That's what I need, she thought, something to raise me up, fill me, make me light and warm and flavorful.

Her attention was drawn to the people at her table. Two older women, widows most likely. A young couple, married, holding hands. A pinched-faced boy with heavy dark eyebrows and a frightened look. She heard him mutter some foreign words to the man next to him. Eastern Europe she guessed.

Sally leaned forward and spoke to their end of the table. "This is my new friend, Alice," she announced. "I promised I would tell her how I've changed since being here at L'Abri."

"Good idea, Sally," said the woman on her left. "We'd all like to hear that."

Alice was glad she didn't have to do any talking, glad these people didn't pry.

"My dad's a Presbyterian minister. I was a good PK," Sally began.

There go those initials again, thought Alice. But Sally turned to her and said, "preacher's kid."

"Oh." She reached for another roll. This was the best meal she'd had in months.

"I was president of I-V at my college—that's a student group, Alice—doing everything expected of me and more."

Kind of the opposite of me, she thought. She did everything they didn't expect. So what was Sally's problem?

"I did all the right things. And because I did I thought I was better than everyone else. But I was a fake. I knew it all in my head, but not in my heart. I knew the right words to say, but I didn't really believe them." Sally's pushed-in face that had struck Alice as homely before now seemed to glow with her earnestness. She wasn't so plain after all.

"I had to come all the way to Switzerland to find out that God is really alive and that he still listens to people and answers their prayers. That he knows all about me. He made me. He knows my worst secrets. He knows I'm just as big a sinner as anyone else. But he cares about me. He will do miracles for me! He already has." When Sally finished she had tears in her eyes.

Alice sank a little lower in her chair and fidgeted with her napkin. What was Sally talking about? What kind of miracles? Everyone else at the table seemed to feel the same way as Sally. She was on the outside as usual. When would lunch be over?

The big bell that she now knew hung from a tall pole outside of Chalet les Mélèzes began to toll.

"Time for our work assignments, Alice. Come with me, I'll point you in the right direction." Sally got up with a leap, energized by her truth bearing, no doubt.

Chapter 57

ALICE FOLLOWED SALLY'S DIRECTIONS to the lower level of another chalet, even higher up the mountain than where they had eaten lunch. A disgruntled looking couple sat on the stoop outside the door. The guy had his arm around the girl and they were whispering to one another. Alice saw the back of someone else sitting on the ground in front of them. He was wearing faded jeans and cowboy boots and a ragged brown tee shirt with the words "Wolf Cub Cabs" printed on the back. He was occupied blowing a chain of smoke rings, one inside the other. She'd always wanted to learn how to do that.

"Is this the laundry?" she asked, feeling a little shy.

"So we're told," said the guy with the girl. His long messy hair and beard hid most of his face. "You new here too?"

"Just got here yesterday," she said. These three certainly didn't have the bright-eyed, bushy-tailed look of most the students. Maybe they were the folks that Helen met the night before.

"Us too," he said. "What a drag. The big hauncho's wife said we could hang out for a week for free, but we've got to work and go to some crappy lectures."

The guy sitting on the ground started to cough. As he turned in her direction, she took a step backwards and nearly fell over. "Will?" It was Will Fowler from freshman philosophy at Michigan, from their trip to Chicago, from the train ride home. Or at least it was a version of him. He was much thinner than a year ago, his hair was half-way down his back and caught in a ponytail. A Fu Manchu mustache encircled his mouth and draggled below his chin.

"Good god, good karma!" He got to his feet and walked toward her with open arms. "My prayers have been answered," he laughed and grabbed her for a hug. She patted his shoulders then tactfully pushed him away. He reeked of cigarettes and curry and dirty hair.

"I can't believe you're here," Alice said. This was even more of a shock than finding Helen in her chalet. "How did you know where to find me?"

"Find you? This is pure fate!" He slapped her on the bottom and laughed again. "You're just what the doctor ordered."

Just then they heard another voice. "Cheerio, chaps!" A small older man dressed in hiking boots, hiking shorts, and a Tyrolean hat strode vigorously around the corner of the building. "I'm Clive. The call me King of Clean. You must be my new ministers of laundry."

"Hello," she said in her voice reserved for adults. "We're all new here."

"Of course, of course. They always send me the three

leaf clovers. But that's fine, that's the way I like it. On your feet. Tell me your names." As he spoke his Irish accent blended with the birdsongs. He pulled out a long line of rope from a compartment in the wall of the chalet and attached it to a pulley system.

"I'm Alice," she said. The others introduced themselves: Mick, Cynthia, and Will.

"Americans. Just as I deduced," Clive said. "Today is Thursday. Thursday tablecloths. An easy job. Tomorrow's crew has napkins and dishtowels. More of a challenge. But let's get to work. I'm sure you're going to enjoy this."

She heard Mick hiss as they ducked into a room full of washtubs and wringers and big wicker baskets full of laundry. "Bet this isn't how your mums do it back home," Clive said.

"No way," said Cynthia. Her voice was deep and gravelly for such a tiny person. She and Mick were both short, but he was sinewy under his black tee shirt and hole-y jeans. She was wraith-like, dressed in a gauzy orange dress with long, bell sleeves. Hippies. But Mick reminded her of someone else. She couldn't think who.

"Cynthia, my dear, you load the tubs. Mick, you man the wringers. Will and Alice, since you've both got a long reach, you two can hang the table clothes on the line. Okay?" He handed them a basket of the morning's wash and a container of clothespins.

They stepped into the bright afternoon sun. Will coughed, then dropped his cigarette and crushed it under his boot. "Let's get back to where we once belonged?" he said, quoting the Beatles. How unreal that he was at L'Abri. She'd only seen him a couple of times after their trip to

Chicago, and both times she'd been with Bruce. He'd written to her in England with a pathetic plea, begging her to travel with him, telling her she was his Muse. She'd never written back.

"So, are you and your friends the ones who are trying to find the Sufi guru?" She shook out a tablecloth and pinned one corner to the line. Best to keep busy.

"That was the plan, but now I've found you! The road to enlightenment takes a lot of twists and turns."

"So you think there's just one road?"

"Huh?" His thinking was slow. He wasn't the same Will from philosophy class, or was he?

"You know, just one way to enlightenment?" she said.

"I don't know. There must be lots of ways, don't you think? That is, if enlightenment is something you can find. Or get." He coughed again.

"My roommate met you last night. I knew her in the States too."

"That chick with the square face?"

"Helen."

"She talked about her roommate and said you were a wild girl. Yup, that's my Alice." She cringed. "Funny thing is, I knew I'd find you," he said from the other side of a tablecloth. "It was destiny."

When they were finished with the basket he poked his head around the fabric hanging between them and whispered, "Let's go sit in the shade. Want a smoke?"

"Maybe Clive has another batch for us." She didn't like the shadowy circles under his eyes.

"What's the rush? I need a rest." He sank down at the base of a tall pine.

"How long have you been traveling? You seem low on energy." She squatted on a flat stone protruding from the hillside.

He squinted and looked off into the distance. "Since the end of June when I totaled my cab. Got out of the country just in time, before the fireworks blew. As for energy," he held up his hand. "Guilty as charged. Low on energy, low on cash, low on dope." He counted out three fingers. "Thought I was low on luck," he stuck out his thumb, "until now."

"But weren't you lucky to find L'Abri? A free place to stay?"

He shrugged. "Don't know about that, but I am lucky to find you." He touched her nose with his finger and her heart skipped back to their train ride from Chicago to Ann Arbor. After he had rescued her from the awful man in the train station, she'd fallen asleep his lap. But she was never quite sure where his fingers had explored. Now his hands were dark and oily, stained with nicotine, and fingernails were black from weeks on the road. "My luck has changed," he was saying but she wasn't listening. She was seeing how reckless she had been back then—and so many times since. "And tomorrow we're hitchhiking over to the next valley to get some weed from a guy who owes Mick. Then things'll really be looking up. You've gotta come. The gods are definitely saying we belong together."

"Ready or not, here's basket number two!" She heard the screen door open to Clive's cheerful call.

"Maybe," she said and went to help Clive with the heavy basket full of wet tablecloths.

Chapter 58

"GOD IS THERE, and He is not silent!" Francis Schaeffer's pinched voice pierced through the chapel and swirled around the hundred or so people gathered for the evening lecture. "...and man is significant...."

"He sounds like an Old Testament prophet," Alice whispered to Helen who was slumped next to her on a wooden bench. She hadn't told her yet that the groovy guy was someone she knew, someone who knew her—almost in the biblical sense. So far she'd been able to avoid seeing Will again since work, study, and meals were all assigned. She was glad he was going away for a day or two. Maybe he wouldn't come back.

"Sure does," agreed Helen. "You should have heard him at my college last year in Illinois. Even the professors were shaking."

"....Western culture is dying," he went on. "We have abandoned rationality for rationalism. We scoff at the concept of truth and become manipulated machines...."

"I don't really get what he's talking about, do you?" Alice said.

"Shhhh!" said a boy behind them.

"Wait awhile, it might sink in—or not!" Helen winked.

"....words have content, communicate meaning. We communicate horizontally with one another. God, too, communicates through words...."

She doodled in her notebook, drawing letters of the alphabet with wings and feet.

"Well how about this?" Her ears perked up when she heard the angry sneer of Mick's voice. He was standing near the front of the semicircle of benches, hand on his hip, a cocky expression on his face. He looked like an Old Testament character too, one of the wicked ones.

"Yes?" Dr. Schaeffer stopped and turned to him. "Do you have something to say?"

"I've got a poem to read. Full of significance and meaning, like you say." Mick snickered as he glanced around the room.

"Go ahead," Dr. Schaeffer said. "Read it. We'll be happy to tell you what we think."

Mick cleared his throat and began. A random pattern of expletives poured from his mouth, two ugly four-letter words repeated over and over.

"Young man," Dr. Schaeffer interrupted. "Is that all you've got to say?"

"I'm not done. There's a whole page more." Mick held a torn piece of notebook paper above his head and waved it at the audience.

"But do you have any additional words, words with content?"

"Hey man, my words have content." Mick stood with his legs spread apart, as if he was getting ready to wrestle.

"Each of those words means something in slang, but you're not saying anything to the rest of us except that you're angry and unhappy."

He's right, Alice thought. Mick is mad. Full of sound and fury, signifying nothing. She remembered Faulkner. And Shakespeare: A tale told by an idiot.

"Just let me finish, man. Then we can take a vote. Democracy and all that pseudo-American crap."

"No, we've heard enough. Now why don't you listen?" Dr. Schaeffer didn't raise his voice but his authority was clear.

"What kind of Christians are you anyway? Don't even let a guy speak."

"We share our homes and our food. But we don't have to let you waste our time."

"Whoa! Come on, Babe," he said pulling on Cynthia's hand. "Come on Will. We don't need this. We're out of here!" He raised his middle finger and turned on his heel. Then she remembered who he reminded her of: Charles Manson.

She watched as the three of them tramped out. A murmur spread through the room as soon as the door closed.

"Wow!" Helen shook her fingers in front of her. "That was cool."

Alice looked at her. "Cool? More like stupid. Obscene. Meaningless."

"You're one to talk, Miss Evolution! I remember you last summer at Outward Bound, going on about the evolution of our culture. Legalizing marijuana. Birth control pills for everyone. You said freedom was the answer to everything. Just do your own thing."

"You're right," Alice said. "But I'm changing."

Lunch was even more elaborate the next day: an authentic Chinese meal with egg drop soup, spring rolls, and pork chow mien.

"Mrs. Schaeffer grew up in China," Sally whispered as Francis Schaeffer began saying grace. Milton, Alice's tutor, was at the head of their table. As soon as Amen was said and they pulled out their chairs to sit down, he started talking about a man he had just met that morning.

"He called himself 'Freedom,'" Milton said. "He lives at a Sufi center over on the next mountain."

That must be the place where Will wanted to go, thought Alice.

"Freedom told me that since he thought he was so enlightened, he rarely talked. He spent hours and hours meditating. People would sit near him and meditate just to hone in on his holy vibrations." Milton was so excited he hadn't even picked up his soup spoon.

"One day last week, Freedom said, he was traveling outside his body on another plane and Sai Baba appeared and demanded to live in Freedom's body."

Astral projection? Alice thought of the voice that had asked her to leave her body on her solo at Outward Bound.

"But Freedom didn't want to give himself away. When he resisted, Sai Baba pressed in on him and it started to hurt. Freedom got desperate and called out for help—not out loud, but in the spiritual realm." Milton stopped and cocked his head, looking around the whole table with his one bright eye. "The pain kept increasing and for some wonderful reason, he called out the name of Jesus. And you know what? Immediately Jesus appeared to him and released him from the grip of Sai Baba."

Everyone at their table had stopped eating.

"But that's not the end of the story," Milton went on. "When Freedom came back to his body he told the people around him what had happened. I love how he explained it. He said there are many moons, but only one sun. The moons reflect the light of the sun but they aren't a source of light in themselves. The only one who is worthy to be worshipped is the source of light." Milton brought his palms together, lifted his hands to his chin, and closed his eyes.

As they were finishing lunch there was a big commotion outside the chalet. People left the tables and went to look out the window into the parking lot below. A shiny black car had pulled up the drive in front of Mélèzes. Out popped a young man and an enormously pregnant woman. People rushed down the stairs from the porch and surrounded them with hugs.

"Who's that VIP?" she asked Sally.

"Calvin. And Martha, his bride. They're just getting back from their honeymoon." Sally beamed in the newlyweds' direction.

"Calvin Schaeffer? Francis and Edith's son?" This must be the friend of Simon's brother.

"Yup. Isn't she pretty?"

"Did you say honeymoon? But she's pregnant!" Alice couldn't believe the girl wasn't at least trying to hide her swelling belly. "If that were me, my parents would banish me from the family."

"Not here," Sally said. "Rumor was that six months ago they were talking about all sorts of bad options, but then they decided to marry. What a work of grace. It's one of the things that proved to me that God the Father is always loving and always kind."

Alice headed to the woodworking shop for her afternoon assignment with yet another mystery to ponder.

Chapter 59

SUNDAY ARRIVED BRIGHT AND CLEAR. After chapel and lunch Sally convinced Alice to join a group taking a long hike above the Rhône valley. "You can see both France and Italy," she said. "And the fresh air will help you sort through all the words you've been hearing."

"But I'm in terrible shape." She looked down at her skinny body. She was wasting away.

"Keep eating the meals around here and you'll have the opposite problem." Sally grabbed a fist of fat around her middle. "That's one reason I'm going hiking. But don't worry, I'll stick with you. We don't have to rush. We'll keep to the footpaths that crisscross the mountain. No fancy stuff."

It was a glorious day and Alice lagged behind, content to let her mind settle softly on the wildflowers at her feet, then drift lazily to the outlines of the distant mountain peaks. Some of the others sang while they walked, or battered theological questions back and forth like a badminton birdie. But she relaxed into the rhythm of her footsteps, happy with the sensation that she was alive and part of the planet. Bruce would like it here, she thought. A letter from him had arrived at L'Abri the day before. "It's time you found the answer," he had scrawled on the blue aerogramme. What did he mean? Was there an answer? She wondered what he was doing right then. She pictured him like one of the distant mountain peaks, firm and strong. He seemed to be there in the background of her life, waiting. She felt that if she kept on going she would eventually reach him. Whereas Rafe—she shuddered—he was a wily, downhill stream rushing under rocks and into dark crannies.

"Hey daydreamer," Sally said. "What are you thinking about?" Sally had stopped to let her catch up. They had walked in a wide loop, first up the mountain behind Huemoz, the village surrounding L'Abri, then down and around beneath it. Now they were heading back.

"If I follow this path will it take me back to our chalet?" Alice asked, not ready to share her thoughts with anyone.

"Yup. This leads into that apple orchard next door to the Wentworth's. You won't get lost."

"Thanks." That was all she needed to say. Sally scurried ahead to catch up with the rest of the group.

She looked over the valley again. An afternoon moon was rising, pale against the blue sky. What had Milton said at lunch? Worship the source of light, not its reflection. Sometimes the moon seemed like it had its own light, but she knew that was a false perception. All the light the moon gave to the earth originated from the sun. She walked on slowly, enjoying the peacefulness of being alone.

A Scottish folk melody rose up from somewhere within

her. Then she realized it was the song two girls had sung in the chapel service that morning. As she hummed some of the words came back to her: "How lovely is thy dwelling place, O Lord of Hosts to me." It was from a Psalm but she didn't know which one. She came to a standstill as the path turned at a split rail fence, and she recognized the apple orchard. This was a lovely dwelling place.

A weatherworn ladder leaned against one of the apple trees. She couldn't resist and climbed up into the spreading branches. Small apples were hanging under clumps of leaves Most were still green, though a few were tinged with pink, promising the deep red of ripeness in the fall. She settled herself on a thick branch and rested against the trunk, holding onto the branches above her. Trees felt so safe. So strong. They were perfectly people-sized, like this one she could sit in, or the lodgepole pine at Outward Bound that had been her shelter for three days during her solo. Or the copper beech back in Ann Arbor that had protected her under its purply-silver leaves when she was a little girl. Even the giant redwood, transplanted from California to Exeter, that hid her while she smoked marijuana, pointed to the heavens like a cathedral. Trees were stable. They knew where they belonged.

Another verse from the song arose from nowhere: "Even the sparrow finds a home where he can settle down." There on a branch just below her was a nest. An intricately woven basket with a perfect half sphere in its center, lined with soft downy feathers. How could a simple bird build something so magnificent, so essential, so nurturing? What was she building with her life? Surely she had more to work with than twigs and dried grass.

"I'd rather be a doorkeeper and serve the Lord all day, than live the life of a sinner and have to stay away." She remembered the harmony of the girls' voices, so beautiful it had made her ache. Even now the song tugged on her and pulled up a long-submerged yearning. She wanted to find her real home. She wanted to know where she belonged.

Alice flopped onto her bed and unlaced her hiking boots. "Man," she said to Helen who was curled up with a romance novel, "I haven't been hiking since Outward Bound."

"Too bad you got suckered in. It was a nice quiet afternoon to stay at home. The Wentworths are up at the big place celebrating the newlyweds." Helen slipped a piece of chocolate in her mouth and held up the triangular Toblerone package. "Sorry, all gone."

"How old are they anyway?" she asked.

"The newlyweds? Seventeen, eighteen? I don't know for sure. Kind of a rush job if you noticed."

"I noticed. But what really surprises me is how accepting everyone seems to be. That's not what would happen where I come from. My mother told me that if I ever got pregnant before I was married, it would kill my father. And in her uncanny motherliness, she threatened that on a day when my period was late. Nice, huh?"

"I never got that threat. Not a likely problem for me." Helen rolled over and set her book on the floor. "My father'd drop dead if he just knew what went on in my head!"

"Like what?"

"Oh like, 'Is Jesus the only way?' 'Is the Bible the infallible Word of God?' Minor things like that. And 'TULIP.'"

"Flowers?"

"No, Calvinist theology. Total depravity, Unconditional election, Limited atonement, Irresistible grace...."

"Pretty heavy concepts—sounds awfully abstract," Alice said.

"That's what I'm afraid of. And then there's P—Perseverance of the saints. Guess I'm failing at that one too."

"Have you given up?" She wished there was something she could say to help Helen. "Sally told me about a prayer meeting tonight. Are you going?"

"The Sunday night snooze fest? It's a bore. Don't bother. Unless, of course, you like to be bored." Helen sat up and stretched. "By the way, no formal meal tonight, just cold cuts from the refrigerator. Want to go get some?"

"But what do they do at the prayer meeting?" She only knew about the Episcopal Book of Common Prayer and Transcendental Meditation.

"Pray. You know, talk to God. Dullsville. Let's go eat."

When they got downstairs Sally was sitting on an arm of the sofa in the living room with a plate of cheese slices and grapes. "Your legs still holding you up?" Sally joked as Alice came into the room with her own plate of food. "That was a longer hike than I'd anticipated."

"It was great," Alice said. "I never knew you could see such detail from the mountainside. How many different wildflowers are there, do you think?"

"I don't know but Edith Schaeffer probably does," Sally laughed. "She adores detail. 'God is in the detail' she always says. You should read her book—and her letters about L'Abri. She sees God's hand in every little coincidence."

"What amazes me," Alice went on, still thinking about the flowers she'd seen, "is that flowers bloom in places where no one sees them."

"So?" Helen said, plopping on the sofa with a plate piled with food. "What's the big deal? Seeds scatter, birds drop them, the rain comes. Voilà."

"But I think those secret flowers are treasures waiting to be found. Like a jelly bean hunt at Easter," Alice said.

Sally stood up. "Time for the prayer meeting. You two coming?"

Helen shook her head. "I've been to one too many already."

"Well, I guess I'll go," Alice said. "Might never get another chance." As she said the word "chance" she thought of John Cage and his unappealing, disorganized music. No secret melody waiting to be found there. She thought of Charles Darwin and his theory of impersonal mutation and selection that made the world feel so competitive, and him so sad.

"Try not to snore when you fall asleep at the meeting!" Helen called as Alice and Sally went out the door together.

Twenty or thirty people were sitting on chairs and sofas and leaning against the walls or other people's knees when the girls slid into the room. Alice found a spot on the big braided rug that covered most of the floor, crossed her feet, and sat down. A man she had seen a few times was reading from a Bible. She looked around. Most faces were familiar but she didn't see anyone she knew except Clive from the laundry. He waved at her.

"So whatever we ask in his name, according to his will, he will do it for us," the man who was leading the meeting said. "Remember, Jesus said his sheep hear his voice, so let's listen and discern his will, and then we will ask." Nobody moved. The room grew still. She looked around. Most people had their eyes closed. Some faces looked tense and scrunched up, others were calm and peaceful, almost smiling. She caught Clive's eye again. He grinned and winked. What a leprechaun, she thought. He makes living seem fun.

After what felt like a very long time, a thin female voice began, "Lord, we're so glad that you are God and not us."

That's strange, thought Alice. Well maybe not. Some people do seem to act like they are god.

"We're so glad you know everything," the girl went on. "You made each one of us. You call us by name."

Is that in the Bible? Alice didn't think she'd heard God call her name. She thought of the times scary voices had spoken to her: like the seductive invitation to leave her body on her solo at Outward Bound and the shrill voices at Abaddon forcing her into danger. She didn't think those were the voice of God.

"We know you love us. You care about every detail of our lives." The girl sounded as if she was really talking to someone, not just reciting memorized phrases. Everyone else was quiet or making low sounds of assent. Alice began to feel peaceful, settled. Her body sank down into itself; her breathing grew still. It was like Transcendental Meditation but without the mantra, like TM but with words that had meaning.

"So Lord...we are bold to come to you for help." It sounded like the girl was going to ask for something. Wasn't that presumptuous? "We lift up Gwendolyn and Sam Wentworth. They are longing for a child." Alice opened her eyes. She hadn't noticed Gwendolyn and her husband sitting on the sofa under the window. Now she watched as people near them reached over and gently rested their hands on them. Other people who were farther away raised their palms in the couple's direction. "You are so good, Lord," the girl went on with her prayer. "If it's your will, please bless them with a baby." A low murmur spread through the room, like an ebb to the wave of her prayer. She wondered how Gwendolyn felt about such a personal thing being talked about so openly. Maybe the reason she was cranky was because she couldn't get pregnant. Alice opened her eyes again and saw a gleam of tears on Gwendolyn's cheeks. And on Sam's.

"We agree on this, Lord," a firm male voice spoke out. "You are mighty. You are the life-giver. You gave Abraham and Sarah a child in their old age. Shine your face upon the Wentworths." Alice knew the story of Abraham and Isaac from Sunday School and from the religion classes she took at boarding school. But did these people actually believe that Sarah was ninety years old when Isaac was born? Did they think the Bible was that true?

More prayers were spoken, a mixture of thanking God for answered prayers and asking him for more things. A good apple crop for the village farmers, a safe car journey for some people who were leaving, healing of someone's cancer, an end to the Vietnam War. That was quite a request!

All through the prayer time Alice sat quietly. Her mind was in a strange state of being, both active as she listened to what people were saying, and passive as if she were a blank piece of paper or an unexposed roll of film.

A time of deep silence dropped on the room like a soft cloak resting on her shoulders. No one spoke. It was not awkward but sweet. She thought of her quiet moments with Bruce. The people in this room were comfortable with God. They really believed he was there.

And then it began. First she felt a tiny flicker somewhere inside her, almost like a knot or butterfly in her stomach. Then the flame spread, hot, up to her chest, down to her loins. Into her bones. She was burning in her bones. It didn't hurt, there was no pain, but she was on fire. She opened her eyes and saw her hands were trembling. She looked around the room. Did others feel it? Everything appeared normal. Then the flame rose up into her throat and into her mouth and she had to speak.

"Lord." The word came out like a whisper. She knew he was listening. "Lord." The fire burned into her fingers and toes. "Forgive me." All of a sudden she saw the ruin of her life. Broken hearts and deceitful words, lying and scheming, selfishness, unfaithfulness. She saw her days littered behind her like scraps of old newspaper and broken kindling, discarded letters that went nowhere, words that added up to nothing.

"Lord...." She said it stronger this time. She knew he was real. He was the one who taught the birds to build their nests. He was the one who made apple blossoms turn into apples. "Help me help others like me who are lost. Help me," she said. "Help me help them find you." They were short, broken sentences. Awkward. Simple. But she knew they were the cry of her heart. And then the fire receded into a soft glow. She felt like flesh once more. Wonderful skin and muscles and bones. Mysterious organs, beating heart and breathing lungs. Voice, touch, hearing, seeing. What a miracle to be alive.

"Alice." The voice was soft and almost imperceptible. She listened intently. "Alice, I am." A tear ran down the side of her nose. She tasted the sea. She tasted the clouds. "Alice, you belong to me."

She felt a hand put a tissue in her lap, another rested lightly on her shoulder. She didn't have to open her eyes to know that she was changed. She was like the lodgepole pine. Fire had burned up the chaff and released seeds of life. A passageway had opened up within her. Her eyes and ears were awakened. Her spirit was alive.

More prayers followed and then there was some singing, quiet a Cappella songs she didn't know but were easy to hum along just the same. She didn't want to move. She wanted to stay right there for the rest of her life. She felt like an embryo in a womb, a happy child in a big, loving family. She was a wildflower on the hillside in the midst of waving grasses and buzzing bees and God was looking at her.

"Will you be coming with us, Alice?" Before she opened her eyes she knew it was Clive speaking. His lilting Irish voice held the same glimmer of joy as his crinkly eyes.

"We've got room for one more in the bus." She glanced around for Sally who raised her hand and gave a nod.

She stood and stretched and felt a new grace about her limbs, like tight elastic had been cut loose so her bones could relax into a more natural position. She followed Clive and some other students outside to a star-sprinkled sky. "Wow, so many!" she whispered.

"As many as the grains of sand," said a voice nearby.

"From every tribe and tongue and nation," someone else added. A shiver ran through her. Those were the same words Angelina had said to her in that office in Ann Arbor, right before she disappeared.

"Such is the family of God." It was Clive. "Hop in here, Alice. We'll take you down the mountain to the Wentworth's."

She climbed into the old VW bus and perched on an upside-down bucket behind the driver's seat. The quietness of the prayer meeting clung to them all like the dew on the windshield. She felt good about just being there. She rested her head against the window and breathed in peace. Clive drove down the winding road and through the small village that separated the Wentworth's chalet from the rest of L'Abri. All of a sudden, as they turned onto a dirt road, she knew she was going to throw up. It was like that time in Exeter, in Joker's room, when she'd first smoked hashish mixed with tobacco. But she wasn't stoned now. What was the matter?

"Clive, stop the bus. I'm going to be sick."

With no questions asked he pulled to a stop and someone opened the door. She ran to the tall grass at the roadside and bent over. Three, four, five times she opened her mouth and the contents of her stomach came out. But it was strange. It wasn't like being sick, but more of a purging. A cleansing.

Clive was by her side with a wet washcloth. Was he magical? she wondered for a moment. How did he always have what she needed?

"Thanks, I feel better now."

"And that you are, that you are," he said gently patting her back.

She climbed into the bus. "That was weird," she spoke into the darkness. "I don't think I was really sick. It was more like something had to get out of me."

Voices in the bus muttered assent. Did they know how she felt?

Clive spoke. "That happens, you know, when darkness is exposed by light. Like cockroaches fleeing when you light a candle in a dark room in the middle of the night."

She wasn't sure what he was talking about but her head felt dizzy and her stomach was still queasy. Maybe there was more darkness still inside her.

"It's nothing to be afraid of," he went on. "The serpent's head has been crushed. It's just his dead carcass lashing about that scares us. He can do you no harm."

She thought of the bull snake at Outward Bound, the one they had killed and eaten. It had been more frightening dead that alive.

"Alice, dear," Clive said as he parked the bus in the Wentworth's drive. "I recommend you lay low for a day or two. Let Gwendolyn bring you the occasional pot of tea. Do her good. Oh yes, have you read Edith's book, *The*

L'Abri Story? Might as well read up on where you are while you're here."

It sounded wonderful to her, a day in bed, time away from the talking, the discussions, the whirlwind of ideas that had swept her into a whole new world. She needed time to let the silence of the prayer meeting sink into her, to let the burning in her bones simmer life in her heart.

Chapter 60

ALICE AWOKE WITH A START. Another bad dream, just like the one yesterday morning, only this time it was Bruce, not Rafe, who left her, who walked away, who would not stay by her side. She rolled over away from the log wall and saw that Helen was still asleep in the bed next to hers. The dreams felt so real. She pulled her nightgown tight around her as she walked into the bathroom with its tiny sink. There on the hook was her toiletry bag, and there in the bag was the round disk of her birth control pills. It was time to start a new cycle.

She looked at herself in the mirror, looked deep into her own green eyes. Her focus went from one eye to the other, as if she was two people. Right, left, right, left. She knew she had to make a decision. The circle of pharmaceutical foil glimmered in her hands. Wasn't this freedom? Wasn't this love? Wasn't this the only way to really connect with another person?

The rejection from Bruce and Rafe that she experienced in her dreams hung heavy over her. She could see she had a choice to make. "Even if they all desert me," she prayed, "I will obey You. I don't know how I'll resist, but I will if You help me. You have to help me." She dropped the pills into the wastebasket under the sink and bent to splash cold water in her face.

"Hey, I've been looking for you!" Will ran up to Alice on the path to the Study Center and grabbed her by the arm. "Remember that energy you were talking about? I've got it." He patted a bulge in his blue jean pocket.

She pulled away from him.

"Hey, it's me. Your old friend, your Spring fever. Your midnight express. Let's go somewhere and take a trip." He bent his elbows and pretended to finger a guitar. "You love the blues." He pranced a little, channeling Keith Richards.

"Not really," she said. "The blues are sad and depressing." There was an odd tension inside her, a yo-yo in her chest. She hadn't been high in over a week and hadn't been with a guy since Rafe left for the States. She pulled in her desires and wound them close to her heart.

"I can make you happy," he said, still playing his invisible instrument. She felt as if she was looking through binoculars the wrong way. Will was a strange marionette far down the road.

"Where have you been the last couple days anyway? I thought you might want to have some fun, now that I've got my energy back." He smiled and did his weird dance again.

"Watch it," she said. "There are lots of people around here."

"Lots of squares, that's for sure. But Mick and Cynthia and me, we're going to cut loose tomorrow. We're skipping that Baba guy and hitching south. We've had enough religion. We're going to Africa, to the heart of it all. You got my letter last winter, right? You should come." He grinned again.

"I don't think so." She shook her head. She might have considered it a few days earlier but now she had other things to do. The two days she'd spent in her room had worked some kind of spell on her. A new sensitivity had opened in her, a view out of the tunnel she'd been in. What Will offered was receding farther and farther in the distance. The excitement of drugs and sexual conquest, even the mystery of exploring a new continent, weren't so glamorous anymore since she'd read the amazing stories in Edith's book. Either the people at L'Abri were psychopathic liars or they had some kind of link with miraculous power. Strange things happened when they prayed.

"You aren't getting converted are you?" Will looked at her quizzically.

"I'm not sure. Something happened to me at the prayer meeting and now I'm seeing things differently. It's as if...."

"Save it, Alice. I've heard enough of those stories already." He turned and scurried up the hill. "I'll catch you in the next lifetime," he shouted as he disappeared around the back of the chapel.

She felt only a slight pang as he left, just a little pull on that yo-yo string inside. She looked out across the valley and suddenly the binoculars in her brain flipped around and she could see her own life from far away. She'd been wandering round in circles and now someone, someone she trusted, had handed her a road map. She skipped down the path and ducked into her carrel space in the Study Center. She needed to answer Bruce's letter and tell him she had found the answer.

Chapter 61

ON THE NIGHT BEFORE Alice was to leave L'Abri, there was a timid tapping on her bedroom door. "Come in," she called quietly so as not to wake Helen.

"It's me, Sally. Are you asleep?"

"No, just lying here worrying. Come in." She sat up cross-legged and motioned for Sally to sit on the end of her bed. "I can't believe I'm going home tomorrow. I'm kind of scared."

"I'm sorry," Sally said. "What are you afraid of?" Sally had proven to be a good friend, a good listener. It was one of the things that surprised her—that she could learn to really enjoy someone who had seemed so unattractive and uninteresting at first.

"I'm scared of what's going to happen. Maybe my nightmares are prophecies—like the ones I had skiing at Zermatt. Maybe they'll come true and everyone will desert me. What will my old friends think of me? And my parents—what will I tell them? But most of all I'm afraid I won't be able to recognize God's voice from all the others."

"You know what Jesus said? His sheep hear his voice."

"But how will I know it's him? I hear lots of things."

"You can tell by the fruit, Alice. An apple tree doesn't grow grapes. God's fruit—and there's a whole list of it in Galatians—is patient and kind and has self-control. You'll be able to judge by that." Sally smiled and pulled a small black book out of the pocket of her bathrobe. "Look at this verse. Philippians 4:6. 'Don't be anxious about anything but pray for everything.' Would you like me to pray with you?" Alice nodded and they held hands and closed their eyes.

Just like the night at the prayer meeting, Alice felt peace come into her like a new thought from outside herself. It was as if by closing her eyes to the circumstances around her she was able to open them in a world of infinite possibilities. When they were done Sally put the book in her hand. "This is a New Testament with the Psalms in the back. I can get another one. I want you to have this."

"You've been so kind to me, Sally. I'll never forget you." She hugged the funny-looking girl who had become beautiful in her eyes. "I hope I'll see you again some day."

"There's no doubt about that," Sally said as she turned and went out the door. "We have eternity!"

Chapter 62

THE TRAIN TO GENEVA was crowded. Alice found a seat next to a distinguished looking man with olive skin and greying temples who was dressed in a well-cut summer suit. "Bonjour," she said. It was hard to know what language to speak in Switzerland.

"Bonjour," he nodded. "Vous êtes Anglaise?" He nodded at the book she was holding. She was making another go at Francis Schaeffer's *The God who is There*.

"Non, je suis Américaine," she said. "Et vous?"

"Espagnol."

Oh, she thought. A Spaniard. A friendly Spaniard.

They carried on together in French. He asked questions and she tried to explain what had happened to her at L'Abri. "*J'ai fait la connaissance de Dieu,*" she told him. I met God. That sounded so preposterous in English. "*Comprenez-vous? Pensez-vous que je suis folle?*" Do you think I'm crazy?

"*Non, non, Mademoiselle. Parce que moi, je suis un ange.*"

What! Un ange? She wondered if her vocabulary was breaking down. "You are an angel?"

"Oui. Un ange."

"*Comment est-ce possible?*" How is that possible?

"*N'avez-vous pas lu le Bible?*" Haven't you read the Bible?

"*Si. J'ai un Bible ici dans ma poche.*" She pulled the little New Testament that Sally had given her out of her pocket.

He took it and opened it to Acts 5:18. "They arrested the apostles and put them in the public jail. But during the night an angel of the Lord opened the doors of the jail and brought them out. 'Go, stand in the temple courts,' he said, 'and tell the people the full message of this new life.'" This *is* a new life, she thought.

"*C'est pareil pour vous, Mademoiselle.* It's the same for you. You have been let out of jail. Now you must go and tell people, just like you told me."

She didn't know what to think or believe. Was this another liar, someone pulling her leg, making fun of her experience? She just couldn't tell. But as they arrived at the station, he offered to drive her to the airport. Then he bought her dinner and even a box of chocolates. She trusted that her "lecher detector" was still in working order. This man was truly kind. Maybe that's the way of the Spanish, she thought. Or maybe....

Safely on the plane she turned back to the beginning of Acts. Even though she had religion classes at boarding school and some theology at Exeter, she'd never read much of the Bible and never even noticed the book of Acts. Now she saw that it was a sequel to the Gospel of Luke, both written to someone named Theophilus, "Lover of God." She read through the first few chapters. They were full of names familiar to her like Peter and Paul. As she read the accounts of those very first Christians, the stories seemed true and plausible and similar to what she had experienced. There were even a couple accounts of people have flames of fire alight on them—not unlike the burning she'd felt in her bones at the prayer meeting. As she kept reading she could hardly believe her eyes. It was almost as if there were real people walking around on the pages of her book. She came to chapter twelve where Peter was again in prison, and again an angel got him out. At first Peter thought he was dreaming, and then his friends wouldn't let him in their house because they thought he was a ghost. She was glad to know she wasn't the only one who needed time to figure out if this strange new world was real.

She couldn't help but remember her last trip home, at Christmas. She had been alone and friendless. She had hated Graham for taking her into the loo at Oliver's party, hated Barb for betraying her at the airport, and she hated her mother for hanging up the phone on her. Her heart had been bitter and hard. She had hated herself. Now she had a Bible in her pocket instead of a chunk of hashish. Now she wanted to find ways to be kind to her parents instead of making life difficult for them. And she wanted to see Bruce. She wanted to be his friend. She wanted to let him off the hook about sex. Whatever she did, she knew now that she needed to be able to do it out in the open, under the eyes of God. If God was really there, then he saw her all the time. So how could she do things she would hide from her parents when there was no way to hide from God? It almost seemed too simple. And humanly impossible. She was scared and excited, as if she was about to take her first really important exam.

She wondered about the new faith she had found in Switzerland. Would there be people in America like the ones she'd met at L'Abri? How would she find them? She was pretty sure she hadn't met any before, except for Annie on the bus to LaGuardia. Or maybe Karl, her ski instructor in Zermatt. What about Canon Shawcross in Exeter? Were people who knew God all around her only she hadn't noticed? She would keep her eyes open from now on. A light had been lit within her. She didn't have to be afraid anymore.

Chapter 63

"ALICE!" This time her mother was at the airport to meet her. "My god, you're so skinny—and you look different. You've got a glow. Alice, are you in love?"

"Oh Mother," she said and gave her a hug.

"I hope it's not some foreigner. He's not black is he?"

"It's not what you think, Mother. I don't have a new boyfriend."

"Then it must be that mountain air. I've told your father we just have to go to the mountains. Something about the altitude retards aging. And I've heard Swiss yogurt prolongs life." Her mother hadn't changed.

"That must be it, Mom. I had to eat a lot of yogurt." She smiled and shook her head. She'd forgotten how important appearances were to her mother.

On the way to the baggage claim they passed a news kiosk with the latest magazines. A picture of Jesus was on the cover of *Time*.

"Do you have the newest issue of *Time* at home?" she asked.

"You mean the one about the Jesus Movement? Isn't it something. First God is dead. Now you young people have resurrected him or something. I'll never understand your generation. You think you've invented everything."

Alice kept her mouth shut.

As soon as she got home she headed for the telephone at her father's desk to call Bruce. She couldn't wait to see him.

"Mrs. Bradford?" she said when a woman answered.

"Alice? Don't tell me you're back already."

His mother hadn't changed either. How was she supposed to be kind to someone like that? "May I speak to Bruce?"

"Hummph." A sound of disgust came over the line. Alice waited. "He's asleep. You don't realize how hard he works. Poor boy slaving away on the night shift. I don't know how he does it."

"When do you expect him to be up? I could call back if you don't want to wake him."

"Of course I won't disturb him. But if you call back, the phone might bother his sleep. Why don't you just write him a letter? I'm sure that would suffice."

"How about if you tell him I'm home and he can call me when he gets up?"

"Alice." Mrs. Bradford made a slight hissing sound at the end of her name. "It's not my place to get involved."

"But Mrs. Bradford," she was beginning to feel a slight wheezing in her chest. "We haven't seen each other for almost seven months. I'm sure he would want to know I'm here."

"Oh you're sure, are you? A lot can happen in seven

months. My Bruce has changed a great deal. He graduated, you know. He has plans."

"Plans?" She couldn't help getting sucked in by this woman.

"I didn't think he'd told you. Why would he bother? He's grown out of his childish ways."

Now she was really having trouble breathing. "But I just got a letter from him last week in Switzerland."

"Well then, why don't you reply to it? Oh, there's the doorbell. Must go. Good bye."

Alice hung up the phone and put her head down on the desk. She wanted to scream, but she felt like something was squeezing its hands around her neck. She let out a short sob and gasped for breath. Back and forth she went like that, crying and wheezing, exhausted from her trip, enraged at Bruce's mother. Mean words flooded her mind. She was shocked by her own thoughts. She hated that woman. "I'm sorry God, I'm sorry. But she's awful," she cried out.

"Is that you, honey?" Her mother stood in the doorway. She'd never called her any term of endearment before. Alice sobbed louder. "Oh no, is something wrong with Bruce?" Her mother came up and put a hand on her shoulder. That was new too. She hardly ever touched Alice, at least not that she could remember. She shook her head.

"Are you all right? Are you having trouble breathing?" Alice lifted her head and nodded.

"Oh my baby. Come. Let's go sit in the living room. You need to calm down." Then, almost the way Bruce had helped her the first time she had an asthma attack at his mother's apartment, her mother led her through the kitchen and dining room and sat down with her on the love seat that faced the big, floor-to-ceiling window looking out into the back yard. She held her hand, stroking it gently with her thumb. "Don't try to talk honey, close your eyes and relax the best you can." She could hardly believe her mother was being so tender. "This is my favorite view," her mother said. "I love it in the fall when the sumac changes color. It always reminds me of your hair." It was Alice's favorite view too. "I remember when you were a little girl, watching you run through the paths out there. I always envied your freedom." Was she really hearing this? "Your father thought you were so bright; I'm afraid I dulled in his eyes by comparison." Could her mother possibly have been jealous of her? That didn't make sense. "It's funny," her mother went on. "I didn't realize how important you were to me until you went away to school. And then it seemed too late. I had already lost you."

"No you haven't, Mother. I'm here now."

Her mother leaned over and gave her a kiss. That was a miracle.

Chapter 64

ALICE FILLED a tall plastic glass with ice cubes, then half orange juice and half lemonade. She balanced three Toll House cookies on top of her notebook and headed out to the back yard. She could faintly hear her John Renbourn album coming through the open window of her room upstairs. *The Lady and the Unicorn.* She had the whole afternoon free. She wanted to put a little pink in her skin and a little flesh on her bones. The July sun was as bright and friendly as the blue sky. The breeze that came up out of the woods wrapped her with the scent of wild raspberries. She was glad her parents' house had so much property. The orchard on the side had been sold for lots, but they had kept the wooded area behind the house where the copper beech was still growing taller. She loved having so much privacy. Today she was the only one home: her mother was at the country club, her father at his office. She needed this time alone, this time under the sky.

She lay back on the chaise lounge and closed her eyes. How glorious to feel so safe, to be in love with blades of grass and dandelions, in love with wind and sun and the open eyes of heaven. A line from *The Four Quartets* drifted into her mind. "At the still point of the turning world." Now she knew what T. S. Eliot meant. Let them all swirl around her, parents and Bruce and a thousand crazy ideas. She knew she was loved.

Love. It made her wonder about Bruce. Had his mother ever told him she called? Had he gotten the letter she'd sent, or would his mother intercept that too? Could he still love her? She wouldn't blame him if he didn't after all the horrible things she had done to him. When he found out the truth, would she look worn out and used up in his eyes? But even if that's what he thought, she knew she was brand new.

She slipped one of her three by five cards out of her notebook and held it up to shade her eyes. She was trying to memorize the nine fruits of the Spirit Sally had told her about. Love, joy, peace. She repeated them again. Patience, kindness, goodness. She tried to remember all six. Faithfulness, gentleness....Just then, from the other side of the house, she heard the sound of a car on the gravel drive. A door slammed shut and then the car rolled away down the long driveway. Someone had been dropped off. But who? Every day she hoped Bruce would come, but she knew this couldn't be him. He would park his car just like anyone coming to see them would, any repairman or family acquaintance. George, corralled in his outside yard, started barking his head off. She darted in through the kitchen door and raced to a spot in the dining room where she could stand unobserved and see the front walk.

She nearly choked with shock. There, just a few feet

from her stood Rafe. Rafe! How did he find her? She thought he would still be in California. She'd only been home for four days and already he was here. She didn't want to see him. Why hadn't he phoned first?

The bell rang and its deep musical notes traveled the length of the long house. From her hiding place behind the drapes she could see he was wearing dirty cutoffs and a bright Hawaiian surfer shirt. On his back was an over-stuffed backpack. His long hair and beard were scragglier than ever. He held his hand over his eyes and tried to look in through the beveled glass window in the front door.

She hesitated. What should she do? Twenty years of manners were telling her to answer the door, invite him in, offer him a glass of lemonade. Then what? A cookie, a hug, a kiss, a lunge to the sofa. A hand up her dress, a bed for the night, for the whole summer? She knew he wasn't flying back to London until the end of September.

The bell rang again. She wanted to cry, to hide, to creep silently back into the kitchen and crouch below the counter tops until he went away. But she had to face the truth. She ran the long way around through the living room so he couldn't see her through the front windows and went to answer the door.

Now he was rapping with the brass knocker. What did he expect, arriving unannounced in the middle of the day? She took a deep breath and opened the door.

"Ah, Alice!" His burliness and his heavy Cockney accent surprised her. It had only been four weeks but already he felt like a stranger. "Alice, me Alice." He threw his sun-tanned arms around her and pulled her tight. "I knew you'd be here. My own sweet princess in her castle." He reached down and squeezed her bottom.

"Rafe!" She wriggled out of his hold and took a breath. He smelled like an overused sleeping bag in desperate need of airing out. "I didn't know you'd be here so soon. Why didn't you call?"

"Call? I've been on the road for five days. Got a great ride from a trucker, all the way from Salt Lake City to Cincinnati. This is one titanic country you've got here."

She looked into his eyes. There was a cold animosity behind his crafted smile. How had she been so fooled?

"Are you going to ask me in? Or aren't I spiffy enough for the likes of you, now that you're back in the grand land of Mummy and Da?"

"It's not that, Rafe, it's just that, well, I didn't expect you. No one's home right now."

He pushed past her, slipping the heavy backpack off his shoulders, and stepped into the cool darkness of the hall.

"This is a frigging palace you've got here Alice. You say the king and queen are gone? Great!" He reached up and cupped her breast. "Take me to your chambers."

"Cut it out, Rafe," she said as she peeled his hand away from her front. "Don't do that. We're not animals, you know."

"What's got into you? It's me, Rafe. You're still Alice, aren't you?" He took her chin in his hand and looked straight into her eyes.

She held his stare.

He dropped his hand and laughed a growly sort of laugh. "Where'd you go? Lose yourself in Switzerland, did you?"

She stepped back. "I didn't lose myself. I found myself."

Just then the dog began barking again and she heard the garage door go up. She recognized the familiar sound of the station wagon. Her mother was home early from the golf course.

She led Rafe out to the kitchen. Might as well tackle her mother head on. Rafe stopped at the sink for a drink of water while she went straight to the laundry room and opened the garage door.

"Mom! Home early?"

"I just couldn't concentrate on my game. Four-putted every hole. The girls said my head must be in the clouds." Mrs. Blankwell set her purse and visor next to the dryer and hung her key ring on the hook. "So I walked back from number five and came home. I guess I'm as worried about dear Bruce as you are. Any word yet?"

Before she had a chance to say anything, Rafe appeared in the doorway.

Mrs. Blankwell put a hand to her chest and took two steps backward. "Who is this?" Her lips curled up in distaste.

Alice and Rafe began to speak at the same time.

"How do you do, Mrs. Blankwell...." Rafe extended his hand.

"Mom, this is Rafe. Remember I told you about him? My friend from England?"

Mrs. Blankwell collected herself. Etiquette ruled. "Of course," she smiled her pursed-lip smile, "Raid—or is it Range?"

"Rafe, Mom. Rafe."

"Yes, yes, so glad to meet you, Rafe." She took his hand

and shook it, grimy fingernails and all. "You'll have to forgive me. Things have been in such a tizzy since Alice came home."

"I'm sure, Ma'am. Alice does that." He winked. "Thank you so much for your kind hospitality. This is far better than any five-star hotel."

"Oh," Mrs. Blankwell gave a little squeak, "So you will be staying?" She glanced at Alice.

"I was going to ask you about that, Mom. Could he stay on the daybed in Dad's office for a night?" She knew how her mother's mind worked: Lincoln's office beyond the garage rather than the guest room at the bottom of the stairs, just a short staircase from Alice's bedroom.

"That sounds like a good plan, Alice. Now why don't we go out on the porch and have something cool to drink?" She stepped past Rafe and went to the small bar sink next the liquor cabinets. "Now where's the Bourbon?" she asked. "I'm sure we've got some beer in the refrigerator for our guest. Why don't you check, Alice?"

"I'm having lemonade and orange juice...." she began.

"Bourbon sounds perfect, Ma'am," Rafe cut in.

"Call me Simone," she said.

"Simone it shall be," Rafe said with his best smile.

Alice sat on her hands and watched in amazement as Rafe, fresh from a quick shower, and her mother chatted and bantered, each one trying to out do the other in charm.

"That's a gorgeous Steinway you've got nestled in there. Does it sound as good as it looks?"

"Do you play?" Simone asked. Alice couldn't believe

her mother was warming up to him so fast. Bourbon paves roads that should be left untraveled.

"A bit. Jazz mostly, though I love Bach. And the French Impressionists."

"All my favorites." Mrs. Blankwell lifted her glass in agreement.

"Their chord progressions are so sophisticated. They weren't stuck in any 18th century harmonic rules." Rafe doesn't believe in any rules, she wanted to warn her mother.

"I don't know those intellectual things." Mrs. Blankwell lolled her head back and forth. "I leave the studying to Alice. All I know is that whenever I'm sad I pour my heart into Debussy. His music wraps me in its arms." Alice remembered the sweet, lonely sounds of Clair de Lune that seeped into her bedroom at night when she was a child, just as she was falling asleep. She'd never considered what her mother might be feeling.

"I'd love to hear you play, Ma'am."

"Simone."

"Simone."

"Maybe after dinner. Tell me, what have you been studying at the University? Not something silly like Alice and her religion I hope."

She knew her mother was going to love his answer.

"The Classics!" Simone gushed and told him Latin was her best subject in school, her only good one. "I'm not brainy like Alice. She gets all that from her father."

"But she got her beautiful eyes from you!" They were talking about her as if she wasn't even in the room.

"Excuse me." Alice unwound her legs and stood up.

"I've got to go check something." Neither Rafe nor her mother even looked in her direction; they just went on, fascinated with themselves.

She felt butterflies circling in her stomach. How was she going to get rid of Rafe? What about Bruce? What if he came over like she'd pleaded with him to in her letter? Her breathing was getting shallow. She went to her bedroom and lay on her four-poster bed. The eyelet canopy hung above her like a cloud. Clouds. I wish I could disappear, she thought, dissolve into thin air. I wish someone would take me out of my body, take me out of this awful mess.

Then, like a flash inside her, she saw through the clouds in her mind to the sky. To God. Even when it's cloudy, she thought, the sun is still shining; it's just out of sight. She rolled over onto her stomach and slid to the floor on her knees. She closed her eyes and began to pray. "I'm in a mess, O God. I need your help. I don't know what to do. You promised to always be with me. Let me know you are here."

A sense of calm came over her. She took in a deep breath and opened her eyes. Across the bed in a chintz-covered chair in the corner of the room was her collection of dolls. Fancy Madame Alexander and Little Ginny and a pink knit baby doll were sitting on the lap of her four-foot-tall Raggedy Ann. Raggedy Ann's arms were spread out around the other dolls as if she were holding them in a big embrace. Her flat saucer face still had a smile. The doll's button eyes looked at her.

I love you.

The words hung in the air.

I was next to you all the time.

She remembered her tiny self laying so frightened in bed.

I took the knife in my side for you.

She shook her head. Was she dreaming? She got up and went over to the chair and picked up Raggedy Ann. Her pinafore was ripped at the waist, its sashes were knotted and dirty, strands of red yarn were missing from her hair. Alice unbuttoned the dress and pulled it down off the doll's shoulders. Where was her heart? She moved her fingers over the flesh-colored fabric. Only the tiniest bit of roughness remained. Her heart was not on the outside any more.

She hugged the doll to her chest and twirled around. Love is inside, she laughed. Love comes down from God and into my heart. It will never end. I will always have enough.

For the third time that afternoon the dog announced an arrival. She knew. He had finally come. She ran out the front door and down the walk. She wanted to greet him in the bright sunshine.

www.ingramcontent.com/pod-product-compliance
Lightning Source LLC
Chambersburg PA
CBHW061923170626
46813CB00006B/2273